Charlotte Mary Yonge

Nuttie´s Father

Outlook

Charlotte Mary Yonge

Nuttie´s Father

1. Auflage | ISBN: 978-3-73261-934-4

Erscheinungsort: Paderborn, Deutschland

Erscheinungsjahr: 2018

Outlook Verlag GmbH, Paderborn.

Reproduction of the original.

Nuttie's Father

by

Charlotte M. Yonge

CHAPTER I.

ST. AMBROSE'S CHOIR.

'For be it known
That their saint's honour is their own.'—SCOTT.

The town of Micklethwayte was rising and thriving. There were salubrious springs which an enterprising doctor had lately brought into notice. The firm of Greenleaf and Dutton manufactured umbrellas in large quantities, from the stout weather-proof family roof down to the daintiest fringed toy of a parasol. There were a Guild Hall and a handsome Corn Market. There was a Modern School for the boys, and a High School for the girls, and a School of Art, and a School of Cookery, and National Schools, and a British School, and a Board School, also churches of every height, chapels of every denomination, and iron mission rooms budding out in hopes to be replaced by churches.

Like one of the animals which zoologists call radiated, the town was constantly stretching out fresh arms along country roads, all living and working, and gradually absorbing the open spaces between. One of these arms was known as St. Ambrose's Road, in right of the church, an incomplete structure in yellow brick, consisting of a handsome chancel, the stump of a tower, and one aisle just weather-tight and usable, but, by its very aspect, begging for the completion of the beautiful design that was suspended above the alms-box.

It was the evening of a summer day which had been very hot. The choir practice was just over, and the boys came out trooping and chattering; very small ones they were; for as soon as they began to sing tolerably they were sure to try to get into the choir of the old church, which had a foundation that fed, clothed, taught, and finally apprenticed them. So, though the little fellows were clad in surplices and cassocks, and sat in the chancel for correctness sake, there was a space round the harmonium reserved for the more trustworthy band of girls and young women who came forth next, followed by four or five mechanics.

Behind came the nucleus of the choir—a slim, fair-haired youth of twenty; a neat, precise, well-trimmed man, closely shaven, with stooping shoulders, at least fifteen years older, with a black poodle at his heels, as well shorn as his master, newly risen from lying outside the church door; a gentle, somewhat drooping lady in black, not yet middle-aged and very pretty; a small eager, unformed, black-eyed girl, who could hardly keep back her words for the outside of the church door; a tall self-possessed handsome woman, with a fine classical cast of features; and lastly, a brown-faced, wiry hardworking clergyman, without an atom of superfluous flesh, but with an air of great energy.

'Oh! vicar, where are we to go?' was the question so eager to break forth.

'Not to the Crystal Palace, Nuttie. The funds won't bear it. Mr. Dutton says we must spend as little as possible on locomotion.'

'I'm sure I don't care for the Crystal Palace. A trumpery tinsel place, all shams.'

'Hush, hush, my dear, not so loud,' said the quiet lady; but Nuttie only wriggled her shoulders, though her voice was a trifle lowered. 'If it were the British Museum now, or Westminster Abbey.'

'Or the Alps,' chimed in a quieter voice, 'or the Ufizzi.'

'Now, Mr. Dutton, that's not what I want. Our people aren't ready for that, but what they have let it be real. Miss Mary, don't you see what I mean?'

'Rather better than Miss Egremont herself,' said Mr. Dutton.

'Well,' said the vicar, interposing in the wordy war, 'Mrs. Greenleaf's children have scarlatina, so we can't go to Horton Bishop. The choice seems to be between South Beach and Monks Horton.'

'That's no harm,' cried Nuttie; 'Mrs. Greenleaf is so patronising!'

'And both that and South Beach are so stale,' said the youth.

'As if the dear sea could ever be stale,' cried the young girl.

'I thought Monks Horton was forbidden ground,' said Miss Mary.

'So it was with the last regime', said the vicar; 'but now the new people are come I expect great things from them. I hear they are very friendly.'

'I expect nothing from them,' said Nuttie so sententiously that all her hearers laughed and asked 'her exquisite reason,' as Mr. Dutton put it.

'Lady Kirkaldy and a whole lot of them came into the School of Art.'

'And didn't appreciate "Head of Antinous by Miss Ursula Egremont,"' was the cry that interrupted her, but she went on with dignity unruffled —'Anything so foolish and inane as their whole talk and all their observations I never heard. "I don't like this style," one of them said. "Such ugly useless things! I never see anything pretty and neatly finished such as we used to do."' The girl gave it in a tone of mimicry of the nonchalant voice, adding, with fresh imitation, '"And another did not approve of drawing from the life —models might be such strange people."'

'My ears were not equally open to their profanities,' said Miss Mary. 'I confess that I was struck by the good breeding and courtesy of the leader of the party, who, I think, was Lady Kirkaldy herself.'

'I saw! I thought she was patronising you, and my blood boiled!' cried Nuttie.

'Will boiling blood endure a picnic in the park of so much ignorance, folly, and patronage?' asked Mr. Dutton.

'Oh, indeed, Mr. Dutton, Nuttie never said that,' exclaimed gentle Mrs. Egremont.

'Whether it is fully worth the doing is the question,' said the vicar.

'Grass and shade do not despise,' said Miss Mary.

'There surely must be some ecclesiastical remains,' said the young man.

'And there is a river,' added the vicar.

'I shall get a stickleback for my aquarium,' cried Nuttie. 'We shall make some discoveries for the Scientific Society. I shall note down every individual creature I see! I say! you are sure it is not a sham waterfall or Temple of Tivoli?'

'It would please the choir boys and G. F. S. girls quite as much, if not more, in that case,' said Miss Mary; 'but you need not expect that, Nuttie. Landscape-gardening is gone by.'

'Even with the county people?' said Nuttie.

'By at least half a century,' said Mr. Dutton, 'with all deference to this young lady's experience.'

'It was out of their own mouths,' cried the girl defiantly. 'That's all I know about county people, and so I hope it will be.'

'Come in, my dear, you are talking very fast,' interposed Mrs. Egremont, with some pain in the soft sweet voice, which, if it had been a little stronger, would have been the best in the choir.

These houses in St. Ambrose's Road were semi-detached. The pair which the party had reached had their entrances at the angles, with a narrow gravel path leading by a tiny grass plat to each. One, which was covered with a rich pall of purple clematis, was the home of Mrs. Egremont, her aunt, and Nuttie; the other, adorned with a Gloire de Dijon rose in second bloom, was the abode of Mary Nugent, with her mother, the widow of a naval captain. Farther on, with adjoining gardens, was another couple of houses, in one of which lived Mr. Dutton; in the other lodged the youth, Gerard Godfrey, together with the partner of the principal medical man. The opposite neighbours were a master of the Modern School and a scholar. Indeed, the saying of the vicar, the Rev. Francis Spyers, was, and St. Ambrose's Road was proud of it, that it was a professional place. Every one had something to do either with schools or umbrellas, scarcely excepting the doctor and the solicitor, for the former attended the pupils and the latter supplied them. Mr. Dutton was a partner in the umbrella factory, and lived, as the younger folk said, as the old bachelor of the Road. Had he not a housekeeper, a poodle, and a cat; and was not his house, with lovely sill boxes full of flowers in the windows, the neatest of the neat; and did not the tiny conservatory over his dining-room window always produce the flowers most needed for the altar vases, and likewise bouquets for the tables of favoured ladies. Why, the very daisies never durst lift their heads on his little lawn, which even bore a French looking-glass globe in the centre. Miss Nugent, or Miss Mary as every one still called her, as her elder sister's marriage was recent, was assistant teacher at the School of Art, and gave private drawing lessons, so as to supplement the pension on which her mother lived. They also received girls as boarders attending the High School.

So did Miss Headworth, who had all her life been one of those people who seem condemned to toil to make up for the errors or disasters of others. First she helped to educate a brother, and soon he had died to leave an orphan daughter to be bred up at her cost. The girl had married from her first situation; but had almost immediately lost her husband at sea, and on this her aunt had settled at Micklethwayte to make a home for her and her child, at first taking pupils, but when the High School was set up, changing these into boarders; while Mrs. Egremont went as daily governess to the children of a family of somewhat higher pretensions. Little Ursula, or Nuttie, as she was called, according to the local contraction, was like the child of all the party, and after climbing up through the High School to the last form, hoped, after passing the Cambridge examination, to become a teacher there in another year.

CHAPTER II.

MONKS HORTON.

'And we will all the pleasures prove,
By shallow rivers, by whose falls
Melodious birds sing madrigals.'—Old Ballad.

It was holiday-time, and liberties were taken such as were not permissible, when they might have afforded a bad precedent to the boarders. Therefore, when two afternoons later Mary Nugent, returning from district visiting, came out into her garden behind the house, she was not scandalised to see a pair of little black feet under a holland skirt resting on a laurel branch, and going a few steps more she beheld a big shady hat, and a pair of little hands busy with a pencil and a blank book; as Ursula sat on the low wall between the gardens, shaded by the laburnum which facilitated the ascent on her own side.

'Oh Miss Mary! Delicious! Come up here! You don't know how charming this is.'

She moved aside so as to leave the ascent—by an inverted flower-pot and a laurel branch—open to her friend, thus knocking down one of the pile of books which she had taken to the top of the wall. Miss Nugent picked it up, 'Marie Stuart! Is this your way of studying her?'

'Now, you know 'tis holiday time, and volunteer work; besides, she was waiting for you, and I could not help doing this.' She held out a hand, which was scarcely needed, and Mary sprang lightly to share her perch upon the wall. 'Look here!'

'Am I to guess the subject as in the game of historic outlines,' said Miss Nugent, as the book was laid on her lap. 'It looks like a modern—no, a mediaeval—edition of Marcus Curtius about to leap into the capital opening for a young man, only with his dogs instead of his horse. That hound seems very rationally to object.'

'Now don't! Guess in earnest.'

'A compliment to your name. The Boy of Egremont, poor fellow, just about to bound across the strid.'

'Exactly! I always feel sure that my father must have done something like this.'

'Was it so heroic?' said Miss Mary. 'You know it was for the hundredth time, and he had no reason to expect any special danger.'

'Oh, but his mother was waiting, and he had to go. Now, I'll tell you how it must have been with my father. You know he sailed away in a yacht before I was born, and poor mother never saw him again; but I know what happened. There was a ship on fire like the Birkenhead, and the little yacht went near to pick up the people, and my father called out, like Sir Humphrey Gilbert—

> "Do not fear, Heaven is as near
> By water as by land."

And the little yacht was so close when the great ship blew up that it got sucked down in the whirlpool, and rescuers and all died a noble death together!'

'Has your mother been telling you?' asked Miss Mary.

'Oh no! she never mentions him. She does not know. No one does; but I am quite sure he died nobly, with no one to tell the tale, only the angels to look on, and that makes it all the finer. Or just suppose he was on a desert island all the time, and came back again to find us! I sometimes think he is.'

'What? When you are *quite sure* of the other theory?'

'I mean I am quite sure while I am thinking about it, or reading Robinson Crusoe, or the Swiss Family.'

'Oh!'

'Miss Mary, has no one ever told you anything about my father?'

'No one.'

'They never tell me. Mother cries, and aunt Ursula puts on her "there's-an-end-of-it look." Do you think there is anything they are waiting to tell me till I am older?'

'If there were, I am sure you had better not try to find it out beforehand.'

'You don't think I would do anything of *that sort*? But I thought you might know. Do you remember their first settling here?'

'Scarcely. I was a very small child then.'

Miss Nugent had a few vague recollections which she did not think it expedient to mention. A dim remembrance rose before her of mysterious whisperings about that beautiful young widow, and that it had been said that the rector of the Old Church had declared himself to know the ladies well, and had heartily recommended them. She thought it wiser only to speak of having been one of their first scholars, telling of the awe Miss Headworth inspired; but the pleasure it was to bring a lesson to pretty Mrs. Egremont, who always rewarded a good one with a kiss, 'and she was so nice to kiss—yes, and is.'

'Aunt Ursel and mother both were governesses,' continued the girl, 'and yet they don't want me to go out. They had rather I was a teacher at the High School.'

'They don't want to trust their Little Bear out in the world.'

'I think it is more than that,' said the girl. 'I can't help thinking that he— my father—must have been some one rather grand, with such a beautiful name as Alwyn Piercefield Egremont. Yes; I know it was that, for I saw my baptismal certificate when I stood for the scholarship; it was Dieppe,—Ursula Alice, daughter of Alwyn Piercefield and Alice Elizabeth Egremont, May 15, 1860. James Everett—I think he was the chaplain at Dieppe.'

Mary Nugent thought it the wisest way to laugh and say: 'You, of all people in the world, to want to make out a connection with the aristocracy!'

'True love is different,' said Ursula. 'He must have been cast off by his family for her sake, and have chosen poverty—

> "To make the croon a pund, my Alwyn gaed to sea,
> And the croon and the pund, they were baith for me."'

Miss Mary did not think a yacht a likely place for the conversion of a croon into a pound, and the utter silence of mother and aunt did not seem to her satisfactory; but she feared either to damp the youthful enthusiasm for the lost father, or to foster curiosity that might lead to some painful discovery, so she took refuge in an inarticulate sound.

'I think Mr. Dutton knows,' proceeded Nuttie.

'You don't mean to ask him?'

'Catch me! I know how he would look at me.'

'Slang! A forfeit!'

'Oh, it's holiday time, and the boarders can't hear. There's Mr. Dutton's door!'

This might in one way be a relief to Miss Nugent, but she did not like being caught upon the wall, and therefore made a rapid descent, though not without a moment's entanglement of skirt, which delayed her long enough to show where she had been, as Mr. Dutton was at the same moment advancing to his own wall on the opposite side of the Nugent garden. Perhaps he would have pretended to see nothing but for Nuttie's cry of glee.

'You wicked elf,' said Miss Mary, 'to inveigle people into predicaments, and then go shouting ho! ho! ho! like Robin Goodfellow himself.'

'You should have kept your elevation and dignity like me,' retorted Ursula; 'and then you would have had the pleasure of seeing Mr. Dutton climbing his wall and coming to our feet.'

'Mischievous elves deserve no good news,' said Mr. Dutton, who was by no means so venerable that the crossing the wall was any effort or compromise of dignity, and who had by this time joined Mary on her grass plat.

'Oh, what is it! Are we to go to Monks Horton?' cried Nuttie.

'Here is a gracious permission from Lord Kirkaldy, the only stipulations being that no vestiges of the meal, such as sandwich papers or gooseberry skins, be left on the grass; and that nobody does any mischief,' he added in an awful tone of personality. 'So if I see anybody rooting up holly trees I shall be bound to interfere.'

'Now, Mr. Dutton, it was only a baby holly in a chink.'

'Only a holly tree! Just like the giant's daughter when she only carried off waggon, peasant, oxen, and all in her pinafore.'

'It is not longer than my finger now!'

'Well, remember, mischief either wanton or scientific is forbidden. You are to set an example to the choir-boys.'

'Scientific mischief is a fatal thing to rare plants,' said Mary.

'If I'm not to touch anything, I may as well stay at home,' pouted Nuttie.

'You may gather as many buttercups and daisies as the sweet child pleases,' said Mr. Dutton; whereupon she threatened to throw her books at his head.

Miss Nugent asked how they were to go, and Mr. Dutton explained that there was only a quarter of a mile's walk from the station; that return tickets would be furnished at a tariff of fourpence a head; and that there would be trains at 1.15 and 7.30.

'How hungry the children will be.'

'They will eat all the way. That's the worst of this sort of outing. They eat to live and live to eat.'

'At least they don't eat at church,' said Nuttie.

'Not since the peppermint day, when Mr. Spyers suspended Dickie Drake,' put in Mary.

And the Spa Terrace Church people said it was incense.'

'No. Nuttie!'

'Indeed they did. Louisa Barnet attacked us about it at school, and I said I wished it had been. Only they mustn't eat peppermint in the train, for it makes mother quite ill.'

'Do you mean that Mrs. Egremont will come?' exclaimed Mr. Dutton.

'Oh yes, she shall. It is not too far, and it will be very good for her. I shall make her.'

'There's young England's filial duty!' said Mary.

'Why, I know what is good for her, and she always does as "I wish."'

'Beneficent despotism!' said Mr. Dutton. 'May I ask if Miss Headworth is an equally obedient subject.'

'Oh! Aunt Ursel is very seldom tiresome.'

'Nuttie! Nuttie! my dear,' and a head with the snows of more than half a century appeared on the other side of the wall, under a cap and parasol. 'I am sorry to interrupt you, but it is cool enough for your mother to go into the town, and I wish you to go with her.'

CHAPTER III.

HEIR HUNTING.

'And she put on her gown of green,
And left her mother at sixteen,
To marry Peter Bell!'—WORDSWORTH.

In the shrubberies of Monks Horton were walking a lady somewhat past middle age, but full of activity and vigour, with one of those bright faces that never grow old, and with her a young man, a few years over twenty, with a grave and almost careworn countenance.

More and more confidential waxed the conversation, for the lady was making fresh acquaintance with a nephew seldom seen since he had been her pet and darling as almost a baby, and he was experiencing the inexpressible charm of tone and manner that recalled the young mother he had lost in early boyhood.

'Then your mind is made up,' she said; 'you are quite right to decide on having a profession; but how does your father take it?'

'He is quite convinced that to repeat my uncle's life, dangling on as heir, would be the most fatal mistake.'

'Assuredly, and all the legal knowledge you acquire is so much in favour of your usefulness as the squire.'

'If I ever am the squire, of which I have my doubts.'

'You expect Mr. Egremont to marry?'

'Not a future marriage, but one in the past.'

'A private marriage! Do you suspect it?'

'I don't suspect it—I know it. I have been hoping to talk the matter over with you. Do you remember our first governess, Miss Headworth?'

'My dear Mark, did I not lose at Pera the charms of your infancy?'

'Then neither my mother nor my grandmother ever wrote to you about her?'

'I do remember that it struck me that immunity from governesses was a compensation for the lack of daughters.'

'Can you tell me no details,' said Mark anxiously. 'Have you no letters? It was about the time when Blanche was born, when we were living at Raxley.'

'I am sorry to say that our roving life prevented my keeping old letters. I have often regretted it. Let me see, there was one who boxed May's ears.'

'That was long after. I think it was that woman's barbarity that made my father marry again, and a very good thing that was. It was wretched before. Miss Headworth was in my own mother's time.'

'I begin to remember something happening that your mother seemed unable to write about, and your grandmother said that she had been greatly upset by "that miserable affair," but I was never exactly told what it had been.'

'Miss Headworth came when I was four or five years old. Edda, as we used to call her in May's language, was the first person who gave me a sense of beauty. She had dark eyes and a lovely complexion. I remember in after times being silenced for saying, "not so pretty as my Edda." I was extremely fond of her, enough to have my small jealousy excited when my uncle joined us in our walks, and monopolised her, turning May and me over to play with his dog!'

'But, Mark, Mr. Egremont is some years older than your father. He could not have been a young man at that time.'

'So much the worse. Most likely he seemed to her quite paternal. The next thing I recollect was our being in the Isle of Wight, we two children, with Miss Headworth and the German nurse, and our being told of our new sister. Uncle Alwyn and his yacht were there, and we went on board once or twice. Then matters became confused with me, I recollect a confusion, papa and grandmamma suddenly arriving, everybody seeming to us to have become very cross, our dear Miss Headworth nowhere to be found, our attendants being changed, and our being forbidden to speak of her again. I certainly never thought of the matter till a month ago. You know my uncle's eyes have been much affected by his illness, and he has made a good deal of use of me. He has got a valet, a fellow of no particular country, more Savoyard than anything else, I fancy. He is a legacy, like other evils, from the old General, and seems a sort of necessity to my uncle's existence. Gregorio they call him. He was plainly used to absolute government, and viewed the coming down amongst us as an assertion of liberty much against his will. We could see that he was awfully jealous of my father and me, and would do anything to keep us out; but providentially he can't write English decently, though he can speak any language you please. Well, the man and I came into collision about a scamp of a groom who was doing intolerable mischief in the village, and whom they put it on me to get discharged. On that occasion Mr. Gregorio grew insolent, and intimated to me that I need not make so sure of the succession. He knew that which might make the Chanoine and me change our note. Well, my father is always for avoiding rows; he said it was an unmeaning threat, it was of no use to complain of Gregorio, and we must digest his insolence. But just after, Uncle Alwyn sent me to hunt up a paper that was missing, and in searching a writing-case I came upon an unmistakable marriage certificate between Alwyn Piercefield Egremont and

Alice Headworth, and then the dim recollections I told you of began to return.'

'What did you do?'

'I thought I had better consult my father, expecting to hear that she was dead, and that no further notice need be taken of the matter. But he was greatly disturbed to hear of the certificate, and would hardly believe me. He said that some friend of my grandmother had written her word of goings on at Freshwater between his brother and the young governess, and that they went off at once to put a stop to it, but found us left with the German maid, who declared that Miss Headworth had gone off with Mr. Egremont in the yacht. No more was heard of my uncle for six weeks, and when he came back there was a great row with the old General, but he absolutely denied being married. I am afraid that was all the old sinner wished, and they went off together in the yacht to the West Indies, where it was burnt; but they, as you know, never came to England again, going straight off to the Mediterranean, having their headquarters at Sorrento, and cruising about till the General's death ten years ago.'

'Yes, I once met them at Florence, and thought them two weary pitiable men. One looked at the General as a curious relic of the old buck of the Regency days, and compassionated his nephew for having had his life spoilt by dangling after the old man. It was a warning indeed, and I am glad you have profited by it, Mark.'

'He came back, after the old man died, to club life in London, and seldom has been near the old place; indeed, it has been let till recently, and he wants to let it again, but it is altogether too dilapidated for that without repairs. So he came down to see about it, and was taken ill there. But to return to what my father told me. He was shocked to hear of the certificate, for he had implicitly believed his brother's denial of the marriage, and he said Miss Headworth was so childish and simple that she might easily have been taken in by a sham ceremony. He said that he now saw he had done very wrong in letting his mother-in-law take all the letters about "that unhappy business" off his hands without looking at them, but he was much engrossed by my mother's illness, and, as he said, it never occurred to him as a duty to trace out what became of the poor thing, and see that she was provided for safely. You know Mrs. Egremont says laissez faire is our family failing, and that our first thought is how *not* to do it.'

'Yes, utter repudiation of such cases was the line taken by the last generation; and I am afraid my mother would be very severe.'

'Another thing that actuated my father was the fear of getting his brother into trouble with General Egremont, as he himself would have been the one to profit by it. So I do not wonder so much at his letting the whole drop without inquiry, and never even looking at the letters, which there certainly were. I could not get him to begin upon it with my uncle, but Mrs. Egremont was strongly on my side in thinking that such a thing ought to be looked into, and as I had found the paper it would be best that I should speak. Besides that there was no enduring that Gregorio should be pretending to hold us in terror by such hints.'

'Well, and has there been a wife and family in a cottage all this time?'

'Aunt Margaret, he has never seen or heard of her since he left her at Dieppe! Would you believe it, he thinks himself a victim? He never meant more than to amuse himself with the pretty little governess; and he took on board a Mr. and Mrs. Houghton to do propriety, shady sort of people I imagine, but that she did not know.'

'I have heard of them,' said Lady Kirkaldy, significantly.

'She must have been a kind friend to the poor girl,' said Mark. 'On some report that Lady de Lyonnais was coming down on her, wrathful and terrible, the poor foolish girl let herself be persuaded to be carried off in the yacht, but there Mrs. Houghton watched over her like a dragon. She made them put in at some little place in Jersey, put in the banns, all unknown to my uncle, and got them married. Each was trying to outwit the other, while Miss Headworth herself was quite innocent and unconscious, and, I don't know whether to call it an excuse for Uncle Alwyn or not, but to this hour he is not sure whether it was a legal marriage, and my father believes it was not, looking on it as a youthful indiscretion. He put her in lodgings at Dieppe, under Mrs. Houghton's protection, while he returned home on a peremptory summons from the General. He found the old man in such a state of body and mind as he tries to persuade me was an excuse for denying the whole thing, and from that time he represents himself as bound hand and foot by the General's tyranny. He meant to have kept the secret, given her an allowance, and run over from time to time to see her, but he only could get there once before the voyage to the West Indies. The whole affair was, as he said, complicated by his debts, those debts that the estate has never paid off. The General probably distrusted him, for he curtailed his allowance, and scarcely let him out of sight; and he—he submitted for the sake of his prospects, and thinking the old man much nearer his end than he proved to be. I declare as I listened, it came near to hearing him say he had sold his soul to Satan! From the day he sailed in the Ninon he has never written, never attempted any communication with the woman whose life he had wrecked, except one inquiry at Dieppe, and that was through Gregorio.'

'What! the valet?'

Yes. I believe I seemed surprised at such a medium being employed, for Uncle Alwyn explained that the man had got hold of the secret somehow—servants always know everything—and being a foreigner he was likely to be able to trace her out.

'I daresay he profited by the knowledge to keep Alwyn in bondage during the old man's lifetime.'

'I have no doubt of it, and he expected to play the same game with me. The fellow reminds me, whenever I look at him, of a sort of incarnate familiar demon. When I asked my uncle whether he could guess what had become of her, he held up his hands with a hideous French grimace. I could have taken him by the throat.'

'Nay, one must pity him. The morals of George IV.'s set had been handed on to him by the General,' said Lady Kirkaldy, rejoicing in the genuine indignation of the young face, free from all taint of vice, if somewhat rigid. 'And what now?'

'He assured me that he could make all secure to my father and me, as if that were the important point; but finally he perceived that we had no right to stand still without endeavouring to discover whether there be a nearer heir, and my father made him consent to my making the search, grinning at its Quixotism all the time.'

'Have you done anything?'

'Yes. I have been to Jersey, seen the register—July 20, 1859—and an old French-speaking clerk, who perfectly recollected the party coming from the yacht, and spoke of her as tres belle. I have also ascertained that there is no doubt of the validity of the marriage. Then, deeply mistrusting Master Gregorio, I went on to Dieppe, where I entirely failed to find any one who knew or remembered anything about them—there is such a shifting population of English visitors and residents, and it was so long ago. I elicited from my uncle that she had an aunt, he thought, of the same name as herself; but my father cannot remember who recommended her, or anything that can be a clue. Has any one looked over my grandmother's letters?'

'I think not. My brother spoke of keeping them till I came to London. That might give a chance, or the Houghtons might know about her. I think my husband could get them hunted up. They are sure to be at some continental resort.'

'What's that?' as a sound of singing was heard.

'"Auld Langsyne." The natives are picnicking in the ravine below there. They used to be rigidly excluded, but we can't stand that; and this is the first experiment of admitting them on condition that they don't make themselves obnoxious.'

'Which they can't help.'

'We have yet to see if this is worse than an Austrian or Italian festival. See, we can look down from behind this yew tree. It really is a pretty sight from this distance.'

'There's the cleric heading his little boys and their cricket, and there are the tuneful party in the fern on the opposite side. They have rather good voices, unless they gain by distance.'

'And there's a girl botanising by the river.'

'Sentimentalising over forget-me-nots, more likely.'

'My dear Mark, for a specimen of young England, you are greatly behindhand in perception of progress!'

'Ah! you are used to foreigners, Aunt Margaret. You have never fathomed English vulgarity.'

'It would serve you right to send you to carry the invitation to go round the gardens and houses.'

'Do you mean it, aunt?'

'Mean it? Don't you see your uncle advancing down the road—there—accosting the clergyman—what's his name—either Towers or Spires—something ecclesiastical I know. We only waited to reconnoitre and see whether the numbers were unmanageable.'

'And yet he does not want to sit for Micklethwayte?'

'So you think no one can be neighbourly except for electioneering! O Mark, I must take you in hand.'

'Meantime the host is collecting. I abscond. Which is the least showy part of the establishment?'

'I recommend the coal cellar—'and, as he went off—'poor boy, he is a dear good fellow, but how little he knows how to be laughed at!'

CHAPTER IV.

A NAME.

'So you have ventured out again,' said Lady Kirkaldy, as her nephew strolled up to her afternoon tea-table under a great cedar tree:

'The coast being clear, and only distant shouts being heard in the ravine—

    '"Like an army defeated
The choir retreated;
And now doth fare well
In the valley's soft swell,"'

said the aunt.

'At least you have survived; or is this the reaction,' said the nephew, putting on a languid air.

'There were some very nice people among them, on whom the pictures were by no means thrown away. What would you say, Mark, if I told you that I strongly suspect that I have seen your lost aunt?'

'Nonsense!' cried Mark, as emphatically as disrespectfully.

'I am not joking in the least,' said Lady Kirkaldy, looking up at him. 'I heard the name of Egremont, and made out that it belonged to a very lady-like pretty-looking woman in gray and white; she seemed to be trying to check and tame a bright girl of eighteen or so, who was in a perfect state of rapture over the Vandykes. I managed to ask the clergyman who the lady was, and he told me she was a Mrs. Egremont, who lives with her aunt, a Miss Headworth, who boards girls for the High School; very worthy people, he added.'

'Headworth?'

'Yes.'

'But if it were, she would have known your name.'

'Hardly. The title had not come in those days; and if she heard of us at all it would be as Kerrs. I ventured further to put out a feeler by asking whether he knew what her husband had been, and he said he believed he had been lost at sea, but he, Mr. Spyers I mean, had only been at Micklethwayte three or four years, and had merely known her as a widow.'

'I suppose it is worth following up,' said Mark, rather reluctantly. 'I wish I had seen her. I think I should know Miss Headworth again, and she would hardly know me.'

'You see what comes of absconding.'

'After all, it was best,' said Mark. 'Supposing her to be the real woman, which I don't expect, it might have been awkward if she had heard my name! How can we ascertain the history of this person without committing ourselves?'

Lord Kirkaldy, an able man, who had been for many years a diplomatist, here joined the party, and the whole story was laid before him. He was new to Micklethwayte, having succeeded a somewhat distant kinsman, and did not know enough of the place to be able to fix on any one to whom to apply for information; but the result of the consultation was that Lady Kirkaldy should go alone to call on Miss Headworth, and explain that she was come to inquire about a young lady of the same name, who had once been governess to the children of her sister, Lady Adelaide Egremont. Mark was rather a study to his uncle and aunt all the evening. He was as upright and honourable as the day, and not only acted on high principle, but had a tender feeling to the beautiful playfellow governess, no doubt enhanced by painful experiences of successors chosen for their utter dissimilarity to her. Still it was evidently rather flat to find himself probably so near the tangible goal of his romantic search; and the existence of a first cousin had been startling to him, though his distaste was more to the taking her from second-rate folk in a country town than to the overthrow of his own heirship. At least so he manifestly and honestly believed, and knowing it to be one of those faiths that make themselves facts, the Kirkaldys did not disturb him in it, nor commiserate him for a loss which they thought the best thing possible for him.

Miss Headworth was accustomed to receive visitors anent boarders, so when Lady Kirkaldy's card was brought to her, the first impression was that some such arrangement was to be made. She was sitting in her pretty little drawing-room alone, for Nuttie and her mother had gone out for a walk with Miss Nugent.

The room, opening on the garden, and cool with blinds, had a certain homely grace about the faded furniture. The drawings on the walls were good, the work quaint and tasteful. There was a grand vase of foxgloves before the empty grate, and some Marshal Nial roses in a glass on the table. The old lady herself—with alert black eyes and a sweet expression—rose from her chair in the window to receive her guest.

Lady Kirkaldy felt reassured as to the refinement of the surroundings, and liked the gentle but self-possessed tones of the old lady. She noticed the foxgloves.

'Yes,' said Miss Headworth, 'they are the fruits of yesterday's expedition. My two children, as I call them, brought them home in triumph. I cannot tell you what pleasure Lord Kirkaldy's kindness gave them—and many more.'

'I am glad,' said the lady, while she said to herself, 'now for it,' and sat forward. 'It struck me,' she said, 'on hearing your name that you might be related to—to a young lady who lived a good while ago in the family of my sister, Lady Adelaide Egremont.'

A strange look came into Miss Headworth's eyes, her lips trembled, she clutched tightly the arm of her chair, but then cast a puzzled glance at her visitor.

'Perhaps if you heard of me then,' said the latter, 'it was as Lady Margaret Kerr.'

'Yes,' said Miss Headworth, then pausing, she collected herself and said in an anxious voice, 'Do I understand that your ladyship is come to inquire for my niece, being aware of the circumstances.'

'I only became aware of them yesterday,' said Lady Kirkaldy. 'I was in Turkey at the time, and no particulars were given to me; but my nephew, Mark Egremont, your niece's old pupil, came to consult us, having just discovered among his uncle's papers evidence of the marriage, of which of course he had been ignorant.'

'Then,' exclaimed Miss Headworth, holding her hands tightly clasped, 'Shall I really see justice done at last to my poor child?'

'It is young Mark's most earnest wish and his father—'Lady Kirkaldy hesitated for a word, and Miss Headworth put in:

'His father! Why would he never even acknowledge either Alice's letters or mine? We wrote several times both to him and Lady Adelaide, and never received any reply, except one short one, desiring he might not be troubled on such a subject. It was cruel! Alice said it was not in his writing. She had done very wrong, and the family might well be offended, but a poor child like her, just eighteen, might have been treated with some pity.'

'My sister was in declining health. He was very much engrossed. He left the matter to—to others,' said Lady Kirkaldy. 'He is very sorry now that he acquiesced in what was then thought right. He did not then know that there had been a marriage.'

'I should have thought in that case a clergyman would have been bound to show the more compassion.'

Lady Kirkaldy knew that the cruel silence had been chiefly the work of the stem Puritan pitilessness of her mother, so she passed this over, saying, 'We are all very anxious to atone, as far as possible, for what is past, but we know little or nothing, only what my nephew Mark has been able to gather.'

'Little Mark! Alice always talked of him with great affection. How pleased she will be to hear of his remembering her.'

'Would you object to telling me what you know of this history?' said Lady Kirkaldy. 'I am afraid it is very painful to you, but I think we should understand it clearly. Please speak to me as a friend, as woman to woman.'

'Your ladyship is very kind,' said the poor old lady. 'I have only mentioned the subject once since we came to settle here, seventeen years ago, but such things one cannot forget. If you will excuse me, I have some dates that will assist my accuracy.'

She hurried away, and came back in a few moments, having evidently dried some tears, perhaps of thankfulness, but she paused as if reluctant to begin.

'I think your niece had no nearer relation than yourself,' said Lady Kirkaldy, anxious to set her off and at ease.

'Oh no, or she never would have been so treated. She was an orphan. My poor brother was a curate. He married—as young men will—on insufficient means, his strength gave way, and he died of diphtheria when this poor child was only two years old. Indeed, two little ones died at the same time, and the mother married again and went to Shanghai. She did not long live there, poor thing, and little Alice was sent home to me. I thought I did my best for her by keeping her at a good school. I have often wished that I had given up my situation, and become an assistant there, so as to have her more under my own eyes; but I fancied it important to receive a salary out of which I could save. I am wearying your ladyship, but I can't but dwell on the excuses for my poor child.'

'Indeed I wish to hear all the details,' was the sincere and gentle answer.

'I had her with me generally in the holidays, and I confess I was absolutely alarmed to see how pretty the child was growing, knowing how great a disadvantage it often is. She was always a good girl, not naturally so studious as could be wished, but docile, merry, gentle, a favourite with every one, and peculiarly innocent and childish. I wished her to remain a few years longer as teacher, but it so happened that Lady Adelaide Egremont, coming to consult the head of the establishment about a nursery-governess, saw Alice, and was so much struck with her sweet face, which was all sunshine then, as to insist on engaging her.'

'Ah! my dear sister, I remember her enthusiastic letter about her pretty governess, and her boy's affection for her, an affection that has lasted—'

'It seemed so safe. A clergyman's family in the country, and so kind a lady at the head, that, though Alice had been educated for a superior governess, it appeared the best beginning she could have. And she was very happy, and met with great kindness. Only, unfortunately, Lady Adelaide was delicate, and for many weeks entirely confined to the sofa. Mr. Egremont's elder brother was much there. He seemed to my poor inexperienced child quite elderly, and his attentions like those of—of an old uncle—she told me afterwards—'

'He must really have been over forty—'

'No doubt my poor Alice was unguarded. We know what a merry, happy, childish girl may be, but I never heard that her conduct was even censured while she remained at Baxley, though I find that Captain Egremont used to join them in their walks, under pretext of playing with the children. Then she was sent to Freshwater with the two eldest children during Lady Adelaide's confinement, and there, most unjustifiably, Captain Egremont continually visited them from his yacht, and offered to take them out in it. Alice knew she ought not to go without a married lady on board, and he brought a Mr. and Mrs. Houghton to call, who were very kind and caressing to her and the children, so that she thought all was right. Oh! Lady Kirkaldy, I don't mean to defend her, I daresay she was very giddy and silly, she reproaches herself, poor dear, but I do say that a wicked advantage was taken of her innocence and ignorance. She says that she had begun to grow a little uneasy at the way people looked when Captain Egremont joined them on the beach; and the nurse, a German, said something that she could not understand. On the 1st of July—yes—but I have the date here—came a telegram to the hotel to have rooms for Lady de Lyonnais and Mr. Egremont ready by the evening. The whole place knew it, and some meddling person burst on Alice with the news, roughly and coarsely given, that they were coming to call her to account for her goings on. Captain Egremont found her crying in the utmost terror, and— she really hardly knew what he said to her—she thinks he offered to shelter her on board the Ninon, from Lady de Lyonnais' first wrath while he and Mrs. Houghton explained matters; but she cannot tell, for she lost her senses with fright, only knew that he was kind and sweet to her in her distress, and thought only of escaping. Well, I don't excuse her. Of course it was the most terrible and fatal thing she could have done, and—' The good old lady was quite overcome, and Lady Kirkaldy had tears in her eyes as she said,

'It was frightful folly—but she was guarded.'

'Yes, her innocence was guarded, thank God,' said Miss Headworth fervently. 'You see she did know that Mr. and Mrs. Houghton were on board, and Mrs. Houghton was a truly kind protector who deserved her confidence, though, poor lady, she admitted to me that her own conduct had not been-strictly correct.'

'How long was it before you heard of her?'

'There was a dreadful letter from Mr. Egremont enclosing what was due of her salary, and then I heard no more for seven months. I went to the Isle of Wight and made all inquiries, but the nurse and children had gone away immediately, and I could obtain no trace of them.'

'Then she—your niece, never wrote.'

'She was afraid, poor dear. She had never been at her ease with me. Her mother had taught her to think me strict and harsh, and she had never opened to me in those days. Besides, he had forbidden her. At last, however, in January, came a letter from this Mrs. Houghton, telling me that my Alice was very unwell at Dieppe, that nothing had been heard of her husband, Captain Egremont, to whom she had been married on the 20th of July at St. Philippe, in Jersey, and that she herself was obliged to leave the place almost immediately; but she would, if possible, wait till my arrival, as Mrs. Egremont was not in a condition to be left alone. My dear friends, with whom I was then living, were as kind as possible, and set me free to go. I was there in three days, and truly the dear, beautiful, merry girl I had parted with only a year before was a sad piteous sight. Mrs. Houghton seemed broken-hearted at leaving her, thinking there was little chance of her living; but Mr. Houghton, who, I am afraid, was a professed gambler, had got into some scrape, and was gone to Paris, where she had to follow him. She told me all about it, and how, when Captain Egremont fancied that a marriage in the Channel Islands was one he could play fast and loose with, she had taken care that the formalities should be such as to make all secure. Foolish and wrong as poor Alice had been, she had awakened all the best side of that poor woman's nature, and no mother could have been more careful and tender. She gave me the certificate —here it is—and assured me that it would hold good. I have shown it to a lawyer, and he said the same; but when I sent a copy to Mr. Egremont, my letter was returned unopened.'

'Captain Egremont had denied the marriage, and they believed him,' said Lady Kirkaldy. 'It is hard to believe that he could be so heartless, but he was in bondage to the old General Egremont, and dreaded losing his inheritance.'

'So he told them in his one visit to Dieppe. He said he must keep his

marriage secret, but promised an allowance, on condition that Alice would live quietly at Dieppe, and not communicate with any one of her own family or his. He had left £100 with her, but that was nearly gone, and she had never heard from him. It had preyed on her, and she was so ill that I never expected, any more than Mrs. Houghton, to see her recover. I stayed there with her; she could not be moved, even if she would have consented, when she was continually expecting him; but at last—four days after her little girl was born
—came the news of the Ninon having been burnt, with all on board, three months before. Do you know, strange to say, though I had feared so much to tell her, she began to revive from that time. The suspense and watching were over. She saw that he had not deserted her, and believed that he had loved her to the last. She cried a great deal, but it was in a peaceful, natural way. I wrote then, as I had already written, to Lady Adelaide and to Mr. Egremont, but was not answered.'

'I can account for that,' said Lady Kirkaldy. 'My sister had been ordered to Madeira in the autumn, and there they remained till her death in May. All the letters were sent to my mother, and she did not think fit to forward, or open, any bearing on the subject. In the meantime Mr. Egremont was presented to the family living, and on his return moved to Bridgefield Egremont. And you came here?'

'Of course I could not part with my poor Alice again. Mr. and Mrs. Fordyce, whose daughter I had long ago educated, had always kept up a correspondence with me, and, knowing all the story, proposed to me to come here. He was then rector of the old church, and by their help and recommendation, with such capital as I had, we were able to begin a little school; and though that has had to give way to the High School, what with boarders, and with Alice's employment as daily governess, we have, I am thankful to say, gone on very well and comfortably, and my dear child has recovered her cheerfulness, though she can never be quite what—I think she was meant to be,' said the old lady, with a sad smile, 'though perhaps she is something better.'

'Do you think she was absolutely convinced of his death?'

'Do you mean that he is alive?' exclaimed Miss Headworth in dismay. 'Oh! he is a wickeder man than even I supposed, to have forsaken her all these years. Is my poor child in his power? Must her peace, now she has attained it, be disturbed?'

'There is a great deal to take into consideration,' said Lady Kirkaldy. 'I had better tell you how this visit of mine came about, and explain some matters about the Egremont family.'

She then told how Captain Egremont, after a brief service in the Life Guards, had been made to retire, that the old General, whose heir he was, might keep him in attendance on him. Already self-indulgent and extravagant, the idleness of the life he led with the worn-out old roue had deadened his better feelings, and habituated him to dissipation, while his debts, his expensive habits, and his dread of losing the inheritance, had bound him over to the General. Both had been saved from the fire in the Ninon, whence they were picked up by a Chilian vessel, and they had been long in communicating with home. The General hated England, and was in broken health. He had spent the remaining years of his life at various continental resorts, where he could enjoy a warm climate, combined with facilities for high play.

When at length, he died, Captain Egremont had continued the life to which he had become accustomed, and had of late manifested an expectation that his nephew Mark should play the same part by him as he had done by the General, but the youth, bred in a very different tone, would on no account thus surrender himself to an evil bondage. Indeed he felt all the severity of youthful virtue, and had little toleration for his uncle's ways of thinking; though, when the old man had come home ill, dejected, and half blind, he had allowed himself to be made useful on business matters. And thus he had discovered the marriage, and had taken up the cause with the ardour stimulated by a chivalrous feeling for the beautiful vision of his childhood, whose sudden disappearance had ended his brightest days.

'I suppose it is right and generous of the young man,' said Miss Headworth. 'But since the—the man is alive, I wish my poor Alice could have been left at peace!'

'You forget that her daughter has rights which must be taken into consideration.'

'Little Nuttie! Dear child! I should so far like her to be provided for, so far as that she need not go out in the world to earn her own livelihood. But no! better be as we are than accept anything from that man!'

'I quite understand and respect your feeling, Miss Headworth,' returned the lady; 'but may I return to my question whether you think your niece has any doubt of her husband being dead.'

Miss Headworth considered. 'Since you ask me, I think she has kept the possibility of the life before her. We have never mentioned the subject, and, as I said, the belief in his death ended a great suspense and sense of wounded affection. She began soon and vigorously to turn her attention to the support of her child, and has found a fair measure of happiness; but at the same time she has shrunk from all notice and society, more than would be natural in so very young a widow and so attractive, more than I should have expected from her original character. And once, when she did apprehend symptoms of admiration, she insisted that I should tell the history, enough, as she said, to make it plain that it was impossible. There was one night too, when she had scarlatina, and was a little lightheaded, only four years ago, when she talked a good deal about his coming back; but that might have been only the old impression on her brain, of that long watching at Dieppe. He—Captain Egremont, does not yet know where she is?'

'No, certainly not. But I fear he must.'

'I suppose he ought,' sighed Miss Headworth; 'but in the meantime, till we know what line he takes, surely she need not be unsettled by the knowledge of his existence.'

'By no means. You had better act as you think best about that. But you will not object to my nephew, her old pupil, Mark, coming to see her? I will make him promise not to enter upon the subject.'

Miss Headworth had only time to make a sign of reluctant acquiescence when the door opened and mother and daughter came in. Nuttie first, eager as usual and open-mouthed, unaware that any one was there, for Lady Kirkaldy, wishing to avoid talk and observation, had left her carriage at the livery stables, and walked to St. Ambrose Road. The girl, whom in a moment she classed as small, dark, and oddly like May Egremont, stopped short at sight of a stranger; the mother would have retreated but for Miss Headworth's nervous call 'Alice, my dear, here is Lady Kirkaldy.'

Very lovely was Lady Kirkaldy's impression as she saw a slender figure in a dark gray linen dress, and a face of refined, though not intellectual, beauty and sweetness, under a large straw hat with a good deal of white gauziness about it, and the curtsey was full of natural grace.

'You do not know me,' said Lady Kirkaldy, taking her hand, 'but I am aunt to some former pupils of yours, one of whom, Mark Egremont, is very anxious to come and see you.'

'Mark! My dear little Mark,' and her face lighted up. 'How very kind of him. But he is not little Mark now.'

'He is not a very big Mark either. Most of the Egremonts are small. I see your daughter takes after them,' said Lady Kirkaldy, shaking hands with Ursula, who looked at her in unmitigated amazement.

Alice faltered something about Lady Adelaide.

'My dear sister fell into a decline, and died while the three children were still babies. Poor things, I believe they had a sad time till their father married a Miss Condamine, who has been an excellent stepmother to them. I have been to see them, but Mark was not then at home, so he has come to me at Monks Horton. When will he find you at home? Or may I bring him in at once. He was to meet me at Micklethwayte.'

'I should like very much to see him,' was the answer. And Miss Headworth was obliged to say something about her ladyship taking a cup of tea. Lady Kirkaldy, knowing that Mark was on the watch, set off in search of him, and found him, as she expected, pacing the pavement in front of the church. There was no great distance in which to utter her explanations and cautions, warning him of her promise that the intelligence of the husband's being alive was to be withheld for a fitter time, but he promised dutifully, and his aunt then took him in with her.

The recognition of her claims was a less stunning shock to Alice Egremont than to her aunt. Shielded by her illness, as well as by her simplicity and ignorance, she had never been aware of her aunt's attempted correspondence with the Egremonts, nor of their deafness to appeals made on her behalf. Far less had it ever occurred to her that the validity of her marriage could be denied, and the heinous error of her elopement seemed to her quite sufficient to account for her having been so entirely cast off by the family. The idea that as wife or widow she had any claims on them, or that Ursula might have rights above those of Mark, had not come into her mind, which, indeed, at the moment was chiefly occupied by the doubt whether the milk was come in, and by ordering in the best teacups, presented by the boarders.

Thus she was in the passage when Mark entered, and his exclamation instantly was 'Oh, Edda, dear old Edda! You aren't a bit altered!' and he put his head under her hat and kissed her, adding, as she seemed rather startled, 'You are my aunt, you know; and where's my cousin? You are Ursula?'

He advanced upon Nuttie, took her by the hand and kissed her forehead before she was aware, but she flashed at him with her black eyes, and looked stiff and defiant. She had no notion of kisses to herself, still less to her pretty mother whom she protected with a half proud, half jealous fondness. How could the man presume to call her by that foolish name? However, that single effusion had exhausted Mark's powers of cordiality, or else Nuttie's stiffness froze him. They were all embarrassed, and had reason to be grateful to Lady Kirkaldy's practised powers as a diplomate's wife. She made the most of Mrs. Egremont's shy spasmodic inquiries, and Mark's jerks of information, such as that they were all living at Bridgefield Egremont, now, that his sister May was very like his new cousin, that Blanche was come out and was very like his mother, etc. etc. Every one was more at ease when Lady Kirkaldy carried the conversation off to yesterday's entertainment, hoping no one had been overtired, and the like. Mrs. Egremont lighted up a little and began telling some of the expressions of delight she had heard, and in the midst, Nuttie, waking from her trance of stiff displeasure, came plump in with 'Oh! and there's a water-soldier, a real Stratiotes aculeatus in your lake. May we get it? Mr. Dutton didn't think we ought, but it would be such a prize!'

'Ursula means a rare water-plant,' said Mrs. Egremont gently, seeing that Lady Kirkaldy had no notion of the treasure she possessed. 'She and some of her friends are very eager botanists.'

'I am sure you may,' said the lady, amused.

'Thank you! Then, O mother! Miss Mary and I will go. And we'll wait till after office hours, and then Gerard Godfrey can come and fish it out for us! Oh, thank you. He wants the pattern of the Abbot's cross for an illumination, and he can get some ferns for the church.'

Soon after this ebullition, Lady Kirkaldy carried off her nephew, and his first utterance outside the door was 'A woman like that will be the salvation of my uncle.'

'Firstly, if you can bring them together,' said his aunt; 'and secondly, if there is stuff enough in that pretty creature.'

CHAPTER V.

SUSPENSE.

Poor Miss Headworth's peace of mind was utterly destroyed. That the niece whom she had nursed back to life and happiness, and brought to love her as a mother, should be at the mercy of a man whom she looked on as a heartless profligate, was dreadful to her beyond measure. And it involved Ursula's young life likewise? Could it be a duty, after these eighteen years, to return to him? What legal rights had he to enforce the resumption of the wife he had deserted. 'I will consult Mr. Dutton,' said the old lady to herself; 'Mr. Dutton is the only person who knows the particulars. He will give me the best advice.'

And while Miss Headworth, over her evening toilette, was coming to this resolution in one bedroom, Nuttie, in another, was standing aghast at her mother's agitation, and receiving a confession which filled her with astonishment.

'I can't think why that gentleman should go and be so affectionate all on a sudden, 'quoth Nuttie;' if he is my cousin, and so fond of you, why couldn't he have come to see us before?'

'Oh, Nuttie, dear, you don't understand why it is so good of him! My dear, now this has come, I must tell you—you must hear—the sad thing your mother did. Yes, my dear, I was their governess—and—and I did not—In short, my dear, I eloped.'

'You, mother! Oh what fun!' cried the girl in the utter extremity of wonder.

'Nuttie!' exclaimed Mrs. Egremont, in a tone of horror and indignation—nay, of apprehension.

'O mother—I didn't mean that! But I can't get to believe it. You, little mother mine, you that are so timid and bashful and quiet. That you—you should have done such a thing.'

'Nuttie, my dear, can't you understand that such a thing would make me quiet? I am always feeling when I see people, or they bring their daughters here. "If they only knew—"'

'No, no, no! They would still see you were the sweetest dear. But tell me all about it. How very much in love you must have been!' said Nuttie, a magnificent vision of a young sailor with curly hair and open throat rising before her.

'I think I was more frightened than in love,' faintly said Mrs. Egremont.

'At least I didn't know it was love, I thought he was only kind to me.'

'But you liked it?' said Ursula magisterially.

'I liked it, oh, I liked it! It gave me a feeling such as nothing else ever did, but I never thought of its being love, he was so much older.'

'Older!' exclaimed Nuttie, much taken aback. 'Oh! as old as Mr. Dutton?'

'Mr. Dutton is thirty-six, I think. Yes, he was older than that.'

'Mother, how could you?' For to be older than Mr. Dutton seemed to the youthful fancy to be near decrepitude; but she added, 'I suppose he was very noble, and had done great things.'

'He was the grandest gentleman I ever saw, and had such, a manner,' said the mother, passing over the latter suggestion. 'Anyway, I never thought what it all meant—all alone with the children as I was—till I found people looking at me, and laughing at me, and then I heard Lady de Lyonnais and Mr. Egremont were coming down, very angry, to send me away. I ought, I know it now, to have waited, for they would have written to my aunt. But I was horribly frightened, and I couldn't bear to think of never seeing him again, and he came and comforted me, and said he would take me to Mrs. Houghton, the kind lady who was staying in the Ninon, and they would make it all square for me—and then—oh! it was very sweet—but I never knew that we were sailing away to Jersey to be married! I knew it was very dreadful without any one's leave, but it was so noble of him to take the poor little governess and defend her, and it wasn't as if my mother had been alive. I didn't know Aunt Ursel then as I did afterwards. And Mrs. Houghton said there was nothing else to be done.'

'O don't leave off, mother. Do tell me. How long did you have him?'

'Six weeks then—and afterwards one fortnight at Dieppe. He was not free. He had an old uncle, General Egremont, who was sick and hot-tempered, and he was obliged to keep everything secret from him, and therefore from everybody else. And so I was to live at Dieppe, while he went out to take care of his uncle, and you know—you know—'

'Yes, I know, dear mother. But I am sure he was saving somebody else, and it was a noble death! And I know how Aunt Ursel came to Dieppe, and how I—your own little Frenchwoman—came to take care of you. And haven't we been jolly without any of these fine relations that never looked after you all this time? Besides, you know he is very likely to be on a lonely coral island, and will come home yet. I often think he is.'

'My dear child, I have been happier than I deserved,' said Alice Egremont, drying her eyes. 'But oh! Nuttie, I hope you will be a wiser woman than your mother.'

'Come, don't go on in that way! Why, I've such advantages! I've Miss Mary, and Aunt Ursel, and Mr. Spyers, and Mr. Dutton, and you, you poor little thing, had nobody! One good thing is, we shall get the water-soldier. Mr. Dutton needn't come, for he's like a cat, and won't soil his boots, but Gerard is dying to get another look at the old ruin. He can't make up his mind about the cross on one of the stone-coffin lids, so he'll be delighted to come, and he'll get it out of the pond for us. I wonder when we can go. To-night is choir practice, and to-morrow is cutting-out day.'

Miss Headworth was not sorry that the small sociabilities of the friends did not leave her alone with her niece all that evening, or the next day, when there was a grand cutting-out for the working party,—an operation always performed in the holidays. Miss Headworth had of late years been excused from it, and it gave her the opportunity she wanted of a consultation with Mr. Dutton. He was her prime adviser in everything, from her investments (such as they were) to the eccentricities of her timepieces; and as the cuckoo-clock had that night cuckooed all the hours round in succession, no one thought it wonderful that she should send a twisted note entreating him to call as early as he could in the afternoon. Of course Nuttie's chatter had proclaimed the extraordinary visitors, and it needed not the old lady's dash under "on an anxious affair" to bring him to her little drawing-room as soon as he could quit his desk. Perhaps he hastened his work with a hope in his heart which he durst not express, but the agitation on the usually placid face forbade him to entertain it for an instant, and he only said, 'So our expedition has led to unforeseen consequences, Miss Headworth.' And then she answered under her breath, as if afraid of being overheard: 'Mr. Dutton, my poor child does not know it yet, but the man is alive!'

Mr. Dutton compressed his lips. It was the greater shock, for he had actually made inquiries at the Yacht Club, but the officials there either had not been made aware of the reappearance of the two Egremonts, or they did not think it worth while to look beyond the record which declared that all hands had perished, and the connection of the uncle and nephew with the Yacht Club had not been renewed. Presently he said, 'Then hers was a right instinct. There is reason to be thankful.'

Miss Headworth was too full of her own anxieties to heed his causes for thankfulness. She told what she had heard from Lady Kirkaldy and from Mark Egremont, and asked counsel whether it could be Alice's duty to return to the man who had deserted her, or even to accept anything from him. There was an impetuous and indignant spirit at the bottom of the old lady's heart, in

spite of the subdued life she had led for so many years, and she hardly brooked
the measured considerate manner in which her adviser declared that all
depended on circumstances, and the manner in which Captain Egremont made
the first move. At present no one was acting but young Mark, and, as Mr.
Dutton observed, it was not a matter in which a man was very likely to submit
to a nephew's dictation.

There was certainly no need for Mrs. Egremont to *force* her presence on
him. But Mr. Dutton did think that for her own sake and her child's there ought
to be full recognition of their rights, and that this should be proved by their
maintenance.

'I imagine that Ursula may probably be a considerable heiress, and her
lights must not be sacrificed.'

'Poor little girl! Will it be for her happiness? I doubt it greatly!'

'Of that I suppose we have no right to judge,' said Mr. Dutton, somewhat
tremulously. 'Justice is what we have to look to, and to allow Nuttie to be
passed over would be permitting a slur to be cast on her and her mother.'

'I see that,' said Miss Headworth, with an effort. 'I suppose I am after all a
selfish, faithless old woman, and it is not in my hands after all. But I must
prepare my poor Alice for what may be coming.'

'If any terms are offered to her, she had better put the matter into a lawyer's
hands. Dobson would be a safe man to deal with.'

Miss Headworth was amazed that he—who had helped her in many a little
question bordering on law—should not proffer his aid now in this greatest
stress. He was a resolute, self-controlled man, and she never guessed at the
feeling that made him judge himself to be no fitting champion for Alice
Egremont against her husband. Ever since, ten years ago, he had learnt that his
beautiful neighbour did not regard herself so certainly a widow as to venture
to open her heart to any other love, he had lived patiently on, content to serve
her as a trustworthy friend, and never betraying the secret hope so long
cherished and now entirely crushed.

He was relieved to escape from the interview, and the poor old lady
remained a little more certain as to her duty perhaps, but with a certainty that
only made her more unhappy, and she was so restless and nervous that, in the
middle of the evening's reading of Archbishop Trench's Lectures on History,
Alice suddenly broke off in the very middle of a sentence and exclaimed, 'Aunt
Ursel! you are keeping something from me.'

Miss Headworth made a faint attempt by saying something about presently,
and glancing with her eyes to indicate that it was to be reserved till

after Nuttie's bedtime, but the young lady comprehended the signs and exclaimed, 'Never mind me, Aunt Ursel,—I know all about mother; she told me last night.'

'It is!' broke in Mrs. Egremont, who had been watching her aunt's face. 'You have heard of *him*.'

'Oh, my father! You really have!' cried Nuttie. 'Then he really was on the desert island all this time; I was quite sure of it. How delightful!' She jumped up and looked at the door, as if she expected to see him appear that instant, clad in skins like Robinson Crusoe, but her aunt's nervous agitation found vent in a sharp reproof: 'Nuttie, hold your tongue, and don't be such a foolish child, or I shall send you out of the room this instant!'

'But aunt?' gasped Alice, unable to bear the suspense.

'Yes, my poor dear child. Captain Egremont with the General got off with some of the crew in a boat when the Ninon was burnt. He spent a good many years abroad with the old man, but he has now inherited the family place, and is living there.' Miss Headworth felt as if she had fired a cannon and looked to see the effect.

'Ah, if we could have stayed at Dieppe!' said Mrs. Egremont. 'But we did write back to say where we could be heard of.'

'That was of no use. Mark found no traces of us when he went thither.'

'Did he send Mark?'

'No. My dear Alice, I must not conceal from you that this is all Mr. Mark Egremont's doing. He seems to have been helping his uncle with his papers when he came on the evidence of your marriage, and, remembering you as he does, he forced the confession of it from the captain, and of his own accord set forth to discover what had become of you and to see justice done to you.'

'Dear little Mark!' said she; 'he always was such an affectionate little boy.'

'And now, my dear, you must consider how you will receive any advances on his part.'

'Oh, Aunt Ursel, don't! I can't talk now. Please let me go to bed. Nuttie, dear, you need not come yet.'

The desire for solitude, in which to realise what she had heard, was overpowering, and she fled away in the summer twilight, leaving Nuttie with wide open eyes, looking after her vanished hero and desert island.

'My poor Alice!' sighed the old lady.

'Aunt Ursel!' exclaimed Nuttie, 'was—I mean—is my father a good or a bad man?'

'My dear, should a daughter ask such a question?'

'Aunt Ursel, I can't help it. I think I ought to know all about it,' said Nuttie gravely, putting away her childishness and sitting down by her aunt. 'I did not think so much of it when mother told me they eloped, because, though I know it was very wrong, people do do odd things sometimes when they are very much in love (she said it in a superior patronising tone that would have amused Miss Headworth very much at any other time); and it has not spoilt mother for being the dearest, sweetest, best thing in the world, and, besides, they had neither of them any fathers or mothers to disobey. But, then, when I found he was so old, and that he kept it a secret, and must have told stories only for the sake of money (uttered with extreme contempt), I didn't like it. And if he left her as Theseus left Ariadne, or Sir Lancelot left Elaine, I—I don't think it is nice. Do you think he only pretended to be lost in the Ninon to get rid of her, or that he could not find her?'

'The Ninon was really reported lost with all on board,' said Miss Headworth. 'That was ascertained. He was saved by a Chilian ship, and seems to have been a good while making his way back to Europe. I had taken care that our address should be known at Dieppe, but it is quite possible that he may not have applied to the right people, or that they may not have preserved my letter, so that we cannot feel sore that he was to blame.'

'If he had been worth anything at all, he would have moved heaven and earth to find her!' cried Nuttie; 'and you said yourself it was all *that* Mark's doing!'

'He seems to be a very upright and generous young man, that Mr. Mark Egremont,' said Miss Headworth, a whole romance as to Nuttie's future destiny sweeping across her mind in an instant, with a mental dispensation to first cousins in such a case. 'I think you will find him a staunch champion even against his own interests.'

Perceptions came across Nuttie. 'Oh, then I am a sort of lost heiress, like people in a story! I see! But, Aunt Ursel, what do you think will happen?'

'My dear child, I cannot guess in the least. Perhaps the Egremont property will not concern you, and only go to male heirs. That would be the best thing, since in any case you must be sufficiently provided for. Your father must do that.'

'But about mother?'

'A proper provision must be insisted on for her,' said Miss Headworth. 'It is no use, however, to speculate on the future. We cannot guess how Mr. Mark

Egremont's communication will be received, or whether any wish will be expressed for your mother's rejoining your father. In such a case the terms must be distinctly understood, and I have full trust both in Mr. Mark and in Lady Kirkaldy as her champions to see that justice is done to you both.'

'I'm sure he doesn't deserve that mother should go to him.'

'Nor do I expect that he will wish it, or that it would be proper; but he is bound to give her a handsome maintenance, and I think most probably you will be asked to stay with your uncle and cousins,' said Miss Headworth, figuring to herself a kind of Newstead Abbey or some such scene of constant orgies at Bridgefield Egremont.

'I shall accept nothing from the family that does not include mother,' said Nuttie.

'Dear child, I foresee many trials, but you must be her protector.'

'That I will,' said Nuttie; and in the gallant purpose she went to bed, to find her mother either asleep or feigning slumber with tears on her cheek.

CHAPTER VI.

THE WATER-SOLDIER.

'Presumptuous maid, with looks intent,
Again she stretched, again she bent,
Nor knew the gulf between.'—GRAY.

It all seemed like a dream to Ursula, perhaps likewise to her mother, when they rose to the routine of daily life with the ordinary interests of the day before them. There was a latent unwillingness in Mrs. Egremont's mind to discuss the subject with either aunt or daughter; and when the post brought no letter, Ursula, after a moment's sense of flatness, was relieved, and returned to her eager desire to hurry after the water-soldier. It was feasible that very afternoon. Mary Nugent came in with the intelligence.

'And can Gerard come? or we shall only look at it.'

'Yes, Gerard can come, and so will Mr. Dutton,' said Mary, who, standing about half-way between Mrs. Egremont and her daughter, did not think herself quite a sufficient chaperon.

'He will look on like a hen at her ducklings,' said Nuttie. 'It is cruel to take him, poor man!'

'Meantime, Nuttie, do you like an hour of "Marie Stuart?"'

'Oh, thank you!' But she whispered, 'Aunt Ursel, may I tell her?'

'Ask your mother, my dear.'

Leave was given, half reluctantly, and with a prohibition against mentioning the subject to any one else, but both mother and aunt had confidence in Mary Nugent's wisdom and discretion, so the two friends sat on the wall together, and Ursula poured out her heart. Poor little girl! she was greatly discomfited at the vanishing of her noble vision of the heroic self- devoted father, and ready on the other hand to believe him a villain, like Bertram Risingham, or 'the Pirate,' being possessed by this idea on account of his West Indian voyages. At any rate, she was determined not to be accepted or acknowledged without her mother, and was already rehearsing magnanimous letters of refusal.

Miss Mary listened and wondered, feeling sometimes as if this were as much a romance as the little yacht going down with the burning ship; and then came back the recollection that there was a real fact that Nuttie had a father, and that it was entirely uncertain what part he might take, or what the girl might be called on to do. Considering anxiously these bearings of the question, she scarcely heard what she was required to assent to, in one of Nuttie's eager, 'Don't you think so?'

'My dear Nuttie,' she said, rousing herself, 'what I do think is that it will all probably turn out exactly contrariwise to our imaginations, so I believe it would be wisest to build up as few fancies as possible, but only to pray that you may have a right judgment in all things, and have strength to do what is right, whatever you may see that to be.'

'And of course that will be to stick by mother.'

'There can be little doubt of that, but the how? No, dear, do not let us devise all sorts of *hows* when we have nothing to go upon. That would be of no use, and only perplex you when the time comes. It would be much better to "do the nexte thinge," and read our "Marie Stuart."'

Nuttie pouted a little, but submitted, though she now and then broke into a translation with 'You know mother will never stand up for herself,' or 'They think I shall be asked to stay with the Egremonts, but I must work up for the exam.'

However, the school habit of concentrating her attention prevailed, and the study quieted Nuttie's excitement. The expedition took place as arranged. There was a train which stopped so that the party could go down by it, and the distance was not too great for walking back.

Mr. Dutton met them on the platform, well armed with his neat silk umbrella, and his black poodle, Monsieur, trotting solemnly after him. Gerard Godfrey bore materials for an exact transcript of the Abbot's monumental cross, his head being full of church architecture, while Nuttie carried a long green tin case, or vasculum as she chose to call it, with her three vowels, U A E, and the stars of the Little Bear conspicuously painted on it in white.

'You did not venture on that the other day,' said Mr. Dutton. 'How much of the park do you mean to carry away in it?'

'Let me take it,' said Gerard politely.

'No, thank you. You'd leave it behind, while you were pottering over the mouldings.'

'You are much more likely to leave it behind yourself.' 'What—

with my soldier, my Stratiotes, in it? I think I see myself.'

'Give it to me,' said Gerard. 'Of course I can't see you carrying a great thing like that.'

'Can't you, indeed?'

'Gently, gently, my dear,' said Miss Mary, as the young people seemed very near a skirmish, and the train was sweeping up. Then there was another small scuffle, for Nuttie had set her heart on the third class; but Mr. Dutton had taken second-class tickets, and was about to hand them into a carriage whence there had just emerged a very supercilious black-moustached valet, who was pulling out a leather-covered dressing-case, while Gerard was consoling Nuttie by telling her that Monsieur never deigned to go third class.

'It is a smoking carriage,' said Miss Nugent, on the step. 'Pah! how it smells,' as she jumped back.

'Beautiful backy—a perfect nosegay,' said Gerard.

'Trust that fellow for having the best.'

'His master's, no doubt,' suggested Mr. Dutton.

'You'd better go in it, to enjoy his reversion,' said Nuttie.

'And where's my escort, then?'

'Oh, I'm sure we don't want you.'

'Nuttie, my dear,' expostulated Miss Nugent, dragging her into the next carriage.

'You may enjoy the fragrance still,' said Nuttie when seated. 'Do you see —there's the man's master; he has stood him up against that post, with his cigar, to wait while he gets out the luggage. I daresay you can get a whiff if you lean out far enough.'

'I say! that figure is a study!' said Gerard. 'What is it that he is so like?'

'Oh! I know,' said Nuttie. 'It is Lord Frederick Verisopht, and the bad gentlefolks in the pictures to the old numbers of Dickens that you have got, Miss Mary. Now, isn't he? Look! only Lord Frederick wasn't fat.'

Nuttie was in a state of excitement that made her peculiarly unmanageable, and Miss Nugent was very grateful to Mr. Dutton for his sharp though general admonition against staring, while, under pretext of disposing of the umbrella and the vasculum, he stood up, so as to block the window till they were starting.

There was no one else to observe them but a demure old lady, and in ten minutes' time they were in open space, where high spirits might work themselves off, though the battle over the botanical case was ended by Miss Nugent, who strongly held that ladies should carry their own extra encumbrances, and slung it with a scarf over Nuttie's shoulders in a knowing knapsack fashion.

The two young people had known one another all their lives, for Gerard was the son of a medical man who had lived next door to Miss Headworth when the children were young. The father was dead, and the family had left the place, but this son had remained at school, and afterwards had been put into the office at the umbrella factory under charge of Mr. Dutton, whose godson he was, and who treated him as a nephew. He was a good-hearted, steady young fellow, with his whole interest in ecclesiastical details, wearing a tie in accordance with 'the colours,' and absorbed in church music and decorations, while his recreations were almost all in accordance therewith.

There was plenty of merriment, as he drew and measured at the very scanty ruins, which were little more than a few fragments of wall, overgrown luxuriantly with ivy and clematis, but enclosing some fine old coffin-lids with floriated crosses, interesting to those who cared for architecture and church history, as Mr. Dutton tried to make the children do, so that their ecclesiastical feelings might be less narrow, and stand on a surer foundation than present interest, a slightly aggressive feeling of contempt for all the other town churches, and a pleasing sense of being persecuted.

They fought over the floriations and mouldings with great zest, and each maintained a date with youthful vigour—both being, as Mr. Dutton by and by showed them, long before the foundation. The pond had been left to the last with a view to the wellbeing of the water-soldier on the return. Here the difficulties of the capture were great, for the nearest plant flourished too far from the bank to be reached with comfort, and besides, the sharp-pointed leaves to which it owes its name were not to be approached with casual grasps.

'Oh Monsieur, I wish you were a Beau,' sighed Nuttie. 'Why, are you too stupid to go and get it?'

'It is a proof of his superior intelligence,' said Mr. Dutton.

'But really it is too ridiculous—too provoking—to have come all this way and not get it,' cried the tantalised Nuttie. 'Oh, Gerard, are you taking off your boots and stockings? You duck!'

'Just what I wish I was,' said the youth, rolling up his trousers.

But even the paddling in did not answer. Mr. Dutton called out anxiously, 'Take care, Gerard, the bottom may be soft,' and came down to the very verge just in time to hold out his hand, and prevent an utterly disastrous fall, for Gerard, in spite of his bare feet, sank at once into mud, and on the first attempt to take a step forward, found his foot slipping away from under him, and would in another instant have tumbled backwards into the slush and weeds. He scrambled back, his hat falling off into the reeds, and splashing Mr. Dutton all over, while Monsieur began to bark 'with astonishment at seeing his master in such a plight,' declared the ladies, who stood convulsed with cruel laughter.

'Isn't it dreadful?' exclaimed Ursula.

'Well! It might have been worse,' gravely said Mr. Dutton, wiping off the more obnoxious of his splashes with his pocket handkerchief.

'Oh I didn't mean you, but the water-soldier,' said Nuttie. 'To have come five miles for it in vain!'

'I don't know what to suggest,' added Gerard. 'Even if the ladies were to retire—'

'No, no,' interposed Mr. Dutton, ''tis no swimming ground, and I forbid the expedient. You would only be entangled in the weeds.'

'Behold!' exclaimed Mary, who had been prowling about the banks, and now held up in triumph one of the poles with a bill-hook at the end used for cutting weed.

'Bravo, Miss Nugent!' cried Gerard.

'Female wit has circumvented the water-soldier,' said Mr. Dutton.

'Don't cry out too soon,' returned Mary; 'the soldier may float off and escape you yet.'

However, the capture was safely accomplished, without even a dip under water to destroy the beauty of the white flowers. With these, and a few waterlilies secured by Gerard for the morrow's altar vases, the party set out on their homeward walk, through plantations of whispering firs, the low sun tingeing the trunks with ruddy light; across heathery commons, where crimson heath abounded, and the delicate blush-coloured wax-belled species was a prize; by cornfields in ear hanging out their dainty stamens; along hedges full of exquisite plumes of feathering or nodding grass, of which Nuttie made bouquets and botanical studies, and Gerard stored for harvest decorations. They ran and danced on together with Monsieur at their heels, while the elders watched them with some sadness and anxiety. Free-masonry had soon made both Mary and Mr. Dutton aware of each other's initiation, and they had discussed the matter in all its bearings, agreed that the man was a scoundrel, and the woman an angel, even if she had once been weak, and that she ought to be very resolute with him if he came to terms. And then they looked after their young companions, and Mr. Dutton said, 'Poor children, what is before them?'

'It is well they are both so young,' answered Mary.

CHAPTER VII.

THAT MAN.

Sundays were the ever-recurring centres of work and interests to the little circle in St. Ambrose's Road. To them the church services and the various classes and schools were the great objects and excitements of the week. A certain measure of hopeful effort and varying success is what gives zest to life, and the purer and higher the aim, and the more unmixed the motives, the greater the happiness achieved by the 'something attempted, something done.'

Setting apart actual spiritual devotion, the altar vases, purchased by a contribution of careful savings, and adorned with the Monks Horton lilies, backed by ferns from the same quarter; the surplices made by the ladies themselves, the chants they had practised, the hymns they had taught, could not but be much more interesting to them than if they had been mere lookers on. Every cross on the markers, every flower on the altar cloth was the work of one or other of them; everything in the church was an achievement, and choir boys, school children, Bible classes, every member of the regular congregation, had some special interest; nay, every irregular member or visitor might be a convert in time—if not a present sympathiser, and at the very least might swell the offertory that was destined to so many needs of the struggling district.

Thus it was with some curiosity mingled with self-reproach that Nuttie, while singing her Benedictus among the tuneful shop-girls, to whom she was bound to set an example, became aware of yesterday's first-class traveller lounging, as far as the rows of chairs would permit, in the aisle, and, as she thought, staring hard at her mother. It was well that Mrs. Egremont's invariable custom was never to lift her eyes from her book or her harmonium, or she surely must have been disconcerted, her daughter thought, by the eyes that must have found her out, under her little black net bonnet and veil, as the most beautiful woman in church,—as she certainly was,—even that fine good-for-nothing gentleman thinking so. Nuttie would add his glances to the glories of her lovely mother!

And she did so, with triumph in her tone of reprobation, as she trotted off, after the early dinner, to her share of Sunday-school work as usual under Miss Nugent's wing. It began with a children's service, and then ensued, in rooms at the factory, lent by Mr. Dutton, the teaching that was to supply the omissions of the Board School; the establishment of a voluntary one being the next ambition of St. Ambrose's.

Coming home from their labours, in the fervent discussion of their scholars, and exchanging remarks and greetings with the other teachers of various calibres, the friends reached their own road, and there, to their amazement, beheld Miss Headworth.

'Yes, it really is!' cried Nuttie. 'We can't be too late? No—there's no bell! Aunt Ursel! What has brought you out? What's the matter? Where's mother?'

'In the house. My dear,' catching hold of her, and speaking breathlessly, 'I came out to prepare you. He is come—your father—'

'Where?' cried Nuttie, rather wildly.

'He is in the drawing-room with your mother. I said I would send you.'

Poor Miss Headworth gasped with agitation. 'Oh! where's Mr. Dutton—not that anything can be done—'

'Is it *that man*?' asked Nuttie, and getting no answer, 'I know it is! Oh Aunt Ursel, how could you leave her with him? I must go and protect her. Gerard—come. No, go and fetch Mr. Dutton.'

'Hush! hush, Nuttie,' cried her aunt, grasping her. 'You know nothing about it. Wait here till I can tell you.'

'Come in here, dear Miss Headworth,' said Mary, gently drawing her arm into hers, for the poor old lady could hardly stand for trembling, and bidding Gerard open the door of her own house with the latch-key.

She took them into the dining-room, so as not to disturb her mother, sent Gerard off after Mr. Dutton in the very uttermost astonishment and bewilderment, and set Miss Headworth down in an easy-chair, where she recovered herself, under Mary's soothing care, enough to tell her story in spite of Nuttie's exclamations. 'Wait! wait, Nuttie! You mustn't burst in on them so! No, you need not be afraid. Don't be a silly child! He won't hurt her! Oh no! They are quite delighted to meet.'

'Delighted to meet?' said Nuttie, as if transfixed.

'Yes,' said her aunt. 'Oh yes, I always knew the poor child cared for him and tried to believe in him all along. He only had to say the word.'

'I wouldn't,' cried the girl, her eyes flashing. 'Why didn't you ask him how he could desert her and leave her?'

'My dear! how can one come between husband and wife? Oh, my poor Alice!'

'How was it, how did they meet, dear Miss Headworth?' asked Mary, administering the wine she had been pouring out.

'You hadn't been gone half an hour, Alice was reading to me, and I was just dozing, when in came Louisa. "A gentleman to see Mrs. Egremont," she said, and there he was just behind. We rose up—she did not know him at once, but he just said "Edda, my little Edda, sweeter than ever, I knew you at once," or something of that sort, and she gave one little cry of "I knew you would come," and sprang right into his arms. I—well, I meant to make him understand how he had treated her, but just as I began "Sir"—he came at me with his hand outstretched—'

'You didn't take it, aunt, I hope?' cried Nuttie.

'My dear, when you see him, you will know how impossible it is. He *has* that high-bred manner it is as if he were conferring a favour. "Miss

Headworth, I conclude," said he, "a lady to whom I owe more than I can express." Just as if I had done it for his sake.' Miss Nugent felt this open expression dangerous on account of the daughter, and she looked her consternation at Mr. Dutton, who had quietly entered, ruthlessly shutting Gerard Godfrey out with only such a word of explanation as could be given on the way.

'Then he comes with—with favourable intentions,' said Mary, putting as much admonition as she could into her voice.

'Oh! no doubt of that,' said Miss Headworth, drawing herself together. 'He spoke of the long separation,—said he had never been able to find her, till the strange chance of his nephew stumbling on her at Abbots Norton.'

'That is—possib—probably true,' said Mr. Dutton.

'It can't be,' broke in Nuttie. 'He never troubled himself about it till his nephew found the papers. You said so, Aunt Ursel! He is a dreadful traitor of a man, just like Marmion, or Theseus, or Lancelot, and now he is telling lies about it! Don't look at me. Aunt Ursel, they are lies, and I *will* say it, and he took in poor dear mother once, and now he is taking her in again, and I can't bear that he should be my father!'

It was so entirely true, yet so shocking to hear from her mouth, that all three stood aghast, as she stood with heaving chest, crimson cheeks, and big tears in her eyes. Miss Headworth only muttered, 'Oh, my poor child, you mustn't!'

Mr. Dutton prevented another passionate outburst by his tone of grave, gentle authority. 'Listen a moment, Ursula,' he said. 'It is unhappily true that this man has acted in an unjustifiable way towards your mother and yourself. But there are, no doubt, many more excuses for him than you know of, and as I found a few years ago that the people at Dieppe had lost the address that had been left with them, he must have found no traces of your mother there. You cannot understand the difficulties that may have been in his way. And there is no use, quite the contrary, in making the worst of him. He has found your mother out, and it seems that he claims her affectionately, and she forgives and welcomes him—out of the sweet tenderness of her heart.'

'She may—but I can't,' murmured Nuttie.

'That is not a fit thing for a daughter, nor a Christian, to say,' Mr. Dutton sternly said.

'"Tis not for myself—'tis for her,—'objected Nuttie.

'That's nonsense; a mere excuse,' he returned. 'You have nothing at all to forgive, since he did not know you were in existence. And as to your mother, whom you say you put first, what greater grief or pain can you give her than by showing enmity and resentment against her husband, when she, the really injured person, loves and forgives?'

'He's a bad man. If she goes back to him, I know he will make her unhappy—'

'You don't know any such thing, but you do know that your opposition will make her unhappy. Remember, there's no choice in the matter. He has legal rights over you both, and since he shows himself ready (as I understand from Miss Headworth that he is) to give her and you your proper position, you have nothing to do but to be thankful. I think myself that it is a great subject of thankfulness that your mother can return so freely without any bitterness. It is the blessing of such as she—'

Nuttie stood pouting, but more thoughtful and less violent, as she said, 'How can I be thankful? I don't want position or anything. I only want him to let my—my own mother, and aunt, and me alone.'

'Child, you are talking of what you do not understand. You must not waste any more time in argument. Your mother has sent for you, and it is your duty to go and let her introduce you to your father. I have little doubt that you will find him very unlike all your imagination represents him, but let that be as it may, the fifth Commandment does not say, "Honour only thy good father," but, "Honour thy father." Come now, put on your gloves—get her hat right, if you please, Miss Mary. There—now, come along, be a reasonable creature, and a good girl, and do not give unnecessary pain and vexation to your mother.' He gave her his arm, and led her away.

'Well done, Mr. Dutton!' exclaimed Miss Nugent.

'Poor Mr. Dutton!' All Aunt Ursel's discretion could not suppress that sigh, but Mary prudently let it pass unnoticed, only honouring in her heart the unselfishness and self-restraint of the man whose long, patient, unspoken hopes had just received a death-blow.

'Oh, Mary! I never thought it would have been like this!' cried the poor old lady. 'I ought not to have spoken as I did before the child, but I was so taken by surprise! Alice turned to him just as if he had been the most faithful, loving husband in the world. She is believing every word he says.'

'It is very happy for her that she can,' pleaded Mary.

'So it is, yes, but—when one knows what he is, and what she is! Oh, Mr. Dutton, is the poor child gone in?'

'Yes, I saw her safe into the room. She was very near running off up the stairs,' said Mr. Dutton. 'But I daresay she is fascinated by this time. That sort of man has great power over women.'

'Nuttie is hardly a woman yet,' said Miss Nugent.

'No, but there must be a strong reaction, when she sees something unlike her compound of Marmion and Theseus.'

'I suppose there is no question but that they must go with him!' said Miss Headworth wistfully.

'Assuredly. You say he—this Egremont—was affectionate,' said Mr. Dutton quietly, but Mary saw his fingers white with his tight clenching of the bar of the chair.

'Oh yes, warmly affectionate, delighted to find her prettier than ever, poor dear; I suppose he meant it. Heaven forgive me, if I am judging him too hardly, but I verily believe he went to church to reconnoitre, and see whether she pleased his fancy—'

'And do you understand,' added Mr. Dutton, 'that he is prepared to do her full justice, and introduce her to his family and friends as his wife, on equal terms? Otherwise, even if she were unwilling to stand up for herself, it would be the duty of her friends to make some stipulations.'

'I am pretty sure that he does,' said the aunt; 'I did not stay long when I saw that I was not wanted, but I heard him say something about his having a home for her now, and her cutting out the Redcastle ladies.'

'Besides, there is the nephew, Mr. Mark Egremont,' said Mary. 'He will take care of her.'

'Yes,' said Mr. Dutton. 'It appears to be all right. At any rate, there can be no grounds for interference on our part.'

Mr. Dutton took his leave with these words, wringing Miss Headworth's hand in mute sympathy, and she, poor old lady, when he was gone, fairly collapsed into bitter weeping over the uncertain future of those whom she had loved as her own children, and who now must leave her desolate. Mary did her best with comfort and sympathy, and presently took her to share her griefs and fears with gentle old Mrs. Nugent.

CHAPTER VIII.

THE FATHER.

Nuttie, in her fresh holland Sunday dress, worked in crewels with wild strawberries by her mother's hands, and with a white-trimmed straw hat, was almost shoved into the little drawing-room by Mr. Dutton, though he was himself invisible.

Her eyes were in such a daze of tears that she hardly saw more at first than that some one was there with her mother on the sofa. 'Ah, there she is!' she heard her mother cry, and both rose. Her mother's arm was round her waist, her hand was put into another, Mrs. Egremont's voice, tremulous with exceeding delight, said, 'Our child, our Ursula, our Nuttie! Oh, this is what I have longed for all these years! Oh, thanks, thanks!' and her hands left her daughter to be clasped and uplifted for a moment in fervent thanksgiving, while Nuttie's hand was held, and a strange hairy kiss, redolent of tobacco-smoking, was on her forehead—a masculine one, such as she had never known, except her cousin Mark's, since the old rector died, and she had grown too big for Mr. Dutton's embraces. It was more strange than delightful, and yet she felt the polish of the tone that said, 'We make acquaintance somewhat late, Ursula, but better late than never.'

She looked up at this new father, and understood instantly what she had heard of his being a grand gentleman. There was a high-bred look about him, an entire ease and perfect manner that made everything he did or said seem like gracious condescension, and took away the power of questioning it at the moment. He was not above the middle size, and was becoming unwieldy; but there was something imposing and even graceful in his deportment, and his bald narrow forehead looked aristocratic, set off between side tufts of white hair, white whiskers, and moustaches waxed into sharp points, Victor Emmanuel fashion, and a round white curly beard. His eyes were dark, and looked dull, with yellow unwholesome corners, and his skin was not of a pleasant colour, but still, with all Nuttie's intentions of regarding him with horror, she was subdued, partly by the grand breeding and air of distinction, and partly by the current of sympathy from her mother's look of perfect happiness and exultation. She could not help feeling it a favour, almost an undeserved favour, that so great a personage should say, 'A complete Egremont, I see. She has altogether the family face.'

'I am so glad you think so,' returned her mother.

'On the whole it is well, but she might have done better to resemble you, Edda,' he said caressingly; 'but perhaps that would have been too much for the Earlsforth natives. William's girls will have enough to endure without a double eclipse!' and he laughed.

'I—I don't want—' faltered the mother.

'You don't want, no, but you can't help it,' he said, evidently with a proud delight in her beauty. 'Now that I have seen the child,' he added, 'I will make my way back to the hotel.'

'Will you—won't you stay to tea or dinner?' said his wife, beginning with an imploring tone which hesitated as she reviewed possible chops and her aunt's dismay.

'Thank you, I have ordered dinner at the hotel,' he answered, 'and Gregorio is waiting for me with a cab. No doubt you will wish to make arrangements with Madame—the old lady—and I will not trouble her further to-night. I will send down Gregorio to-morrow morning, to tell you what I arrange. An afternoon train, probably, as we shall go no farther than London. You say Lady Kirkaldy called on you. We might return her visit before starting, but I will let you know when I have looked at the trains. My compliments to Miss Headworth. Good evening, sweetest.' He held his wife in a fond embrace, kissing her brow and cheeks and letting her cling to him, then added, 'Good evening, little one,' with a good-natured careless gesture with which Nuttie was quite content, for she had a certain loathing of the caresses that so charmed her mother. And yet the command to make ready had been given with such easy authority that the idea of resisting it had never even entered her mind, though she stood still while her mother went out to the door with him and watched him to the last.

Coming back, she threw her arms round her daughter, kissed her again and again, and, with showers of the glad tears long repressed, cried, 'Oh, my Nuttie, my child, what joy! How shall I be thankful enough! Your father, your dear father! Now it is all right.' Little sentences of ecstasy such as these, interspersed with caresses, all in the incoherence of overpowering delight, full of an absolute faith that the lost husband had loved her and been pining for her all these years, but that he had been unable to trace her, and was as happy as she was in the reunion.

The girl was somewhat bewildered, but she was carried along by this flood of exceeding joy and gladness. The Marmion and Theseus images had been dispelled by the reality, and, with Mr. Dutton's sharp reproof fresh upon her, she felt herself to have been doing a great injustice to her father; believed all that her mother did, and found herself the object of a romantic recognition—if not the beggar girl become a princess, at any rate, the little school-teacher a county lady! And she had never seen her mother so wildly, overpoweringly happy with joy. That made her, too, feel that something grand and glorious had happened.

'What are we going to do?' she asked, as the vehemence of Mrs. Egremont's emotion began to work itself off.

'Home! He takes us to his home! *His* home!' repeated her mother, in a trance of joy, as the yearnings of her widowed heart now were fulfilled.

'Oh, but Aunt Ursel!'

'Poor Aunt Ursel! Oh, Nuttie, Nuttie, I had almost forgotten! How could I?' and there was a shower of tears of compunction. 'But he said he owed everything to her! She will come with us! Or if she doesn't live with us, we will make her live close by in a dear little cottage. Where is she? When did she go? I never saw her go.'

The sound of the front door was heard, for the visitor had been watched away and Miss Headworth was returning to her own house to be there received with another fervent gush of happiness, much more trying to her, poor thing, than to Nuttie.

There was evensong imminent, and the most needful act at the moment was to compose the harmonium-player sufficiently for her to take her part. Miss Headworth was really glad of the necessity, since it put off the discussion, and made a reason for silencing Nuttie until all should be more recovered from the first agitation. Alice Egremont herself was glad to carry her gratitude and thankfulness to the Throne of Grace, and in her voluntary, and all her psalms, there was an exulting strain that no one had thought the instrument capable of producing, and that went to the heart of more than one of her hearers. No one who knew her could doubt that hers was simply innocent exultation in the recovery of him whom she so entirely loved and confided in. But there could not but be terrible doubts whether he were worthy of that trust, and what the new page in her life would be.

Miss Headworth had said they would not talk till after church, but there was no deferring the matter then. She was prepared, however, when her niece came up to her in a tender deprecating manner, saying, 'Aunt Ursel, dear Aunt Ursel, it does seem very ungrateful, but—'

'He is going to take you away? Yes, I saw that. And it ought to be, my dear. You know where?'

'Yes; to London first, to be fitted out, and then to his own home. To Bridgefield Egremont. I shall have to see Mr. Egremont,' and her voice sank with shame. 'But Mark will be good to me, and why should I care when I have him.'

'It is quite right. I am glad it should be so,' firmly said the old lady.

'And yet to leave you so suddenly.'

'That can't be helped.'

'And it will only be for a little while,' she added, 'till you can make arrangements to come to us. My dear husband says he owes you everything. So you must be with us, or close to us.'

'My dear, it's very dear and good of you to think of it, but I must be independent.' She put it in those words, unwilling again to speak unguardedly before Nuttie.

'Oh, dear auntie, indeed you must! Think what you are to us, and what you have done for us. We can't go away to be happy and prosperous and leave you behind. Can we, Nuttie? Come and help me to get her to promise. Do—do dearest auntie,' and she began the coaxing and caressing natural to her, but Nuttie did not join in it, and Miss Headworth shook her head and said gravely —

'Don't, Alice. It is of no use. I tell you once for all that my mind is made up.'

Alice, knowing by long experience that, when her aunt spoke in that tone, persuasion was useless, desisted, but looked at her in consternation, with eyes swimming in tears. Nuttie understood her a little better, and felt the prickings of distrust again.

'But, aunt, dear aunt, how can we leave you? What will you do with all the boarders,' went on Mrs. Egremont.

'I shall see my way, my dear. Do not think about that. It is a great thing to see you and this child receive justice.'

'And only think, after all the hard things that have been said of him, that we should meet first at church! He would not wait and send letters and messages by Mark. You see he came down himself the first moment. I always knew he would. Only I am so sorry for him, that he should have lost all those sweet years when Nuttie was a tiny child. She must do all she can to make up to him.'

'Oh dear!' broke out Nuttie. 'It is so strange! It will be all so strange!'

'It will be a very new life,' said her aunt, rather didactically; 'but you must do your best to be a good daughter, and to fill your new position, and I have no doubt you will enjoy it.'

'If I could but take all with me!' said Nuttie. 'Oh dear! whatever will you do, Aunt Ursel? Oh mother, the choir! Who will play the harmonium? and who will lead the girls? and whatever will Mr. Spyers do? and who will take my class? Mother, couldn't we stay a little longer to set things going here?'

'It is nice of you to have thought of it, my dear,' said Mrs. Egremont, 'but your father would not like to stay on here.'

'But mightn't I stay, just a few days, mother, to wish everybody good-bye? Mr. Dutton, and Miss Mary, and Gerard, and all the girls?'

There was some consolation in this plan, and the three women rested on it that night, Mrs. Egremont recovering composure enough to write three or four needful notes, explaining her sudden departure. The aunt could not talk of a future she so much dreaded for her nieces, losing in it the thought of her own loneliness; Alice kept back her own loving, tender, undoubting joy with a curious sense that it was hard and ungrateful towards the aunt; but it was impossible to think of that, and Nuttie was in many moods.

Eager anticipation of the new unseen world beyond, exultation in finding herself somebody, sympathy with her mother's happiness, all had their share, but they made her all the wilder, because they were far from unmixed. The instinctive dislike of Mr. Egremont's countenance, and doubt of his plausible story, which had vanished before his presence, and her mother's faith, returned upon her from time to time, caught perhaps from her aunt's tone and looks. Then her aunt had been like a mother to her—her own mother much more like a sister, and the quitting her was a wrench not compensated for as in Mrs. Egremont's case by a more absorbing affection. Moreover, Nuttie felt sure that poor Gerard Godfrey would break his heart. As the mother and daughter for the last time lay down together in the room that had been theirs through the seventeen years of the girl's life, Alice fell asleep with a look of exquisite peace and content on her face, feeling her long term of trial crowned by unlooked-for joy, while Ursula, though respecting her slumbers too much to move, lay with wide-open eyes, now speculating on the strange future, now grieving over those she left—Aunt Ursel, Gerard, Mary, and all such; the schemes from which she was snatched, and then again consoling herself with the hope that, since she was going to be rich, she could at once give all that was wanted—the white altar cloth, the brass pitcher—nay, perhaps finish the church and build the school! For had not some one said something about her position? Oh yes, she had not thought of it before, but, since she was the elder brother's daughter, she must be the heiress! There was no doubt a grand beautiful story before her; she would withstand all sorts of fascinations, wicked baronets and earls innumerable, and come back and take Gerard by the hand, and say, 'Pride was quelled and love was free.' Not that Gerard had ever uttered a word tending in that direction since he had been seven years old, but that would make it all the prettier; they would both be silently constant, till the time came, perhaps when she was of age. Mother would like it, though *that* father would certainly be horrid. And how nice it would be to give Gerard everything, and they would go all over the Continent, and see pictures, and buy them, and see all the cathedrals and all the mountains. But perhaps, since Mark Egremont had really been so generous in hunting up the cousin who was displacing him, she was bound in duty to marry him; perhaps he reckoned on her doing so. She would be generous in her turn, give up all the wealth to him, and return to do and be everything to Micklethwayte. How they would admire and bless her. And oh! she was going to London to- morrow—London, which she so much wished to see—Westminster Abbey, British Museum, All Saints, National Gallery, no end of new dresses.

Half-waking, half-dreaming, she spent the night which seemed long enough, and the light hours of the summer morning seemed still longer, before she could call it a reasonable time for getting up. Her splashings awoke her mother, who lay smiling for a few moments, realising and giving thanks for her great joy, then bestirred herself with the recollection of all that had to be done on this busy morning before any summons from her husband could arrive.

Combining packing and dressing, like the essentially unmethodical little woman she was, Mrs. Egremont still had all her beautiful silky brown hair about her shoulders when the bell of St. Ambrose's was heard giving its thin tinkling summons to matins at half-past seven. She was disappointed; she meant to have gone for this last time, but there was no help for it, and Nuttie set off by herself.

Gerard Godfrey was at his own door. He was not one of the regular attendants at the short service, being of that modern species that holds itself superior to 'Cranmer's prayers,' but on this morning he hastened up to her with outstretched hand.

'And you are going away!' he said.

'I hope to get leave to stay a few days after mother,' she said.

'To prolong the torment?' he said.

'To wish everybody good-bye. It is a great piece of my life that is come to an end, and I can't bear to break it off so short.'

'And if you feel so, who are going to wealth and pleasure, what must it be to those who are left behind?'

'Oh!' said Nuttie, 'some one will be raised up. That's what they always say.'

'I shall go into a brotherhood,' observed Gerard desperately.

'Oh, don't,'began Nuttie, much gratified, but at that moment Miss Nugent came out at her door, and Mr. Spyers, who was some way in advance, looked round and waited for them to come up. He held out his hands to her and said, 'Well, Nuttie, my child, you are going to begin a new life.'

'Oh dear! I wish I could have both!' cried Nuttie, not very relevantly as far as the words went.

'Scheiden und weiden thut weh!' quoted Mary.

'If his place was only Monks Horton. What will Aunt Ursel do?'

'I think perhaps she may be induced to join us,' said Mary. 'We mean to do our best to persuade her.'

'And there's the choir! And my class, and the harmonium,' went on Nuttie, while Gerard walked on disconsolately.

'Micklethwayte has existed without you, Nuttie,' said Mr. Spyers, taking her on with him alone. 'Perhaps it will be able to do so again. My dear, you had better look on. There will be plenty for you to learn and to do where you are going, and you will be sure to find much to enjoy, and also something to bear. I should like to remind you that the best means of going on well in this new world will be to keep self down and to have the strong desire that only love can give to be submissive, and to do what is right both to God and your father and mother. May I give you a text to take with you? "Children, obey your parents in the Lord, for this is right."'

They were at the door and there was no time for an answer, but Nuttie, as she took her place, was partly touched and partly fretted at the admonition.

The question as to her remaining a day or two after her mother was soon disposed of. Mrs. Egremont sent a pretty little note to make the request, but the elegant valet who appeared at ten o'clock brought a verbal message that his master wished Mrs. and Miss Egremont to be ready by two o'clock to join him in calling on Lady Kirkaldy at Monks Horton, and that if their luggage was ready by four o'clock, he (Gregorio) would take charge of it, as they were all to go up to town by the 4.40 train.

'Did he have my note?' faltered Alice, stimulated by the imploring glances of aunt and daughter, but anticipating the answer.

'Yes, madame, but he wishes that Miss Egremont should accompany you immediately.'

'Of course,' was Alice's comment, 'now that he has found his child, he cannot bear to part with her.'

And all through the farewells that almost rent the gentle Alice's heart in two, she was haunted by the terror that she or her daughter should have red eyes to vex her husband. As to Mr. Dutton, he had only come in with Gerard in a great hurry just after breakfast, said there was much to do to-day at the office, as they were going to take stock, and they should neither of them have time to come home to luncheon. He shook the hands of mother and daughter heartily, promised to 'look after' Miss Headworth, and bore off in his train young Gerard, looking the picture of woe, and muttering 'I believe he has got it up on purpose;' while mother and daughter thought it very odd, and rather unkind.

CHAPTER IX.

NEW PLUMES.

The very best open fly and pair of horses, being the equipage most like a private carriage possessed by the Royal Hotel, came to the door with Mr. Egremont seated in it, at a few minutes after two o'clock, and found Alice in her only black silk, with a rose in her bonnet, and a tie to match on her neck, hastily procured as signs of her wifehood.

She had swallowed her tears, and Nuttie was not a crying person, but was perfectly scarlet on her usually brown cheeks. Her father muttered some civility about back seats, but it was plain that it was only in words, and she never thought of anything but looking back, with her last wave to her aunt and the two maids, one crying at the gate, the other at the door.

'There,' said Mr. Egremont, as they drove away, 'that is over!'

'My dear aunt,' said his wife. 'Who can express her goodness to me?'

'Cela va sans dire,' was the reply. 'But these are connections that happily Ursula is young enough to forget and leave behind.'

'I shall never forget!' began Nuttie, but she saw her father composing himself in his corner without paying the slightest heed to what she was saying, and she encountered a warning and alarmed glance from her mother, so she was forced to content herself with uttering silent vows of perpetual recollection as she passed each well-known object,—the unfinished church, with Mr. Spyers at the door talking to old Bellman; the Town Hall, whose concerts, lectures, and S. P. G. meetings had been her chief gaiety and excitement; the School of Art, where Lady Kirkaldy's appearance now seemed to her to have been like that of a bird of omen; past the shops in the High Street, with a little exultation at the thought of past desires which they had excited. Long could she have rattled away, her hopes contradicting her regrets, and her regrets qualifying her anticipations, but she saw that her mother was nervous about every word and gesture, and fairly looked dismayed when she exclaimed, 'Oh, mother, there's Etta Smith; how surprised she will be!' bowing and smiling with all her might.

There was a look of bare toleration on Mr. Egremont's face, as if he endured because it would soon be over, as Nuttie bowed several times, and his wife, though less quick to catch people's eyes, sometimes also made her recognition. When the streets were past and Nuttie had aimed her last nods at the nursery parties out walking on the road, she became aware that those cold, lack-lustre, and yet sharply critical eyes of her father were scanning her all over.

'She has been educated?' he presently said to his wife.

'Oh yes,' was the eager answer. 'She is in the highest form at the High School, and has to go up for the Senior Local Examination. Miss Belper makes sure that she will get a first class.'

Mr. Egremont gave a little wave of the hand, as dismissing something superfluous, and said, 'I hope she has some accomplishments.'

'She has done very fairly in French and German—'

'And Latin,' put in Ursula.

'And she has had several prizes at the School of Art.'

'And music? That's the only thing of any value in society,' he said impatiently, and Mrs. Egremont said more timidly, 'She has learnt music regularly.'

'But I don't care about it,' broke in Nuttie. 'I haven't mother's ear nor her voice. I learnt the science in case I should have to teach, and they make me practise. I don't mind classical music, but I can't stand rubbish, and I think it is waste of time.'

Mr. Egremont looked fairly amused, as at the outspoken folly of an enfant terrible, but he only said, either to his wife or to himself, 'A little polish, and then she may be fairly presentable.'

'We have taken great pains with her,' answered the gentle mother, evidently taking this as a great compliment, while the daughter was tingling with indignation. She, bred up by mother, and aunt, and Mary Nugent, to be barely presentable. Was not their society at Micklethwayte equal in good manners to any, and superior, far superior, in goodness and intelligence to these stupid fashionable people, who undervalued all her real useful acquirements, and cared for nothing but trumpery music.

The carriage entered the park, and Nuttie saw lake and woods from a fresh point of view. The owners were both at home, and Nuttie found herself walking behind her parents into a cheerful apartment, half library, half morning-room. Mrs. Egremont was by far the most shy and shrinking of the party, but it was an occasion that showed her husband's complete tact and savoir favre. He knew perfectly well that the Kirkaldys knew all about it, and he therefore took the initiative. 'You are surprised to see us,' he said, as he gave his hand, 'but we could not leave the country without coming to thank Lady Kirkaldy for her kindness in assisting in following up the clue to Mrs. Egremont's residence.'

'I am very happy,' said Lady Kirkaldy, while all were being seated.

'I think it was here that my nephew Mark first met one whom, child as he was, he could not but remember.'

'I don't think you met him here,' said Lady Kirkaldy to Mrs. Egremont; 'but he heard the name and was struck by it.'

'Dear Mark!' was the response. 'He was so kind.'

'He is a dear good boy,' chimed in my lady.

'Yes,' said her lord, 'an excellent good fellow with plenty of brains.'

'As he well knows,' said Mr. Egremont. 'Oh yes; I quite agree with all you say of him! One ought to be thankful for the possession of a rare specimen.'

It was in the tone in which Falstaff discussed that sober boy, Lord John of Lancaster. Lord Kirkaldy asked if the visitors were going to remain long in the neighbourhood.

'We are due in London to-night,' replied Mr. Egremont. 'We shall spend a day or two there, and then go home. Alice,' he added, though his wife had never heard him call her so before, 'Lady Kirkaldy knows your inexperience. Perhaps she would be good enough to give you some addresses that might be useful.'

'I shall be delighted,' said the lady, cordially looking at the blushing Mrs. Egremont.

'Dressmaker, and all the rest of it,' said Mr. Egremont. 'You know better than she does what she will require, and a little advice will be invaluable. Above all, if you could tell her how to pick up a maid.'

Lady Kirkaldy proposed to take the mother and daughter up to her dressing-room, where she kept her book of addresses to London tradesmen; and Mr. Egremont only begged that they would remember the 4.40 train. Then Lord Kirkaldy was left to entertain him, while the ladies went up the broad staircase to the pleasant room, which had a mingled look of refinement and usefulness which struck Nuttie at once. Lady Kirkaldy, as soon as the door was shut, took her visitor by the hand, kissed her forehead, and said, 'You must let me tell you how glad I am.'

The crystal veil at once spread over Alice's eyes.

'Oh, thank you. Lady Kirkaldy! I am *so* happy, and yet I am so afraid. Please tell me what we shall *do* so that we may not vex him, so high bred and fastidious as he is?'

'Be yourself! That's all, my dear,' said Lady Kirkaldy tenderly. 'Don't be afraid. You are quite incapable of doing anything that could distress the most fastidious taste.'

It was perfectly true of the mother, perhaps less so of the daughter; but Lady Kirkaldy only thought of her as a mere girl, who could easily be modelled by her surroundings. The kind hostess applied herself to giving the addresses of the people she thought likely to be most useful in the complete outfit which she saw would be necessary, explaining to which establishments she applied with confidence if she needed to complete her wardrobe in haste, feeling certain that nothing would be sent her that she disliked, and giving leave to use her name. She soon saw that the mother was a little dazed, while Ursula's eyes grew rounder at the unlimited vista of fine clothes, and she assented, and asked questions as to the details. As to a maid, Lady Kirkaldy would write to a person who would call on Mrs. Egremont at the hotel in London, and who might be what was wanted; and in conclusion, Lady Kirkaldy, with some diffidence, begged to be written to—'if—if,' she said, 'there happened to be any difficulty about which you might not like to consult Mrs. William Egremont.' Nuttie hardly knew whether to be grateful or not, for she did not believe in any standard above that of Micklethwayte, and she was almost angry at her mother's grateful answer—'Oh, thank you! I should be so grateful! I am so afraid of annoying him by what he may think small, ignorant, country-town ways! You will understand—'

Lady Kirkaldy did understand, and she dreaded what might be before the sweet little yielding woman, not from want of breeding so much as from the long-indulged selfishness of her husband; but she encouraged her as much as possible, and promised all possible counsel, bringing her downstairs again just in time.

'Pretty little soul!' said Lord Kirkaldy, as the fly clattered away. 'I wonder whether Mark has done her a kindness!'

'It is just what she is, a pretty, nay, a beautiful soul, full of tenderness and forgiveness and affection and humility, only I doubt whether there is any force or resolution to hold her own. You smile! Well, perhaps the less of that she has the better she may get on with him. Did he say anything about her?'

'No; I think he wants to ignore that they have not spent the last twenty years together.'

'That may be the best way for all parties. Do you think he will behave well to her?'

'No man could well do otherwise to such a sweet little thing,' said Lord Kirkaldy; 'especially as she will be his most obedient slave, and will make herself necessary to him. It is much better luck than he deserves; but I pity her when she comes to make her way with yon ladies!'

'I wish I was there! I know she will let herself be trodden on! However, there's Mark to stand up for her, and William Egremont will do whatever he thinks right and just. I wish I knew how his wife will take it!'

CHAPTER X.

BRIDGEFIELD EGREMONT.

'Let us see these handsome houses
Where the wealthy nobles dwell.'—TENNYSON.

'Mother, mother!' cried two young people, bursting open the door of the pretty dining-room of Bridgefield Rectory, where the grown-up part of the family were lingering over a late breakfast.

'Gently, gently, children,' said the dignified lady at the head of the table. 'Don't disturb papa.'

'But we really have something to say, mother!' said the elder girl, 'and Fraulein said you ought to know. Uncle Alwyn is come home, and Mrs. Egremont. And please, are we to call her Aunt Egremont, or Aunt Alwyn, or what?'

The desired sensation was produced. Canon Egremont put down his newspaper. The two elder sisters looked from one to the other in unmitigated astonishment. Mark briefly made answer to the final question, 'Aunt Alice,' and Mrs. Egremont said gravely, 'How did you hear this, Rosalind? You know I always forbid you to gossip.'

'We didn't gossip, mother. We went up to the gardens to get some mulberries for our half-holiday feast; and Ronaldson came out and told us we must ask leave first, for the ladies were come. The Squire came home at nine o'clock last night, and Mrs. Egremont and all, and only sent a telegram two hours before to have the rooms got ready.'

'Has Uncle Alwyn gone and got himself married?' exclaimed one of the young ladies, in utter amazement.

'Not just now, Blanche,' said her father. 'It is an old story now. Your uncle married this lady, who had been governess to May and Mark, many years ago, and from—circumstances in which she was not at all to blame, he lost sight of her while he was abroad with old General Egremont. Mark met her about a fortnight ago, and this has led to your uncle's going in quest of her, though he has certainly been more sudden in his proceedings than I expected.'

The mother here succeeded in sending Rosalind and Adela, with their wondering eyes, off the scene, and she would much have liked to send her two stepdaughters after them, but one-and-twenty and eighteen could not so readily be ordered off as twelve and ten; and Mark, who had been prohibited from uttering a word to his sisters, was eagerly examining Margaret whether she remembered their Edda; but she had been only three years old at the time of the adventures in the Isle of Wight, and remembered nothing distinctly but the aspect of one of the sailors in the yacht.

'Well,' said Mrs. Egremont, 'this has come very suddenly upon us. It would have been more for her own dignity if she had held out a little before coming so easily to terms, after the way in which she has been treated.'

'When you see her, mother, you will understand,' said Mark.

'Shall we have to be intimate with her?' asked May.

'I desire that she should be treated as a relation,' said the Canon decidedly. 'There is nothing against her character,' and, as his wife was about to interrupt,—'nothing but an indiscretion to which she was almost driven many years ago. She was cruelly treated, and I for one am heartily sorry for having let myself be guided by others.'

Mrs. William Egremont felt somewhat complacent, for she knew he meant Lady de Lyonnais, and there certainly had been no love lost between her and her step-children's grandmother; but she was a sensible woman, and forbore to speak, though there was a mental reservation that intimacy would a good deal depend upon circumstances. Blanche cried out that it was a perfect romance, and May gravely said, 'But is she a lady?'

'A perfect lady,' said Mark. 'Aunt Margaret says so.'

'One knows what a perfect lady means,' returned May.

'Come, May,' said Mrs. Egremont, 'do not let us begin with a prejudice. By all accounts the poor thing has conducted herself with perfect respectability all this time. What did you tell me, Mark? She has been living with an aunt, keeping a school at Micklethwayte.'

'Not quite,' said Mark. 'She has been acting as a daily governess. She seemed to be on friendly terms with the clerical folk. I came across the name at a school feast, or something of the kind, which came off in the Kirkaldys' park.'

'Oh, then, I know exactly the sort of person!' returned May, pursing up her lips.

Mark laughed and said, 'I wonder whether it is too soon to go up and see them. I wonder what my uncle thinks of his daughter.'

'What! You don't mean to say there is a daughter?' cried May.

'Even so. And exactly like you too, Miss May.'

'Then you are cut out, Mark!'

'You are cut out, I think, May. You'll have to give her all your Miss Egremont cards.'

'No,' said the young lady; 'mother made me have my Christian name printed. She said all but the daughters of the head of the family ought to have it so. I'm glad of it.'

'How old is she?' asked Blanche.

'About a year younger than you.'

'I think it is very interesting,' said Blanche. 'How wonderful it must all be to her! I will go up with you, Mark, as soon as I can get ready.'

'You had better wait till later in the day, Blanche,' said the mother. She knew the meeting was inevitable, but she preferred having it under her own eye, if she could not reconnoitre.

She was a just and sensible woman, who felt reparation due to the newly-discovered sister-in-law, and that harmony, or at least the appearance of it, must be preserved; but she was also exclusive and fastidious by nature, and did not look forward to the needful intercourse with much satisfaction either on her own account or that of her family.

She told Mark to say that she should come to see Mrs. Egremont after luncheon, since he was determined to go at once, and moreover to drag his father with him. Canon Egremont was a good and upright man, according to his lights, which were rather those of a well-beneficed clergyman of the first than of the last half of the century, intensified perhaps that the passive voice was the strongest in him. All the country knew that Canon Egremont could be relied on to give a prudent, scholarly judgment, and to be kind and liberal, when once induced to stir mind or body—but how to do that was the problem. He had not been a young man at the time of his first marriage, and was only a few years' junior to his brother, though he had the fresh, wholesome look of a man who kept regular hours and lived much in the air.

Alice knew him at once, and thought eighteen years had made little change, as, at Nuttie's call to her, she looked from the window and saw the handsome, dignified, gray-haired, close-shaven rosy face, and the clerical garb unchanged in favour of long coats and high waistcoats.

The mother and daughter were exploring the house together. Mr. Egremont had made it known that he preferred having his breakfast alone, and not being disturbed in the forenoon. So the two ladies had breakfasted together at nine, the earliest hour at which they could prevail on the household to give them a meal. Indeed Nuttie had slept till nearly that time, for between excitement and noise, her London slumbers had been broken; and her endeavour to keep Micklethwayte hours had resulted in a long, weary, hungry time in the sitting-room of the hotel, with nothing to do, when the gaze from the window palled on her, but to write to her aunt and Mary Nugent. The rest of the day had been spent in driving about in a brougham with her mother shopping, and this she could not but enjoy exceedingly, more than did the timid Mrs. Egremont, who could not but feel herself weighted with responsibility; and never having had to spend at the utmost more than ten pounds at a time, felt bewildered at the cheques put into her hands, and then was alarmed to find them melting away faster than she expected.

There was a very late dinner, after which Mr. Egremont, on the first day, made his wife play bezique with him. She enjoyed it, as a tender reminiscence of the yachting days; but Nuttie found herself de trop, and was reduced to the book she had contrived to purchase on her travels. The second night Mr. Egremont had picked up two friends, not yet gone out of town, whose talk was of horses and of yachts, quite incomprehensible to the ladies. They were very attentive to Mrs. Egremont, whom they evidently admired, one so visibly as to call up a blush; but they disregarded the daughter as a schoolgirl. Happily they appeared no more after the dinner; but Nuttie's first exclamation of astonished disgust was silenced at once by her mother with unusual determination, 'You must not speak so of your father's friends.'

'Not when—'

'Not at all,' interrupted Mrs. Egremont.

The only sense of promotion to greatness that Ursula had yet enjoyed was in these fine clothes, and the maid whom Lady Kirkaldy had recommended, a grave and severe-looking person, of whom both stood somewhat in awe. The arrival at Bridgefield had been too late for anything to be taken in but a general impression of space and dreariness, and the inevitable dinner of many courses, after which Nuttie was so tired out that her mother sent her to bed.

Since the waking she had made some acquaintance with the house. There was no show of domestics, no curtseying housekeeper to parade the new mistress over the house; Mr. Egremont had told his wife that she must fill up the establishment as she pleased, but that there was an admirable cook downstairs, and he would not have her interfered with—she suited his tastes as no one else did, and she must be left to deal with the provisions and her own underlings. There was a stable establishment, and a footman had been hired in town, but there was besides only one untidy-looking housemaid, who began by giving warning; and Alice and Nuttie had roamed about without meeting any one from the big wainscotted dining-room with faded crimson curtains and family portraits, the older grimy, the younger chalky, to the two drawing-rooms, whose gilding and pale blue damask had been preserved by pinafores of brown holland; the library, which looked and smelt as if Mr. Egremont was in the habit of sitting there, and a big billiard-room, all opening into a shivery-feeling hall, with Scagliola columns and a few dirty statues between them; then upstairs to a possible morning-room, looking out over a garden lawn, where mowing was going on in haste, and suites of dreary shut- up fusty bedrooms. Nuttie, who had notions of choosing her own bower, could not make up her mind which looked the least inviting. It did not seem as if girls could ever have laughed together, or children clattered up and down the stairs. Mrs. Egremont begged her to keep possession for the present at least of the chamber where the grim housemaid had chosen to put her, and which had the advantage of being aired.

The two windows looked out over the park, and thence it was that while Morris, the maid, was unpacking and putting away the new purchases, and Nuttie was standing, scarcely realising that such pretty hats and bonnets could be her very own, when her mother beheld the Canon and Mark advancing up the drive. It was with a great start that she called Ursula to come down directly with her, as no one would know where to find them, hastily washing the hands that had picked up a sense of dustiness during the exploration, and taking a comprehensive glance in the cheval glass, which showed her some one she felt entirely unfamiliar to her in a dainty summer costume of pale gray silk picked out with a mysterious shade of pink. Ursula too thought Miss Egremont's outer woman more like a Chelsea shepherdess than Nuttie's true self, as she tripped along in her buckled shoes and the sea green stockings that had been sent home with her skirt. With crimson cheeks and a throbbing heart, Alice was only just at the foot of the stairs when the newcomers had made their way in, and the kind Canon, ignoring all that was past, held out his hands saying, 'Well, my dear, I am glad to see you here,' kissing Mrs. Egremont on each cheek. 'And so this is your daughter. How do you do, my dear—Ursula? Isn't that your name?' And Ursula had again to submit to a kiss, much more savoury and kindly than her father's, though very stubbly. And oh! her uncle's dress was like that of no one she had ever seen except the rector of the old church, the object of unlimited contempt to the adherents of St. Ambrose's.

As to Mark, he only kissed his aunt, and shook hands with her, while his father ran on with an unusual loquacity that was a proof of nervousness in him.

'Mrs. Egremont—Jane, I mean—will be here after luncheon. She thought you would like to get settled in first. How is Alwyn? Is he down yet?'

'I will see,' in a trembling voice.

'Oh no, never mind, Alwyn hates to be disturbed till he has made himself up in the morning. My call is on you, you know. Where are you sitting?'

'I don't quite know. In the drawing-room, I suppose.'

The Canon, knowing the house much better than she did, opened a door into a third drawing-room she had not yet seen, a pretty little room, fitted up with fluted silk, like a tent, somewhat faded but not much the worse for that, and opening into a conservatory, which seemed to have little in it but some veteran orange trees. Nuttie, however, exclaimed with pleasure at the nicest room she had seen, and Mark began unfastening the glass door that led into it. Meantime Alice, with burning cheeks and liquid eyes, nerved her voice to say, 'Oh, sir—Mr. Egremont—please forgive me! I know now how wrong I was.'

'Nonsense, my dear. Bygones are bygones. You were far more sinned against than sinning, and have much to forgive me. There, my dear, we will say no more about it, nor think of it either. I am only too thankful that poor Alwyn should have some one to look after him.'

Alice, who had dreaded nothing more than the meeting with her former master, was infinitely relieved and grateful for this kindness. She had ejaculated, 'Oh, you are so good!' in the midst, and now at the mention of her husband, she exclaimed, 'Oh! do you think he is ill? I can't help being afraid he is, but he will not tell me, and does not like to be asked.'

'Poor fellow, he has damaged his health a good deal,' was the answer. 'He had a sharp attack in the spring, but he has pretty well got over it, and Raikes told me there was no reason for uneasiness, provided he would be careful; and that will be a much easier matter now. I should not wonder if we saw him with quite a renewed youth.'

So the Canon and Mrs. Egremont were getting on pretty well together, but there was much more stiffness and less cordiality between the two cousins, although Mark got the window open into the conservatory, and showed Nuttie the way into the garden, advising her to ask Ronaldson, the gardener, to fill the conservatory with flowers. The pavilion, as this little room was called, always seemed to have more capacities for being lived in than any other room in the house. It had been fitted up when such things were the fashion for the shortlived bride of 'our great uncle.'

'The colour must have been awful then,' said Mark, looking up at it, 'enough to set one's teeth on edge; but it has faded into something quite orthodox—much better than could be manufactured for you.'

Mark had evidently some ideas of art, and was besides inclined to do the honours to the stranger; but Nuttie was not going to encourage him or anybody else to make up to her, while she had that look of Gerard Godfrey's in her mind's eye. So she made small answer, and he felt rebuffed, but supposed her shy, and wondered when he could go back to her mother, who was so much more attractive.

Presently his father went off to storm the den of the master of the house, and there was a pleasant quarter of an hour, during which the three went out through the conservatory, and Mark showed the ins-and-outs of the garden, found out Ronaldson, and congratulated him on having some one at last to appreciate his flowers, begging him to make the conservatory beautiful. And Mrs. Egremont's smile was so effective that the Scot forthwith took out his knife and presented her with the most precious of the roses within his reach.

Moreover Mark told the names and ages of all his sisters, whole and half. He was the only son, except a little fellow in the nursery. And he exhorted his aunt not to be afraid of his step-mother, who was a most excellent person, he declared, but who never liked to see any one afraid of her.

There was something a little alarming in this, but on the whole the visit was very pleasant and encouraging to Mrs. Egremont; and she began rejoicing over the kindness as soon as the Canon had summoned his son, and they had gone away together.

'I am sure you must be delighted with your uncle and cousin, my dear,' she said.

'He's not a bit my notion of a priest,' returned Nuttie. 'And I don't believe he has any daily prayers!'

'He is old-fashioned, my dear.'

'One of the stodgey old clergymen in books,' observed Nuttie. 'I didn't think there were any of that sort left.'

'Oh, my dear, pray don't take fancies into your head! He is a very, very good man, and has been most kind to me, far more than I deserve, and he is your uncle, Nuttie. I do so hope you will get on well with your cousins.'

Here a gong, a perfectly unknown sound to Nuttie, made itself heard, and rather astonished her by the concluding roar. The two ladies came out into the hall as Mr. Egremont was crossing it. He made an inclination of the head, and uttered a sort of good morning to his daughter, but she was perfectly content to have no closer salutation. Having a healthy noonday appetite, her chief wish was at the moment that those beautiful little cutlets, arranged in a crown form, were not so very tiny; or that, with two men-servants looking on, it were possible to attain to a second help, but she had already learnt that Gregorio would not hear her, and that any attempt to obtain more food frightened her mother.

'So his reverence has been to see you,' observed Mr. Egremont. 'William, if you like it better.'

'Oh yes, and he was kindness itself!'

'And how did Master Mark look at finding I could dispense with his assistance?'

'I think he is very glad.'

Mr. Egremont laughed. 'You are a simple woman, Edda! The pose of virtuous hero was to have been full compensation for all that it might cost him! And no doubt he looks for the reward of virtue likewise.'

Wherewith he looked full at Ursula, who, to her extreme vexation, felt herself blushing up to the ears. She fidgeted on her chair, and began a most untrue 'I'm sure—' for, indeed, the poor girl was sure of nothing, but that her father's manner was most uncomfortable to her. His laugh choked whatever she might have said, which perhaps was well, and her mother's cheeks glowed as much as hers did.

'Did the Canoness—Jane, I mean—come up?' Mr. Egremont went on.

'Mrs. Egremont? No; she sent word that she is coming after luncheon.'

'Hm! Then I shall ride out and leave you to her majesty. Now look you, Alice, you are to be very careful with William's wife. She is a Condamine, you know, and thinks no end of herself, and your position among the women- folk of the county depends more on how she takes you up than anything else. But that doesn't mean that you are to let her give herself airs and domineer over you. Remember you are the elder brother's wife—Mrs. Egremont of

Bridgefield Egremont—and she is nothing but a parson's wife, and I won't have her meddling in my house. Only don't you be absurd and offend her, for she can do more for or against you in society than any one else—more's the pity!'

'Oh! won't you stay and help me receive her?' exclaimed the poor lady, utterly confused by these contrary directions.

'Not I! I can't abide the woman! nor she me!' He added, after a moment, 'You will do better without me.'

So he went out for his ride, and Ursula asked, 'Oh, mother! what will you do?'

'The best I can, my dear. They are good people, and are sure to be kinder than I deserve.'

Nuttie was learning that her mother would never so much as hear, far less answer, a remark on her husband. It was beginning to make a sore in the young heart that a barrier was thus rising, where there once had been as perfect oneness and confidence as could exist between two natures so dissimilar, though hitherto the unlikeness had never made itself felt.

Mrs. Egremont turned the conversation to the establishing themselves in the pavilion, whither she proceeded to import some fancy-work that she had bought in London, and sent Nuttie to Ronaldson, who was arranging calceolarias, begonias, and geraniums in the conservatory, to beg for some cut-flowers for a great dusty-looking vase in the centre of the table.

These were being arranged when Mrs. William Egremont and Miss Blanche Egremont were ushered in, and there were the regular kindred embraces, after which Alice and Nuttie were aware of a very handsome, dignified-looking lady, well though simply dressed in what was evidently her home costume, with a large shady hat and feather, her whole air curiously fitting the imposing nickname of the Canoness. Blanche was a slight, delicate- looking, rather pretty girl in a lawn-tennis dress. The visitor took the part of treating the newcomers as well-established relations.

'We would not inundate you all at once,' she said, 'but the children are all very eager to see their cousin. I wish you would come down to the Rectory with me. My ponies are at the door. I would drive you, and Ursula might walk with Blanche.' And, as Alice hesitated for a moment, considering how this might agree with the complicated instructions that she had received, she added, 'Never mind Alwyn. I saw him going off just before I came up, and he told William he was going to look at some horses at Hale's, so he is disposed of for a good many hours.'

Alice decided that her husband would probably wish her to comply, and she rejoiced to turn her daughter in among the cousins, so hats, gloves, and parasols were fetched, and the two mothers drove away with the two sleek little toy ponies. By which it may be perceived that Mrs. William Egremont's first impressions were favourable.

'It is the shortest way through the gardens,' said Blanche. 'Have you been through them yet?'

'Mark walked about with us a little.'

'You'll improve them ever so much. There are great capabilities. Look, you could have four tennis courts on this one lawn. We wanted to have a garden-party up here last year, and father said we might, but mother thought Uncle Alwyn might think it a liberty; but now you'll have some delicious ones? Of course you play lawn-tennis?'

'I have seen it a very few times,' said Nuttie.

'Oh, we must teach you! Fancy living without lawn-tennis!' said Blanche. 'I always wonder what people did without it. Only'—with an effort at antiquarianism—'I believe they had croquet.'

'Aunt Ursula says there weren't garden-parties before croquet came in.'

'How dreadful, Ursula! Your name's Ursula, isn't it? Haven't you some jolly little name to go by?'

'Nuttie.'

'Nuttie! That's scrumptious! I'll call you Nuttie, and you may call me Pussycat.'

'That's not so nice as Blanche.'

'Mother won't have me called so when strangers are there, but you aren't a stranger, you know. You must tell me all about yourself, and how you came never to learn tennis!'

'I had something else to do,' said Nuttie, with dignity.

'Oh, you were in the schoolroom! I forgot. Poor little Nuts!'

'At school,' said Ursula.

'Ah, I remember! But you're out now, aren't you? I've been out since this spring. Mother won't let us come out till we are eighteen, isn't it horrid? And we were so worked there! I can tell you a finishing governess is an awful institution! Poor little Rosie and Adey will be in for one by and by. At present they've only got a jolly little Fraulein that they can do anything they please with.'

'Oh, I wonder if she would tell me of some German books!'

'You don't mean that you want to read German!' and Blanche stood still, and looked at her cousin in astonishment.

'Why, what else is the use of learning it?'

'Oh, I don't know. Every one does. If one went abroad or to court, you know,' said Blanche vaguely; but Ursula had now a fresh subject of interest; for, on emerging from the shrubbery, they came in sight of a picturesque but not very architectural church, which had the smallest proportion of wall and the largest of roof, and a pretty oriel-windowed schoolhouse covered with clematis. Nuttie rushed into inquiries about services and schools, and was aghast at hearing of mere Sundays and saints' days.

'Oh no! father isn't a bit Ritualistic. I wish he was, it would be so much prettier; and then he always advertises for curates of moderate views, and they are so stupid. You never saw such a stick as we have got now, Mr. Edwards; and his wife isn't a lady, I'm sure.'

Then as to schools, it was an absolute amazement to Nuttie to find that the same plans were in force as had prevailed when her uncle had come to the living and built that pretty house—nay, were kept up at his sole expense, because he liked old-fashioned simplicity, and did not choose to be worried with Government inspection.

'And,' said Blanche, 'every one says our girls work ever so much better, and make nicer servants than those that are crammed with all sorts of nonsense not fit for them.'

As to the Sunday school. Mother and the curate take care of that. I'm sure, if you like it, you can have my class, for I always have a headache there, and very often I can't go. Only May pegs away at it, and she won't let me have the boys, who are the only jolly ones, because she says I spoil them. But you must be my friend—mind, Nuttie, not May's, for we are nearer the same age. When is your birthday? You must put it down in my book!'

Nuttie, who had tolerable experience of making acquaintance with new girls, was divided between a sense of Blanche's emptiness, and the warmth excited by her friendliness, as well as of astonishment at all she heard and saw.

Crossing the straggling, meandering village street, the cousins entered the grounds of the Rectory, an irregular but well-kept building of the soft stone of the country, all the garden front of it a deep verandah that was kept open in summer, but closed with glass frames in the winter—flower-beds lying before it, and beyond a lawn where the young folk were playing at the inevitable lawn-tennis.

Margaret was not so pretty as Blanche, but had a more sensible face, and her welcome to Ursula was civil but reserved. Rosalind and Adela were bright little things, in quite a different style from their half-sisters, much lighter in complexion and promising to be handsomer women. They looked full of eagerness and curiosity at the new cousin, whom Blanche set down on a bank, and proceeded to instruct in the mysteries of the all-important game by comments and criticisms on the players.

As soon as Mark and Adela had come out conquerors, Ursula was called on to take her first lesson. May resigned her racket, saying she had something to do, and walked off the field, and carrying off with her Adela, who, as Blanche said, 'had a spine,' and was ordered to lie down for an hour every afternoon. The cheerfulness with which she went spoke well for the training of the family.

Nuttie was light-footed and dexterous handed, and accustomed to active amusements, so that, under the tuition of her cousins, she became a promising pupil, and thawed rapidly, even towards Mark.

She was in the midst of her game when the two mothers came out, for the drive had been extended all round the park, under pretext of showing it to its new mistress, but really to give the Canoness an opportunity of judging of her in a tete-a-tete. Yet that sensible woman had asked no alarming questions on the past, still less had offered any advice that could seem like interference. She had only named localities, mentioned neighbours, and made little communications about the ways of the place such as might elicit remarks; and, as Alice's voice betrayed less and less constraint, she ventured on speaking of their daughters, so as to draw forth some account of how Ursula might have been educated.

And of this, Alice was ready and eager to talk, telling how clever and how industrious Nuttie had always been, and how great an advantage Miss Nugent's kindness was, and how she was hoping to go up for the Cambridge examination; then, detecting some doubt in her companion's manner, she said, 'It would be a great disappointment to her not to do so now. Do you think she had better not?'

'I don't think she will find time to go on with the preparation! And, to tell the truth, I don't think we are quite ripe for such things in this county. We are rather backward, and Ursula, coming in fresh upon us, might find it a disadvantage to be thought much cleverer than other people.'

'Ah! I was not quite sure whether her father would like it.'

'I do not think he would. I am sure that if my little Rose were to take it into her head, I should have hard work to get her father's consent, though no doubt the world will have progressed by the time she is old enough.'

'That settles it,' said Alice. 'Thank you, Mrs. Egremont. I own,' she added presently, 'that I do somewhat regret that it cannot be, for I thought that a motive for keeping up her studies would be helpful to my child;—I do not mean for the sake of the studies, but of the—the balance in all this change and novelty.'

'You are quite right, I have felt it myself,' said her sister-in-law. 'Perhaps something could be done by essay societies. May belongs to one, and if Ursula is an intellectual girl, perhaps you could keep her up to some regular employment in the morning. I succeeded in doing so when May came out, but I can accomplish nothing regular but music with Blanche; and an hour's steady practice a day is better than nothing.'

The drive was on the whole a success, and so was the tea-drinking in the verandah, where Aunt Alice and little five-years old Basil became fast friends and mutual admirers; the Canon strolled out and was installed in the big, cushioned basket-chair that crackled under his weight; Blanche recounted Nuttie's successes, and her own tennis engagements for the week; Mark lay on a rug and teased her, and her dachshund; Nuttie listened to the family chatter as if it were a play, and May dispensed the cups, and looked grave and severe.

'Well?' said the Canon anxiously, when Mark, Blanche, and little Basil had insisted on escorting the guests home, and he and his wife were for a few minutes tete-a-tete.

'It might have been much worse,' said the lady. 'She is a good little innocent thing, and has more good sense than I expected. Governessy, that's all, but she will shake out of that.'

'Of course she will. It's the best thing imaginable for Alwyn!'

His wife kept back the words, 'A hundred times too good for Alwyn!'

CHAPTER XI.

LAWN-TENNIS.

A garden-party, Mrs. William Egremont decided, would be the best mode of testifying her approbation of her sister-in-law, and introducing the newcomers to the neighbourhood. So the invitations were sent forth for an early day of the coming week.

From how many points of view was Mrs. William Egremont's garden- party regarded, and how different! There was Basil, to whom it meant wearing his velvet suit and eating as many ices as mother would allow. To Blanche, it was an occasion for triumph on the tennis ground for herself, and for hopes for her pupil; and Ursula herself looked forward to it and practised for it like a knight for his first encounter in the lists, her sole care being to distinguish herself with her racket. To her mother, it was an ordeal, where she trusted not to be a mortification to her husband and his family; while to the hostess, it was a not unwelcome occasion of exercising honest diplomacy and tact, not without a sense of magnanimity. To May, it was a bore to be endured with dutiful philosophy; to her good-natured father an occasion for hospitality, where he trusted that his brother would appear, and appear to advantage, and was ready even to bribe him thereto with that wonderful claret that Alwyn had always envied, and declared to be wasted on a parson. And Mark, perhaps he viewed the occasion with different eyes from any one else. At any rate, even the denizens of Bridgefield mustered there with as many minds as Scott ascribes to the combatants of Bannockburn, and there were probably as many other circles of feeling more or less intersecting one another among the more distant guests, most of them, however, with the same feeling of curiosity as to what this newly-discovered wife and daughter of Alwyn Egremont might be like.

Externally, in her rich black silk, trimmed with point lace, and her little straw-coloured bonnet with its tuft of feathery grass and blue cornflower, she was so charming that her daughter danced round her, crying, 'O mammy, mammy, if they could but see you at home'—then, at a look: 'Well then— Aunt Ursel, and Miss Mary, and Mr. Dutton!'

Nuttie was very much pleased with her own pretty tennis dress; but she had no personal vanity for herself, only for her mother. The knowledge that she was no beauty was no grievance to her youthful spirits; but when her father surveyed them in the hall, she looked for his verdict for her mother as if their relations were reversed.

'Ha! Well, you certainly are a pretty creature, Edda,' he said graciously.

'You'll pass muster! You want nothing but style. And, hang it! you'll do just as well without it, if the Canoness will only do you justice. Faces like that weren't given for nothing.'

She blushed incarnadine and accepted one of his kisses with a pleasure, at which Nuttie wondered, her motherly affection prompting her to murmur in his ear—

'And Ursula?'

'She'll not cut you out; but she is Egremont enough to do very fairly. Going already?'

'If you would come with us,' she said wistfully, to the horror of Nuttie, who was burning to be at the beginning of all the matches.

'I? oh no! I promised old Will to look in, but that won't be till late in the day, or I shall have to go handing all the dowagers into the dining-room to tea.'

'Then I think we had better go on. They asked us to come early, so as to see people arrive and know who they are.'

They was a useful pronoun to Alice, who felt it a liberty to call her grand-looking sister-in-law, Jane—was too well-bred to term her Mrs. William.

The mother and daughter crossed the gardens, Nuttie chattering all the way about the tennis tactics she had picked up from Blanche, while her mother answered her somewhat mechanically, wondering, as her eye fell on the square squat gray church tower, what had become of the earnest devotion to church work and intellectual pursuits that used to characterise the girl. True, always both mother and daughter had hitherto kept up their church-going, and even their Sunday-school habits, nor had any hindrance come in their way, Mr. Egremont apparently acquiescing in what he never shared. But these things seemed, in Ursula's mind, to have sunk out of the proportion they held at Bridgefield, no longer to be the spirit of a life, but mere Sunday duties and occupations.

Was this wicked world getting a hold of the poor child? Which was duty? which was the world? This was the thought that perplexed Alice, too simple as yet to perceive that Ursula's former absorption had been in the interests that surrounded her and her companions, exactly as they were at present, and that the real being had yet to work itself out.

For herself, Alice did not think at all. She was rejoicing in her restored husband, and his evident affection. Her duty towards him was in her eyes plain. She saw, of course, that he had no religion, but she accepted the fact like that of bad weather; she loved him, and she loved her daughter; she said her prayers with all her heart for them, she hoped, and she did her best, without trying to go below the surface.

There was the Rectory gate wide open. There was Basil rushing up to greet his dear Aunt Alice, there were all the windows and doors of the Rectory open, and the nearer slopes covered with chairs and seats of all dimensions, some under trees, some umbelliferous, and glowing Afghan rugs, or spotted skins spread for those who preferred the ground. There was Blanche flitting about wild with excitement, and pouncing on Nuttie to admire her outfit, and reiterate instructions; there were the two younger girls altering the position of chairs according to their mother's directions; there were actually two guests— not very alarming ones, only the curate and his wife, both rather gaunt, bony people. He was button-holing the Canon, and she was trying to do the same by the Canoness about some parish casualty. The Canon hoped to escape in the welcome to his sister-in-law and niece, but he was immediately secured again, while his wife found it requisite to hurry off else where, leaving Mrs. Edwards to tell her story to Mrs. Egremont. In point of fact, Alice really liked the good lady, was quite at ease with her, and felt parish concerns a natural element, so that she gave full heed and attention to the cruelty of Mrs. Parkins' depriving Betsy Butter (with an old father and mother to support) of her family washing, on the ground of a missing pocket handkerchief, the which Mrs. Edwards believed to have been abstracted by the favourite pickle of Miss Blanche's class, if only a confession could be elicited from him when undefended by his furious mother. Mrs. Egremont was listening with actual interest and sympathy to the history of Betsy Butter's struggles, and was inquiring the way to her cottage, when she was called off to be introduced to the arrivals who were beginning to flood the lawn. She presently saw May, who had just come down, walking up and down with Mrs. Edwards, evidently hearing the story of the handkerchief. She thought it had been Nuttie for a moment. There was a general resemblance between the cousins that made them be mistaken for one another several times in the course of the day, since their dresses, though not alike, were of the same make and style.

Thus it was that as Nuttie was sitting on the grass in earnest contemplation of Blanche's play, a hand was familiarly laid on her shoulder, and a voice said, 'I haven't seen that horrid girl yet!'

After so many introductions, Nuttie had little idea whom she knew, or whom she did not know. She looked up and saw a small person in light blue, with the delicate features, transparent skin, and blue eyes that accompany yellow hair, with an indescribable glitter of mirth and joyousness about the whole creature, as if she were part and parcel of the sunbeam in which she stood.

'What horrid girl?' said Nuttie.

'The interloper, the newly-discovered savage, come to upset—Ah!'—with a little shriek—'It isn't May! I beg your pardon.'

'I'm May's cousin,' said Nuttie, 'Ursula Egremont.'

'Oh, oh!' and therewith the fact burst on both girls at once. They stood still a moment in dismay, then the stranger went into a fit of laughter. 'Oh, I beg your pardon! I can't help it! It is so funny!'

Nuttie was almost infected, though somewhat hurt. 'Who said I was horrid?' she asked.

'Nobody! Nobody but me—Annaple Ruthven—and they'll all tell you, May and all, that I'm always putting my foot in it. And I never meant that you were horrid—you yourself—you know—only—'

'Only nobody wanted us here,' said Nuttie; 'but we could not help it.'

'Of course not. It was shocking, just my way. Please forgive me!' and she looked most pleading. Nuttie held out her hand with something about 'No one could mind;' and therewith Annaple cried, 'Oh, if you don't mind, we can have our laugh out!' and the rippling laughter did set Nuttie off at once. The peal was not over when May herself was upon them demanding what was the joke.

'Oh, there she is! The real May! Why,' said Annaple, kissing her, 'only think here I've been and gone and thought this was you, and inquired about— What was it?—the awful monster—the chimera dire—that Mark had routed up—'

'No; you didn't say that,' said Nuttie, half provoked.

'Never mind what I said. Don't repeat it. I only wish myself and everyone else to forget it. Now it is swept to the winds by a good wholesome giggling. But what business have you two to be so inconveniently alike? You are as bad as the twin Leslies!'

'There's an old foremother on the staircase in white satin who left her looks to us both,' said May.

'You'll have to wear badges,' said Annaple. 'You know the Leslies were so troublesome that one had to be shipped off to the East Indies and the other to the West.'

'They married, that's all,' said May, seeing Nuttie looking mystified; and at that moment, Blanche's side coming out victorious, Nuttie descended into the arena to congratulate and be asked to form part of the next set.

'Well, that was a scrape!' said Annaple; 'but she wasn't bad about it! I must do something to make up for it somehow—get Janet to invite her, but really Janet is in such a state of mind that I am mildness itself compared with her. She would not have come, only John was curious, and declared he should go whether we did or not.'

'Ah!' said May, 'I saw him, like the rest of mankind, at madame's feet.'

'Oh! is she of that sort?'

'No,' said May, 'not at all. Mother and father too both think she is good to the backbone; but she is very pretty, with just the inane soft sweetness that men rave about—innocent really. All accounts of her are excellent, and she has nice parish ways, and will be as helpful as Uncle Alwyn will let her.'

'But she couldn't always have been nice?'

'Well, I verily believe it was all Uncle Alwyn's and grandmamma's fault. I know Mark thinks so.'

'When the women of a family acquit a woman it goes for something,' said Annaple. 'That's not original, my dear, I heard old Lady Grosmede say so to Janet when she was deliberating over the invitation, "For a good deal more than Mr. Mark's, at any rate."'

'Mark is very fond of her—the mother, I mean. He says when he was a little fellow her loss was worse to him than even our mother's.'

'Do you remember the catastrophe?'

'Not a bit. Only when she is petting Basil it strikes me that I have heard the tones before. I only remember the time of misery under the crosspatches grandmamma got for us.'

'Well, it was a splendid cutting of his own throat in Mark,' said Annaple, 'so it ought to turn out well.'

'I don't know how it is to turn out for Mark,' answered May. 'Oh, here he comes!'

'Will you come into this set, Annaple?' he asked. 'They want another couple,' and, as she accepted, 'How do you get on with May's double?'

'I pity May for having such a double.'

'Don't encourage her by misplacedpity.'

'It's abominable altogether! I want to fly at somebody!'

'Exhaust your feelings on your racket, and reflect that you see a man released from bondage.'

'Is that philosophy or high-faluting?' she said in a teasing tone as the game began.

The Ruthvens had very blue blood in their veins, but as there were nine of the present generation, they possessed little beyond their long pedigree; even the head of the family, Lord Ronnisglen, being forced to live as a soldier, leaving his castle to grouse shooters. His seven brothers had fared mostly in distant lands as they could, and his mother had found a home, together with her youngest child, at Lescombe, where her eldest was the wife of Sir John Delmar. Lady Ronnisglen was an invalid, confined to the house, and Lady Delmar had daughters fast treading on the heels of Annabella, so christened, but always called Annaple after the old Scottish queens, her ancestors. She had been May Egremont's chief friend ever since her importation at twelve years old, and the intimacy had been promoted by her mother and sister. Indeed, the neighbourhood had looked on with some amusement at the competition ascribed to Lady Delmar and to the wealthy parvenu, Mrs. West, for the heir-presumptive of Bridgefield Egremont.

Annaple's lightness and dexterity rendered her the best of the lady tennis-players, and the less practised Ursula found herself defeated in the match, in spite of a partner whose play was superior to Mark's, and with whom she shyly walked off to eat ices.

'I see,' said Annaple, 'it is a country-town edition of May. I shan't blunder between them again.'

'She will polish,' said Mark, 'but she is not equal to her mother.'

'Whom I have not seen yet. Ah, there's Mr. Egremont! Why, he looks quite renovated!'

'Well he may be!'

'But Mark, not to hurt your feelings, he must have behaved atrociously.'

'I'm not going to deny it,' said Mark.

'I always did think he looked like it,' said Annaple.

'When have you seen him before?'

'Only once, but it was my admirable sagacity, you understand? I always see all the villains in books just on his model. Oh, but who's that? How very pretty! You don't mean it is she! Well, she might be the heroine of anything!'

'Isn't she lovely?'

'And has she been keeping school like Patience on a monument all these years? It doesn't seem to have much damaged her damask cheek!'

'It was only daily governessing. She looks much better than when I first saw her; and as to the damask—why, that's deepened by the introduction to old Lady Grosmede that is impending.'

'She is being walked up to the old Spanish duck with the red rag round her leg to receive her fiat. What a thing it is to be a bearded Dowager, and rule one's neighbourhood!'

'I think she approves. She has made room for her by her side. Is she going to catechise her?'

Annaple made an absurd sound of mingled pity and disgust.

'Not that she—my aunt, I mean—need be afraid. The shame is all on the other side.'

'And I think Lady Grosmede has too much sense to think the worse of her for having worked for herself,' added Annaple. 'If it was not for mother I should long to begin!'

'You? It's a longing well known to me!—but you!'

'Exactly! As the Irishman felt blue moulded for want of a bating, so do I feel fagged out for want of an honest day's work.'

'If one only knew what to turn to,' said Mark so wearily that Annaple exclaimed,

'We seem to be in the frozen-out state of mind, and might walk up and down singing "I've got no work to do,"'—to which she gave the well known intonation.

'Too true,' said he, joining in the hum.

'But I thought you were by way of reading law.'

'One must see more than only "by way of" in these days to do any good.'

At that moment Basil ran up with a message that Lady Delmar was ready to go home.

They walked slowly up the terrace and Mark paused as they came near Mrs. Egremont to say, 'Aunt Alice, here is Miss Ruthven, May's great friend.'

Annaple met a pleasant smile, and they shook hands, exchanging an observation or two, while a little way off Lady Grosmede was nodding her strong old face at Lady Delmar, and saying, 'Tell your mother I'll soon come and see her, my dear. That's a nice little innocent body, lady-like, and thoroughly presentable. Alwyn Egremont might have done worse.'

'The only wonder is he did not!' returned Lady Delmar. 'They make the best of it here.'

'Very good taste of them. But, now I've seen her, I don't believe there's anything behind. Very hard upon the poor young man, though it was all his doing, his mother says. I congratulate you that it had not gone any farther in that quarter.'

'Oh, dear no! Never dreamt of it. She is May's friend, that's all.'

Nevertheless Lady Delmar made a second descent in person to hurry Annaple away.

'Isn't it disgusting?' said May, catching her stepmother's smile.

'You will see a good deal more of the same kind,' said the Canoness; 'I am afraid more mortification is in store for Mark than he guesses. I wish that girl were more like her mother.'

'Mamma! a girl brought up among umbrella-makers! Just fancy! Why, she has just nothing in her!'

'Don't set Mark against her, May; he might do worse.'

'Her head is a mere tennis ball,' said May, drawing her own higher than ever, 'and no one would know her from a shop girl.'

'She is young enough,' said the Canoness. 'Don't class me with Lady Delmar, May—I only say—if—and that I don't think you realise the change Mark will feel.'

'Better so than sell himself,' muttered May.

CHAPTER XII.

OUT OF WORK.

Society recognised the newcomers. Lady Grosmede's card appeared the next day, and was followed by showers of others, and everybody asked everybody 'Have you seen Mrs. Egremont?'

It was well for Alice's happiness even at home that she was a success. When Alwyn Egremont had been lashed by his nephew's indignant integrity into tardy recognition of the wife of his youth, it had been as if he had been forced to pick up a flower which he had thrown away. He had considerable doubts whether it would answer. First, he reconnoitred, intending, if he found a homely or faded being, to pension her off; but this had been prevented by her undeniable beauty and grace, bringing up a rush of such tender associations as he was capable of. Yet even then, her position depended on the impression she might make on those about him, on her own power of self- assertion, and on her contributing to his comfort or pleasure.

Of self-assertion Alice had none, only a gentle dignity in her simplicity, and she was so absolutely devoted to him that he found his house far more pleasant and agreeable for her presence and unfailing attention, though still his estimation of her was influenced more than he owned to himself by that of the world in general, and the Rectory in particular.

And the Rectory did its part well. The Canon was not only charmed with the gentle lady, but felt an atonement due to her; and his wife, without ever breathing into any ears, save his, the mysterious adjective 'governessy,' praised her right and left, confiding to all inquirers the romance of the burnt yacht, the lost bride, and the happy meeting under Lady Kirkaldy's auspices, with the perfect respectability of the intermediate career, while such was the universal esteem for, and trust in herself and the Canon, that she was fully believed; and people only whispered that probably Alwyn Egremont had been excused for the desertion more than he deserved.

The subject of all this gossip troubled herself about it infinitely less than did the good Canoness. In effect she did not know enough of the world to think about it at all. Her cares were of a different order, chiefly caused by tenderness of conscience, and solicitude to keep the peace between the two beings whom she best loved.

Two things were in her favour in this latter respect, one that they saw very little of each other, since Mr. Egremont seldom emerged from his own rooms till after luncheon; and the other that Ursula's brains ran to little but lawn-tennis for the ensuing weeks. To hold a champion's place at the tournaments, neck and neck with her cousin Blanche, and defeat Miss Ruthven, and that veteran player, Miss Basset, was her foremost ambition, and the two cousins would have practised morning, noon, and night if their mothers would have let them. There need have been no fear of Ursula's rebellion about the Cambridge honours, she never seemed even to think of them, and would have had no time in the more important competition of rackets. Indeed, it was almost treated as a hardship that the pair were forbidden to rush together before twelve o'clock, and that Ursula's mother insisted on rational home occupation until that time, setting the example herself by letter-writing, needlework, and sharing in the music which was a penance to the girl, only enforced by that strong sense of protecting affection which forbade rebellion. But Alice could hope that their performances were pleasant to her husband in the evening, if only to sleep by, and so she persisted in preparing for them.

Nuttie's rage for tennis, and apparent forgetfulness of her old life and aspirations, might be disappointing, but it conduced to make her mother's task easier than if she had been her original, critical, and protesting self. In the new and brilliant surroundings she troubled herself much less than could have been expected at the failure of her father, his house, nay, and of the parish itself, in coming up to the St. Ambrose standard. How much was owing to mere novelty and intoxication, how much to a yet unanalysed disappointment, how much to May's having thrown her upon the more frivolous Blanche, could not be guessed. The effect was unsatisfactory to her mother, but a certain relief, for Nuttie's aid would have been only mischievous in the household difficulties that weighed on the anxious conscience. Good servants would not stay at Bridgefield Hall for unexplained causes, which their mistress believed to be connected with Gregorio, or with the treasure of a cook-housekeeper over whom she was forbidden to exercise any authority, and who therefore entirely neglected all meals which the master did not share with the ladies. Fortunately, Mr. Egremont came in one day at their luncheon and found nothing there but semi-raw beef, upon which there was an explosion; and being by this time convinced that his wife both would and could minister to his comfort, her dominion was established in the female department, though, as long as Gregorio continued paramount with his master, and the stables remained in their former state, it was impossible to bring matters up to the decorous standard of the Rectory, and if ever his mistress gave an order he did not approve, Gregorio overruled it as her ignorance. In fact, he treated both the ladies with a contemptuous sort of civility. Meantime Mr. Egremont was generally caressing and admiring in his ways towards his wife, with only occasional bursts of temper when anything annoyed him. He was proud of her, gave her a liberal allowance, and only refused to be troubled; and she was really happy in his affection, for which she felt a gratitude only too humble in the eyes of her daughter.

They had parties. Blanche's ambition of tennis courts all over the lawn was fulfilled, and sundry dinners, which were crosses to Alice, who had neither faculty nor training for a leader and hostess, suffered much from the menu, more from the pairing of her guests, more again in catching her chief lady's eye after, and most of all from her husband's scowls and subsequent growls and their consequence, for Ursula broke out, 'It is not fair to blame my mother. How should she have all the savoir-faire, or what you may call it, of Aunt Jane, when she has had no practice?'

'Perhaps, Mrs. Egremont,' he retorted with extreme suavity, 'you will also attend to your daughter's manners.' Otherwise he took little notice of Ursula, viewing her perhaps, as did the neighbourhood, as a poor imitation of May, without her style, or it may be with a sense that her tongue might become inconvenient if not repressed. When he began to collect sporting guests of his own calibre in the shooting season, the Canoness quietly advised her sister-in-law to regard them as gentlemen's parties, and send Ursula down to spend the evening with her cousins; and to this no objection was made. Mr. Egremont wanted his beautiful wife at the head of his table, and his guests never comported themselves unsuitably before her; but nobody wanted the unformed girl, and she and Blanche were always happy together.

The chief restraint was when Mark was at home, and that was not always. He made sundry visits and expeditions, and was altogether in an uncomfortable condition of reaction and perplexity as to his future. He was a good and conscientious fellow, and had never been actually idle, but had taken education and life with the easiness of the prospective heir to a large property; and though he had acquitted himself creditably, it was with no view of making his powers marketable. Though he had been entered at the Temple, it was chiefly in order to occupy himself respectably, and to have a nominal profession, so as not to be wholly dependent on his uncle; and all that he had acquired was the conviction that it would be half a lifetime, if not a whole one, before the law would afford him a maintenance.

His father wished him to take Holy Orders with a view to the reversion of the Rectory, but Mark's estimate of clerical duty and vocation was just such as to make him shrink from them. He was three-and-twenty, an awkward age for all those examinations that stand as lions in the face of youth intended for almost any sort of service, and seldom or never to be gagged by interest. For one indeed, he went up and failed, and in such a manner as to convince him that cramming had more to do than general culture with success.

He had a certain consciousness that most people thought another way open to him, most decidedly his gentle aunt, and perhaps even his parents. The matter came prominently before him one day at luncheon, when, some parochial affairs being on hand and Mr. Egremont out for the day, Alice, whose free forenoons enabled her to take a share in church and parish affairs, was there, as well as the curate and his wife.

These good people were in great commotion about a wedding about to take place between a young farmer and his delicate first cousin, the only survivor of a consumptive family.

'"Proputty, proputty,"' quoted the Canon. 'James Johnson is what they call a warm man.'

'It is a sin and a shame,' said Mrs. Edwards. 'What can they expect? George Johnson looks strong enough now, but they tell me his brother undoubtedly died of decline, though they called it inflammation; but there was tubercular disease.'

'I am afraid it is strong in the family,' said the Canoness, 'they all have those clear complexions; but I do believe George is heartily in love with poor little Emily.'

'First cousins ought to be in the table of degrees,' said Mr. Edwards.

'It is always a question whether the multiplying of prohibitions without absolute necessity is expedient,' said the Canon.

He spoke quite dispassionately, but the excellent couple were not remarkable for tact. Mrs. Edwards gave her husband such a glance of warning and consternation as violently inclined May to laugh, and he obediently and hesitatingly began, 'Oh yes, sir, I beg your pardon. Of course there may be instances,' thereby bringing an intense glow of carnation into Alice's cheeks, while the Canon, ready for the occasion, replied, 'And George Johnson considers himself one of them. He will repair the old moat house, I suppose.'

And his wife, though she would rather have beaten Mrs. Edwards, demanded how many blankets would be wanted that winter.

The effect of this little episode was that Mark announced to his father that evening his strong desire to emigrate, an intention which the Canon combated with all his might. He was apparently a hale and hearty man, but he had had one or two attacks of illness that made him doubt whether he would be long-lived; and not only could he not bear to have his eldest son out of reach, but he dreaded leaving his family to such a head as his brother. Mark scarcely thought the reasons valid, considering the rapidity of communication with Canada, but it was not possible to withstand the entreaties of a father with tears in his eyes; and though he could not bring himself to consent to preparing to be his father's curate, he promised to do nothing that would remove him to another quarter of the world, and in two or three days more, started for Monks Horton to see what advice his uncle and aunt there could give him; indeed, Lord Kirkaldy's influence was reckoned on by his family almost as a sure card in the diplomatic line.

The Kirkaldys were very fond of Mark, and had an odd feeling of being accountable for the discovery which had changed his prospects. They would have done anything for him that they could, but all Lord Kirkaldy's interest was at the foreign office, or with his fellow-diplomates, and here he soon found an insuperable bar. Mark's education had stood still from the time of Miss Headworth's flight till his father's second marriage, his energies having been solely devoted to struggles with the grim varieties of governess purveyed by his grandmother, and he had thus missed all chance of foundation of foreign languages, and when once at school, he had shared in the average English boy's contempt and aversion for the French masters who outscreamed a whole class.

In consequence, Lord Kirkaldy, an accurate and elegant scholar in European tongues, besides speaking them with the cosmopolitan ease of an ambassador's son, was horrified, not only at Mark's pronunciation, but at his attempts at letter-writing and translation, made with all the good will in the world, but fit for nothing but to furnish the good stories which the kind uncle refrained from telling any one but his wife. Unluckily, too, a Piedmontese family, some of them not strong in their English, were on a visit at Monks Horton, and the dialect in which the old marquis and Mark tried at times to interchange ideas about pheasants was something fearful. And as in the course of a week Mark showed no signs of improvement in vernacular French or Italian, Lord Kirkaldy's conscience would let him give no other advice than that his nephew should stick to English law living still on the allowance his father gave him, and hoping for one of the chance appointments open to an English barrister of good family and fair ability.

Of course Mark had gone at once to carry tidings of 'Aunt Alice,' as he scrupulously called her, to old Miss Headworth, whom his aunt had continued to visit at intervals. That good lady had given up her boarders, having realised enough to provide for her own old age, and she had joined forces with the Nugents, Mary being very thankful to have her companionship for Mrs. Nugent, who was growing too blind and feeble to be satisfactorily left alone all day.

Mark delighted the old ladies by his visits and accounts of their darling's success and popularity, which he could paint so brightly that they could not help exulting, even though there might be secret misgivings as to the endurance of these palmy days. He was a great hero in their eyes, and they had too good taste to oppress him with their admiration, so that he really was more at ease in their little drawing-room than anywhere at Monks Horton, whither the Italians could penetrate. The marchesino spoke English very well, but that was all the worse for Mark, since it gave such a sense of inferiority. He was an intelligent man too, bent on being acquainted with English industries of all kinds; and thus it was that a party was organised to see the umbrella factory. It was conducted by Mr. Dutton, with whom Lord Kirkaldy, between charities and public business, had become acquainted.

To Mark's secret shame, this manufacturer spoke French perfectly, and even got into such a lively conversation with the old marquis about Cavour, that Lord Kirkaldy begged him to come to dinner and continue it. They were all surprised, not only by the details of the manufacture and the multitude of artizans, male and female, whom it employed, but by the number of warehouse-clerks whom they found at work, and who, it appeared, were in correspondence with agencies and depots in London and all the principal towns in the kingdom. Gerard Godfrey was there,—casting looks askance at the young Egremont, whom he regarded as a kind of robber.

The marchesino asked from what class these young men were taken, and Mr. Dutton made reply that most of them were sons of professional men. If they could obtain a small capital and take shares in the business they were encouraged to do so, and rose to the headship of the agencies, obtaining a fair income.

'And you don't exact an examination,' said Mark.

'Except in handwriting and book-keeping,' said Mr. Dutton.

'Poor Mark, you look for your bugbear everywhere!' sighed his aunt.

They went over the Institute, coffee-rooms, eating-rooms, and lodging-houses, by which the umbrella firm strove to keep their hands respectable and contented, and were highly pleased with all, most especially with Mr. Dutton, who, though his name did not come prominently forward, had been the prime mover and contriver of all these things, and might have been a wealthier man if he had not undertaken expenses which he could not charge upon the company.

Gerard Godfrey came in to Mrs. Nugent's that evening in the lowest spirits. He had a sister married to a curate in the same county with Bridgefield, and she had sent him a local paper which 'understood that a marriage was arranged between Mark de Lyonnais Egremont, Esquire, and Ursula, daughter of Alwyn Piercefield Egremont, Esquire, of Bridgefield Egremont,' and he could not help coming to display it to Miss Headworth in all its impertinence and prematurity.

'Indeed he said nothing to me about it,' said Miss Headworth, 'and I think he would if it had been true.'

'No doubt he intends it, and is trying to recommend himself through you,' said Gerard.

'I should not think he needed that,' returned Aunt Ursel, 'though I should be very glad, I am sure. He is an excellent young man, and it is quite the obvious thing.'

'People don't always do the obvious thing,' put in Mary Nugent.

'Certainly it didn't look like it,' said Miss Headworth,' when he told us about the great annual Hunt Ball at Redcastle that Nuttie and his sister Blanche are to come out at; he said he did not intend to go home for it if he could help it.'

'Struggling against fate,' said Miss Nugent.

'The puppy!' burst out Gerard.

Having ascertained the particulars of this same Hunt Ball, Gerard became possessed with a vehement desire to visit his sister, and so earnestly solicited a few days' leave of absence that it was granted to him. 'Poor boy, he may settle down when he has ascertained what an ass he is,' said Mr. Dutton.

'Ah!' said Mary. 'I thought he was very bad when I saw he had not changed the green markers for St. Luke's Day.'

CHAPTER XIII.

DETRIMENTALS.

'That tongue of yours at times wags more than charity allows;
And if you're strong, be merciful, great woman of three cows.'—J. O. MANGAN.

Nine miles was a severe distance through country lanes in November to go to a ball; but the Redcastle Hunt Ball was the ball of the year, uniting all the county magnates; and young ladies were hardly reckoned as 'come out' till they had appeared there. Mrs. Egremont's position would hardly be established till she had been presented to the notabilities who lived beyond calling intercourse; and her husband prepared himself to be victimised with an amount of grumbling that was intended to impress her with the magnitude of the sacrifice, but which only made her offer to forego the gaiety, and be told that she would never have any common sense.

So their carriage led the way, and was followed by the Rectory waggonette containing the ladies and Mark, who had been decisively summoned home, since his stepmother disliked public balls without a gentleman in attendance, and his father was not to be detached from his fireside.

And in a group near the door, got up as elaborately as his powers could accomplish, stood Gerard Godfrey. He knew nobody there except a family in his sister's parish, who had good-naturedly given him a seat in their fly, and having fulfilled his duty by asking the daughter to dance, he had nothing to disturb him in watching for the cynosure whose attraction had led him into these unknown regions, and, as he remembered with a qualm, on the eve of St. Britius. However, with such a purpose, one might surely grant oneself a dispensation from the vigil of a black letter saint.

There at length he beheld the entrance. There was the ogre himself, high bred, almost handsome, as long as he was not too closely scrutinised, and on his arm the well-known figure, metamorphosed by delicately-tinted satin sheen and pearls, and still more by the gentle blushing gladness on the fair cheeks and the soft eyes that used to droop. Then followed a stately form in mulberry moire and point lace, leaning on Gerard's more especial abhorrence,
—'that puppy,' who had been the author of all the mischief; and behind them three girls, one in black, the other two in white, and, what was provoking, he really could not decide which was Ursula. The carefully-dressed hair and stylish evening dress and equipments had altogether transformed the little homely schoolgirl, so that, though he was sure that she was not the fair-haired damsel with pale blue flowers, he did not know how to decide between the white and daisies and the black and grasses. Indeed, he thought the two whites most likely to be sisters, and all the more when the black lace halted to exchange greetings with some one, and her face put on an expression so familiar to him, that he started forward and tried to catch her eye; but in vain, and he suffered agonies of doubt whether she had been perverted by greatness.

It was some comfort that, when presently a rush of waiters floated by, she was not with her cousin; but to provoke him still more, as the daisies neared him, he beheld for a moment in the whirl the queer smile, half-frightened, half-exultant, which he had seen on Nuttie's face when swinging sky-high!

When the pause came and people walked about, the black lady stood talking so near him that he ventured at last on a step forward and an eager 'Miss Egremont,' but, as she turned, he found himself obliged to say, 'I beg your pardon.'

'Did you mean my cousin. We often get mistaken for each other,' said May civilly.

He brightened. 'I beg your pardon,' he said, 'I knew her at Micklethwayte. I am here—quite by accident. Mrs. Elmore was so good as to bring me.'

May was rather entertained. 'There's my cousin,' she said, 'Lord Philip Molyneux is asking her to dance,' and she left him most unnecessarily infuriated with Lord Philip Molyneux.

A steward introduced him to a dull-looking girl, but fortune favoured him, for this time he did catch the real Nuttie's eye, and all herself, as soon as the dance was over, she came up with outstretched hands, 'Oh Gerard! to think of your being here! Come to mother!'

And, beautiful and radiant, Mrs. Egremont was greeting him, and there were ten minutes of delicious exchange of news. But 'pleasures are as poppies fled,' Nuttie had no dance to spare, her card was full, and she had not learnt fashionable effrontery enough to play tricks with engagements, and just then Mr. Egremont descended on them—'I wish to introduce you to the Duchess,' he said to his wife; and on the way he demanded—'Who is that young cub?'

'Gerard Godfrey—an old neighbour.'

'I thought I had seen him racketing about there with Ursula. I'll not have those umbrella fellows coming about!'

'Does he really make umbrellas, Nuttie?' asked Blanche, catching her hand.

'No such thing!' said Nuttie hotly, 'he is in the office. His father was a surgeon; his sisters married clergymen!'

'And he came here to meet you,' said Annaple Ruthven. 'Poor fellow, what a shame it is! Can't you give him one turn!

'Oh dear! I'm engaged all through! To Mark this time.'

'Give him one of the extras! Throw Mark over to me! No,' as she looked at the faces of the two girls, 'I suppose that wouldn't do, but I'm free this time— I'm not the fashion. Introduce me; I'll do my best as consolation.'

Nuttie had just performed the feat, with great shyness, when Mark appeared, having been sent in quest of his cousin, when her father perceived that she had hung back.

Poor Gerard led off Miss Ruthven the more gloomily, and could not help sighing out, 'I suppose that is an engagement!'

'Oh! you believe that impertinent gossip in the paper,' returned Annaple. 'I wonder they don't contradict it; but perhaps they treat it with magnificent scorn.'

'No doubt they know that it is only premature.'

'If *they* means the elders, I daresay they wish it, but we aren't in France or Italy.'

'Then you don't think, Miss Ruthven, that it will come off?'

'I don't see the slightest present prospect,' said Annaple, unable to resist the kindly impulse of giving immediate pleasure, though she knew the prospect might be even slighter for her partner.

However, he 'footed it' all the more lightly and joyously for the assurance, and the good-natured maiden afterwards made him conduct her to the tea-room, whither Mark and Nuttie were also tending, and there all four contrived to get mixed up together; and Nuttie had time to hear of Monsieur's new accomplishment of going home for Mr. Dutton's luncheon and bringing it in a basket to the office, before fate again descended; Mr. Egremont, who had been at the far end of the room among some congeners, who preferred stronger refreshment, suddenly heard her laugh, stepped up, and, with a look of thunder towards her, observed in a low voice, 'Mark, you will oblige me by taking your cousin back to her mother.'

'The gray tyrant father,' murmured Annaple in sympathy. 'That being the case, I may as well go back in that direction also.'

This resulted in finding Lady Delmar and the two Mrs. Egremonts together, comparing notes about the two different roads to Redcastle from their several homes.

Lady Delmar was declaring that her coachman was the most obstinate man in existence, and that her husband believed in him to any extent.

'Which way did you come?' she asked.

'By Bankside Lane,' said the Canoness.

'Over Bluepost Bridge! There, Janet,' said Annaple.

'So much the worse. I know we shall come to grief over Bluepost Bridge, and now there will be treble weight to break it down. I dreamt it, I tell you, and there's second sight in the family.'

'Yes, but you should tell what you did dream, Janet,' said her sister. 'She thought Robinson, the coachman, was waltzing with her over it, and they went into a hole and stuck fast, while the red-flag traction engineman prodded her with an umbrella till she was all over blood. Now, if it had been anything rational, I should have thought something of her second sight! I tell her 'twas suggested by—

> "London Bridge is broken down,
> Dance o'er my lady Lee!"'

'Well, I am quite certain those traction-engines will break it some time or other,' said Lady Delmar. 'I am always trying to get John to bring it before the magistrates, but he only laughs at me, and nothing will induce Robinson to go the other way, because they have just been mending the road on Lescombe Hill! Annaple, my dear, I can't allow you another waltz; Mark must excuse you—I am going. It is half-past two, and the carriage was ordered at two! Robinson will be in a worse temper than ever if we keep him waiting.'

She bore her sister off to the cloak-room, and there, nearly an hour later, the Egremonts found them still waiting the pleasure of the implacable Robinson; but what was that in consideration of having kept her sister from such a detrimental as poor Mark had become? So muttered Mr. Egremont, in the satisfaction of having himself, with gentlemanly severity, intimated the insuperable gulf between Miss Egremont of Bridgefield and the Man of Umbrellas.

Moreover, his sister-in-law took care that he should hear that the Duchess of Redcastle had pronounced his wife sweetly pretty and lady-like, and talked of inviting them for a visit of a few nights.

'A bore,' observed he ungratefully, ''tis as dull as ditchwater.' But, in truth, though the Canon's family, when in residence, were intimate with the ducal family, Alwyn Egremont had never been at the castle since the days of his earliest youth, and he was not quite prepared to owe his toleration there to his wife's charms, or the Canoness's patronage of her.

And innocent Alice only knew that everybody had been very kind to her, and it was only a pity that her husband did not like her to notice poor Gerard Godfrey.

CHAPTER XIV.

GOING AGEE.

'Gin ye were a brig as auld as me.'—BURNS.

>

'What's the matter?' exclaimed Mrs. Egremont, waking from a doze, —'that bridge?'

'Bridge! Don't be such a fool! We aren't near it yet.'

The servant, his face looking blurred through the window, came to explain that the delay was caused by an agricultural engine, which had chosen this unlucky night, or morning, to travel from one farm to another. There was a long delay, while the monster could be heard coughing frightfully before it could be backed with its spiky companion into a field so as to let the carriages pass by; and meantime Mr. Egremont was betrayed into uttering ejaculations which made poor Nuttie round her eyes in the dark as she sat by his feet on the back seat, and Alice try to bury her ears in her hood in the corner.

On they went at last, for about a mile, and then came another sudden stop —another fierce growl from Mr. Egremont, another apparition of the servant at the window, saying, in his alert deferential manner, 'Sir, the bridge have broke under a carriage in front. Lady Delmar's, sir. The horse is plunging terrible.'

The door was torn open, and all three, regardless of ball costumes, precipitated themselves out.

The moon was up, and they saw the Rectory carriage safe on the road before them, but on the bridge beyond was a struggling mass, dimly illuminated by a single carriage lamp. Mr. Egremont and the groom hurried forward where Mark and the Rectory coachman were already rendering what help they could. May standing at the horses' heads, and her mother trying to wrap everybody up, since stay in their carriages they could not. Transferring the horses to Nuttie, the two sisters hurried on towards the scene of action, but Blanche's white satin boots did not carry her far, and she turned on meeting her uncle. He spoke with a briskness and alacrity that made him like another man in this emergency, as he assured the anxious ladies that their friends were safe, but that they could not be extricated till the carriage was lifted from the hole into which it had sunk amid bricks, stones, and broken timbers. He sent his own coachman to assist, as being the stronger man, and, mounting the box, turned and drove off in quest of further help, at a wayside cottage, or from the attendants on the engine, whose weight had probably done the mischief, and prepared the trap for the next comer.

As May came near, her brother made her available by putting the lamp into her hand, bidding her hold it so as to light those who were endeavouring to release the horse, which had cleared the portion of the bridge before the break-down under the brougham, and now lay on the road, its struggles quelled by a servant at its head. Nearly the whole of the hind wheels and most of the door had disappeared on one side, and, though more was visible on the other, it was impossible to open the door, as a mass of rubbish lay on it. Annaple was on this side, and her voice was heard calling to May in fits of the laughter which is perhaps near akin to screams—

 '"London bridge is broken down,
 Dance o'er my lady Lee!"

Janet will go in for second-sight ever after. Yes, she's all right, except a scratch from the glass, and that I'm sitting on her more or less. How are they getting on?' 'The horse is all but out. Not hurt, they think. Here's another man come to help—a gentleman—my dear, it is your partner, Nuttie's umbrella man.' 'Oh, making it complete—hopes, Janet—I'm sorry, but I can't help squashing you! I can't help subsiding on you! What is it now?' as the lamp-light vanished.

'They are looking for something to make levers of,' returned May; 'these wooden rails are too rotten.'

'Can't they get us through the window?' sighed a muffled voice.

'Not unless we could be elongated, like the Hope of the Katzekopfs.'

'We shall manage now,' cried Mark; 'we have found some iron bars to the hatch down there. But you must prepare for a shock or two before you can be set free.'

The two gentlemen and three servants strove and struggled, hoisted and pushed, to the tune of suppressed sounds, half of sobs, half of laughter, till at last the carriage was heaved up sufficiently to be dragged backwards beyond the hole; but even then it would not stand, for the wheels on the undermost side were crushed, neither could either door be readily opened, one being smashed in, and the other jammed fast. Annaple, however, still tried to keep up her own spirits and her sister's, observing that she now knew how to sympathise with Johnnie's tin soldiers in their box turned upside down.

Two sturdy labourers here made their appearance, having been roused in the cottage and brought back by Mr. Egremont, and at last one door was forced open by main force, and the ladies emerged, Annaple, helping her sister, beginning some droll thanks, but pausing as she perceived that Lady Delmar's dress was covered with blood.

'My dear Janet. This is worse than I guessed. Why did you not speak?'

'It is not much,' said the poor lady, rather faintly. 'Myneck—'

The elder ladies came about her, and seated her on cushions, where, by the light of May's lamp, Alice, who had been to an ambulance class at Micklethwayte, detected the extent of the cut, extracted a fragment of glass, and staunched the bleeding with handkerchiefs and strips of the girls' tulle skirts, but she advised her patient to be driven at once to a surgeon to secure that no morsel of glass remained. Mr. Egremont, gratified to see his wife come to the front, undertook to drive her back to Redcastle. Indeed, they must return thither to cross by the higher bridge. 'You will go with me,' entreated Lady Delmar, holding Alice's hand; and the one hastily consigning Nuttie to her aunt's care, the other giving injunctions not to alarm her mother to Annaple, who had declared her intention of walking home, the two ladies went off under Mr. Egremont's escort.

Just then it was discovered that the Delmar coachman, Robinson, had all this time been lying insensible, not dead, for he moaned, but apparently with a broken leg, if nothing worse. Indeed, the men had known it all along, but, until the ladies had been rescued, nothing had been possible but to put his cushion under his head and his rug over him. The ladies were much shocked, and Mrs. William Egremont decided that he must be laid at the bottom of the waggonette, and that she would take him straight to the hospital.

They were only a mile and a half from Lescombe, and it was pronounced safe to cross on foot by the remains of the bridge, so that Annaple, who had a pair of fur boots, had already decided on going home on foot. The other girls wanted to accompany her, and, as May and Nuttie both had overshoes, they were permitted to do so, and desired to go to bed, and wait to be picked up by the waggonette, which must return to Bridgefield by the Lescombe road. Blanche, having a delicate throat, was sentenced to go with her stepmother. Mark undertook to ride the horse through the river, and escort the three girls, and Gerard Godfrey also joined them. The place where he was staying lay a couple of miles beyond Lescombe, and when Mrs. Elmore's fly had been met and turned back by Mr. Egremont, he had jumped off to render assistance, and had done so effectively enough to win Mark's gratitude.

It was by this time about half-past five, as was ascertained by the light of the waning moon, the carriage-lamp having burnt out. It was a fine frosty morning, and the moon was still powerful enough to reveal the droll figures of the girls. May had a fur cloak, with the hood tied over her head by Mrs. Egremont's lace shawl; Nuttie had a huge white cloud over her head, and a light blue opera cloak; Annaple had 'rowed herself in a plaidie' like the Scotch girl she was, and her eyes flashed out merrily from its dark folds. They all disdained the gentlemen's self-denying offers of their ulsters, and only Nuttie consented to have the carriage-rug added to her trappings, and ingeniously tied on cloak-fashion with her sash by Gerard. He and Mark piloted the three ladies over the narrow border of the hole, which looked a very black open gulf. Annaple had thanked the men, and bidden them come to Lescombe the next day to be paid for their assistance. Then they all stood to watch Mark ride through the river, at the shallowest place, indicated both by her and the labourers. It was perfectly fordable, so Annaple's were mock heroics when she quoted—

> 'Never heavier man and horse
> Stemmed a midnight torrent's force.'

And Nuttie responded in a few seconds—

> 'Yet through good heart and our Ladye's grace

They were both in high spirits, admiring each other's droll appearance, and speculating on the ghosts they might appear to any one who chanced to look out of window. Annaple walked at the horse's head, calling him poor old Robin Hood, and caressing him, while Gerard and Nuttie kept together.

May began to repent of her determination to walk; Lescombe seemed very far off, and she had an instinct that she was an awkward fifth wheel. Either because Robin Hood walked too fast for her weary limbs, or because she felt it a greater duty to chaperon Nuttie than Annaple, she fell back on the couple in the rear, and was rather surprised at the tenor of their conversation.

This 'umbrella man' was telling of his vicar's delight in the beautiful chalice veil that had been sent by Mrs. Egremont, and Nuttie was communicating, as a secret she ought not to tell, that mother was working a set of stoles, and hoped to have the white ones ready by the dedication anniversary; also that there was a box being filled for the St. Ambrose Christmas tree. They were trying to get something nice for each of the choir boys and of the old women; and therewith, to May's surprise, this youth, whom she regarded as a sort of shopman, fell into full narration of all the events of a highly-worked parish,—all about the choral festival, and the guilds, and the choir, and the temperance work. A great deal of it was a strange language to May, but she half-disapproved of it, as entirely unlike the 'soberness' of Bridgefield ways, and like the Redcastle vicar, whom her father commonly called 'that madman.' Still, she had a practical soul for parish work, and could appreciate the earnestness that manifested itself, and the exertions made for people of the classes whom she had always supposed too bad or else too well off to come under clerical supervision. And her aunt and cousin and this young man all evidently had their hearts in it! For Nuttie— though her new world had put the old one apparently aside—had plunged into all the old interests, and asked questions eagerly, and listened to their answers, as if Micklethwayte news was water to the thirsty. The two were too happy to meet, and, it must be confessed, had not quite manners enough, to feel it needful to include in their conversation the weary figure that plodded along at a little distance from them, hardly attending to the details of their chatter, yet deriving new notions from it of the former life of Ursula and her mother, matters which she had hitherto thought beneath her attention, except so far as to be thankful that they had emerged from it so presentable. That it was a more actively religious, and perhaps a more intellectual one than her own, she had thought impossible, where everything must be second-rate. And yet, when her attention had wandered from an account of Mr. Dutton's dealings with a refractory choir boy bent on going to the races, she found a discussion going on about some past lectures upon astronomy, and Nuttie vehemently regretting the not attending two courses promised for the coming winter upon electricity and on Italian art, and mournfully observing, 'We never go to anything sensible here.'

May at first thought, 'Impertinent little thing,' and felt affronted, but then owned to herself that it was all too true. Otherwise there was hardly anything said about the contrast with Nuttie's present life; Gerard knew already that the church atmosphere was very different, and with the rector's daughter within earshot, he could not utter his commiseration, nor Nuttie her regrets.

Once there was a general start, and the whole five came together at the sight of a spectrally black apparition, with a huge tufted head on high, bearing down over a low hedge upon them. Nobody screamed except Nuttie, but everybody started, though the next moment it was plain that they were only chimney-sweepers on their way.

'Retribution for our desire to act ghosts!' said Annaple, when the sable forms had been warned of the broken bridge. 'Poor May, you are awfully tired! Shouldn't you like a lift in their cart?'

'Or I could put you up on Robin Hood,' said Mark.

'Thank you, I don't think I could stick on. Is it much farther?'

'Only up the hill and across the park,' said Annaple, still cheerily.

'Take my arm, old woman,' said Mark, and then there was a pause, before Annaple said in an odd voice, 'You may tell her, Mark.'

'Oh, Annaple! Mark! is it so?' cried May joyously, but under her breath; and with a glance to see how near the other couple were.

'Yes,' said Annaple between crying and laughing. 'Poor Janet, she'll think we have taken a frightfully mean advantage of her, but I am sure I never dreamt of such a thing; and the queer thing is, that Mark says she put it into his head!'

'No, no,' said Mark; 'you know better than that—'

'Why, you told me you only found it out when she began to trample on the fallen—'

'I told you I had only understood my own heart.'

'And I said very much the same—she made me so angry you see.'

'I can't but admire your motives!' said May, exceedingly rejoiced all the time, and ready to have embraced them both, if it had not been for the spectators behind. 'In fact, it was opposition you both wanted. I wonder how long you would have gone on not finding it out, if all had been smooth?'

'The worst of it is,' said Annaple, 'that I'm afraid it is a very bad thing for Mark.'

'Not a bit of it,' retorted he. 'It is the only thing that could have put life into my work, or made me care to find any! And find it I will now! Must we let the whole world in to know before I have found it, Annaple?'

'I could not but tell my mother,' said Annaple. 'It would come out in spite of me, even if I wished to keep it back.'

'Oh yes! Lady Ronnisglen is a different thing,' said Mark. 'Just as May here is—'

'And she will say nothing, I know, till we are ready—my dear old minnie,' said Annaple. 'Only, Mark, do pray have something definite to hinder Janet with if there are any symptoms of hawking her commodity about.'

'I *will*,' said Mark. 'If we could only emigrate!'

'Ah, if we could!' said Annaple. 'Ronald is doing so well in New Zealand, but I don't think my mother could spare me. She could not come out, and she must be with me, wherever I am. You know—don't you—that I am seven years younger than Alick. I was a regular surprise, and the old nurse at Ronnisglen said 'Depend upon it, my Leddy, she is given to be the comfort of your old age.' And I have always made up my mind never to leave her. I don't think she would get on with Janet or any of them without me, so you'll have to take her too, Mark.'

'With all my heart,' he answered. 'And, indeed, I have promised my father not to emigrate. I must, and will, find work at hand, and wake a home for you both!'

'But you will tell papa at once?' said May. 'It will hurt him if you do not.'

'You are right, May; I knew it when Annaple spoke of her mother, but there is no need that it should go further.'

The intelligence had lightened the way a good deal, and they were at the lodge gates by this time. Gerard began rather ruefully to take leave; but Annaple, in large-hearted happiness and gratitude, begged him to come and rest at the house, and wait for daylight, and this he was only too glad to do, especially as May's secession had made the conversation a little more personal.

Nuttie was in a certain way realising for the first time what her mother's loyalty had checked her in expressing, even if the tumult of novelties had given her full time to dwell on it.

'Everybody outside is kind,' she said to Gerard; 'they are nice in a way, and good, but oh! they are centuries behind in church matters and feeling, just like the old rector.'

'I gathered that; I am very sorry for you. Is there no one fit to be a guide?'

'I don't know,' said Nuttie. 'I didn't think—I must, somehow, before Lent.'

'There is Advent close at hand,' he said gravely. 'If you could only be at our mission services, we hope to get Father Smith!'

'Oh, if only I could! But mother never likes to talk about those kind of things. She says our duty is to my father.'

'Not the foremost.'

'No, she would not say that. But oh, Gerard! if he should be making her worldly!'

'It must be your work to hinder it,' he said, looking at her affectionately.

'Oh, Gerard! but I'm afraid I'm getting so myself. I have thought a great deal about lawn-tennis, and dress, and this ball,' said Nuttie. 'Somehow it has never quite felt real, but as if I were out on a visit.'

'You are in it, but not of it,' said Gerard admiringly.

'No, I'm not so good as that! I like it all—almost all. I thought I liked it better till you came and brought a real true breath of Micklethwayte. Oh! if I could only see Monsieur's dear curly head and bright eyes!'

This had been the tenor of the talk, and these were the actual last words before the whole five—just in the first streaks of dawn—coalesced before the front door, to be admitted by a sleepy servant; Mark tied up the horse for a moment, while Annaple sent the man to waken Sir John Delmar, and say there had been a slight accident, but no one was much hurt; and, as they all entered the warm, dimly-lighted hall, they were keenly sensible that they had been dancing or walking all night.

Rest in the chairs which stood round the big hearth and smouldering wood-fire was so extremely comfortable, as they all dropped down, that nobody moved or spoke, or knew how long it was before there was a voice on the stairs—'Eh? what's this, Annaple? An accident? Where's Janet?' and a tall burly figure, candle in hand, in a dressing-gown and slippers, was added to the group.

'Janet will be at home presently, I hope,' said Annaple, 'but she got a cut with some broken glass, and we sent her round by Dr. Raymond's to get it set to rights. Oh, John! we came to grief on Bluepost Bridge after all, and I'm afraid Robinson has got his leg broken!'

Sir John was a good-natured heavy man, whose clever wife thought for him in all that did not regard horses, dogs, and game. He looked perfectly astounded, and required to have all told him over again before he could fully take it in. Then he uttered a suppressed malediction on engines, insisted that all his impromptu guests should immediately eat, drink, and sleep, and declared his intention of going off at once to Redcastle to see about his wife.

The two gentlemen were committed to the charge of the butler, and Annaple took Nuttie and May to her sister's dressing-room, where she knew she should find fire and tea, and though they protested that it was not worth while, she made them undress and lie down in a room prepared for them in the meantime. It was a state chamber, with a big bed, far away from the entrance, shuttered and curtained up, and with double doors, excluding all noise. The two cousins lay down, Nuttie dead asleep almost before her head touched the pillow, while May was aching all over, declaring herself far too much tired and excited to sleep; and, besides that it was not worth while, for she should be called for in a very short time. And she remained conscious of a great dread of being roused, so that when she heard her cousin moving about the room, she insisted that they had scarcely lain down, whereupon Nuttie laughed, declared that she had heard a great clock strike twelve before she moved, and showed daylight coming in through the shutters.

'We can't lie here any longer, I suppose,' said May, sitting up wearily; 'and yet what can we put on? It makes one shiver to think of going down to luncheon in a ball dress!'

'Besides, mine is all torn to pieces to make bandages,' said Nuttie. 'I must put on the underskirt and my cloak again.'

'Or Annaple might lend us something. I must get out somehow to know how poor Lady Delmar is, and what has become of everybody. Ring, Ursula, please, and lie down till somebody comes.'

The bell was answered by a maid, who told them that my lady had been brought home by Mr. and Mrs. Egremont about an hour after their arrival. She was as well as could be expected, and there was no cause for anxiety. Mr. and Mrs. Egremont had then gone on to Bridgefield, leaving word that Mrs. William Egremont and Miss Blanche were sleeping at Redcastle, having sent home for their own dresses and the young ladies', and would call for the rest of their party on the way. Indeed, a box for the Miss Egremonts had been deposited by the Canon from the pony-carriage an hour ago, and was already in the dressing-room; but Miss Ruthven would not have them disturbed. Miss Ruthven,—oh yes, she was up, she had not been in bed at all.

CHAPTER XV.

A CASTLE OF UMBRELLAS.

No, Annaple Ruthven could not have slept, even if she had had time. Her first care had been to receive her sister, who had been met at the entrance of Redcastle by her husband. There had been profuse offers of hospitality to Mr. and Mrs. Egremont, the latter of whom looked tired out, and offers of sending messengers to Bridgefield; but Mr. Egremont would not hear of them, and every one suspected that he would not incur the chance of rising without Gregorio and all his appliances.

By the time they were disposed of, and Lady Delmar safe in bed, it was time to repair to her mother's room, so as to prevent her from being alarmed. Lady Ronnisglen was English born. She was not by any means the typical dowager. Her invalid condition was chiefly owing to an accident, which had rendered her almost incapable of walking, and she was also extremely susceptible of cold, and therefore hardly ever went out; but there was so much youth and life about her at sixty-three that she and Annaple often seemed like companion sisters, and her shrewd, keen, managing eldest-born like their mother.

Annaple lay down beside her on her bed in the morning twilight, and gave her the history of the accident in playful terms indeed. Annaple could never help that, but there was something in her voice that made Lady Ronnisglen say, when satisfied about Janet's hurt, 'You've more to say, Nannie dear.'

'Yes, minnie mine, I walked home with Mark Egremont.'

'And—?'

'Yes, minnie. He is going to work and make a home—a real, true, homely home for you and me.'

'My child, my child, you have not hung the old woman about the poor boy's neck!'

'As if I would have had him if he did not love her, and make a mother of her!'

'But what is he going to do, Nan? This is a very different thing from—'

'Very different from Janet's notions!' and they both laughed, the mother adding to the mirth by saying—

'Poor Janet, congratulating herself that no harm had been done, and that you had never taken to one another!'

'Did she really now?'

'Oh yes, only yesterday, and I bade her not crow too soon, for I thought I saw symptoms—'

'You dear darling minnie! Think of that! Before we either of us knew it, and when he is worth ever so much than he was before! Not but that I am enraged when people say he has acted nobly, just as if there had been anything else for him to do!'

'I own that I am glad he has proved himself. I was afraid he would be dragged in the way of his uncle. Don't be furious, Nannie. Not at all into evil, but into loitering; and I should like to know what are his prospects now.'

'Well, mother, I don't think he has any. But he means to have. And not a word is to be said to anybody except you and his father and May till he has looked over the top of the wall, and seen his way. We need not bring Janet down on us till then.'

'I must see him, my dear. Let me see him before he goes away. He always has been a very dear lad, a thoroughly excellent right-minded fellow. Only I must know what he means to do, and whether there is any reasonable chance of employment or fixed purpose.'

Lady Ronnisglen's maid here arrived with her matutinal cup of tea; and Annaple, beginning to perceive that she was very stiff, went off in hopes that her morning toilette would deceive her hardworked little frame into believing it had had a proper night's rest.

She was quite ready to appear at the breakfast table, though her eldest niece, a long-haired, long-limbed girl, considerably the bigger of the two, was only too happy to preside over the cups. All the four young people were in the greatest state of excitement, welcoming, as the heroes of the night, Mark and Mr. Godfrey, and clamouring to be allowed to walk down after breakfast with their father and the gentlemen to see the scene of the catastrophe and the remains of the carriage and the bridge.

Sir John made a courteous reference to the governess, but there was a general sense that the cat was away, and presently there was a rush upstairs to prepare for the walk. Annaple had time in the course of all the bustle, while the colour came back to her cheeks for a moment, to tell Mark that her mother had been all that was good, and wanted to see him.

He must manage to stay till after eleven o'clock; she could not be ready before. Then he might come to her sitting-room, which, as well as her bedroom, was on the ground floor.

Mark had to work off his anxiety by an inspection of the scene of the disaster and a circumstantial explanation of the details to the young Delmars, who crowded round him and Mr. Godfrey, half awed, half delighted, and indeed the youngest—a considerable tomboy—had nearly given the latter the opportunity of becoming a double hero by tumbling through the broken rail, but he caught her in time, and she only incurred from Sir John such a scolding as a great fright will produce from the easiest of fathers.

Afterwards Mark put Gerard on the way to his brother-in-law's living, asking him on the road so many questions about the umbrella business that the youth was not quite sure how to take it, and doubted whether the young swell supposed that he could talk of nothing else; but his petulance was mitigated when he was asked, 'Supposing a person wished to enter the business, to whom should he apply?'

'Do you know any one who wishes for anything of the kind?' he asked. 'Are you making inquiries for any one?' and on a hesitating affirmation, 'Because I know there is an opening for a man with capital just at present. Dutton won't advertise—'tis so risky; and he wants some knowledge of a person's antecedents, and whether he is likely to go into it in a liberal, gentlemanly spirit, with good principles, you see, such as would not upset all we are doing for the hands.'

'What amount of capital do you mean?'

'Oh, from five hundred to a thousand! Or more would not come amiss. If I only had it! What it would be to conduct an affair like that on true principles! But luck is against me every way.'

Mark was at the sitting-room door as the four quarters began to strike in preparation for eleven, but Lady Ronnisglen had been in her chair for nearly half-an-hour, having been rapid and nervous enough to hurry even the imperturbable maid, whom Annaple thought incapable of being hastened. She was a little slight woman, with delicate features and pale complexion, such as time deals with gently, and her once yellow hair now softened with silver was turned back in bands beneath the simple net cap that suited her so well. There was a soft yet sparkling look about her as she held out her hands and exclaimed, 'Ah, Master Mark, what mischief have you been doing?'

Mark came and knelt on one knee beside her and said: 'Will you let me work for you both, Lady Ronnisglen? I will do my best to find some.'

'Ah! that is the point, my dear boy. I should have asked and wished for definite work, if you had come to me before that discovery of yours; and now it is a mere matter of necessity.'

'Yes,' said Mark; then, with some hesitation, he added: 'Lady Ronnisglen, do you care whether I take to what people call a gentleman's profession? I could, of course, go on till I am called to the bar, and then wait for something to turn up; but that would be waiting indeed! Then in other directions I've taken things easy, you see, till I'm too old for examinations. I failed in the only one that was still open to me. Lord Kirkaldy tried me for foreign office work, and was appalled at my blunders. I'm not fit for a parson.'

'I should have thought you were.'

'Not I,' said Mark. 'I'm not up to the mark there. I couldn't say honestly that I was called to it. I wish I could, for it would be the easiest way out of it; but I looked at the service, and I can't. There—that's a nice confession to come to you with! I can't think how I can have been so impudent.'

'Mark, you are a dear good lad. I respect and honour you ever so much more than before all this showed what stuff was in you! But the question is, What's to be done? My child is verily the "penniless lass with a high pedigree," for she has not a poor thousand to call her own.'

'And I have no right to anything in my father's lifetime, though I have no doubt he would give me up my share of my mother's portion—about £3000. Now this is what has occurred to me: In the place where I found my uncle's wife—Micklethwayte, close to Monks Horton—there's a great umbrella factory, with agencies everywhere. There are superior people belonging to it. I've seen some of them, and I've been talking to the young fellow who helped us last night, who is in the office. I find that to go into the thing with such capital as I might hope for, would bring in a much larger and speedier return than I could hope for any other way, if only my belongings would set aside their feelings. And you see there are the Kirkaldys close by to secure her good society.'

Lady Ronnisglen put out her transparent-looking, black-mittened hand, and gave a little dainty pat to his arm. 'I like to see a man in earnest,' said she. Her little Skye terrier was seized with jealousy at her gesture, and came nuzzling in between with his black nose. 'Mull objects!' she said, smiling; but then, with a graver look, 'And so will your father.'

'At first,' said Mark; 'but I think he will give way when he has had time to look at the matter, and sees how good you are. That will make all the difference.'

So Annaple, who had been banished for a little while, was allowed to return, and mother, daughter, and lover built themselves a little castle of umbrellas, and bestowed a little arch commiseration on poor Lady Delmar; who, it was agreed, need know nothing until something definite was arranged, since Annaple was clearly accountable to no one except her mother. She would certainly think the latter part of her dream only too well realised, and consider that an unfair advantage had been taken of her seclusion in her own room. In spite of all loyal efforts to the contrary, Mark, if he had been in a frame of mind to draw conclusions, would have perceived that the prospect of escaping from the beneficent rule of Lescombe was by no means unpleasant to Lady Ronnisglen. The books that lay within her reach would hardly have found a welcome anywhere else in the house. Sir John was not brilliant, and his wife had turned her native wits to the practical rather than the intellectual line, and had quite enough to think of in keeping up the dignities of Lescombe with a large family amid agricultural difficulties.

Annaple remembered at last that she ought to go and look after her guests, assisted therein by the pleasure of giving May a hearty kiss and light squeeze, with a murmur that 'all was right.'

She brought them downstairs just as the gong was sounding, and the rush of girls descending from the schoolroom, and Lady Ronnisglen being wheeled across the hall in her chair. Nuttie, who had expected to see a gray, passive, silent old lady like Mrs. Nugent, was quite amazed at the bright, lively face and voice that greeted the son-in-law and grandchildren, May and herself, congratulating these two on having been so well employed all the morning, and observing that she was afraid her Nannie could not give so good an account of herself.

'Well,' said Sir John, 'I am sure she looks as if she found plodding along the lanes as wholesome as sleeping in her bed! Nan Apple-cheeks, eh?'

Whereupon Annaple's cheeks glowed all the more into resemblance of the baby-name which she had long ceased to deserve; but May could see the darkness under her eyes, betraying that it was only excitement that drove away fatigue.

Sir John had not gone far in his circumstantial description of the injuries to his unfortunate carriage when the Canon arrived, with his wife and Blanche. Mark would have given worlds in his impatience to have matters settled between the two parents then and there; but Lady Ronnisglen had already warned him that this would not be possible, and assured him that it would be much wiser to prepare his father beforehand.

Then he fixed his hopes on a solitary drive with his father back in the pony carriage, but he found himself told off to take that home, and had to content himself with May as a companion. Nor was his sister's mode of receiving the umbrella plan reassuring. She had smiled too often with her stepmother over Nuttie's having been brought up among umbrellas to be ready to accept the same lot for her brother and her friend, and she was quite sure that her father would never consent. 'An Egremont an umbrella-maker! how horrible! Just fancy seeing Dutton, Egremont and Co. on the handle of one's umbrella!'

'Well, you need not patronise us,' said Mark.

'But is it possible that Lady Ronnisglen did not object?' said May.

'She seemed to think it preferable to driving pigs in the Texas, like her son Malcolm.'

'Yes, but then that *was* the Texas.'

'Oh May, May, I did not think you were such a goose!'

'I should have thought the folly was in not being patient. Stick to your profession, and something must come in time.'

'Ay, and how many men do you think are sticking to it in that hope? No, May, 'tis not real patience to wear out the best years of my life and hers in idleness, waiting for something not beneath an Egremont to do!'

'But is there nothing to do better than that?'

'Find it for me, May.'

CHAPTER XVI.

INFRA DIG.

'Till every penny which she told,
Creative Fancy turned to gold.'—B. LLOYD.

The Blueposts Bridge had produced a good deal of effect. Ursula Egremont in special seemed to herself to have been awakened from a strange dream, and to have resumed her real nature and affections. She felt as if she would give all her partners at the ball for one shake of Monsieur's fringed paws; her heart yearned after Aunt Ursel and Miss Mary; she longed after the chants of the choir; and when she thought of the effort poor Gerard Godfrey had made to see her, she felt him a hero, and herself a recreant heroine, who had well-nigh been betrayed into frivolity and desertion of him, and she registered secret resolutions of constancy.

She burned to pour out to her mother all the Micklethwayte tidings, and all her longings to be there; but when the Rectory party set her down at the door, the footman, with a look of grave importance, announced that Mr. Egremont was very unwell. 'Mr. Gregory thinks he has taken a chill from the effect of exposure, sir, and Dr. Hamilton has been sent for.'

The Canon and his wife both got out on this intelligence, and Mrs. Egremont was summoned to see them. She came, looking more frightened than they thought the occasion demanded, for she was appalled by the severe pain in the head and eyes; but they comforted her by assuring her that her husband had suffered in the same manner in the spring, and she saw how well he had recovered; and then telling Nuttie to bring word what the doctor's report was, and then spend the evening at the Rectory, they departed, while poor Nuttie only had one kiss, one inquiry whether she were rested, before her mother fled back to the patient.

Nor did she see her again till after the doctor's visit, and then it was only to desire her to tell her uncle that the attack was pronounced to be a return of the illness of last spring, and that it would be expedient to go abroad for the winter.

Go abroad! It had always been a vision of delight to Nuttie, and she could not be greatly concerned at the occasion of it; but she did not find the Rectory in a condition to converse and sympathise. Blanche was lying down with a bad headache. The Edwardses and a whole party of semi-genteel parish visitors had come in to inquire about the accident, and had to be entertained with afternoon tea; and May, though helping her stepmother to do her devoir towards them, seemed more preoccupied than ever.

As indeed she was, for she knew that Mark was putting his fate to the touch with his father in the study.

The Canon heard the proposal with utter consternation and dismay at the perverseness of the two young people, who might have been engaged any time these two years with the full approbation of their families, and now chose the very moment when every one was rejoicing at their freedom.

'When a young man has got into a pickle,' he said, 'the first thing is to want to be married!'

'Exactly so, sir, to give him a motive for getting out of the pickle.'

'Umbrellas! I should like to hear what your grandfather would have said!'

'These are not my grandfather's days, sir.'

'No indeed! There was nothing to do but to give a hint to old Lord de Lyonnais, and he could get you put into any berth you chose. Interest was interest in those days! I don't see why Kirkaldy can't do the same.'

'Not unless I had foreign languages at my tongue's end.'

Whereat the Canon groaned, and Mark had to work again through all the difficulties in the way of the more liberal professions; and the upshot was that his father agreed to drive over to Lescombe the next day and see Lady Ronnisglen. He certainly had always implicitly trusted his son's veracity, but he evidently thought that there must have been much warping of the imagination to make the young man believe the old Scottish peeress to have consented to her daughter's marrying into an umbrella factory.

Nuttie was surprised and gratified that both Mark and May put her through an examination on the habits of Micklethwayte and the position of Mr. Godfrey, which she thought was entirely due to the favourable impression Gerard had produced, and she felt proportionably proud of him when Mark pronounced him a very nice gentlemanly young fellow. She could not think why her uncle, with more testiness than she had ever seen in that good-natured dignitary, ordered May not to stand chattering there, but to give them some music.

The Canon drove to Lescombe the next day under pretext of inquiring after Lady Delmar, and then almost forgot to do so, after he had ascertained that she was a prisoner to her dressing-room, and that Sir John was out shooting. The result of his interview filled him with astonishment. Lady Ronnisglen having had a large proportion of sons to put out in life on very small means had learnt not to be fastidious, and held that the gentleman might ennoble the vocation instead of the vocation debasing the gentleman. Moreover, in her secret soul she felt that her daughter Janet's manoeuvres were far more truly degrading than any form of honest labour; and it was very sore to her to have no power of preventing them, ridicule, protest, or discouragement being all alike treated as the dear mother's old-world unpractical romance. It galled her likewise that she could perceive the determination that Annaple Ruthven should be disposed of before Muriel Delmar came on the scene; and the retiring to ever so small a home of their own had been discussed between mother and daughter, and only put aside because of the pain it would give their honest-hearted host and their hostess, who really loved them.

Thus she did her best to persuade her old friend that there were few openings for a man of his son's age, and that if the Micklethwayte business were all that Mark imagined, it was not beneath the attention even of a well-born gentleman in these modern days, and would involve less delay than any other plan, except emigration, which was equally dreaded by each parent. Delay there must be, not only in order to ascertain the facts respecting the firm, but to prove whether Mark had any aptitude for the business before involving any capital in it. However, every other alternative would involve much longer and more doubtful waiting. And altogether the Canon felt that if a person of Lady Ronnisglen's rank did not object, he had scarcely a right to do so. However, both alike reserved consent until full inquiry should have been made.

The Canon wrote to Lord Kirkaldy, and in the meantime wanted to gather what information he could from his sister-in-law; but he found her absolutely engrossed as her husband's nurse, and scarcely permitted to snatch a meal outside the darkened room. He groaned and grumbled at his brother's selfishness, and declared that her health would be damaged, while his shrewder lady declared that nothing would be so good for her as to let Alwyn find her indispensable to his comfort, even beyond Gregorio.

This absorption of her mother fell hard on Ursula, especially when the first two days' alarm was over, and her mother was still kept an entire prisoner, as companion rather than nurse. As before, the rheumatic attack fastened upon the head and eyes, causing lengthened suffering, and teaching Mr. Egremont that he had never had so gentle, so skilful, so loving, or altogether so pleasant a slave as his wife, the only person except Gregorio whom, in his irritable state, he would tolerate about him.

His brother could not be entirely kept out, but was never made welcome, more especially when he took upon himself to remonstrate on Alice's being deprived of air, exercise, and rest. He got no thanks; Mr. Egremont snarled, and Alice protested that she was never tired, and needed nothing. The Rectory party were, excepting the schoolroom girls, engaged to make visits from home before going into residence at Redcastle, and were to begin with Monks Horton. They offered to escort Ursula to see her great aunt at Micklethwayte —Oh joy of joys!—but when the Canon made the proposition in his brother's room, Mr. Egremont cut it short with 'I'm not going to have her running after those umbrella-mongers.'

The Canon's heart sank within him at the tone, and he was really very sorry for his niece, who was likely to have a fortnight or three weeks of comparative solitude before her father was ready to set out on the journey.

'Can't she help you, in reading to her father—or anything?' he asked

Alice, who had come out with him into the anteroom to express her warm thanks for the kind proposal.

She shook her head. 'He would not like it, nor I, for her.'

'I should think not!' exclaimed the Canon, as his eye fell on the title of a yellow French book on the table. 'I have heard of this! Does he make you read such as this to him, Alice?'

'Nothing else seems to amuse him,' she said. 'Do you, think I ought not? I don't understand much of that kind of modern French, but Nuttie knows it better.'

'Not *that kind*, I hope,' said the Canon hastily. No, no, my dear,' as he saw her colour mantling, 'small blame to you. You have only to do the best you can with him, poor fellow! Then we'll take anything for you. We've said nothing to Nuttie, Jane said I had better ask you first.'

'Oh, that was kind! I am glad she is spared the disappointment.'

Not that she was. For when she learnt her cousins' destination, she entreated to go with them, and had to be told that the proposal had been made and refused.

There is no denying that she behaved very ill. It was the first real sharp collision of wills. She had differed from, and disapproved of, her father all along, but what had been required of her had generally been pleasant to one side at least of her nature; but here she was condemned to the dulness of the lonely outsider to a sick room, when her whole soul was leaping back to the delights of her dear old home at Micklethwayte.

She made her mother's brief meal with her such a misery of protests and insistences on pleadings with her father that poor Alice was fain to rejoice when the servants' presence silenced her, and fairly fled from her when the last dish was carried out.

When they met again Nuttie demanded, 'Have you spoken to my father?'

'I told you, my dear, it would be of no use?'

'You promised.'

'No, Nuttie, I did not.'

'I'm sure I understood you to say you would if you could.'

'It was your hopes, my dear child. He is quite determined.'

'And you leave him so. Mother, I can't understand your submitting to show such cruel ingratitude!'

Nuttie was very angry, though she was shocked at the burning colour and hot tears that she beheld as, half choked, her mother said: 'Oh, my dear, my dear, do not speak so! You know—you know it is not in my heart, but my first duty, and yours too, is to your father.'

'Whatever he tells us?' demanded Nuttie, still hot and angry.

'I did not say that,' returned her mother gently, 'but you know, Nuttie, Aunt Ursel herself would say that it is our duty to abide by his decision here.'

'But you could speak to him,' still argued Nuttie, 'what's the use of his being so fond of you if he won't do anything you want?'

'Hush! hush, Nuttie! you know that is not a right way of speaking. I cannot worry him now he is ill. You don't know what that dreadful pain is!'

Happily Nuttie did refrain from saying, 'No doubt it makes him very cross;' but she muttered, 'And so we are to be cut off for ever from Aunt Ursel, and Miss Mary, and—and—every thing good—and nice—and catholic?'

'I hope not, indeed, I hope not. Only he wants us to get the good society manners and tone—like your cousins, you know. You are young enough for it, and a real Egremont, you know Nuttie, and when you have learnt it, he will trust you there,' said the mother, making a very mild version of his speech about the umbrella-mongers.

'Yes, he wants to make me worldly, so that I should not care, but that he never shall do, whatever you may let him do to you.'

His bell rang sharply, and away hurried Alice, leaving her daughter with a miserably sore and impatient heart, and the consciousness of having harshly wounded the mother whom she had meant to protect. And there was no hugging and kissing to make up for it possible. They would not meet till dinner-time, and Nuttie's mood of stormy repentance had cooled before that time into longing to be more tender than usual towards her mother, but how was that possible during the awful household ceremony of many courses, with three solemn men-servants ministering to them?

And poor Alice jumped up at the end, and ran away as if afraid of fresh objurgations, so that all Nuttie could do was to rush headlong after her, catch her on the landing, kiss her face all over, and exclaim, 'Oh, mother, mother, I was dreadfully cross!'

'There, there! I knew you would be sorry, dear, dear child, I know it is very hard, but let me go. He wants me!'

And a very forlorn and deplorable person was left behind, feeling as if her father, after carrying her away from everything else that she loved, had ended by robbing her of her mother.

She stood on the handsome staircase, and contrasted it with the little cosy entrance at her aunt's. She felt how she hated all these fine surroundings, and how very good and unworldly she was for so doing. Only, was it good to have been so violent towards her mother?

The Rectory folks were dining out, so she could only have recourse to Mudie's box to try to drive dull care away.

A few days more and they were gone. Though Mr. Egremont was gradually mending, he still required his wife to be in constant attendance. In point of fact Alice could not, and in her loyalty would not, tell her dignified brother-in-law, far less her daughter, of the hint that the doctor had given her, namely, that her husband was lapsing into the constant use of opiates, founded at first on the needs of his malady, but growing into a perilous habit, which accounted for his shutting himself up all the forenoon.

While under medical treatment it was possible to allowance him, and keep him under orders, but Dr. Hamilton warned her not to allow the quantity to be exceeded or the drugs to be resorted to after his recovery, speaking seriously of the consequences of indulgence. He spoke as a duty, but as he looked at the gentle, timid woman, he saw little hope of her doing any good!

Poor Alice was appalled. All she could do was to betake herself to 'the little weapon called All-Prayer,' and therewith to use all vigilance and all her arts of coaxing and cheering away weariness and languor, beguiling sleeplessness, soothing pain by any other means. She had just enough success to prevent her from utterly despairing, and to keep her always on the strain, and at her own cost, for Mr. Egremont was far more irritable when he was without the narcotic, and the serenity it produced was an absolute relief. She soon found too that Gregorio was a contrary power. Once, when he had suggested the dose, and she had replied by citing the physician's commands, Mr. Egremont had muttered an imprecation on doctors, and she had caught a horrible grin of hatred on the man's face, which seemed to her almost diabolical. She had prevailed then, but the next time her absence was at all prolonged, she found that the opiate had been taken, and her dread of quitting her post increased, though she did not by any means always succeed. Sometimes she was good-humouredly set aside, sometimes roughly told to mind her own business; but she could not relinquish the struggle, and whenever she did succeed in preventing the indulgence she felt a hopefulness that—in spite of himself and Gregorio, she might yet save him.

Another hint she had from both the Canon and his wife. When they asked what place was chosen, Mr. Egremont said he had made Alice write to inquire of the houses to be had at various resorts—Mentone, Nice, Cannes, and the like. She was struck by the ardour with which they both began to praise Nice, Genoa, Sorrento, any place in preference to Mentone, which her husband seemed to know and like the best.

And when she went downstairs with them the Canon held her hand a moment, and said, 'Anywhere but Mentone, my dear.'

She looked bewildered for a moment, and the Canoness added, 'Look in the guide-books.'

Then she remembered Monte Carlo, and for a moment it was to her as shocking a warning as if she had been bidden to keep her husband out of the temptation of thieving.

She resolved, however, to do her best, feeling immediately that again it was a pull of her influence against Gregorio's. Fortune favoured her so far that the villa favoured by Mr. Egremont was not to be had, only the side of the bay he disliked, and that a pleasant villa offered at Nice.

Should she close with it? Well—was there great haste? Gregorio knew a good many people at Mentone, and could ascertain in his own way if they could get the right side of the bay by going to the hotel and waiting. Alice, however, pressed the matter—represented the danger of falling between two stools, pleaded personal preference, and whereas Mr. Egremont was too lazy for resistance to any persuasion, she obtained permission to engage the Nice villa. The next day Gregorio announced that he had heard that the proprietor of Villa Francaleone at Mentone was giving up hopes of his usual tenants, and an offer might secure it.

'Villa Eugenie at Nice is taken,' said Alice, and she received one of those deadly black looks, which were always like a stab.

Of all this Nuttie knew nothing. She was a good deal thrown with the schoolroom party and with the curate's wife for companionship. Now Mrs. Edwards did not approve of even the canonical Egremonts, having an ideal far beyond the ritual of Bridgefield; and she was delighted to find how entirely Miss Egremont sympathised with her.

Nuttie described St. Ambrose's as a paradise of church observances and parish management, everything becoming embellished and all shortcomings forgotten in the loving mists of distance. The harmonium was never out of tune; the choir-boys were only just naughty enough to show how wisely Mr. Spyers dealt with them; the surplices, one would think, never needed washing; Mr. Dutton and Gerard Godfrey were paragons of lay helpers, and district visitors never were troublesome. Mrs. Edwards listened with open ears, and together they bewailed the impracticability of moving the Canon to raising Bridgefield to anything approaching to such a standard; while Nuttie absolutely cultivated her home sickness.

According to promise Blanche wrote to her from Monks Horton, and told her thus much—'We have been all over your umbrella place. It was very curious. Then we called upon Miss Headworth, who was quite well, and was pleased to hear of you.'

Blanche was famous for never putting into a letter what her correspondent wanted to hear, but her stepmother wrote a much longer and more interesting letter to Mrs. Egremont.

'You will be glad to hear that we found your aunt quite well. I suppose it is not in the nature of things that you should not be missed; but I should think your place as well supplied as could be hoped by that very handsome and superior Miss Nugent, with whom she lives. I had a good deal of conversation with both; for you will be surprised to hear that the Canon has consented to Mark's making the experiment of working for a year in Greenleaf and Dutton's office, with a view to entering the firm in future. I was very anxious to understand from such true ladies what the position would be socially. I longed to talk it over with you beforehand; but Alwyn could never spare you, and it was not a subject to be broached without ample time for discussion. We felt that though the Kirkaldys could tell us much, it was only from the outside, whereas Miss Headworth could speak from within. The decision is of course a blow to his father, and will be still more so to the De Lyonnais family, but they have never done anything to entitle them to have a voice in the matter, and the Kirkaldys agree with us that, though not a path of distinction, it is one of honourable prosperity; and with this, if Mark is content, we have no right to object, since his mind is set on present happiness rather than ambition.'

It was a letter gratifying to Alice in its confidential tone, as well as in the evident approval of those surroundings which she loved so well. She read it to her husband, as she was desired to give him a message that the Canon had not written out of consideration for his eyes. He laughed the laugh that always jarred on her. 'So Master Mark has got his nose to the grindstone, has he?' was his first exclamation, and, after some cogitation, 'The fellow wants to be married, depend on it!'

'Do you think so?' returned Alice wistfully.

'Think! Why, you may see it in Jane's letter! I wonder who it is! The little yellow Ruthven girl, most likely! The boy is fool enough for anything! I thought he would have mended his fortunes with Ursula, but he's too proud to stomach that, I suppose!'

'I did wish that!' said Alice. 'It would have set everything straight, and it would have been so nice for her.'

'You should have cut out your daughter after your own pattern,' he answered; 'not let her be such a raw insignificant little spitfire. 'Tis a pity. I don't want the estate to go out of the name, though I won't leave it to an interfering prig like Mark unless he chooses to take my daughter with it!'

The latter part of this amiable speech was muttered and scarcely heard or attended to by Alice in her struggle to conceal the grief she felt at the uncompromising opinion of her child. Nuttie might outgrow being raw, but there seemed less rather than more prospect of a better understanding with her father. About a week later Mark made his appearance, timing it happily when his uncle was making his toilette, so that his aunt was taking a turn on the sunny terrace with Nuttie when the young man came hurrying up the garden.

'Mark! What? Are you come home?'

'Not the others. They are at Mr. Condamine's, I came last night—by way of Lescombe. Edda, dear, it is all right! Oh, I forgot you did not know! There was no seeing you before we went away. Ah! by the by, how is my uncle?'

'Much better, except that using his eyes brings on the pain. 'What is it, Mark? Ah! I can guess,' she said, aided no doubt by that conjecture of her husband's.

'Yes, yes, yes!' he answered, with a rapidity quite unlike himself. 'Why, Nuttie, how mystified you look!'

'I'm sure I don't wonder at any one being glad to live at dear old Micklethwayte,' said Nuttie slowly. 'But, somehow, I didn't think it of you, Mark.'

'My dear, that's not all!' said her mother.

'Oh!' cried Nuttie, with a prolonged intonation. 'Is it?—Oh, Mark! did you *do it* that night when you led the horse home?'

'Even so, Nuttie! And, Aunt Alice, Lady Ronnisglen is the best and bravest of old ladies, and the wisest. Nobody objects but Lady Delmar, and she declares she shall not consider it an engagement till Ronnisglen has been written to in Nepaul, as if he had anything to do with it; but that matters the less, since they all insist on our waiting till I've had a year's trial at the office! I suppose they could not be expected to do otherwise, but it is a pity, for I'm afraid Lady Delmar will lead Annaple and her mother a life of it.'

'Dear Mark, I am delighted that it is all going so well.'

'I knew you would be! I told them I must tell *you*, though it is not to go any farther.'

So that hope of Mark's restoration to the inheritance faded from Alice, and yet she could not be concerned for him. She had never seen him in such good spirits, for the sense of failure and disappointment had always been upon him; and the definite prospect of occupation, gilded by his hopes of Annaple, seemed to make a new man of him.

CHAPTER XVII.

AN OLD FRIEND.

'My heart untravelled still returns to thee.'—GOLDSMITH.

To go abroad! Such had been the fairy castle of Nuttie's life. She had dreamed of Swiss mountains, Italian pictures, Rheinland castles, a perpetual panorama of delight, and here she was in one of the great hotels of Paris, as little likely to see the lions of that city as she had been to see those of London.

The party were halting for two days there because the dentist, on whom Mr. Egremont's fine show of teeth depended, practised there; but Nuttie spent great part of the day alone in the sitting-room, and her hand-bag and her mother's, with all their books and little comforts, had been lost in the agony of landing. Her mother's attendance was required all the morning, or what was worse, she expected that it would be, and though Nuttie's persistence dragged out the staid, silent English maid, who had never been abroad before, to walk in the Tuilleries gardens, which they could see from their windows, both felt half-scared the whole time. Nuttie was quite unused to finding her own way unprotected, and Martin was frightened, cross, and miserable about the bags, which, she averred, had been left by Gregorio's fault. She so hated Gregorio that only a sort of adoration which she entertained for Mrs. Egremont would have induced her to come tete-a-tete with him, and perhaps he was visiting his disappointment about Mentone on her. In the afternoon nothing was achieved but a drive in the Bois de Boulogne, when it was at once made evident that Mr. Egremont would tolerate no questions nor exclamations.

His mouth was in no condition for eating in public, and he therefore decreed that his wife and daughter should dine at the table d'hote, while he was served alone by Gregorio. This was a great boon to Nuttie, and to her mother it recalled bridal days long past at Dieppe; but what was their astonishment when on entering the room they beheld the familiar face of Mr. Dutton! It was possible for him to place himself between them, and there is no describing the sense of rest and protection his presence imparted to them, more especially to Nuttie.

He had come over, as he did from time to time, on business connected with the materials he used, and he was beguiled into telling them of his views of Mark, whom he had put in the way of learning the preliminaries needful to an accountant. He had a deep distrust of the business capacities and perseverance of young gentlemen of family, especially with a countess-aunt in the neighbourhood, and quoted Lord Eldon's saying that to make a good lawyer of one, it was needful for him to have spent both his own and his wife's fortune to begin with, but he allowed that young Mr. Egremont was a very favourable specimen, and was resolutely applying himself to his work, and that he himself felt it due to him to give all the assistance possible.

Miss Headworth, he could not deny, had aged, but far less than Mrs. Nugent in the past year, and it really was a great comfort to Miss Mary to have the old ladies together. He told too how the mission, now lately over, had stirred the Micklethwayte folk into strong excitement, and how good works had been undertaken, evil habits renounced, reconciliations effected, religious services frequented. Would it last? Nobody, he said, had taken it up so zealously as Gerard Godfrey, who seemed as if he would fain throw everything up, and spend his whole life in some direct service as a home missionary or something of the kind. 'He is a good fellow,' said Mr. Dutton, 'and it is quite genuine, but I made him wait at least a year, that he may be sure that this is not only a passing impulse.'

Nuttie thought that she knew what was the impulse that had actuated him, and felt a pleasant elation and self-consciousness even while she repressed a sigh of pity for herself and for him. Altogether the dip into the Micklethwayte world was delightful, but when Mr. Dutton began to ask Nuttie what she had seen, she burst out with, 'Nothing—nothing but just a walk and a drive in the Bois de Boulogne;' and her mother explained that 'in Mr. Egremont's state of health,' etc.

'I wonder,' asked Mr. Dutton, 'if I might be allowed—'

Nuttie's eyes sparkled with ecstasy.

It ended in her mother, who had been wondering how Mr. Egremont could be amused all the long evening, arranging that Mr. Dutton should come in an hour's time to call on him, on the chance of being admitted, and that then the offer might be made when she had prepared him for it, advising Nuttie to wait in her own room. She was beginning to learn how to steer between her husband and her daughter, and she did not guess that her old friend was sacrificing one of the best French plays for the chance.

It turned out well; Mr. Egremont was conscious of a want of variety. He demanded whether it was the young fellow, and being satisfied on that part, observed in almost a good-humoured tone, 'So, we are in for umbrellas, we may as well go in for the whole firm!' caused the lights to be lowered under pretext of his eyes—to conceal the lack of teeth—did not absolutely refuse to let Nuttie take advantage of the escort, and when Mr. Dutton did come to the anteroom of the apartment, he was received with full courtesy, though Gregorio looked unutterable contempt. Mr. Dutton was a man who could talk, and had seen a good deal of the world at different times. Mr. Egremont could appreciate intelligent conversation, so that they got on wonderfully well together, over subjects that would have been a mere weariness to Nuttie but for the exceeding satisfaction of hearing a Micklethwayte voice. At last Mr. Dutton said something about offering his escort to the ladies, or to Miss Egremont, who used, he said in a paternal way, to be a little playfellow of his; Mr. Egremont really smiled, and said, 'Ay, ay, the child is young enough to run after sights. Well, thank you, if you are so good as to take the trouble, they will be very grateful to you, or if her mother cannot go with her, there's the maid.'

Nuttie thought she had never known him so amiable, and hardly durst believe her good fortune would not turn the wheel before morning. And it so far did that her mother found, or thought she found, that it would not do to be out of call, and sent the silent Martin in her stead. But Mr. Dutton had set telegraphs to work and recovered the bags, which Gregorio had professed to give up in despair.

A wonderful amount of lionising was contrived by Mr. Dutton, who had lived a few years at Paris in early youth, and had made himself acquainted alike with what was most worth seeing, and the best ways and means of seeing it, so that as little time as possible was wasted on the unimportant. It was one of the white days of Nuttie's life, wanting nothing but her mother's participation in the sight of the St. Michael of the Louvre, of the Sainte Chapelle, of the vistas in Notre Dame, and of poor Marie Antoinette's cell,— all that they had longed to see together.

She had meant to tell Mr. Dutton that it was all her father's selfishness, but somehow she could not say so, there was something about him that hindered all unbefitting outbreaks of vexation.

And thus, when she mentioned her disappointment at not being allowed to go to Micklethwayte with her uncle, he answered, 'You could not of course be spared with your father so unwell.'

'Oh, he never let me come near him! I wasn't of the slightest use to him!'

'Mrs. Egremont would have missed you.'

'Really he never gave her time. He perfectly devours her, body and soul. Oh dear, no! 'Twas for no good I was kept there, but just pride and ingratitude, though mother tried to call it being afraid for my manners and my style.'

'In which, if you lapse into such talk, you fully justify the precaution. I was just thinking what a young lady you had grown into,' he answered in a tone of banter, under which, however, she felt a rebuke; and while directing her attention to the Pantheon, he took care to get within hearing again of Martin.

And in looking at these things, he carried her so far below the surface. St. Michael was not so much Raffaelle's triumph of art as the eternal victory over sin; the Sainte Chapelle, spite of all its modern unsanctified gaudiness, was redolent of St. Louis; and the cell of the slaughtered queen was as a martyr's shrine, trod with reverence. There were associations with every turn, and Nuttie might have spent years at Paris with another companion without imbibing so many impressions as on this December day, when she came home so full of happy chatter that the guests at the table d'hote glanced with amusement at the eager girl as much as with admiration at the beautiful mother. Mr. Dutton had been invited to come and take coffee and spend the evening with them again, but Mr. Egremont's affairs with the dentist had been completed, and he had picked up, or, more strictly speaking, Gregorio had hunted up for him, a couple of French acquaintances, who appeared before long and engrossed him entirely.

Mr. Dutton sat between the two ladies on a stiff dark-green sofa on the opposite side of the room, and under cover of the eager, half-shrieking, gesticulating talk of the Frenchmen they had a quiet low-toned conversation, like old times, Alice said. 'More than old times,' Nuttie added, and perhaps the others both agreed with her.

When the two Englishwomen started at some of the loud French tones, almost imagining they were full of rage and fury, their friend smiled and said that such had been his first notion on coming abroad.

'You have been a great deal abroad?' Mrs. Egremont asked; 'you seem quite at home in Paris.'

'Oh, mamma, he showed me where the school was that he went to, and the house where he lived! Up such an immense way!'

Mr. Dutton was drawn on to tell more of his former life than ever had been known to them. His father, a wine merchant, had died a bankrupt when he was ten years old, and a relation, engaged in the same business at Paris, had offered to give him a few years of foreign schooling, and then make him useful in the business.

His excellent mother had come with him, and they had lived together on very small means, high up in a many-storied lodging-house, while he daily attended the Lycie. His reminiscences were very happy of those days of cheerful contrivance, of her eager desire to make the tiny appartement a home to her boy, of their pleasant Sundays and holidays, and the life that in this manner was peculiarly guarded by her influence, and the sense of being all she had upon earth. He had scarcely ever spoken of her before, and he dwelt on her now with a tenderness that showed how she had been the guiding spirit of his life.

At fifteen he was taken into the office at Marseilles, and she went thither with him, but the climate did not agree with her; she drooped, and, moreover, he discovered that the business was not conducted in the honourable manner he had supposed. After a few months of weighing his obligations to his kinsman against these instincts, the question was solved by his cousin's retiring. He resolved to take his mother back to England at any loss, and falling in with one of the partners of the umbrella firm in quest of French silk, he was engaged as foreign correspondent, and brought his mother to Micklethwayte, but not in time to restore her health, and he had been left alone in the world just as he came of age, when a small legacy came to him from his cousin, too late for her to profit by it. It had been invested in the business, and he had thus gradually risen to his present position. Mrs. Egremont was amazed to hear that his mother had only been dead so short a time before she had herself come to Micklethwayte; and fairly apologised for the surprise she could not help betraying at finding how youthful he had then been, and Nuttie exclaimed, in her original unguarded fashion:

'Why, Mr. Dutton, I always thought you were an old bachelor!'

'Nuttie, my dear!' said her mother in a note of warning, but Mr. Dutton laughed and said:

'Not so far wrong! They tell me I never was a young man.'

'You had always to be everything to your mother,' said Mrs. Egremont softly.

'Yes,' he said, 'and a very blessed thing it was for me.'

'Ah! you don't regret now all that you must have always been giving up for her,' returned Alice.

'No, indeed. Only that I did not give up more.'

'That is always the way.'

'It is indeed. One little knows the whips that a little self-will prepares.'

Nuttie thought he said it for her admonition, and observed, 'But she was good,' only, however, in a mumble, that the other two thought it inexpedient to notice, though it made both hearts ache for her, even Alice's—with an additional pang of self-reproach that she herself was not good enough to help her daughter better.

Neither of them guessed at the effect that a glimpse of the lovely young seeming widow had had on the already grave self-restrained young man in the home lately made lonely, how she had been his secret object for years, and how, when her history was revealed to him, he had still hoped on for a certainty which had come at last as so fatal a shock and overthrow to all his dreams.

A life of self-restraint and self-conquest had rendered it safe for him to thoroughly enjoy the brief intercourse, which had come about by the accident of his having come to dine at the Hotel de Louvre, to meet a friend who had failed him.

These were two completely happy hours to all the three, and when they said 'good-night' there was a sense of soothing and invigoration on Alice's mind; and on Nuttie's that patience and dutifulness were the best modes of doing justice to her Micklethwayte training, although he had scarcely said a word of direct rebuke or counsel.

While Mr. Dutton sped home to tell Miss Headworth that Mrs. Egremont looked lovelier than ever, and was—yes she was—more of an angel, that her husband had been very pleasant, much better than he expected, and, indeed, might come to anything good under such influence; and as to little Nuttie— she was developing fast, and had a brave constant heart, altogether at Micklethwayte. But that servant who was acting as courier was an insolent scoundrel, who was evidently cheating them to the last degree.

CHAPTER XVIII.

A FRIEND IN NEED.

All the preliminaries of the sojourn at Nice had been settled in correspondence, and the Egremont family had nothing to do, after arriving at the station, but to drive up to Villa Eugenie, whose flower-wreathed balconies were like a vision of beauty. Servants had been hired through agencies known to Mr. Egremont, and Gregorio looked very black at his mistress keeping the reins in her hand, and tried to make her feel herself inefficient.

It was not an eventful or very interesting part of Ursula's life. She was almost wild with the novelty and beauty of the South at first, but except for what she could thus see, there was little variety. The mould of the day was as much as possible after the Bridgefield fashion, except that there were no cousins at the Rectory, no parish interests, very little society, as far as the ladies were concerned. Mr. Egremont had old acquaintance and associates with whom he spent afternoons and evenings, after his own fashion, but they were not people to whom he wished to introduce his wife and daughter.

And the superior English habitues of Nice, the families who formed the regular society, knew Mr. Egremont's reputation sufficiently to feel by no means disposed to be cordial to the fair wife and grown-up daughter whom he so unexpectedly produced on the scene. It had been different at home, where he had county standing, and the Canon and Canoness answered for the newcomers; but here, where all sorts of strange people came to the surface, the respectable felt it needful to be very cautious, and though of course one or two ladies had been asked to call through the intervention of Lady Kirkaldy or of Mrs. William Egremont, and had been assured on their authority that it was 'all right,' their attentions were clogged by doubt, and by reluctance to involve their mankind in intimacy with the head of the family. Thus very little of the proverbial gaiety of Nice offered itself to Nuttie and her mother, and, except by a clerical family who knew Mr. Spyers, they were kept at a distance, which Mr. Egremont perceived and resented by permitting no advances. The climate suited him so well that, to his wife's great relief, he seemed to have dropped his inclination for sedatives; but his eyes would not bear much, and she felt bound to be always on the alert, able to amuse him and hinder his feeling it dull. Gregorio highly disapproved of the house and servants, and was always giving hints that Mentone would agree far better with his master; but every day that Mr. Egremont seemed sufficiently amused at Nice was so much gain, and she had this in her favour, that he was always indolent and hard to move. Moreover, between his master's levee and late dinner Gregorio was hardly ever to be found. No doubt he knew the way to Monte Carlo well enough, and perhaps preferred that the family should be farther off, for he soon ceased to show himself discontented with their present abode. Once when his absence was inconvenient, Mr. Egremont abused him roundly as a good-for-nothing gambler, but when Alice hoped that he might be called to a reckoning, the wrath had subsided with the immediate vexation, and as usual she was told 'All those fellows were alike.'

The foreign servants were not to be induced to give the early-rising ladies more than a roll and cup of coffee, and Nuttie felt ravenous till she learned to lay in a stock of biscuits, and, with Martin's connivance, made tea on her own account, and sustained her mother for the morning's walk before the summons to Mr. Egremont.

He always wanted his wife much earlier in the day, during his hours of deshabille, and letting her write his letters and read the papers to him. She was pleased with this advance, but it gave Nuttie a great deal more solitude, which was sometimes judiciously spent, but it was very hard not to be desultory in spite of learning lessons in French, Italian, and drawing.

Later in the day came the drive or the visit to the public gardens when the band was playing, but this became less frequent as Mr. Egremont observed the cold civility shown to his wife, and as he likewise grew stronger and made more engagements of his own. Then Nuttie had happy afternoons of driving, donkey-riding, or walking with her mother, sketching, botanising, admiring, and laying up stores for the long descriptive letters that delighted the party in St. Ambrose's Road, drinking in all the charm of the scenery, and entering into it intelligently. They spent a good many evenings alone together likewise, and it could not but give Alice a pang to see the gladness her daughter did not repress when this was the case, even though to herself it meant relaxation of the perpetual vigilance she had to exert when the father and daughter were together to avert collisions. They were certainly not coming nearer to one another, though Nuttie was behaving very well and submissively on the whole, and seldom showing symptoms of rebellion. This went on through the early part of their stay, but latterly there was a growing sense upon the girl that she and her mother were avoided by some young ladies to whom they had been introduced, and whom they saw regularly at the daily services at St. Michael's Church. They were pleasant-looking girls, with whom Nuttie longed to fraternise, and she was mortified at never being allowed to get beyond a few frigidly civil words in the street, more especially when she came upon sketching parties and picnics in which she was never included.

It was all very well for her mother to answer her murmurs and wonderings with 'You know people are very exclusive, my dear.' Nuttie began to guess that her father and her name were the real reason, and her eyes were further opened later in the spring when Mr. Egremont, who had recovered unusual health and vigour, took his ladies to Mentone to spend a day or two in the newer beauties there. Alice had her misgivings, but the visit was avowedly to show the place to her, and she could not reasonably object. He was in unusual good humour, and even tolerated their ecstasies at the scenery and the flowers, dined at the table d'hote and found acquaintance, enjoyed himself, and in the forenoon, while Nuttie was out wondering and admiring, and going as far as she could drag Martin, he expressed to his wife that she would be astonished at the gardens and the music of Monte Carlo.

There, however, Alice made a stand. 'Thank you, it is very kind, but if you please, I should not like to take Ursula to Monte Carlo, or to go there myself,' she said in an apologetic tone.

He laughed. 'What! you are afraid of making the little one a confirmed gambler?'

'You know I am not, but—'

'You think the little prig will be contaminated, eh?'

'Well, I think it will be happier for her if she never sees anything—of the kind.'

'You little foolish Edda, as if her eyes or ears need see anything but flowers and music and good company.'

'I know that, but I had so much rather not. It was a sweet face and caressing voice that implored, and he still was good humoured.

'Well, well, I don't want to drag you, old lady, against your will, though I fancy you would be rather surprised at the real aspect of the abode of iniquity your fancy depicts.'

'Oh, thank you, thank you so much!'

'What an absurd little woman it is! I wonder if you would thank me as heartily supposing I cleared a round thousand and gave you—say a diamond necklace?'

'I am sure I should not!'

'No, I don't believe you would. That restless little conscience of yours would be up on end. After all, I don't know that you are the worse for it, when it looks so prettily out of your brown eyes. I wonder what you expect to see? The ruined gamester shooting himself on every path, eh?'

'No, no; I don't suppose I should see anything horrid or even disagreeable. I know it is all very beautiful; but then every person who goes for the innocent pleasures' sake only helps to keep up the whole thing—evil and all.'

'And what would the old women of all sorts here and at Nice do without such a choice temple of scandal to whet their teeth upon? Well, I suppose you and your precious daughter can take care of yourselves. There are the gardens, or you can tell Gregorio to order you a carriage.'

'Then you are going?'

'Yes, I promised Grafton. Don't be afraid, Mistress Edda, I'm not going to stake Bridgefield and reduce you to beggary. I'm an old hand, and was a cool one in my worst days, and whatever I get I'll hand over to appease you.'

That was all she could obtain, and she secretly hoped there would be no winnings to perplex her. Thankful that she had not made him angry by the resistance for which she had prepared herself with secret prayer ever since the Mentone scheme had been proposed, she placed herself at Nuttie's disposition for the rest of the day.

They had a charming donkey-ride, and, still unsatiated with beauty, Ursula made her mother come out again to wonder at the trees in the public gardens. Rather tired, they were sitting on a shaded bench, when a voice close to them exclaimed, 'It is; yes, it must be; 'tis the voice—yes, and the face prettier than ever. Little Alice—ah! you don't know me. Time has been kinder to you than to me.'

'Oh! I know you now! I beg your pardon,' cried Alice, recognising in the thin nutcracker parchment visage and shabbily-dressed figure the remnant of the brilliant aquiline countenance and gay attire of eighteen years ago. 'Mrs. Houghton! I am so glad to have met you, you were so kind to me. And here she is.'

'What! is this the child? Bless me, what a proof how time goes! Young lady, you'll excuse my not knowing you. You were a very inconvenient personage not quite born when I last met your mother. What a likeness! I could have known her for Alwyn Egremont's daughter anywhere!'

'Yes, they all say she is a thorough Egremont.'

'Then it is all right. I saw Alwyn Egremont, Esquire, and family among the arrivals at Nice, but I hardly durst expect that it was you. It seemed too good to be true, though I took care the knot should be tied faster than my gentleman suspected.'

'Oh, please!' cried Alice deprecatingly, at first not apprehending the force of the words, having never known the gulf from which Mrs. Houghton had saved her, and that lady, seeing that the girl was listening with all her ears, thought of little pitchers and restrained her reminiscences, asking with real warm interest, 'And how was it? How did you meet him again?'

'He came and found me out,' said Alice, with satisfaction in her voice.

'Indeed! Not at Dieppe; for he was en garcon when I nearly came across him ten years ago at Florence.'

'Oh no! He inquired at Dieppe, but they had lost the address my aunt left.'

'Indeed! I should not have thought it of old Madame Leroux, she seemed so thoroughly interested in la pauvre petite. What did you do? Your aunt wrote to me when your troubles were safely over, and she thought him lost in the poor Ninon, that she meant to settle in a place with an awfully long Yorkshire name.'

'Micklethwayte; yes, we lived there, and got on very well. We had boarders, and I had some dear little pupils; but last year Mark Egremont—you remember dear little Mark—was in the neighbourhood, and hearing my name, he told his uncle, who had been seeking us ever since. And he came, Mr. Egremont, and took us home, and oh, the family have been so kind!'

'What? The parson, and that awful old she-lion of a grandmother, whose very name scared you out of your wits?'

'She is dead, and so is dear good Lady Adelaide. Canon Egremont is kindness itself. It was all the old lady's doing, and he knew nothing about it. He was gone to Madeira with Lady Adelaide and got none of our letters, and he never knew that his brother was married to me.'

'Trust Alwyn for that,' Mrs. Houghton muttered. 'Well, all's well that ends well, and I hope he feels due gratitude to me for doing him a good turn against his will. I tried to get at him at Florence to find out what he had done with you, but unluckily I was ill, and had to send through poor Houghton, and he mismanaged it of course, though I actually wrote down that barbarous address, Mickle something, on a card. I believe he only got as far as the man instead of the master.'

'Ah! I wanted to ask for Captain Houghton,' said Alice, glad to lead the conversation away from revelations of which she had an instinctive dread.

'Gone, my dear! two years ago. Poor fellow! it was low fever, but quite as much want of luck, I shall always believe,' she said.

'Oh, I am sorry! He was so kind to me!' said Alice, squeezing her hand, and looking up with sweet tender commiseration.

'There, there, don't, you pretty creature!' said Mrs. Houghton, putting her hand across her eyes. 'I declare, you've almost made me cry—which I've not done—well, hardly, since I parted with you at Dieppe, thinking you a sweet little flower plucked and thrown away to die, though I had done my best to bind it to him. What care I took not to let Houghton disabuse him about Jersey marriages!'

There is a difference between hearing and hearkening, and Alice Egremont's loving and unsuspecting heart was so entirely closed against evil thoughts of her husband, and so fully occupied with her old friend's condition, that she never took in the signification of all this, while Nuttie, being essentially of a far more shrewd and less confiding nature, and already imbued with extreme distrust of her father, was taking in all these revelations with an open-eyed, silent horror of conviction that her old impressions of the likeness to Marmion or Theseus had been perfectly correct. It was all under her hat, however, and the elder ladies never thought of her, Alice bringing back the conversation to Mrs. Houghton herself. 'Oh, my dear, I drag on as I can. I've got a fragment of our old income, and when that's run too low, I go up to Monte Carlo—I always had the lucky hand, you know, and 'tis only restitution after all! I'm sick of it all though, and sometimes think I'll take my good sister Anne's offers and go home.'

'Oh do, do!' cried Alice.

'But,' went on the poor woman, 'humble pie goes against me, and think what an amount would be before me—heigh ho!—after nearly five-and-twenty years; yes, five-and-twenty years it is—since Houghton, poor fellow, told me I was too bright and winsome for a little country lawyer's house in a poky street. What would they think of me now?' and she laughed with a sound that was painful to hear. 'Well, Sycorax had done one good deed, and when I look at you, queening it there, I feel that so have I.'

'You were very good to me, I know; but oh, if you would go home to your sister!'

'My dear, you little know what you ask! Anne! Why, she is the prime district lady, or whatever you call it, of Dockforth. Think what it would be to her to have this battered old vaurien thrown on her hands, to be the stock subject for all the righteous tongues. Besides,' as she coughed, 'the English climate would make an end of me outright. I'm in a bad way enough here, where I can sit among the lemon trees half the days in the winter, but the English fireside in a stuffy parlour—' and she shuddered.

That shiver reminded all that it was getting late, too late for Mrs. Houghton to be out of doors, and near the time when Mr. Egremont was to meet his ladies at the hotel. Alice begged for Mrs. Houghton's address, and it was given with a short ironical laugh at her promise to call again if possible. 'Ay, if possible,' the poor woman repeated. 'I understand! No, no,' as Alice was about to kiss her. 'I won't have it done.'

'There's no one in sight.'

'As if that made a difference! Alice, child, you are as innocent as the little dove that flew aboard the Ninon. How have you done it? Get along with you! No kisses to such as me! I don't know whether it breaks my heart, or binds it up to look at the face of you. Anyway, I can't bear it.'

She hurried away, and made some steps from them. A terrible paroxysm of coughing came on, and Mrs. Egremont hurried towards her, but she waved back all help, shook her head, and insisted on going home. Alice kept her in sight, till she dived into a small side street.

'Mother,' said Nuttie. Then there was a pause. 'Mother, did you know all this?'

'Don't talk of it, Nuttie. It is not a thing to be talked about to any one or by any one. I wish you had not been there.'

'But, mother, this once! Did you know?'

'I knew that I knew not what I did when I went on board that yacht, but that God's kind providence was over me in a way that I little deserved. That is all I care to know, and, Ursula, I will have not another word about it. No, I will not hear it.'

'I was only going to ask whether you would tell my father.'

'Certainly; but not before you.'

The tone of decision was unwonted, and Nuttie knew she must abide by it, but the last shreds of filial respect towards Mr. Egremont were torn away by what Mrs. Houghton had implied, and the girl dashed up and down her bedroom muttering to herself, 'Oh, why have I such a father? And she, she will not see it, she is wilfully blind! Why not break with him and go home to dear Aunt Ursel and Gerard and Mr. Dutton at once, instead of this horrid, horrid grandeur? Oh, if I could fling all these fine things in his face, and have done with him for ever. Some day I will, when I am of age, and Gerard has won his way.'

Meantime Alice, in some trepidation, but with resolution at the bottom, had told her husband of the meeting with Mrs. Houghton, of her widowhood, sickness, and poverty.

He did not like the intelligence of their meeting, and hoped no one had seen it; then, when reassured on this score, he hummed a little and exclaimed, 'Poor old Flossy Houghton! I don't wonder! They went the pace! Well, what do you want? Twenty pounds for her! Why, 'twill all be at Monte Carlo in three days' time.'

'It is very good of you, but I want more than that. She is so ill and wretched, you know.'

'I can't have you visiting her, if that's what you mean. Why, after all the pains I've been at to get you on your proper level at home, here's my Lady Louisa and all her crew, in their confounded insolence, fighting shy of you, and you can't give them a better colour for it than by running after a woman like that—divorced to begin with, and known at every gambling table in Europe.'

'I know that, Alwyn, dear Alwyn' (it was very seldom that she called him so, and she put her clasped hands on his shoulder); 'but I am sure she is dying, and she was so good to me, I can't bear doing nothing for her.'

'Well, there's twenty—fifty, if you like.'

'Thank you, thank you, but you know I never meant to visit her—like—like society; only to go sometimes privately and—'

'And how about your daughter?'

'I would not take her on any account. What I want to do is this. Mrs. Houghton spoke of her sister, a kind good woman in England, who would take her home, and love her, if only she could bring herself to go. Now, I think I could persuade her to write, or let me write to the sister—and if only the two were together again! It is very dreadful to think of her dying alone, in the way she is going on!'

'What, little saint, you want to try your hand on her? I should say she was too tough an old sinner for you.'

'Oh, Alwyn! her heart was very near, though she tried to keep it back. I do not want to—to do what you mean—only to get her to let her sister come. I'm sure that would do the rest.'

'If any sister does more than you, you little witch,' he said.

Alice pressed him no more then, but a day or two later, when she knew he had an engagement, she arranged to dispose of Nuttie with the clergyman's wife, and then begged permission to go by train to Mentone, and come back in the evening. He did not like it—no more did she—for she was perfectly unaccustomed to travelling alone, but there was a deep sense of sacred duty upon her, only strengthened by her unwillingness to realise how much she owed to Mrs. Houghton.

She telegraphed that she was coming, and found her friend more touched than she chose to allow at the fact of her visit, declaring that she must have wonderful power over Alwyn Egremont, if she knew how to use it; indeed, the whole tone was of what Alice felt flattery, intended to turn away anything more serious. Poor woman, she was as careful of doing no injury to her young friend's reputation as Mr. Egremont could have desired. Alice had come resolved that she should have one good meal, but she would not hear of eating anywhere in public where either could be recognised, and the food was brought to a private room in the hotel. To her lodgings she still would not take Alice, nor would she give her sister's address. Except for a genuine shower of tears when Alice insisted on kissing her there seemed no ground gained.

But Alice went again on her husband's next visit to Mentone. He was, to a certain degree, interested in her endeavours, and really wished the poor woman to be under the charge of her relations, instead of dying a miserable lonely death among strangers.

This time Alice had to seek her friend in the dreary quatrieme of the tall house with the dirty stone stairs. It was a doleful empty room, where, with a mannish-looking dressing-gown and a torn lace scarf tied hood-fashion over her scanty hair, Mrs. Houghton sat over a pan of charcoal oppressive to Alice's English lungs.

'Come again!' she cried. 'Well, I really shall begin to think that angels and ministers of grace exist off the stage! You pretty thing! Let me look at you. Where did you get that delicious little bonnet?'

'Why, it is perfectly plain!'

'So it is! 'Tis only the face that is in it. Now if some folks put this on— sister Anne, for example, what dowdies they would be. Poor old Anne, you must know she had a turn for finery, only she never knew how to gratify it. To see the contortions of her crinolines was the delight of all the grammar school. It was a regular comedy for them to see her get into our pew edgeways, and once unconsciously she carried off a gentleman's hat on her train.'

So she went on talking, coughing at intervals, and generally using a half-mocking tone, as if defying the tenderness that awoke in spite of her, but always of her original home, and especially of her sister. Alice ventured to ask whether they often heard from one another.

'Good soul, she always writes at Christmas and on my birthday. I know as well as possible that I shall find a letter poste restante wherever she heard of me last, and that she hasn't done—I'm ashamed to say for how long—really, I think not since I let her know that I couldn't stand Ivy Lodge, Dockforth, at any price, when she wrote to Monaco on seeing poor Houghton's death in the paper.'

There was a good deal of rambling talk of this kind, to which Alice listened tenderly and compassionately, making no attempt at persuasion, only doing what was possible for the poor lady's comfort. She had procured on her way some fruit and jelly, and some good English tea, at which Mrs. Houghton laughed, saying, 'Time was, I called it cat-lap! Somehow it will seem the elixir of life now, redolent, even milkless, of the days when we were young.'

Then she revealed something of her long, suffering, almost ghastly nights, and Alice gently told how her old friend, Mrs. Nugent, suffered from sleeplessness, and kept a store of soothing psalms and hymns in her memory. There was a little laugh. 'That's for you good folk. I haven't such a thing about me! Come, Par exemple!' and Alice repeated the first thing she could remember, the verse beginning 'God, who madest earth and heaven.'

'That's one of your charms, is it? Well, it would not be too much for me if my poor old memory would hold it. Say it again.'

Alice generally had about her a tiny prayer-book with 'Hymns, Ancient and Modern,' attached. It had been a gift from Mary Nugent, and she was fond of it, but the opportunity was not to be lost, and she took it out, saying she would bring a larger one and reclaim it. And, as she was finally taking leave, she said with a throbbing heart, 'Do you know that you have betrayed your sister's address? I shall write to her now.'

'If you do—!' cried Mrs. Houghton, in a tone like threatening deprecation, but with a little of her strange banter in it besides. Alice's mind had been made up to do the thing, and she had not felt it honest not to give due warning of her intentions. Even now she was not certain of the lady's surname, but she trusted to her husband's knowledge of Mrs. Houghton's previous history; and not in vain. Mr. Egremont amused himself with a little ridicule at his wife's quixotry, and demanded whether Flossy Houghton was a promising convert; but confessed himself very glad that the poor thing should be off their hands, declaring that it was quite time her own people looked after her, and happily he recollected her maiden name. So the letter was written, after numerous attempts at expressing it suitably, explaining Mrs. Houghton's illness and the yearnings she was too proud and ashamed to express to her sister, and was answered at once by a few short words of earnest gratitude, and an assurance that Miss Reade was preparing to start at once. Could Mrs. Egremont meet her and prepare her sister?

To Alice's disappointment this could not be. Mr. Egremont had invited some friends to the villa, and would not spare her. She could only send a note, assuring Miss Reade that she believed that preparation would do more harm than good, and she waited and watched anxiously. A card came by the post in Mrs. Houghton's scrawled writing. 'Naughty little wretch!' was all it said, but thence she gathered hope.

The spring was advancing, and Mr. Egremont was in haste to be gone, but Alice obtained one more run to Mentone, and once more climbed up the dark and dirty stairs to the room, where the well-known voice answered her tap, 'Come in! Ah, there she is, the wicked little angel!'

A substantial little roly-poly business-like little woman hurried forward with tearful eyes and outstretched hands. 'Oh, Mrs. Egremont! can I ever thank you enough?'

'You can't, Anne, so don't try. It will be a relief to all parties,' interposed Mrs. Houghton. 'Sentiment is not permitted here.'

Nevertheless she hugged Alice almost convulsively. She was sitting in a comfortable arm-chair, one about which Mrs. Egremont knew something, and the whole aspect of the room had changed indescribably for the better, as much indeed as Mrs. Houghton's own personal array, which had no longer the desolate neglected look of old.

A little stool was close to her chair, as if the two sisters could not bear to be far apart, and the look of love and content in their eyes as they turned to one another was perfect joy to Alice. She had no longer any doubt that Anne Reade, who had found the wanderer yet a great way off, would yet bring her back to the home, spiritually if not outwardly.

Mrs. Houghton spoke, of better rooms when the winter visitors had fled, Anne spoke of her being able to return to Dockforth. Whether that would ever be seemed entirely doubtful to Alice's eyes, especially as the patient's inclination was evidently otherwise. There was nothing to be done but to leave the sisters together, obtaining Miss Reade's ready promise to write, and putting into her hands a sum of money which could be sincerely called 'only a debt of gratitude from my husband and me,' and which would smooth the way either to remaining or returning to England.

Nor was there any return. Ere many weeks had passed Mrs. Egremont heard from Miss Reade how a fresh cold had made it impossible to move, and summer heat had brought on low fever, which had destroyed the feeble strength, but not till 'childhood's star' had again arisen, and a deeply and truly repentant woman had passed away, saved, as it seemed, through that one effort on behalf of the young girl whose innocence she had protected.

CHAPTER XIX.

THE VORTEX.

The rebuffs that society had bestowed on his wife and daughter at Nice had rendered Mr. Egremont the more determined on producing them in London and establishing their position. He secured a furnished house in Westburnia before leaving Nice, and, travelling leisurely home without visiting Bridgefield, he took possession the second week in May.

There had not been much correspondence with the Rectory, and on the first forenoon, as Mrs. Egremont and Nuttie were trying to enliven the drawing-room with the flowers sent up to meet them, they were surprised by the entrance of Blanche, full of kisses and welcomes.

'Oh! didn't you know? I'm with the Kirkaldys just round the corner. Aunt Margaret has undertaken to do the part of a noble aunt by me.'

'Then you are here for the season? And May?'

'May wouldn't come, except just for a week to see the pictures, and lay in a stock of talk. She's grown more parochial than ever, and we believe it is all Hugh Condamine. Oh! I forgot you were gone before we came home last autumn. He is mamma's nephew, you know, and was ordained last year to the curacy of the next parish to his father's place. If the Edwardses only would take themselves off, we would have him at home, and then we should have flowers on the altar, and all sorts of jolly things. Papa would stand ever so much more from him than from the old Edwardses.'

'But is he engaged to May, then?'

'Well, no, not exactly. I believe he does not think it right till he has done preparing for priest's orders. He's ever so strict, you know, and he hasn't got much either; but he means it. Lucy, his sister, you know, told me all about it, and that altogether the elders had settled it was better for both that he should attend to his preparation, and May should not bind herself, though they really understand one another, and so she won't come to London.'

'Oh, that's very good of her!' cried Nuttie; 'but why won't they let them settle their minds and be engaged?'

'People are always tiresome,' said Blanche; 'and I do believe the living is at the bottom of it, at least Lucy thought so. I mean everybody wants to wait

—all the old ones, I mean—not Hugh or May, of course—to know whether Mark will stick to the umbrellas, or turn back and be a clergyman, because, then, of course, he would have the living; and if he doesn't, they want to be certain whether Uncle Alwyn, or you, Nuttie, would promise it to Hugh if he married May!'

'Me!' exclaimed Nuttie.

'My dear, I don't like to hear you talk of such things,' said Mrs. Egremont gently.

'Oh yes, I know—it's all very dreadful. I was only telling you what is in the old people's heads, and what would settle it, and make it all right with them.'

'And how is Mark? Is Miss Ruthven in London?' asked Mrs. Egremont, glad to turn away the conversation from the contingencies of which Blanche spoke with the hardness of youth, as yet not realising sorrow.

'I daresay you know nearly as much of Mark as we do, now the Kirkaldys are up here. All his letters go to Lescombe. Oh no, Annaple is not in London. The Delmars can't afford it, you know, though I believe my lady would have made a stretch if Annaple hadn't been bespoke—but now she reserves herself for Muriel.'

Alice looked with some discomfort at the soft fair-haired creature who was uttering all this worldly jargon in a tone that would have been flippant if it had not been so childish. She asked if Lord. Ronnisglen had written.

'Oh yes, long ago. Lady Delmar had tried to make him nasty about it, but he wouldn't be, so that's all right; and Mark seems to get on very well, though it must be horridly dull for him now the Kirkaldys are away, and he can't spend all his Sundays at Monks Horton.'

'He will get more into the spirit of the place,' said Nuttie, whereat Blanche shrugged her shoulders a little, and exclaimed:

'You've got out of it at any rate, Nuttie!'

'I hope not!'

'Well, then, the look of it! I never saw any one so improved! Isn't she, Aunt Alice? She's grown, I declare! Yes'—measuring herself against her cousin—'I was a leetle bit taller when you came, and now you've got above me! and what a duck of a way of doing your hair! You must show me! I must tell May there's no fear of your being taken for one another now; Aunt Margaret will be quite surprised.'

It was true that Ursula had developed a good deal during the last year, and, under the experienced hands of Martin, had lost her schoolgirl air, and turned into a young lady capable of becoming the Paris outfit which her father had enjoined. Without positive beauty, she was a pleasing, intelligent, animated girl, with the reputation of being an heiress, with a romance in the background, and there was nothing to prevent her from being a success. The family connections, with Lady Kirkaldy to set the example, had determined on giving full support to Mrs. Egremont, and, as of course every one liked to look at so lovely a face, the way of both was smoothed in a manner that delighted her husband when they encountered any of those who had looked coldly on her at Nice.

He would have had her presented, but her own reluctance and the united counsels of Lady Kirkaldy and the Canoness prevailed on him to drop the idea; and then there was a fight with Ursula, who declared that she would not go to court if her mother did not; but she was overruled at last by that mother's tears at her defiance; and let herself be presented, together with Blanche, by Lady Kirkaldy.

To Ursula it was altogether a strange time, full of the same kind of reckless swing and sense of intoxication that had possessed her at Bridgefield. Not that there was an excessive amount of actual gaiety. Hot rooms and late hours were soon found not to agree with Mrs. Egremont. She looked faded and languid after evening parties; and, as her husband really cared more to have her ready to wait upon him and amuse him than for anything else, he did not insist on her going out more than might be needful to establish her position, or when it suited him to show her off. The other purposes were quite as well served by letting Ursula go out with Lady Kirkaldy, who was warmly interested in mother and daughter, glad of a companion for Blanche, and still more glad of a companion for herself. For she was not slow to discover that exhibitions, which were merely fashionable gapeseed to her niece, were to Nuttie real delights, viewed intelligently, and eliciting comments and questions that Lady Kirkaldy and even her husband enjoyed in their fresh interest, but which were unendurable weariness to Blanche, unless she had some one to chatter with. Lectures and lessons, which the aunt hoped to render palatable by their being shared by the two cousins, only served to show the difference between a trained and eager, and an untrained and idle, nature. With the foreign society to be met at Lord Kirkaldy's, Blanche was less at a loss than her brother, and could get on by the help of nods and becks and wreathed smiles; but Nuttie, fresh from her winter abroad, could really talk, and was often in request as a useful person to help in entertaining. She thus saw some of the choicest society in London, and, in addition, had as much of the youthful gaiety as Lady Kirkaldy thought wholesome for the two girls. Also there were those ecclesiastical delights and privileges which had been heard of at Micklethwayte, and were within reach, greatly enjoyed by Mrs. Egremont whenever she could share them, though her daughter chafed at her treating all except the chief service on Sunday as more indulgence than duty.

Nuttie was strong, with that spring of energy which unbroken health and a quiet life lays up, and, in her own phrase, she went in for everything, from early services to late balls, thinking all right because it was seldom that her day did not begin with matins or Celebration, and because she was not taken to more than two balls a week, and conversed at times with superior people, or looked at those with world-famed names. Possibly the whirl was greater than if it had been mere gaiety, for then the brain would not have participated in it. Church functions, with the scurry to go at all, or to obtain a seat, fine music, grand sermons, religious meetings, entertainments for the poor, lectures, lessons, exhibitions, rides, drives, kettle-drums, garden-parties, concerts, theatres, operas, balls, chattering, laughing, discussing, reading up current subjects, enjoying attention, excitement as to what should be done and how,— one thing drove out another in perpetual succession, and the one thing she never did or could do was to sit still and think! Rest was simply dreamless sleep, generally under the spell of a strong will to wake at the appointed hour for church. The short intervals of being alone with her mother were spent in pouring out histories of her doings, which were received with a sympathy that doubled their pleasure, excepting when Nuttie thought proper to grumble and scold at her mother's not coming to some Church festival at an hour when she thought Mr. Egremont might want her.

Of him Nuttie saw very little. He did not want her, and cared little what she did, as long as she was under the wing of Lady Kirkaldy, whose patronage was a triumphant refutation of all doubts. He went his own way, and had his own club, his own associates, and, with his wife always at his beck and call, troubled himself very little about anything else.

Alice spent a good deal of time alone, chiefly in waiting his pleasure; but she had her own quiet occupations, her books, her needlework, her housekeeping, and letter-writing, and was peacefully happy as long as she did not displease Nuttie. There were no collisions between father and daughter, and the household arrangements satisfied that fastidious taste. She was proud of Ursula's successes, but very thankful not to be dragged out to share them, though she was much less shy, and more able on occasion to take her place.

One pain she had. Good old Mrs. Nugent was rapidly decaying, and she shared with all her loving heart in the grief this was to Mary and to Miss Headworth, and longed to help them in their nursing. She would not grieve Nuttie by dwelling constantly on the bad accounts, and the girl hardly attended to them in the tumult of occupations; and so at last, when the final tidings came in the second week in July, they were an absolute shock to Nuttie, and affected her as the first grief sometimes does. Mrs. Nugent was really the first person of her own intimate knowledge who had died, and in the excited state in which she was, the idea of the contrast between her own occupations and Mary's was so dreadful to her that she wept most bitterly, with the sobs of childhood, such as she really did not know how to restrain.

It was an unfortunate day, for it was one of the few on which Mr. Egremont wanted to take out his ladies. There was to be a great garden-party at Richmond, given by one of his former set, who had lately whitewashed himself by marrying a very fast and fashionable lady. Nuttie had heard strong opinions on the subject at Lord Kirkaldy's; but her father was quite elated at being in a position to countenance his old friends. Alice, in the midst of her sorrow, recollected this with consternation.

'My dear, my dear, hush! You must stop yourself! Remember we have to go out.'

'Go—out,' cried Nuttie, her sobs arrested by very horror. 'You wouldn't go —!'

'I am afraid your father would be very much vexed—'

'Let him! It is a horrid wicked place to go to at all; and now—when dear, dear old Mrs. Nugent is lying there—and—'

The crying grew violent again, and in the midst in walked Mr. Egremont with an astonished 'What is all this?'

'We have lost one of our dear kind old friends at Micklethwayte,' said Alice, going towards him; 'dear old Mrs. Nugent,' and she lifted up her tear- stained face, which he caressed a little and said, 'Poor old body;' but then, at a sob, 'Can't you stop Ursula from making such a row and disfiguring herself? You must pick up your looks, Edda, for I mean you to make a sensation at Jerningham's.'

'Oh, Alwyn, if you could let us stay at home! Mrs. Nugent was so good to us, and it does seem unkind—'The tears were in her eyes again.

'Nonsense!' he said impatiently. 'I promised Jerningham, and it is absurd to have you shutting yourself up for every old woman at Micklethwayte.'

Thereupon Ursula wiped away her tears, and stood up wrathful before him. 'I am not going,' she said.

'Oh, indeed!' he returned in a tone that made her still more angry. 'Hein'! a French ejaculation which he had the habit of uttering in a most exasperating manner.

'No,' she said. 'It is scarcely a place to which we even ought to be asked to go, and certainly not when—'

'Do you hear that, Mrs. Egremont?' he asked.

'Oh, Nuttie, Nuttie, dear!' she implored; 'don't.'

'No, mother,' said Nuttie, with flashing eyes; 'if you care so little for your best friends as to let yourself be dragged out among all sorts of gay, wicked people when your dear friend is lying dead, I'm sure I shan't go with you.'

Her father laughed a little. 'A pretty figure you are, to make a favour of accompanying us!'

'Oh, go away, go away, Nuttie,' entreated her mother. 'You don't know what you are saying.'

'I do know,' said Nuttie, exasperated perhaps by the contrast in the mirror opposite between her own swelled, disfigured face, and the soft tender one of her mother with the liquid eyes. 'I know how much you care for the dear friends who took care of us when we were forsaken!'

And with this shaft she marched out of the room, while her father again laughed, and said, 'Have they been training her for the tragic stage? Never mind, Edda, the little vixen will come to her senses upstairs, and be begging to go.'

'I don't think she will,' said Alice sadly; 'she is not that sort of stuff, and she was very fond of Mrs. Nugent. Oh, Alwyn! if you could let us off.'

'Not after that explosion, certainly,' he said. 'Besides, I promised Jerningham, and such an excuse would never hold water. She is not even a relation.'

'No, but she was very good to me.'

'The more reason why you should not stay at home and be hipped. Never mind that silly girl. She will be all right by and by.'

On the contrary, she did not come down to luncheon, and when, about an hour later, Alice, after writing a few tender loving words to the mourners, went up to her daughter's room, it was to find a limp and deplorable figure lying across the bed, and to be greeted with a fresh outburst of sobs and inarticulate exclamations.

'Oh, Nuttie, dear, this will not do! It is not right. Dear good Mrs. Nugent herself would tell you that this is not the way any one so good and so suffering should be grieved for. Think—'

'Oh, I know all that!' cried Nuttie, impatiently; 'but she—she was the dearest—and nobody cares for her but me. Not even you—'

Again Alice tried to debate the point, and urge on her the duties of moderation, self-control, and obedience, but the poor gentle mother was at a great disadvantage.

In the first place, she respected and almost envied her daughter's resistance, and really did not know whether it was timidity or principle that made it her instinct to act otherwise; in the next, Ursula could always talk her down; and, in the third, she was, and greatly she reproached herself for that same, in great dread of setting herself off into tears that might become hysterical if she once gave way to them. And what would be her husband's feelings if she too collapsed and became unpresentable.

So, having once convinced herself that even if Nuttie had been a consenting party, no amount of cold water and eau-de-cologne would bring those bloodshot eyes, swollen lids, and mottled cheeks to be fit to be seen, she fled as fast as possible from the gasps of barbed reproaches which put her own composure in peril, and dressed with the heaviest of hearts, coupled with the utmost solicitude to look her best. If she had not thought it absolutely wrong, she would even have followed Martin's suggestion, and put on a soupcon of rouge; but by the time she was summoned to the carriage the feverishness of her effort at self-control had done the work, and her husband had paid her the compliment of observing that she looked pretty enough for two.

Nuttie heard them drive off, with a burst of fresh misery of indignation against her mother—now as a slave and a victim—now as forgetting her old home. It was chiefly in mutterings; she had pretty well used up her tears, for, unconsciously perhaps, she had worked them up as a defensive weapon against being carried to the party; and now that the danger was over, her head throbbed, her eyes burnt, and her throat ached too much for her to wish to cry any more. She had not felt physically like this, since the day, seven years ago, when she and Mildred Sharpe had been found suspiciously toying with the key of the arithmetic, and had been debarred from trying for the prize. Then she felt debased and guilty; now she felt, or ought to feel, like a heroine maintaining the right.

She got up and set herself to rights as well as she could. Martin, who had been allowed to know that she had lost an old friend, petted and pitied her, and brought her a substantial meal with her tea, after which she set out to evensong at the church at the end of the square, well veiled under a shady hat, and with a conviction that something ought to happen.

Nothing did, however, happen; she met no one whom she knew, the psalms were not particularly appropriate, and her attention wandered away to the scene at home. She did not come back, as she was sure she ought to have done, soothed, exhilarated, and refreshed, but rather in a rasped state of mind, and a conscience making a vehement struggle to believe itself in the right—a matter in which she thoroughly succeeded.

She wrote a long letter to Mary Nugent, and shed some softer tears over it, then she built a few castles on her future escape from the power of her father; and then she picked up Reata, and became absorbed in it, regretting only the weakness of her eyes, and the darkening of the summer evening.

She was still reading when the others came home. Her mother kissed her, but looked so languid and tired-out that Nuttie was shocked, and Martin declared that she ought not to go down to dinner.

A tete-a-tete dinner between father and daughter was too dreadful to Alice's imagination to be permitted, so she dressed and went down, looking like a ghost. Mr. Egremont scowled at Nuttie, Nuttie scowled at him, each considering it the fault of the other, and when at last it was over, Alice gave up the struggle, and went off to bed, leaving a contrite message that her headache would be better to-morrow.

'All your accursed folly and obstinacy,' observed Mr. Egremont, when Nuttie, with a tone of monition gave him the message.

'I should call it the consequence of being dragged out with a sore heart,' returned Nuttie—a little speech she had prepared ever since she had seen how knocked up her mother was.

'Then I should recommend keeping your ideas to yourself,' he answered, looking at her in his annihilating manner.

She was put down. She thought afterwards of a hundred things that she could have said to him, but she was crushed for the present, and when he went out she could only betake herself to Reata, and forget all about it as much as she could.

When she went upstairs, at the end of the third volume, Martin was on the watch, and would not let her go into the room.

'I have been at hand, ma'am, without her guessing it, and I am happy to say her tears has had a free course when she was in bed. Yes, ma'am, suppressed grief is always dangerous.'

Mrs. Egremont was still prostrate with fatigue and headache the next day, and Nuttie had all the quiet luxuriating in reminiscences she desired. Her father was vexed and angry, and kept out of the way, but it must be confessed that Nuttie's spirits had so much risen by the afternoon that it was a sore concession to consistency when she found herself not expected at Blanche's last little afternoon dance at Lady Kirkaldy's!

CHAPTER XX.

WOLF.

'If I cannot once or twice in a quarter bear out a knave against
an honest man, I have but very little credit with your Worship.'—II. King Henry IV.

Another cause besides Ursula's recalcitrance and her mother's ailment contributed to disturb Mr. Egremont, and bring him home. His agent, by name Bulfinch, a solicitor at Redcastle, came to him with irrefragable proofs of gross peculation on the part of the bailiff who managed the home farm which supplied the house and stables, and showed him that it was necessary to make a thorough investigation and change of system.

In point of fact, Mr. Egremont greatly preferred being moderately cheated to exerting himself to investigate, but this was going beyond moderation, and the explosion had been too public to be passed over. So he came home and sat by, while his wife and Mr. Bulfinch did the work for him, and made it evident to him that the frauds had been of long standing, and carried on with the connivance of the coachman, of Gregorio,—who had before Mrs. Egremont's arrival acted as house steward,—and of the former cook. Indeed, it was the housekeeper whom Mrs. Egremont had left in charge, whose refusal to connive had brought about the discovery.

Gregorio's share in all was sufficiently evident, and Alice's heart leapt with hope. Her husband would be wholly her own if his evil genius were once departed, but Mr. Egremont would not see it. He had no objection to sacrifice the coachman and all his underlings, with the bailiff and his entire family, and felt none of the pity that Alice had for the pretty, silly, half-educated daughters; but as to the valet—Pooh! pooh! the poor fellow had been out of the way all this time—whatever he had done had been in the dark, ages long ago, before Bridgefield knew its mistress; he was a foreigner, and that was enough to prevent him from forgathering with the English. It was all their English prejudice.

'I can show you facts and figures, sir,' said Mr. Bulfinch.

'I daresay, a year or more old. Why, I was an unprotected carcase then—a mere prey—the fellow only did after his kind.'

Alice held her tongue then, but made an effort in private. 'Indeed, I don't think you know; I am afraid Gregorio is not altered. I found him out in his charges about the wine, and the servants' wages at Nice, only you wouldn't listen.'

'His little perquisites, my dear child! Come, nonsense, these foreign fellows don't pretend to have the morals you ascribe to the native flunkey— generally without foundation either—they are much of a muchness as to that; but your Frenchman or Italian does it more neatly, and is a dozen times better servant than the other is.'

'But—'

'Oh, ay! I know you don't like him. But he knows his manners to you, I hope?' said Mr. Egremont, with a suddenness that made her wish she could truthfully say he did not.

'Yes, he always is—is respectful, but somehow I see it is under protest.'

Mr. Egremont laughed. 'Rivals—yes, I see; why, you don't consider the sore trial of having a full-grown mistress turned in upon him! Look here, you keep the keys already, but the new fellow at the farm and all the rest of them shall account to you for everything—Gregorio and all. Won't that satisfy you?'

''Tis not only the money, but I think Gregorio is a bad—not a good—man.'

'Ho, ho! she wants to advertise for a pious footman and coachman! eh? No, I thank you, my dear Edda, I agree with—who was it who said, "Volez moi, mais sans m'ennuyer."'

The Rectory likewise had hoped for Gregorio's dismissal, and there were grave looks when Alice had to confess that nothing would move her husband against him. The Canon even lashed himself up to say, 'I tell you how it is, Alwyn, you'll never do any good with your household, while you keep that fellow.'

'I am not aware what description of good you expect me to do with it, Will,' coolly answered the elder brother in a disconcerting tone.

Poor Alice, on her side, thought of the Little Master, and then wondered if it was uncharitable to do so. For she knew it had become war to the knife with Gregorio! Whether his master told him, or whether it were his own evil conscience, or the wonderful intuition of servants, he certainly knew of the pressure for his dismissal, and he visited it on her as much as he durst.

Outwardly deferential, he could thwart and annoy her in a hundred ways, from making love to the housemaids to making evil suggestions to his master, yet never giving her any overt cause of complaint. He could worry and sting her under the politest exterior, and he knew very well that the most effectual form of annoyance was the persuading his master that any discomfort or lassitude was to be removed by some form of narcotic. This would have the further advantage of stupefying Mr. Egremont, and making him more ready to lapse under the old influence; while the duration and strength of the new one was already a surprise to Gregorio.

But there was no doubt that Mrs. Egremont had profited by her year of training. She looked tired, and less youthful and pretty, but she had gained in grace and importance as well as in style, and was much more really the mistress of Bridgefield. Her shyness had passed away, and she knew now to take her place in society, though still she was somewhat silent. And her husband depended upon her entirely for all his correspondence, for much of his occupation and amusement, and even for the regulation of his affairs. In the household, Gregorio was little more than his personal attendant, and she had the general management, even of the other men-servants. The Canoness might well say it had turned out better than she expected.

And Nuttie had become more womanly, and had acquired the indefinable polish given by a London season. She had learnt the art of conversation, and could make herself agreeable to her uncle, or to any one else who came in her way. Even May allowed that she had something in her, and cultivated her more than before; but, on the other hand, even the Rectory could perceive that there was now an absolute alienation between her and her father, and what might before have been fear had become dislike. If she had to refer to him, especially if her plans for herself or her mother were crossed, there was always a tone of bitterness or of sarcasm about her; and her greater boldness and freedom of speech would occasionally manifest itself towards him. This was not indeed often, since not only did his cool contempt make her come off the worst in the encounters, but the extreme distress they gave to her mother made her refrain whenever her temper, or what she thought her conscience, would let her; but still there was always a danger which kept poor Alice on thorns whenever there was a possible difference of schemes or opinions.

Mrs. William Egremont was seriously considering of representing to Ursula that her conduct was bad taste, bad policy, and, moreover, was doing her mother's spirits and health serious harm; but it was a delicate matter in which to meddle, and the good lady could not make up her mind how far to surrender her brother-in-law's character and allow a partial justification to

Ursula. She was a cautious woman, and waited and watched her opportunities.

In the beginning of October Mr. and Mrs. Egremont were invited to a great shooting party at Sir James Jerningham's. The invitation did not include Ursula. Perhaps she had never dawned on their hostess's imagination; perhaps it was that Lady Jerningham was well known to dislike girls, or any one who might absorb young men's attention. At any rate the omission was a cause of thankfulness to the party concerned, and she did not neglect to worry her mother by a protest against keeping such company as would be met at Waldicotes.

Alice smiled a little faintly and said, 'I don't think it hurts me, my dear; I don't understand half of what they talk about, and they are always kind to me.'

'I don't think you ought to go among them or countenance them.'

'My dear child,'—and the colour rose—'I don't feel as if I had a right to set myself above any one.'

'Mother!'

'People might have said just the same of me.'

'And whose fault was that?' muttered Nuttie under her breath, but Mrs. Egremont would not hear. She only pleaded, as perhaps mother ought not to have done with child.

'You know, Nuttie, it is not for my own pleasure, but your father's eyesight makes him dislike to go anywhere without me now; and I really should be uneasy about him.'

'Yes; he is all you care for,' said Nuttie. 'You sacrifice everything you used to think essential, just to his will and pleasure.'

'Oh, Nuttie, I hope not; I don't think I do!'

'If I thought it was doing him any good I should not so much mind,' went on the girl; 'but he is just the same, and I am always thinking of "As the husband is, the wife is—"'

'Hush! hush! You have no right to think in that way of your father. I will not hear it. I have let you say too much already, Nuttie.' Then after a pause she added, gently and wistfully, 'You have been better taught, and are clearer headed than ever I was, my Nuttie, and it is quite right that you should hate what seems evil to you. I can only go on trying to do what seems my duty from day to day. I know,' she added with rising tears, 'that the sin and folly of my younger days worked a difficult position for us both; but we can only act according to our lights, and pray God to direct us; and please—please bear with me, my dear one, if the same course does not always seem right to us both.'

Nuttie had never heard her say anything so fully showing that she realised these difficulties, and, greatly touched, she asked pardon, kissed and caressed her mother. There was a calm over them for the next few days, and Nuttie actually refrained from bitter comments when her mother was not allowed to go to evensong on Sunday, on the plea of her being tired, but, as the girl believed, in order that she might read the newspapers aloud.

She knew that her silence was appreciated by the way her mother kissed her and called her a dear, good, considerate girl.

On Monday Mr. and Mrs. Egremont went away at what was a strangely early hour for the former, Nuttie spending her days at the Rectory.

On the Tuesday Blanche went with her little sister and the governess on a shopping expedition to Redcastle, and in relating her adventures on her return, she said, 'Oh, by the bye, I met Annaple in Park's shop!'

'Full of Micklethwayte news, I suppose,' said May.

'Yes, of course. Did you know, Nuttie, that your aunt was ill?'

'No, indeed, I did not. What was the matter?'

'Bronchitis, I believe—brown titus, as Betty Butter calls it.'

'Bronchitis! Oh dear! oh dear! Are you quite sure, Blanche?'

'Oh yes! I am quite certain Annaple said Mark told her that Miss Headworth was laid up with bronchitis.'

'And nobody has written to us all this week!' sighed Nuttie.

'I should think that a sign there could not be much in it,' observed May; 'it may be only a bad cold.'

'But Aunt Ursel had bronchitis four years ago, and was very ill indeed,' persisted Nuttie. 'I'm sure it is bronchitis, and that she won't let Miss Mary write to us.'

She was in much distress about it, though May privately told her that she ought to know Blanche's way better than to trust implicitly to any of her reports; and her aunt said much the same thing in more general terms, even proposing that if she did not hear the next morning she should go over to Lescombe to ascertain what Mark had really said.

This pacified her a little, but on her way home the alarm grew upon her, and, moreover, she recollected the opposition that she believed that her father was certain to make to either her mother or herself going to nurse her aunt. It flashed upon her that if she were to hasten to Micklethwayte on this alarm before there could be a prohibition, it would be no disobedience, and perfectly justifiable, not to say noble. Her parents were to return on Thursday evening, and she made up her mind that, unless she were fully reassured as to Miss Headworth's state, she would go off at once to Micklethwayte before any one could gainsay her. She had plenty of money, and she consulted the time-table in the hall before going upstairs. It only concerned the nearest line, but she calculated that if she caught the express, she should reach her destination in time to write to her mother at Waldicotes, and prevent needless shocks. Her eagerness for the plan grew upon her, so that it seemed like liberation; she could hardly sleep for thinking of it, and certainly was not as much disappointed as she believed herself when the post came in—a blank.

Martin was away with her mistress, so Nuttie explained matters to the upper housemaid, who was very sympathetic, carried down her orders for the carriage, procured for her both breakfast and provision for the journey, and packed her clothes. Ursula would fain have been off before the Rectory was aware, but the two little girls came up with a message about the plans for the day, just as she was beginning an explanatory note, and she entrusted to them the information that she was so uneasy about Miss Headworth that she had decided on going to see for herself.

So in dashed Adela and Rosalind to their mother's room full of excitement with the news that Cousin Nuttie was gone off by the train, because her aunt was very ill indeed.

'Gone, Adela? are you sure? Really gone?'

'Oh yes, mamma! The dogcart was coming round, and she said she wanted to catch the 10.05 train, and was very sorry she had not time to write a note to you.'

'Was there a letter? What had she heard?'

'Oh, only that her aunt was so very ill! She did not tell us—did she, Rosie?'

'There was something about being in time to write to Aunt Alice,' suggested Adela.

'I am very sorry about this. I am afraid it will be a great shock to Alice,' observed the mother, as she imparted the news at her husband's dressing- room door.

'Young girls are so precipitate!' said the Canon.

'Your brother won't like it at all,' the lady continued.

'Not he. But after all, it is just as well that he was not asked. They do owe that poor old lady a good deal, and Alwyn's not the man to see it. I'm not sorry the girl took the matter into her own hands, though I couldn't have advised it.'

'Except that it will all fall on Alice.'

'He is very fond of Alice. She has done more with him than I ever thought possible. Kept him respectable this whole year, and really it grows on him. He makes ever so much more of her now than when he first brought her home— and no wonder. No, no; he won't fall foul of her.'

'Perhaps not; but it is just as bad, or worse, for her if he falls foul of her daughter. Besides, she is very much attached to her aunt. I wish I knew what the account was, or whether she knows anything about it.'

CHAPTER XXI.

URSULA'S RECEPTION.

'Thy wish was father, Harry, to that thought.'—SHAKESPEARE.

It was at half-past seven o'clock that Ursula Egremont's cab stopped at St. Ambrose's Road. She had missed the express train, and had to come on by a stopping one. But here at last she was, with eyes even by gaslight full of loving recognition, a hand full of her cab-fare, a heart full of throbbing hope and fear, a voice full of anxiety, as she inquired of the astonished servant, 'Louisa, Louisa, how is Aunt Ursel!' and, without awaiting the reply, she opened the adjoining door. There sat, with their evening meal on the table, not only Mary Nugent, but Miss Headworth herself.

Nuttie rushed at her, and there was an incoherency of exclamations, the first thing that made itself clear to the senses of the traveller being, 'Ill, my dear? No such thing! Only I had a bad cold, and Mary here is only too careful of me.'

'But Mark said you had bronchitis.'

'What could have put that into his head? He did not write it, surely?'

'He wrote it to Annaple Ruthven, and she told Blanche.'

'Oh!' and Mary Nugent's tone was rather nettling.

'And then it was such a terrible time since we had heard anything,' added Nuttie, on the defensive.

'Did not your mother get my letter?' said Miss Headworth. 'I wrote to her at—what's the name of that place? I hope I addressed it right.'

'Oh, but I was not there. I didn't go with them.'

'Ah, yes, I remember. Then did not she send you?'

'No, I came off this morning. I heard this yesterday evening, and I determined that nothing should stop me if there was no news by the post.'

'Dear child! But will your father not be displeased?' said Miss Headworth.

'He hasn't any right to object,' cried Nuttie, with flashing eyes and a look that made Miss Nugent anxious; but at the moment there could be little thought save of welcome to the warm-hearted girl. Louisa was already brewing fresh tea, and extemporising additions to the meal, and Nuttie was explaining how she hoped to have arrived a couple of hours sooner.

'By the bye, I meant to have written to mother for her to have it to-morrow before leaving Waldicotes. Is there time?'

No, the pillar at hand was cleared at seven, and the regular post-office could not be reached in time; so they satisfied themselves with the knowledge that Mrs. Egremont must have had Aunt Ursel's cheerful letter, and Mary recommended telegraphing to the Canon the first thing in the morning. Then they gave themselves up to enjoyment.

'At any rate, I'm here,' said Nuttie, 'and I'll make the most of it.'

And her handsome furs were laid aside, and her boots taken off, and she resigned herself to absolute ease and luxury, while Mary poured out the tea, and her aunt heaped her plate with eggs and rashers 'such as one doesn't get anywhere else,' said Nuttie, declaring herself quite voracious, while her aunt fondly admired her growth and improvement, and she inquired into the cold, not quite gone yet; and there were speculations over what Mark could have got into his head. Mary remembered having met him coming to call, and having told him that she had persuaded Miss Headworth to keep her bed because her colds were apt to be severe, and it was agreed to lay the exaggeration at the door of the lovers and Blanche. Miss Headworth laughed, and said she ought to be flattered that an old woman's sore throat should be thought worthy of mention by a fine young gentleman like Mr. Mark. 'A very good young man he is,' she added. 'You would never have thought how kind he is in coming in here to tell me everything he hears about your dear mother,

Nuttie.'

'He makes himself very useful while Mr. Dutton is away,' added Mary, 'taking his young men's class and all.'

'Oh! is Mr. Dutton away?'

'Yes; he has had to be in London a great deal of late. I am afraid he may have to live there altogether.'

'What a grievous pity!'

'He won't be anywhere without doing good,' said Miss Headworth, 'but I sometimes wish we had his cool good sense here.'

'And how is Mr. Spyers,' asked Nuttie. She felt shy of asking for Gerard Godfrey, or perhaps she thought she ought to be shy of his name, and kept hoping that it would come in naturally.

'Mr. Spyers is very well. Very busy of course, and very much delighted with your mother's gifts to the church. All her own work, isn't it, Nuttie?'

'Yes; every bit. She does lots of embroidery and work of all kinds when she is waiting for *him* or sitting with him, and luckily it has never occurred to him to ask what it is for.'

The two ladies knew well what was meant by him, but they would not pursue the subject, and proceeded to put Nuttie au courant with St. Ambrose affairs—how last year's mission had produced apparently an immense effect in the town, and how the improvement had been ebbing ever since, but had left various individual gains, and stirred up more than one good person who had hitherto thought it enough to save one's own soul and let other people alone; how Mr. Spyers was endeavouring to bind people together in a guild; how a violent gust of temperance orators had come down upon the place, and altogether fascinated and carried away Gerard Godfrey.

There was his name at last, and Nuttie was rather gratified to feel herself blushing as she asked, 'Ah! poor Gerard—how is he?'

'As good and sincere as ever,' said Miss Nugent, 'but not much wiser. He is so excitable and vehement.'

'Yes,' said Miss Headworth. 'I don't understand the kind of thing. In my time a steady young clerk used to be contented after hours with playing at cricket in the summer, or learning the flute in the winter—and a great nuisance it was sometimes, but now Gerard must get himself made a sort of half clergyman.'

'A reader,' suggested Mary.

'Minor orders. Oh, how delightful!' cried Nuttie.

'People, don't half understand it,' added Miss Headworth. 'Mrs. Jeffreys will have it that he is no better than a Jesuit, and really I did not know what to say, for he talked, to me by the hour about his being an external brother to something.'

'Not to the Jesuits, certainly,' said Nuttie.

'Yes, I told her that; but she thinks all monks are Jesuits, you know, and that all brothers are monks; and he does wear his cassock—his choir cassock, I mean—when he has his service in the iron room at the sandpits. And now he has taken up temperance, and flies about giving the pledge, and wanting one to wear bits of blue ribbon. I told him I never did take, and never had taken, more than a little hot wine and water when I had a cold, and I couldn't see what good it would do to George Jenkins and the poor fellows at the Spread Eagle if I took ever so many vows.'

'There's a regular blue-ribbon fever set in,' said Miss Nugent. 'Gerard told me I was supporting the cause of intemperance yesterday because I was so wicked as to carry the rest of your bottle of port, Miss Headworth, to poor Anne Crake.'

'Well! he is a dear boy, and youth wouldn't be youth if it were not sometimes rather foolish,' said Miss Headworth, 'and it is better it should be for good than evil.'

'Eager in a cause and not for selfishness,' said Mary. 'Poor Gerard, I wonder where he will be safely landed!'

So did Nuttie, who had a secret flattering faith in being the cause of all the poor young fellow's aberrations, and was conscious of having begun the second volume of her life's novel. She went to bed in the elated frame of mind proper to a heroine. There was a shade over all in the absence of dear old Mrs. Nugent, and in Mary's deep mourning, but there is more tenderness than poignancy in sorrow for shocks of corn gathered in full season, and all was cheerful about her.

She had quite a triumph the next day, as old friends dropped in for the chance of seeing her. The least agreeable encounter was that with Mark, who came in on his way to the office, having just received by the second post a letter from his father inquiring into Miss Headworth's state. He met Nuttie in the vestibule, with her hat on, and in a great hurry, as she wanted to walk with Mary to the School of Art, Gerard Godfrey accompanying them as far as the office; and she did not at all like the being called to account, and asked what could have possessed her to take alarm.

'Why, you wrote yourself!'

'I!'

'To Annaple Ruthven.'

'What am I supposed to have written?'

'That Aunt Ursel was very ill with bronchitis.'

'I'll be bound that Miss Ruthven said no such thing. You don't pretend that you heard it from herself?'

'No; but Blanche did.'

'Blanche! Oh, that accounts for it! Though I should have thought you knew Blanche by this time.'

'But what did you say?'

'I believe I said I couldn't get a knitting pattern Miss Headworth was to send Lady Ronnisglen because she was in bed with a cold. What you and Blanche could contrive to make of a simple thing like that—'

'And Annaple!'

'Well,' but checking himself with a smile, 'we will not fight about that. I only hope it has not brought you into an awkward scrape, Nuttie.'

'I can't help that,' she answered with her head rather high.

'You have written and explained?' he said anxiously.

'To my mother, of course.'

'If I were you,' he said, lowering his voice, 'I should write or send a special message to your father.'

'I can't see why. It was a mistake.'

'Yours was a strong measure, and he won't like it. Be advised, Nuttie. Recollect your mother. The best way would be to go home at once. I could get a day to take you—if you would start this afternoon.'

'Thank you; I'm not going back till I hear,' she said proudly.

Time being up, Mark took his leave hastily, and as he shut the door, Nuttie uttered half aloud the words she had scarcely repressed, 'No, I thank you, Mr. Mark, I am not going back like a dog in a string.'

'What, was that what he expected of you?' said Gerard Godfrey, whom she had not intended to hear her, but who had come out of the sitting-room on the sounds of departure.

'He said he would take me home if I could go at once.'

'Wouldn't he have liked it!' exclaimed Gerard.

'It might be the best way,' said Miss Nugent, who had followed young Godfrey.

'Now, Miss Mary,' cried Nuttie, 'as if I could shorten my holiday now that I have it.'

'And I don't see what business he had to call you to account,' said Gerard. 'A stuck-up fellow.'

'Of course all the Egremonts are set against my being here,' said Nuttie.

'I thought the Canon offered to bring you last year,' said Mary gently.

'Oh, that was only to Monks Horton! It would have been simply tantalising.'

'Lady Kirkaldy is an excellent person,' said Miss Nugent.

'Is she at home now?' asked Ursula.

'Coming next week, they tell me,' said Gerard.

'He—your cousin—will always be loafing up there now, giving up all that he had undertaken, I suppose.'

'Not very likely,' said Mary quietly.

It is a mere Scottish anti-church influence,' said Gerard, turning round at the swing-door of his office. 'Why else will Egremont not take the pledge?'

Wherewith he disappeared, blue ribbon and all, while Mary smiled, though she was vexed; and Nuttie observed, 'Poor Gerard; but I can't see why he should be jealous of Mark *now*.'

Mary did not choose to understand what Nuttie implied in her simplicity, and made answer, 'He is rather blue ribbon mad. Besides, I am afraid the fact of being a "swell" does not conduce to your cousin's popularity among the clerks.'

'Surely he does not give himself airs,' said Ursula, her family feelings awaking.

'No; but I fancy he is rather reserved.'

'What's this about giving up what he has undertaken? What is it?'

'When Mr. Dutton went to London, he asked Mark to take his Sunday afternoons with the big lads. He thought they wanted some one with more resources and variety than there is in poor Gerard, who didn't at all like being passed over.'

'I never should have thought it of Mark. He never dreamt of teaching anybody at home.'

'Very likely not, but there is an atmosphere at St. Ambrose's.'

'And oh, how glad I am to be in it! I wonder how long they will let me stay! The dear little mother will try to get me a Sunday here, if she dares. Indeed, I can't hear before Saturday, and then there would hardly be time to get home! Oh, that's jolly! I'll go to the nursery gardens, and get *such* flowers for the vases!'

Saturday brought Nuttie a letter, but not from her mother—

> 'My Dear Ursula—I write because we are anxious to keep your mother as quiet as possible. It was a serious shock to her to find that you had left home, and she naturally supposed that Miss Headworth was in great danger. Your father was greatly displeased, and she has been much overcome, and very unwell, but we hope by keeping her perfectly quiet that worse consequences may be prevented. Your father desires you to remain where you are for the present, as he will not have her disturbed again. Your mother sends her love both to you and to your aunt, and desires me to say that she will write in a day or two, and that she thinks you had better not come back till she is better and your father's vexation has diminished.
>
> 'I wish you had informed us of your intentions, as then we could have ascertained the grounds of the report that terrified you so strangely.—I remain your affectionate aunt,
>
> JANE M. EGREMONT.'

'Poor mother! he has been sneering at us all in his dreadful cynical way, and knocked her up into one of her awful headaches,' said Nuttie, who felt extremely angered by the grave tone of rebuke in the letter, and tossed it over to her aunt without absolutely reading it all. Miss Headworth was a good deal distressed, and anxious to know what Mrs. William Egremont meant; but Nuttie positively declared, 'Oh, it is her headaches! You know she always had them more or less, and they have grown a great deal worse since she has taken to sitting in that horrid, stuffy, perfumy, cigar-ry room, and doesn't take half exercise enough.'

And when Miss Headworth showed herself much concerned about the state of things, Nuttie coaxed her, and declared that she should fancy herself unwelcome, and have to go and beg a lodging somewhere instead of enjoying her reprieve. And Aunt Ursel was far less impervious to coaxing than she used to be when she was the responsible head of a boarding house. She did most thoroughly enjoy the affection of her great niece, and could not persuade herself to be angry with her, especially when the girl looked up smiling and said, 'If the worst came to the worst and he did disinherit me, the thing would only right itself. I always meant to give it back to Mark.'

No great aunt in the world could fail to admire the generous spirit of the girl who came back from the great world of luxury, so loving and happy in her humble surroundings. The only sighs were for poor Alice, in the hands of a man of whom Miss Headworth knew so much evil. If she were not wretched and a victim—and Nuttie did not think her such—she must surely be getting spoilt and worldly. Her daughter implied fears of this kind, yet who could read her letters and think so?

Nuttie was fortunately too much in awe of the Canoness to write all the pertnesses that tingled at her fingers' ends, and she sent a proper and fairly meek letter, intimating, however, that she was only too happy to remain at Micklethwayte.

It was two or three days more before she heard again.

'My Own Dear Child—They have let me write at last, and I can say how much I like to think of your nestling up to dear Aunt Ursel, and how glad I am to find that she was well enough to enjoy you. It is almost like being there to hear of you, and the only thing that grieves me is that your father was very much vexed at your setting off in that sudden way, and at my being so foolish about it. His eyes have been very bad, and he missed me sadly while I was laid up. We are neither of us very strong, and we think—if Aunt Ursel and Mary can keep you for a little longer —it will be better for you to stay on with them, as it might be as dreary for you as it was last winter, especially as the Rectory folk will soon be going into residence. I will write to them about it and persuade them to take something for your board, so as to make it easy for them. And then you can have a fire in your room; you must not leave it off now you are used to it. My dear, I wish you would write a little apology to your father. I ought not to conceal that he is really very angry, and I think it would be well if you expressed some regret, or if you cannot truthfully do that, asked his pardon for your impetuosity; for you know he cannot be expected to realise all that dear Aunt Ursel is to us. You cannot think how kind your Aunt Jane has been to me; I did not think she could have been so tender. This is the first letter I ever had to write to you, my own dear child. I miss you every moment, but after all it is better you should be away till your father has overlooked this hurried expedition of yours. I am sure he would if you wrote him a real nice letter, telling how you were really frightened, and that it was not a mere excuse. Pray do, and then you can come back to your loving little mother.

'A. E.'

'As if I would or could,' quoth Nuttie to herself. 'Apologise to him indeed, for loving the aunt who toiled for us when he deserted us. Poor little mother, she can't really expect it of me. Indeed, I don't think she quite knows what she wants, or whether she likes me to be here or at Bridgefield! My belief is that he bullies her less when I am out of the way, because she just gives way to him, and does not assert any principle. I've tried to back her up, and it is of no use, and I am sure I don't want such a winter as the last. So I am much better here; and as to begging pardon, when I have done nothing wrong, I am sure I won't, to please anybody. I shall tell her that she ought to know me better than to expect it!'

But Nuttie did not show the letter either to Aunt Ursel or Mary Nugent; nor did she see that in which Alice had satisfied them that it might be better that her daughter should pay them a long visit, while Mr. Egremont's health required constant attendance, and the Canon's family were at Redcastle. And as her husband was always open-handed, she could make Ursula's stay with them advantageous to their slender means, without hurting their feelings.

She told them as much as she could, but there was more that no living creature might know, namely, the advantage that Gregorio had gained over that battlefield, his master, during her days of illness. The first cold weather had brought on pain, and anger and anxiety, nervous excitement and sleeplessness, which the valet had taken upon him to calm with a narcotic under a new name that at first deceived her till she traced its effects, and inquired of Dr. Hammond about it. Unwillingly, on her account, he enlightened her, and showed her that, though the last year's care had done much to loosen the bonds of the subtle and alluring habit, yet that any resumption of it tended to plunge its victim into the fatal condition of the confirmed opium-eater, giving her every hope at the same time that this propensity might be entirely shaken off, and that the improvement in Mr. Egremont's health and habits which had set in might be confirmed, and raise him above the inclination.

Could she have been rid of Gregorio, she would have felt almost sure of victory; but as it was, she believed the man absolutely meant to baffle her, partly out of a spiteful rivalry, partly because his master's torpid indolence could be used to his own advantage. She was absolutely certain that his sneering tone of remark made her husband doubly disinclined to let any religious book be near, or to permit her to draw him to any Sunday observance.

The battle must be fought out alone. The gentle woman could have no earthly helper in the struggle. The Canon and Mark, the only persons who could have given her the slightest aid, were both at a distance, even if her loyal heart could have brooked confession to them, and she only hoped that Nuttie would never know of it. Only aid from above could be with her in the daily, hourly effort of cheerfulness, patience, and all the resources of feminine affection, to avert the temptation; and she well knew that the presence of the ardent, unsubdued, opinionative girl would, alas! only double the difficulties. So she acquiesced, at least for the present, in Nuttie's grand achievement of having broken away from all the wealth and luxury of Bridgefield to return to her simple home and good old aunt. Mark was a good deal vexed, but Nuttie did not care about that, attributing this displeasure to Egremont clanship; Mary Nugent was doubtful and anxious, and thought it her duty to reconcile herself to her father; but Miss Headworth, who, be it remembered, had reason to have the worst impressions of Mr. Egremont, rejoiced in her young niece having escaped from him for the time, and only sighed over the impossibility of Alice's doing the same. And when Nuttie described, as she constantly did, the various pleasures she had enjoyed during the past year, the good old lady secretly viewed her as a noble Christian heroine for resigning all this in favour of the quiet little home at Micklethwayte, though reticent before her, and discussed her excellence whenever she was alone with Mary.

Nor would Miss Nugent vex her with contradictions or hints that what Nuttie was giving up at present might be a dull house, with her mother engrossed by an irritable semi-invalid, and the few gaieties to be enjoyed by the help of the Canon's family at Redcastle. She did ask the girl whether Mrs. Egremont, being avowedly not quite well, might not need her assistance; but Nuttie vehemently disavowed being of any possible use to her father; he never let her read to him! oh no! he called her music schoolgirly, a mere infliction; he never spoke to her if he could help it, and then it was always with a sort of sneer; she believed he could not bear the sight of her, and was ashamed of it, as well he might be! For Mrs. Houghton's disclosures had rankled ever since within her, and had been confirmed by her aunt.

'But that is very sad,' said Mary. 'I am so sorry for you. Ought you not to try hard to conquer his distaste?'

'I—why, he cares for nothing good!'

'Nay,' smiling. 'Not for your mother?'

'Oh! She's pretty, you know; besides, she makes herself a regular slave to him, and truckles to him in everything, as I could never do.'

'Perhaps she is overcoming evil with good.'

'I am afraid it is more like being overcome of evil. No, no, dear Miss Mary, don't be shocked. The dear little mother never would be anything but good in her own sweet self, but it is her nature not to stand up for anything, you know. She seems to me just like a Christian woman that has been obliged to marry some Paynim knight. And it perfectly provokes me to see her quite gratified at his notice, and ready to sacrifice anything to him, now I know how he treated her. If I had been in her place, I wouldn't have gone back to him; no, not if he had been ready to crown me after I was dead, like Ines de Castro.'

'I don't know that you would have had much choice in that case.'

'My very ghost would have rebelled,' said Nuttie, laughing a little.

And Mary could believe that Mrs. Egremont, with all her love for her daughter, might find it a relief not to have to keep the peace between the father and child. 'Yet,' she said to herself, 'if Mr. Dutton were here, he would have taken her back the first day.'

CHAPTER XXII.

DISENCHANTMENT.

'He promised to buy me a bunch of blue ribbons.'

St. Ambrose's road was perfectly delightful as long as there was any expectation of a speedy recall. Every day was precious; every meeting with an old face was joyful; each interchange of words with Mr. Spyers or Gerard Godfrey was hailed as a boon; nothing was regretted but the absence of Monsieur and his master, and that the favourite choir boy's voice was cracked.

But when there was reason to think that success had been complete, when Miss Headworth had been persuaded by Mary that it was wiser on all accounts not to mortify Alice by refusing the two guineas a week offered for Miss Egremont's expenses; when a couple of boxes of clothes and books had arrived, and Ursula found herself settled at Micklethwayte till after Christmas, she began first to admit to herself that somehow the place was not all that it had once been to her.

Her mother was absent, that was one thing. Mrs. Nugent was gone, that was another. There was no Monsieur or Mr. Dutton to keep her in awe of his precision, even while she laughed at it. There were no boarders to patronise and play with, and her education at the High School was over. If she saw a half-clothed child, it was not half so interesting to buy an ulster in the next shop, as it was to turn over the family rag-bag, knit, sew, and contrive!

Somehow things had a weariness in them, and the little excitements did not seem to be the exquisite delights they used to be. After having seen Patience at the Princess's it was not easy to avoid criticising a provincial Lady Jane, and it was the like with other things of more importance. Even the ritual of St. Ambrose's Church no longer struck her as the ne plus ultra of beauty, and only incited her to describe London churches.

She resumed her Sunday-school classes, and though she talked at first of their raciness and freedom, she soon longed after the cleanliness, respectfulness, and docility of the despised little Bridgefordites, and uttered bitter things of Micklethwayte turbulence, declaring—perhaps not without truth—that the children had grown much worse in her absence.

And as Mr. Godfrey had been superintendent during the latter half of the time, this was a cruel stroke. He wanted to make her reverse her opinions. And they never met without 'Now, Ursula, don't you remember Jem Burton putting on Miss Pope's spectacles, and grinning at all the class.'

'Yes; and how Mr. Dutton brought him up to beg her pardon. Now, was any notice taken when that horrid boy—I don't know his name—turned the hymn they were saying to her into "Tommy, make room for your uncle"?'

'Oh, Albert Cox! It is no use doing anything to him, he would go off at once to the Primitives.'

'Let him!'

'I cannot make him a schismatic.'

'I wonder what he is now!'

'Besides, Miss Pope perfectly provokes impertinence.'

'Then I wouldn't give her work she can't do.'

Such an argument as this might be very well at the moment of provocation, but it became tedious when recurred to at every meeting. Nuttie began to wonder when Monks Horton would be inhabited again, and how much notice Lady Kirkaldy would take of her, and she was a good deal disappointed when Mark told her that Lord Kirkaldy had been begged to undertake a diplomatic mission which would keep them abroad all the winter.

There was a certain weariness and want of interest. It was not exactly that there was nothing intellectual going on. There were the lectures, but they were on chemistry, for which Nuttie cared little. There were good solid books, and lively ones too, but they seemed passe to one who had heard them discussed in town. Mary and Miss Headworth read and talked them over, and perhaps their opinions were quite as wise, and Miss Nugent's conversation was equal to that of any of Nuttie's London friends, but it was only woman's talk after all—the brilliancy and piquancy, the touch and go, she had enjoyed in Lady Kirkaldy's drawing-room was lacking.

Mr. Spyers was too much immersed in parish matters to read anything secular, and neither he nor Gerard Godfrey seemed ever to talk of anything but parish matters. There was not the slightest interest in anything beyond. Foreign politics, European celebrities,—things in which Nuttie had learnt to take warm interest when with the Kirkaldys, were nothing to them. Even Mary wondered at her endeavours to see the day's paper, and she never obtained either information or sympathy unless she came across Mark. It seemed to her that Gerard cared less for the peace or war of an empire than for a tipsy cobbler taking the pledge. The monotony and narrowness of the world where she had once been so happy fretted and wearied her, though she was ashamed of herself all the time, and far too proud to allow that she was tired of it all. Aunt Ursel at her best had always been a little dry and grave, an authority over the two nieces; and though softened, she was not expansive, did not invite confidences, and home was not home without the playfellow- mother.

And most especially was she daily tired of Gerard Godfrey! Had he always talked of nothing but 'the colours,' chants, E. C. U., classes, and teetotalism? Whatever she began it always came back to one or other of these subjects, and when she impatiently declared that she was perfectly sick of hearing of the Use of Sarum, he looked at her as guilty of a profanity.

Perhaps it was true that he was narrower than he had been. He was a good, honest, religiously-minded lad, but with no great depth or grasp of intellect; Ursula Egremont had been his companion first and then his romance, and the atmosphere of the community in which he lived had been studious and intelligent. His expedition to Redcastle had convinced him that the young lady lived in a different world, entirely beyond his reach, and in the reaction of his hopelessness, he had thrown himself into the excitement of the mission, and it had worked on him a zealous purpose to dedicate himself totally to a religious life, giving up all worldly aims, and employing the small capital he could call his own in preparing for the ministry. Mr. Dutton had insisted that he should test his own steadfastness and resolution by another year's work in his present situation before he took any steps.

He had submitted, but still viewed himself as dedicated, and so far as business hours permitted, gave his services like a clerical pupil to St. Ambrose's with the greatest energy, and perhaps somewhat less judgment than if Mr. Dutton had been at hand. Being without natural taste for intellectual pursuits, unless drawn into them by his surroundings, he had dropped them entirely, and read nothing but the ephemeral controversial literature of his party, and not much of that, for he was teaching, preaching, exhorting, throughout his spare time; while the vicar was in too great need of help to insist on deepening the source from which his zealous assistant drew. As Miss Nugent observed, teetotalism was to him what dissipation was to other young men.

On this vehemence of purpose descended suddenly Ursula Egremont once more; and the human heart could not but be quickened with the idea, not entirely unfounded, that it was to him that she had flown back, and that her exile proved that she cared for him more than for all the delights she had enjoyed as heiress of Bridgefield. The good youth was conscientious to the back-bone, and extremely perplexed between his self-dedication and the rights that their implied understanding might give to her. Was she to be the crowning blessing of his life, to be saved partly through his affection from worldly trials and temptations, and bestowing on him a brilliant lot in which boundless good could be effected? Or was she a syren luring him to abandon his higher and better purposes?

The first few days of her stay, the former belief made him feel like treading on air, or like the hero of many a magazine story; but as time went on this flattering supposition began to fail him, when Nuttie showed her weariness of the subjects which, in his exclusiveness, he deemed the only ones worthy of a Christian, or rather of a Catholic. Both of them had outgrown the lively, aimless chatter and little jests that had succeeded the games of childhood, and the growth had been in different directions, so that Ursula felt herself untrue to her old romance when she became weary of his favourite topics, disappointed by his want of sympathy and comprehension, fretted by his petty disapprovals, and annoyed by his evident distaste for Mark, to whom she turned as to one of her proper world.

At last, after many tossings, Gerard fixed upon a test. If she endured it she would be the veritable maiden of his imagination, and they would stand by one another, come what would; if not, he would believe that the past had been fancy, not love, or love that had not withstood the attractions of fashionable life. A great temperance meeting was coming on, and Gerard, eager at once to fill the room, and to present a goodly roll of recruits, watched anxiously for his moment, and came on Nuttie with his hands full of bills in huge letters, and his pockets of badges.

'Excellent speakers,' he cried. 'We shall have the hall crowded. You'll come, Ursula?'

'I don't know what Miss Mary will do. I don't think she means it.'

'Oh, if you insist, if we both insist, she will. Look at the paper—we are to have some splendid experiences.'

Nuttie made a face. 'I've heard all about those,' she said. 'That man,' pointing to one of the names, 'regularly rants about it; he is like a madman.'

'He does go rather far, but it is quite necessary, as you will hear. Oh, Nuttie, if you would only be one of us! I've brought a card! If you would!'

'Why, what's the use, Gerard! I don't like wine, I never do drink it, except a little claret-cup sometimes when I can't get water.'

'Then it would cost you nothing.'

'Yes, it would. It would make me ridiculous.'

'You used not to heed the sneers of the world.'

'Not for anything worth doing—but this is not.'

'It is the greatest cause of the day!' he cried, in an eager exalted manner, which somewhat inclined her to laugh. 'Do away with alcohol and you would do away with crime!'

'Thank you for the compliment, Gerard; I never found that the infinitesimal drop of alcohol that I suppose there is in a tumbler of claret-cup disposed me to commit crimes.'

'Why won't you understand me, Ursula! Can't you give up that for the sake of saving others!'

'I wonder whom it would save.'

'Example saves! If you put on this'—taking out the badge 'how many should you not lead at your home?'

'Just nobody! Mother and I should have a bad time of it, that's all.'

'And if you endured, what would not your testimony effect in the household and village?'

'Nothing! I have nothing to do with the men-servants, and as to the village, it is very sober. There's only one public house, and that is kept by Uncle William's old butler, and is as orderly as can be.'

'Ah! that's the way you all deceive yourselves. Moderate drinkers are ten times more mischievous than regular drunkards.'

'Thank you, Gerard! And outrageous abstainers are more mischievous than either of them, because they make the whole thing so utterly foolish and absurd.' She was really angry now, and so was Gerard.

'Is that your ultimatum?' he asked, in a voice that he strove to render calm.

'Certainly; I'm not going to take the pledge.'

Having quarrelled in childhood, made quarrelling now easier, and Gerard answered bitterly:

'Very well, I hope you will have no cause to repent it.'

''Tis not the way to make me repent it, to see how it seems to affect some people's common sense. It is just as if all your brains had run to water!' said Nuttie, laughing a little; but Gerard was desperately serious, and coloured vehemently.

'Very well, Miss Egremont, I understand. I have had my answer,' he said, gathering up his papers and marching out of the room.

She stood still, offended, and not in the least inclined to run after him and take back her words. He, poor fellow, stumbled down the steps, and held by the garden rail to collect his senses and compose himself.

'What's the matter, Gerard, are you ill or giddy?' asked Miss Nugent, coming up in the winter twilight.

'No, oh no! Only the dream of my life is over,' he answered, scarce knowing what he said.

'You haven't—' cried Mary aghast.

'Oh no,' he said, understanding the blank, 'only she won't take the pledge!'

'I don't see how she could or ought,' responded Mary. 'Is that all?'

'I had made it the test,' muttered poor Gerard. 'It is right! It is all over now. I shall know how to go on my way. It is best so—I know it is—only I did not know whether anything was due to her.' It was almost a sob.

'Dear old Gerard,' said Mary, 'I see you meant to do right. It is well your mind should be settled. I think you'll find comfort in your good work.'

He wrung her hand, and she went in, half amused, for she was fully aware of the one-sidedness of the mania for temperance under which he acted, yet honouring his high, pure motives, and rejoicing that he had found this indirect mode of gauging Nuttie's feelings towards him—that is, if he was right about them, and there was no revulsion.

Far from it. Nuttie was still angry. 'Gerard had been so ridiculous,' she said, 'teasing her to take the pledge, and quite incapable of understanding her reasons. I can't think why Gerard has grown so stupid.'

'Enthusiasms carry people away,' returned Mary.

'If Mr. Dutton had only stayed, he would have kept Gerard like himself,' said Nuttie.

But there was no relenting. The two young people avoided each other; and perhaps Nuttie was secretly relieved that the romance she had outgrown no longer entangled her.

CHAPTER XXIII.

A FAILURE.

'Would I had loved her more!'—Mrs. Hemans.

'On the 14th of January, at Bridgefield Egremont, the wife of Alwyn Piercefield Egremont, Esquire, a son and heir.'

Ursula had been prepared for this event for about a fortnight by a long tender letter from her mother, mourning over the not meeting at Christmas, and the long separation, but saying that she had wished to spare the long anxiety, and that it had been a trying time which she felt herself able to cope with better alone, than even with her dear Nuttie, knowing her to be happy and safe with Aunt Ursel. Now, if all went well, they would have a happy meeting, and begin on a new score. 'If the will of God should be otherwise,' added Alice, 'I am sure I need not entreat my Nuttie to do and be all that she can to her father. My child, you do not know how sorely he needs such love and tendance and prayer as you can give him. I know you have thought I have set you aside—if not better things, for his sake. Indeed I could not help it.' Then there was something tear-stained and blotted out, and it ended with, 'He is beginning to miss your step and voice about the house. I believe he will really be glad to see you, when the bright spring days come, and I can kiss my own Nuttie again.'

Nuttie was very much delighted, but a little hurt that her aunt and Mary should have been in the secret, and pledged to say nothing to her till her mother should write. She found, moreover, that Miss Headworth was extremely anxious and not altogether reassured by Mrs. William Egremont's letter of announcement, which filled Nuttie with delight. How happy the little mother must be to have a baby in her arms again, and though she herself did not profess to have a strong turn for infant humanity, it was the greatest possible relief to be no longer an heiress, excepting that the renunciation in favour of Mark was no longer practicable.

The residence at Redcastle was not over, but the Canoness had come to nurse her sister-in-law, and kept up the correspondence. The son and heir was reported to be a perfect specimen, and his father was greatly elated and delighted, but the letters showed anxiety about the mother, who did not get on as she ought, and seemed to have no power of rally about her. At length came a letter that seemed to burn itself into Nuttie's brain—

'My Dear Ursula—Your mother is longing to see you. You had better come home directly. Your aunt saved her before. Tell her if she will come, she shall have my deepest gratitude. I shall send to meet the 5.11 train.—Your affectionate father,

A. P. EGREMONT.'

Mrs. William Egremont wrote at more length. Symptoms had set in which filled the doctors and nurses with double anxiety. Advice had been sent for from London, and Mr. Egremont was in an uncontrollable state of distress. She had undertaken to summon Ursula home, and to beg Miss Headworth to undertake the journey. She evidently did not know that her brother-in-law had written himself, and before they could start a telegram terrified them, but proved to contain no fresh tidings, only a renewed summons.

Miss Headworth forgot all her resolutions about Mr. Egremont's hospitality—her Alice was her only thought, and all the remedies that had been found efficacious at Dieppe. The good lady had a certain confidence in her own nursing and experience of Alice, which buoyed her up with hope, while Ursula seemed absolutely stunned. She had never thought of such a frightful loss or grief, and her mental senses were almost paralysed, so that she went through the journey in a kind of surface trance, observing all around her much as usual, looking out for the luggage and for the servant who had come to meet them with the report 'No change.' She did the honours of the carriage, and covered Miss Headworth with the fur rug. They wanted it, for they were shivering with anxiety.

Canon Egremont came out to the front hall to meet them, and put his arms round Nuttie tenderly, saying, 'My poor dear child!' then as he saw he had frightened them, 'No, no! She is alive—conscious they say, only so very weak.' Then with something of his usual urbane grace, he held out his hand, 'Miss Headworth, it is very good in you to come. You have a great deal to forgive.'

He took them into the tent-room, where tea was standing, interrupting himself in the account he was giving to bid Nuttie let her aunt have some. It was plain from his manner that he had given up hope, and in another minute in hurried his brother, looking terribly haggard and with bloodshot eyes, giving his hand to each, with, 'That's right, Miss Headworth, thank you. Come, let me know what you think of her!'

'Does she know they are come?' said the Canon. 'No? Then, Alwyn, let them have some tea, and take off their things. I can tell you, the nurses will never let them in just off a journey.'

Miss Headworth seconded this, and Mr. Egremont submitted, allowing that she had not asked for Nuttie since the morning, and then had smiled and squeezed his hand when he said she was coming with her aunt; but he walked up and down in direful restlessness, his whole mind apparently bent on extracting from Miss Headworth that she had been as ill or worse at Dieppe.

Alas! when Mrs. William Egremont came down to fetch Nuttie; there was no question that matters were much worse. The sweet face was perfectly white and wasted, and the heavy lids of the dark eyes scarcely lifted themselves, but the lips moved into a smile, and the hand closed on that of the girl, who stood by her as one frozen into numbness. There was the same recognition when her aunt was brought to her side, the poor old lady commanding herself with difficulty, as the loving glance quivered over the face.

Time passed on, and she still held Nuttie's hand. Once, when a little revived by some stimulant at her lips, she made an effort and said, 'Stay with him! Take care of him! *Love* him! And your little brother, my Nuttie! Promise!'

'I promise,' the girl answered, scarce knowing what she said.

And the eyes closed with an air of peace and rest.

Again when Miss Headworth was doing something to ease her position she said, 'Thank you,' and then more vigorously, 'Thank you, dear aunt, for all you have been to us.'

There was little more. She asked Nuttie for 'her hymn,' the evening hymn with which mother and daughter used nightly to go to sleep, and which, in her strange dreamy way, the girl managed to say.

Then a little murmur and sign passed between the elder ladies, and Mrs. William Egremont fetched her husband. As he opened his book to find the commendatory prayer, thinking her past all outward consciousness, and grieved by the look of suffering, her eyes again unclosed and her lips said,

'Failed.'

'Don't think of that! God can make failures success.'

There was a half smile, a look of peace. '*He* makes up,' she said; and those were the last audible words before it was over, and the tender spirit was released from its strife, some time later, they only knew when by the failure of the clasp on her husband's hand.

Old Miss Headworth did not understand the meaning of that sad word till the next forenoon. Then,—as she sat in the darkened tent-room, crying over her letters,—while the stunned and bewildered Nuttie was, under her Aunt Jane's direction, attending to the needful arrangements, Canon Egremont wandered in upon her in the overflow of confidence of a man with a full heart, wanting to talk it all out, communicating the more, because she was a discreet woman, and asked no questions. He had tried to see his brother, but Gregorio had not admitted him. He was aware now of the whole state of things. Dr. Hammond had told him, when first beginning to be alarmed for his patient, that the principal cause for anxiety was the exhaustion caused by the long strain on her spirits and strength consequent on her efforts to wean her husband from his fatal propensity. There had been other 'complications,' as the doctor called them, and more immediate causes of danger, but both he and his colleague, summoned from London, believed that she would have surmounted them if she had had more strength to rally. But her nurses dated the decided turn for the worse from the day when she had gazed up into Mr. Egremont's face, and detected the look in his eyes that she had learnt too well to understand.

She would fain have lived, and, according to her obedient nature, had submitted to all the silence and stillness enforced on her; but she had told Dr. Hammond that she must see her brother-in-law before she was too far gone. And the doctor, knowing all, took care it should be brought about.

And then she had spoken of her failure in the effort of these years. 'If I had begun better,' she said, 'it might not have been so with him.'

'My dear, indeed you have nothing to blame yourself for. You were grievously sinned against by us all. Alwyn was no saint when he drew you into it—and you, you have been his good angel, doing all and more too,' said the Canon, almost breaking down.

'I tried—but if I had been a better woman—And to leave him to that man!'

'Child, child, victories sometimes come this way!' he cried, scarce knowing how it was put into his mouth, but glad to see the light in her eye.

'Thanks,' she replied. 'No, I ought not to have said that. I leave him to

God, and my poor Nuttie. I want you to tell her, if I can't, what she must try to do. If I had but brought them together more! But I tried for the best.'

Then she begged for her last communion, saying, 'I do pray for that poor Gregorio. Isn't that forgiving him?' And the attempt to exchange forgiveness with the Canon for their mutual behaviour at the time of her marriage overcame them both so much that they had to leave it not half uttered. Indeed, in speaking of the scene, William Egremont was utterly overwhelmed.

'And that's the woman that I treated as a mere outcast!' he cried, walking about the little room. 'Oh God, forgive me! I shall never forgive myself.'

Poor Miss Headworth! In past days she had longed for any amount of retribution on Alice's hard-hearted employers, but it was a very different thing to witness such grief and self reproach. He had in truth much more developed ideas of duty, both as man and priest, than when he had passively left a disagreeable subject to his mother-in-law, as lying within a woman's province; and his good heart was suffering acutely for the injustice and injury in which he had shared towards one now invested with an almost saintly halo.

In the gush of feeling he had certainly revealed more to Miss Headworth, than his wife, or even he himself, in his cooler moments, would have thought prudent, and he ended by binding her to secrecy; and saying that he should only tell his niece what was necessary for her to know.

Nuttie was going about, dry-eyed and numbed, glad of any passing occupation that would prevent the aching sense of desolation at her heart from gaining force to overwhelm her; courting employment, and shunning pity and condolence, but she could not escape when her uncle took her hand, made her sit down by him, with 'I want to speak to you, my dear;' and told her briefly and tenderly what her mother's effort had been, and of the message and task she had bequeathed. The poor girl's heart fainted within her.

'Oh! but, Uncle William, how can I? How can I ever? Mother could do things I never could! He *did* care for her! He does not care for me!'

'You must teach him to do so, Nuttie.'

'Oh!' she said, with a hopeless sound.

The Canon did think it very hopeless in his heart, but he persevered, as in duty bound. 'I told your dear mother that perhaps you would succeed where she thought she had failed, though indeed she had done much. It made her happy. So, my dear child, you are bound to do your best.'

'Yes;' then, after a pause—'But mother could coax him and manage him. Mother was with him day and night; she could always get at him. What can I do?'

'I think you will find that he depends upon you more,' said the Canon, 'and it may be made easier to you, if you only set your will to it.'

'If I ought, I'll try,' said poor Nuttie, more humbly perhaps than she had ever spoken before, but in utter dejection, and her uncle answered her like a child.

'There, that's a good girl. Nobody can do more.'

For the Canon had one hope. He had not thought it becoming to speak to her of the counter influence, but he could not help thinking it possible that if he and his son, backed by doctor and lawyer, made a long pull, a strong pull, and a pull altogether, they might induce his brother to part with Gregorio, and this would render Ursula's task far less impossible.

He was confirmed in this hope by finding that Mark's arrival was not unwelcome to Mr. Egremont, who seemed to have forgotten the unpleasantness with which he had regarded the engagement, and only remembered that his nephew had been Alice's champion, resuming old customs of dependence, making him act as amanuensis, and arraigning the destiny that had restored so lovely and charming a creature only to snatch her away, leaving nothing but a headstrong girl and a helpless baby.

That poor little fellow was all that could be desired at his age, but Nuttie felt her beautiful mother almost insulted when the elder ladies talked of the wonderful resemblance that the Canoness declared to have been quite startling in the earlier hours of his life. For the convenience of one of the sponsors, he was to be christened in the afternoon following the funeral, the others being— by his mother's special entreaty—his sister and Mark. Egremont customs were against the ladies going to the funeral, so that Nuttie was kept at home, much against her will; but after the luncheon she escaped, leaving word with her aunts that she was going to walk down to church alone, and they were sorry enough for her to let her have her own way, especially as her father, having been to the funeral, had shut himself up and left all the rest to them.

The Egremont family had a sort of enclosure or pen with iron rails round it close to the church wall, where they rested under flat slabs. The gate in this was open now, and the new-made grave was one mass of white flowers,— wreaths and crosses, snowdrops, hyacinths, camellias, and the like,—and at the feet was a flowerpot with growing plants of the white hyacinth called in France 'lys de la Vierge.' These, before they became frequent in England, had been grown in Mr. Dutton's greenhouse, and having been favourites with Mrs. Egremont, it had come to be his custom every spring to bring her the earliest plants that bloomed. Nuttie knew them well, the careful tying up, the neat arrangement of moss over the earth, the peculiar trimness of the whole; and as she looked, the remembrance of the happy times of old, the sick longing for all that was gone, did what nothing had hitherto effected—brought an overwhelming gush of tears.

There was no checking them now that they had come. She fled into church on the first sounds of arrival and hid herself in the friendly shelter of the great family pew; but she had to come out and take her place, though she could hardly utter a word, and it was all that she could do to keep from sobbing aloud; she could not hand the babe, and the Canon had to take on trust the name 'Alwyn Headworth,' for he could not hear the words that were on her trembling lips.

It was soon over; and while the baby and his attendants, with Miss Headworth, were being packed into the carriage, and her uncle and aunt bowing off the grand god-father, she clutched her cousin's arm, and said, 'Mark; where's Mr. Dutton?'

'I—I didn't know he was coming, but now you ask, I believe I saw him this morning.'

'I know he is here.'

'Do you want to see him?' said Mark kindly.

'Oh, if I might!'

Then, with a sudden impulse, she looked back into the church, and recognised a black figure and slightly bald head bowed down in one of the seats. She pointed him out. 'No doubt he is waiting for us all to be gone,' said Mark in a low voice. 'You go into the Rectory, Nuttie; there's a fire in the study, and I'll bring him to you there. I'll get him to stay the night if I can.'

'Oh, thank you!' and it was a really fervent answer.

Mark waited, and when Mr. Dutton rose, was quite shocked at his paleness and the worn look on his face, as of one who had struggled hard for resignation and calm. He started, almost as if a blow had been struck him, as Mark uttered his name in the porch, no doubt having never meant to be perceived nor to have to speak to any one; but in one moment his features had recovered their usual expression of courteous readiness. He bowed his head when Mark told him that Ursula wanted to shake hands with him, and came towards the Rectory, but he entirely declined the invitation to sleep there, declaring that he must return to London that night.

Mark opened the study door, and then went away to secure that the man whom he had learnt to esteem very highly should at least have some refreshment before he left the house.

Those few steps had given Mr. Dutton time to turn from a mourner to a consoler, and when Nuttie came towards him with her hand outstretched, and 'Oh, Mr. Dutton, Mr. Dutton!' he took it in both his, and with a calm broken voice said, 'God has been very good to us in letting us know one like her.'

'But oh! what can we do without her?'

'Ah, Nuttie! that always comes before us. But I saw your work and your comfort just now.'

'Poor little boy! I shall get to care about him, I know, but as yet I can only feel how much rather I would have *her*.'

'No doubt, but it is *her* work that is left you.'

'Her work? Yes! But oh, Mr. Dutton, you don't know how dreadful it is!'

He did not know what she meant. Whether it was simply the burthen on any suddenly motherless girl, or any special evil on her father's part, but he was soon enlightened, for there was something in this old friend that drew out her confidence beyond all others, even when he repressed her, and she could not help telling him in a few murmured furtive words such as she knew she ought not to utter, and he felt it almost treason to hear. 'Opiates! she was always trying to keep my father from them! It was too much for her! My uncle says I must try to do it, and I can't.'

'Poor child!' said Mr. Dutton kindly, though cut to the heart at the revelation of sweet Alice's trial; 'at least you can strive, and there is always a blessing on resolution.'

'Oh, if you knew! and he doesn't like me. I don't think I've ever been nice to him, and that vexed her! I haven't got her ways.'

'No,' said Mr. Dutton, 'but you will learn others. Look here, Nuttie. You used to be always craving for grand and noble tasks, the more difficult the better. I think you have got one now, more severe than ever could have been thought of—and very noble. What are those lines about the task "bequeathed from bleeding sire to son"? Isn't it like that? You are bound to go on with her work, and the more helpless you feel, and the more you throw yourself on God, the more God will help you. He takes the will for the deed, if only you have will enough; and, Nuttie, you can pray that you may be able to love and honour him.'

Teacups were brought in, followed by Mark, and interrupted them; and, after a short interval, they parted at the park gate, and Ursula walked home with Mark, waked from her dull numb trance, with a crushed feeling as if she had been bruised all over, and yet with a purpose within her.

CHAPTER XXIV.

FARMS OR UMBRELLAS.

'He tokin into his handis
His londis and his lode.'—CHAUCER.

'Mark! Mark!' A little figure stood on the gravel road leading through Lescombe Park, and lifted up an eager face, as Mark jumped down from his horse. 'I made sure you would come over.'

'Yes, but I could not get away earlier. And I have so much to say to you and your mother, Annaple; there's a great proposition to be considered.'

'Oh dear! and here is John bearing down upon us. Never mind. We'll get into the mither's room and be cosy!'

'Well, Mark,' said Sir John's hearty voice, 'I thought you would be here. Come to luncheon? That's right! And how is poor Egremont? I thought he looked awful at the funeral.'

'He is fairly well, thank you; but it was a terrible shock.'

'I should think so. To find such a pretty sweet creature just to lose her again. Child likely to live, eh?'

'Oh yes, he is a fine fellow, and has never had anything amiss with him.'

'Poor little chap! Doesn't know what he has lost! Well, Nannie,' as they neared the house, 'do you want a tete-a-tete or to take him in to your mother? Here, I'll take the horse.'

'Come to her at once,' said Annaple; 'she wants to hear all, and besides she is expecting me.'

Mark was welcomed by Lady Ronnisglen with inquiries for all concerned, and especially for that 'poor girl. I do pity a young thing who has to take a woman's place too soon,' she said. 'It takes too much out of her!'

'I should think Ursula had plenty of spirit,' said Annaple.

'I don't know whether spirit is what is wanted,' said Mark. 'Her mother prevailed more without it than I am afraid she is likely to do with it.'

'Complements answer better than parallels sometimes, but not always,' said Lady Ronnisglen.

'Which are we?' asked Annaple demurely.

'Not parallels certainly, for then we should never meet,' responded Mark. 'But here is the proposal. My father and all the rest of us have been doing our best to get my uncle to smooth Ursula's way by getting rid of that valet of his.'

'The man with the Mephistopheles face?'

'Exactly. He is a consummate scoundrel, as we all know, and so does my uncle himself, but he has been about him these twelve or fourteen years, and has got a sort of hold on him—that—that— It is no use to talk of it, but it did not make that dear aunt of mine have an easier life. In fact I should not be a bit surprised if he had been a hindrance in the hunting her up. Well, the fellow thought proper to upset some arrangements my mother had made, and then was more insolent than I should have thought even he could have been towards her. I suppose he had got into the habit with poor Aunt Alice. That made a fulcrum, and my father went at my uncle with a will. I never saw my father so roused in my life. I don't mean by the behaviour to his wife, but at what he knew of the fellow, and all the harm he had done and is doing. And actually my uncle gave in at last, and consented to tell Gregorio to look out for another situation, if he has not feathered his nest too well to need one, as I believe he has.'

'Oh, that will make it much easier for Ursula!' cried Annaple.

'If he goes,' put in her mother.

'I think he will. I really had no notion how much these two years have improved my uncle! To be sure, it would be hard to live with such a woman as that without being the better for it! But he really seems to have acquired a certain notion of duty!'

They did not smile at the simple way in which Mark spoke of this vast advance, and Lady Ronnisglen said, 'I hope so, for the sake of his daughter and that poor little boy.'

'I think that has something to do with it,' said Mark. 'He feels a responsibility, and still more, I think he was struck by having a creature with him to whom evil was like physical pain.'

'It will work,' said Lady Ronnisglen.

'Then,' went on Mark, 'he took us all by surprise by making me this proposal—to take the management of the estate, and become a kind of private secretary to him. You know he gets rheumatism on the optic nerve, and is almost blind at times. He would give me £300 a year, and do up the house at the home farm, rent free. What do you say to that, Annaple?'

There was a silence, then Annaple said: 'Give up the umbrellas! Oh! What do you think, Mark?'

'My father wishes it,' said Mark. 'He would, as he had promised to do, make over to me my share of my own mother's fortune, and that would, I have been reckoning, bring us to just what we had thought of starting upon this spring at Micklethwayte.'

'The same now,' said Lady Ronnisglen, after some reckoning, 'but what does it lead to?'

'Well—nothing, I am afraid,' said Mark; 'as you know, this is all I have to reckon upon. The younger children will have hardly anything from their mother, so that my father's means must chiefly go to them.'

'And this agency is entirely dependent on your satisfying Mr. Egremont?'

'True, but that's a thing only too easily done. However, as you say, this agency has no future, and if that came to an end, I should only have to look out for another or take to farming.'

'And ask poor John if that is a good speculation nowadays!' said Annaple.

'Fortunes are and have been made on the umbrellas,' said Mark. 'Greenleaf has a place almost equal to Monks Horton, and Dutton, though he makes no show, has realised a considerable amount.'

'Oh yes, let us stick to the umbrellas!' cried Annaple; 'you've made the plunge, so it does not signify now, and we should be so much more independent out of the way of everybody.'

'You would lose in society,' said Mark, 'excepting, of course, as to the Monks Horton people; but they are often away.'

'Begging your pardon, Mark, is there much to lose in this same neighbourhood?' laughed Annaple, 'now May will go.'

'It is not so much a question of liking,' added her mother, 'as of what is for the best, and where you may wish to be—say ten years hence.'

Looked at in this way, there could be no question but that the umbrella company promised to make Mark a richer man in ten years' time than did the agency at Bridgefield Egremont. He had a salary from the office already, and if he purchased shares in the partnership with the portion his father would resign to him, his income would already equal what he would have at Bridgefield, and there was every prospect of its increase, both as he became more valuable, and as the business continued to prosper. If the descent in life had been a grievance to the ladies, the agency would have been an infinite boon, but having swallowed so much, as Annaple said, they might as well do it in earnest, and to some purpose. Perhaps, too, it might be detected that under the circumstances Annaple would prefer the living in a small way out of reach of her sister's visible compassion.

So the matter was settled, but there was an undercurrent in Mark's mind on which he had not entered, namely, that his presence at home might make all the difference in that reformation in his uncle's habits which Alice had inaugurated, and left in the hands of others. With him at hand, there was much more chance of Gregorio's being dispensed with, Ursula's authority maintained, little Alwyn well brought up, and the estate, tenants, and household properly cared for, and then he smiled at his notion of supposing himself of so much importance. Had he only had himself to consider, Mark would have thought his duty plain; but when he found Miss Ruthven and her mother so entirely averse, he did not deem it right to sacrifice them to the doubtful good of his uncle, nor indeed to put the question before them as so much a matter of conscience that they should feel bound to consider it in that light. He did indeed say, 'Well, that settles it,' in a tone that led Annaple to exclaim: 'I do believe you want to drop the umbrellas!'

'No,' he answered, 'it is not that, but my father wished it, and thought it would be good for my uncle.'

'No doubt,' said Annaple, 'but he has got a daughter, also a son, and a brother, and agents are plentiful, so I can't see why all the family should dance attendance on him.'

Lady Ronnisglen, much misdoubting Mr. Egremont's style of society, and dreading that Mark might be dragged into it, added her word, feeling on her side that it was desirable and just to hinder the family from sacrificing Mark's occupation and worldly interest to a capricious old roue, who might very possibly throw him over when it would be almost impossible to find anything else to do. Moreover, both she and Annaple believed that the real wish was to rescue the name of Egremont from association with umbrellas, and they held themselves bound to combat what they despised and thought a piece of worldly folly.

So Mark rode home, more glad that the decision was actually made than at the course it had taken. His father was disappointed, but could not but allow that it was the more prudent arrangement; and Mr. Egremont showed all the annoyance of a man whose good offer has been rejected.

''Tis that little giggling Scotch girl!' he said. 'Well, we are quit of her, anyway. 'Tis a pity that Mark entangled himself with her, and a mother-in-law into the bargain! I was a fool to expect to get any good out of him!'

This was said to his daughter, with whom he was left alone; for Miss

Headworth could not bear to accept his hospitality a moment longer than needful, and besides had been so much shaken in nerves as to suspect that an illness was coming on, and hurried home to be nursed by Mary Nugent. Canon Egremont was obliged to go back to Redcastle to finish his residence, and his wife, who had been absent nearly a month from her family, thought it really wisest to let the father and daughter be thrown upon one another at once, so that Ursula might have the benefit of her father's softened mood.

There could be no doubt that he was softened, and that he had derived some improvement from the year and a half that his wife had been with him. It might not have lifted him up a step, but it had arrested him in his downward course. Selfish and indolent he was as ever, but there had been a restraint on his amusements, and a withdrawal from his worst associates, such as the state of his health might continue, above all if Gregorio could be dispensed with. The man himself had become aware of the combination against him, and, though reckoning on his master's inertness and dependence upon him, knew that a fresh offence might complete his overthrow, and therefore took care to be on his good behaviour.

Thus Nuttie's task might be somewhat smoothed; but the poor girl felt unspeakably desolate as she ate her breakfast all alone with a dull post-bag, and still more so when, having seen the housekeeper, who, happily for her, was a good and capable woman, and very sorry for her, she had to bethink herself what to do in that dreary sitting-room during the hour when she had always been most sure of her sister-mother's dear company. How often she had grumbled at being called on to practise duets for her father's evening lullaby! She supposed she ought to get something up, and she proceeded to turn over and arrange the music with a sort of sick loathing for whatever was connected with those days of impatient murmurs, which she would so gladly have recalled. Everything had fallen into disorder, as Blanche and May had left it the last time they had played there; and the overlooking it, and putting aside the pieces which she could never use alone, occupied her till Gregorio, very meek and polite, came with a message that Mr. Egremont would be glad if she would come to his room. In some dread, some distaste, and yet some pity and some honest resolution, she made her way thither.

There he sat, in dressing-gown, smoking-cap, and blue spectacles, with the glittering February sunshine carefully excluded. He looked worse and more haggard than when she had seen him at dinner in the evening, made up for company, and her compassion increased, especially as he not only held out his hand, but seemed to expect her to kiss him, a thing she had never done since their first recognition. It was not pleasant in itself, but it betokened full forgiveness, and indeed he had never spoken to her in his sneering, exasperating voice since her mournful return home.

'Have you seen the boy?' he asked.

'Yes; they are walking him up and down under the south wall,' said Nuttie, thankful that she had peeped under the many wraps as he was carried across the hall.

'Here! I want you to read this letter to me. A man ought to be indicted for writing such a hand!'

It was really distinct penmanship, though minute; but, as Nuttie found, her father did not like to avow how little available were his eyes. He could write better than he could read, but he kept her over his correspondence for the rest of the morning, answering some of the letters of condolence for him in her own name, writing those of business, and folding and addressing what he himself contrived to write. Her native quickness stood her in good stead, and, being rather nervous, she took great pains, and seldom stumbled; indeed, she only once incurred an exclamation of impatience at her stupidity or slowness.

She guessed rightly that this forbearance was owing to tender persuasions of her mother, and did not guess that a certain fear of herself was mingled with other motives. Her father had grown used to woman's ministrations; he needed them for his precious little heir, and he knew his daughter moreover for a severe judge, and did not want to alienate her and lose her services; so they got on fairly well together, and she shared his luncheon, during which a message came up about the carriage; and as there had been an application for some nursery needment, and moreover black-edged envelopes had run short, there was just purpose enough for a drive to the little town.

Then Nuttie read her father to sleep with the newspaper; rushed round the garden in the twilight to stretch her young limbs; tried to read a little, dressed, dined with her father; finished what he had missed in the paper, then offered him music, and was told 'if she pleased,' and as she played she mused whether this was to be her life. It looked very dull and desolate, and what was the good of it all? But there were her mother's words, 'Love him!' How fulfil them? She could pity him now, but oh! how could she love one from whom her whole nature recoiled, when she thought of her mother's ruined life? Mr. Dutton too had held her new duties up to her as capable of being ennobled. Noble! To read aloud a sporting paper she did not want to understand, to be ready to play at cards or billiards, to take that dawdling drive day by day, to devote herself to the selfish exactions of burnt-out dissipation. Was this noble? Her mother had done all this, and never even felt it a cross, because of her great love. It must be Nuttie's cross if it was her duty; but could the love and honour possibly come though she tried to pray in faith?

CHAPTER XXV.

THE GIGGLING SCOTCH GIRL.

'For every Lamp that trembled here,
And faded in the night,
Behold a Star serene and clear
Smiles on me from the height.'—B. M.

Nuttie was not mistaken in supposing that this first day would be a fair sample of her life, though, of course, after the first weeks of mourning there were variations; and the return of the Rectory party made a good deal of brightening, and relieved her from the necessity of finding companionship and conversation for her father on more than half her afternoons and evenings.

He required her, however, almost every forenoon, and depended on her increasingly, so that all her arrangements had to be made with reference to him. It was bondage, but not as galling in the fact as she would have expected if it had been predicted to her a few months previously. In the first place, Mr. Egremont never demanded of her what was actually against her conscience, except occasionally giving up a Sunday evensong to read the paper to him, and that only when he was more unwell than usual. He was, after all, an English gentleman, and did not ask his young daughter to read to him the books which her mother had loathed. Moreover, Gregorio was on his good behaviour, perfectly aware that there was a family combination against him, and having even received a sort of warning from his master, but by no means intending to take it, and therefore abstaining from any kind of offence that could furnish a fresh handle against him; and thus for the present, Dr. Hammond's regimen was well observed, and Mr. Egremont was his better self in consequence, for, under his wife's guardianship, the perilous habit had sufficiently lost strength to prevent temper and spirits from manifestly suffering from abstinence.

The first time Nuttie found herself obliged to make any very real sacrifice to her father's will was on the occasion of Mark's marriage at Easter. Things had arranged themselves very conveniently for him at Micklethwayte, though it seemed to Nuttie that she only heard of affairs there in a sort of distant dream, while such events were taking place as once would have been to her the greatest possible revolutions.

Aunt Ursel reached home safely, but her expectations of illness were realised. She took to her bed on arriving, and though she rose from it, there was reason to think she had had a slight stroke, for her activity of mind and body were greatly decayed, and she was wholly dependent on Mary Nugent for care and comfort. Mary, remembering the consequences of the former alarm, made the best of the old lady's condition; and Nuttie, ashamed of having once cried 'wolf,' did not realise the true state of the case, nor indeed could she or would she have been spared to go to Micklethwayte.

The next news told that Gerard Godfrey, at the end of the year required by Mr. Dutton, had resigned his situation, and at the close of his quarter's notice was going to prepare for Holy Orders under the training of a clergyman who would employ him in his parish, and assist him in reading up to the requirements for admission to a theological college. Poor dear old Gerard! It gave Nuttie a sort of pang of self-reproach to own how good and devoted he was, and yet so narrow and stupid that she could never have been happy with him. Was he too good, or was he too dull for her? Had she forsaken him for the world's sake, or was it a sound instinct that had extinguished her fancy for him? No one could tell, least of all the parties concerned. He might be far above her in spiritual matters, but he was below her in intellectual ones, and though they would always feel for one another that peculiar tenderness left by the possibilities of a first love, no doubt the quarrel over the blue ribbon had been no real misfortune to either.

The next tidings were still more surprising. Mr. Dutton was leaving the firm. Though his father had died insolvent, and he had had to struggle for himself in early life, he was connected with wealthy people, and change and death among these had brought him a fair share of riches. An uncle who had emigrated to Australia at the time of the great break up had died without other heirs, leaving him what was the more welcome to him that Micklethwayte could never be to him what it had been in its golden age. He had realised enough to enable him to be bountiful, and his parting gift to St Ambrose's would complete the church; but he himself was winding up the partnership, and withdrawing his means from Greenleaf and Co. in order to go out to Australia to decide what to do with his new possessions.

Mark Egremont purchased a number of the shares, though, to gratify the family, the shelter of the Greenleaf veiled his name under the 'Co.,' and another, already in the firm, possessed of a business-like appellation, gave designation to the firm as Greenleaf, Goodenough, and Co.

Mr. Dutton's well-kept house, with the little conservatory and the magnolia, was judged sufficient for present needs, and the lease was taken off his hands, so that all was in order for the marriage of Mark and Annaple immediately after Easter.

Lady Delmar had resigned herself to the inevitable, and the wedding was to take place at Lescombe. Nuttie, whose chief relaxation was in hearing all the pros and cons from May and Blanche, was asked to be one of the bridesmaids by Annaple, who had come over to the Rectory in a droll inscrutable state of mischief, declaring that she had exasperated Janet to the verge of insanity by declaring that she should have little umbrellas like those in the Persian inscriptions on her cards, and that Mark was to present all the bridesmaids with neat parasols. If crinolines had not been gone out they could have all been dressed appropriately. Now they must wear them closely furled. All this banter was hardly liked by May and Blanche, whose little sisters were laughed at again for needing the assurance that they were really to wear white and rowan leaves and berries—the Ronnisglen badge. Nuttie, who had drawn much nearer to May, refrained from relating this part of the story at home, but was much disappointed when, on telling her father of the request, she was answered at once:

'Hein! The 24th? You'll be in London, and a very good thing too.'

'Are we to go so soon?'

'Yes. Didn't I tell you to take that house in Berkshire Road from the 20th?'

'I did not think we were to start so soon. Is there any particular reason?'

'Yes. That Scotch girl ought to have known better than to ask you in your deep mourning. I thought women made a great point of such things.'

'Aunt Jane did not seem to think it wrong,' said Nuttie, for she really wished much for consent. Not only had she grown fond both of Mark and Annaple, but she had never been a bridesmaid, and she knew that not only the Kirkaldys but Mr. Dutton had been invited; she had even ventured on offering to lodge some of the overflowing guests of the Rectory.

'Their heads are all turned by that poverty-stricken Scotch peerage,' returned Mr. Egremont; 'or the Canoness should have more sense of respect.'

Nuttie's wishes were so strong that she made one more attempt, 'I need not be a bridesmaid. They would not mind if I wore my black.'

'I should, then!' said her father curtly. 'If they don't understand the proprieties of life, I do. I won't have you have anything to do with it. If you are so set upon gaiety, you'll have enough of weddings at fitter times!'

It was the old sneering tone. Nuttie felt partly confounded, partly indignant, and terribly disappointed. She did care for the sight of the wedding

—her youthful spirits had rallied enough for that, but far more now she grieved at missing the sight of Mr. Dutton, when he was going away, she knew not where, and might perhaps come on purpose to see her; and it also made her sore and grieved at being accused of disregard to her mother. She was silenced, however, and presently her father observed, in the same unpleasant tone, 'Well, if you've digested your disappointment, perhaps you'll condescend to write to the agent, that I expect the house to be ready on the 21st.'

Nuttie got through her morning's work she hardly knew how, though her father was dry and fault-finding all the time. Her eyes were so full of tears when she was released that she hardly saw where she was going, and nearly ran against her aunt, who had just walked into the hall. Mrs. Egremont was too prudent a woman to let her burst out there with her grievance, but made her come into the tent-room before she exclaimed, 'He is going to take me away to London; he won't let me go to the wedding.'

'I am sorry for your disappointment,' said her aunt quietly, 'but I am old-fashioned enough to be glad that such strong respect and feeling should be shown for your dear mother. I wish Annaple had spoken to me before asking you, and I would have felt the way.'

'I'm sure it is not want of feeling,' said Nuttie, as her tears broke forth.

'I did not say it was,' returned her aunt, 'but different generations have different notions of the mode of showing it; and the present certainly errs on the side of neglect of such tokens of mourning. If I did not think that Annaple and her mother are really uncomfortable at Lescombe, I should have told Mark that it was better taste to wait till the summer.'

'If I might only have stayed at home—even if I did not go to the wedding,' sighed Nuttie, who had only half listened to the Canoness's wisdom.

'Since you do not go, it is much better that you should be out of the way,' said Mrs. Egremont. 'Is your father ready to see me?'

So Nuttie had to submit, though she pouted to herself, feeling grievously misjudged, first as if she had been wanting in regard to the memory of her mother, who had been so fond of Mark, and so rejoiced in his happiness; and then that her vexation was treated as mere love of gaiety, whereas it really was disappointment at not seeing Mr. Dutton, that good, grave, precise old friend, who could not be named in the same breath with vanity. Moreover, she could not help suspecting that respect to her mother was after all only a cloak to resentment against Mark and his marriage.

However, she bethought herself that her mother had often been disappointed and had borne it cheerfully, and after having done what Aunt Ursel would have called 'grizzling' in her room for an hour, she wrote her note to Miss Ruthven and endeavoured to be as usual, feeling keenly that there was no mother now to perceive and gratefully commend one of her only too rare efforts for good humour. On other grounds she was very sorry to leave Bridgefield. May had, in her trouble, thawed to her, and they were becoming really affectionate and intimate companions, by force of propinquity and relationship, as well as of the views that May had imbibed from Hugh Condamine. Moreover Nuttie felt her aunt's watch over the baby a great assistance to her own ignorance.

However the Canoness had resigned to the poor little heir the perfect and trustworthy nurse, whom Basil had outgrown, and who consented to the transfer on condition of having her nursery establishment entirely apart from the rest of the household. Her reasons were known though unspoken, namely, that the rejection of one or two valets highly recommended had made it plain that there had been no dislodgment of Gregorio. The strong silent objection to him of all good female servants was one of the points that told much against him. Martin and the housekeeper just endured him, and stayed on for the present chiefly because their dear lady had actually begged them not to desert her daughter if they could help it, at least not at first.

Nuttie bound over her cousins to give her a full account of the wedding, and both of them wrote to her. Blanche's letter recorded sundry scattered particulars,—as to how well the rowan-trimmed tulle dresses looked—how every one was packed into the carriages for the long drive—how there had been a triumphal arch erected over the Bluepost Bridge itself, and Annaple nearly choked with laughing at the appropriateness—how, to her delight, a shower began, and the procession out of the church actually cried out for umbrellas—how papa, when performing the ceremony, could not recollect that the bride's proper name was Annabella, and would dictate it as Anna- Maria, Sir John correcting him each time sotto voce—how Basil and little Hilda Delmar walked together and 'looked like a couple of ducks,' which, it was to be hoped, was to be taken metaphorically—how dreadfully hard the ice on the wedding-cake was, so that when Annaple tried to cut it the knife slipped and a little white dove flew away and hit May, which everyone said was a grand omen that she would be the next bride, while of course Annaple was perfectly helpless with mirth. Every one said it was the merriest wedding ever seen, for the bride's only tears were those of laughter. What Nuttie really cared for most came just at the end, and not much of that. 'Your Mr. Dutton is just gone. He got on famously with Hugh Condamine, and I forgot to tell you that he has given Mark such a jolly present, a lovely silver coffee-pot, just the one thing they wanted, and Lady Delmar said he didn't look near so like a tradesman as she expected. I see May is writing too, but I don't know what you will get out of her, as Hugh Condamine came for the day.'

Nuttie, however, had more hopes from May. Her letter certainly was fuller of interest, if shorter.

'My Dear Nuttie—Blanche has no doubt told you all the externals. I suppose there never was a brighter wedding, for as Annaple keeps her mother with her, there was no real rending asunder of ties. Indeed I almost wish her excitement did not always show itself in laughing, for it prevents people from understanding how much there is in her.

(Plainly Hugh Condamine had been rather scandalised by the 'giggling Scotch girl.')

'Dear old Lady Ronnisglen was delightful. If there were any tears, they were hers, and Lady Delmar was very cordial and affectionate. Of course Hugh and Mr. Dutton missed much that one would have liked in a wedding. I drove back with them afterwards, and it was very interesting to listen to their conversation about church matters. Hugh is very much struck with your friend; he had heard a good deal about Micklethwayte before, and says that such a lay worker is perfectly invaluable. It is a great pity that he is not going on in the firm, it would make it so much nicer for Mark, but he says he has duties towards his new property. I think he was sorry not to find you at home, but he plainly never thought it possible you should be at the wedding. I don't know whether I ought to tell you this, but I think you ought to know it. There is a lovely new wreath of Eucharis lilies and maiden-hair at dear Aunt Alice's grave, close against the rails at the feet, and Hugh told me that he looked out of his window very early yesterday morning and saw Mr. Dutton standing there, leaning on the rail, with his bare head bowed between his hands. You can't think how it impressed Hugh. He said he felt reverent towards him all through that day, and he was quite angry with Rosalind and Adela for jesting because, when the shower began as we were coming out of church, Mr. Dutton rushed up with an umbrella, being the only person there who had one, I believe. Hugh says you may be proud of such a friend. I wish you could have seen Hugh.— Your affectionate cousin,

'MARGARET EGREMONT.'

CHAPTER XXVI.

THREE YEARS LATER.

'There's something rotten in the State.'—Hamlet.

On an east-windy afternoon in March Mary Nugent emerged from the School of Art, her well-worn portfolio under her arm, thinking how many successive generations of boys and girls she had drilled through 'free-hand,' 'perspective,' and even 'life' with an unvarying average of failure and very moderate success, and how little talent or originality had come to the front, though all might be the better for knowing how to use eyes and fingers.

On the whole her interest as well as her diligence did not flag; but a sense of weariness and monotony would sometimes come after a recurrence of well-known blunders of her pupils, and she missed the sense of going home to refreshment and enjoyment which had once invigorated her. St. Ambrose's Road had had its golden age, but the brightness had been dimmed ever since that festival at Monks Horton. One after another of the happy old society had dropped away. The vicar had received promotion, and she only remained of the former intimates, excepting old Miss Headworth, who was no longer a companion, but whom affection forbade her to desert in feeble old age. Had her thoughts of the old times conjured up a figure belonging to them? There was the well-brushed hat, the natty silk umbrella, the perfect fit of garments, the precise turn-out, nay, the curly lion-shaven poodle, with all his fringes, leaping on her in recognition, and there was that slightly French flourish of the hat, before—with a bounding heart—she met the hand in an English grasp.

'Miss Nugent!'

'Mr. Dutton!'

'I thought I should meet you here!'

'When did you come?'

'Half an hour ago. I came down with George Greenleaf, left my things at the Royal Hotel, and came on to look for you.'

'You will come and spend the evening with us?'

'If you are so good as to ask me. How is Miss Headworth?'

'Very feeble, very deaf; but she will be delighted to see you. There is no fear of her not remembering you, though she was quite lost when Mrs. Egremont came in yesterday.'

'Mrs. Egremont!' he repeated with a little start.

'Mrs. Mark. Ah! we have got used to the name—the Honourable Mrs. Egremont, as the community insist on calling her. What a sunny creature she is!'

'And Miss Egremont, what do you hear of her?'

'She writes long letters, poor child. I hope she is fairly happy. Are you come home for good, or is this only a visit?'

'I have no intention of returning. I have been winding up my good cousin's affairs at Melbourne.'

Mary's heart bounded again with a sense of joy, comfort, and protection; but she did not long keep Mr. Dutton to herself, for every third person they met gladly greeted him, and they were long in getting to St. Ambrose's Road, now dominated by a tall and beautiful spire, according to the original design. They turned and looked in at the pillared aisles, stained glass, and handsome reredos.

'Very different from our struggling days,' said Mr. Dutton.

'Yes,' said Mary, with half a sigh. 'There's the new vicar,' as he passed with a civil nod. 'He has three curates, and a house of Sisters, and works the parish excellently.'

'You don't speak as if you were intimate.'

'No. His womankind are rather grand—quite out of our beat; and in parish work I am only an estimable excrescence. It is very well that I am not wanted, for Miss Headworth requires a good deal of attention, and it is only the old Adam that regrets the days of importance. Ah, do you see?'

They were passing Mr. Dutton's old home. On the tiny strip of lawn in front was a slender black figure, with yellow hair, under a tiny black hat, dragging about a wooden horse whereon was mounted a sturdy boy of two, also yellow-locked and in deep mourning under his Holland blouse.

'Billy-boy is riding to meet his daddy!' was merrily called out both by mother and son before they perceived the stranger.

'Mr. Dutton,' said Mary.

Annaple bowed, but did not put out her hand, and such a flush was on her face that Miss Nugent said, 'I am sure that is too much for you!'

'Oh no—' she began; but 'Allow me,' said Mr. Dutton, and before she could refuse he was galloping round and round the little lawn, the boy screaming with delight as Monsieur raced with them.

'So he is come!' she said in a low doubtful voice to Mary.

'Yes. He has met Mr. Greenleaf in London. I always think he has the contrary to the evil eye. Whatever he takes in hand rights itself.'

'I'll hope so. Oh, thank you! Billy-boy, say thank you! What a ride you have had!'

'Why are they in such deep mourning?' asked Mr. Dutton, after they had parted.

'Oh, did you not know? for good old Lady Ronnisglen. She had a bad fall about two years ago, and never left her bed again; and this last autumn she sank away.'

'They have had a great deal of trouble, then. I saw the death of Canon Egremont in the Times soon after I went out to Australia.'

'Yes; he had heart disease, and died quite suddenly. The living is given to Mr. Condamine, who married the eldest daughter, and the widow is gone to live under the shadow of Redcastle Cathedral.'

Therewith Miss Nugent opened her own door, and Miss Headworth was soon made aware of the visitor. She was greatly changed, and had the indescribable stony look that tells of paralysis; and though she knew Mr. Dutton, and was delighted to see him, his presence made her expect to see Alice and Nuttie come in, though she soon recollected herself and shed a few helpless tears. Then—in another mood—she began to display with pride and pleasure the photographs of 'Alice's dear little boy.' She had a whole series of them, from the long-clothed babe on his sister's knee to the bright little fellow holding a drum—a very beautiful child, with a striking resemblance to his mother, quite startling to Mr. Dutton, especially in the last, which was coloured, and showed the likeness of eyes and expression.

'Nuttie always sends me one whenever he is taken,' said the old lady. 'Dear Nuttie! It is very good for her. She is quite a little mother to him.'

'I was sure it would be so,' said Mr. Dutton.

'Yes,' said Mary, 'he is the great interest and delight of her life. Her letters are full of his little sayings and doings.'

'Is she at home now?'

'No; at Brighton. Her father seems to have taken a dislike to Bridgefield since his brother's death, and only goes there for a short time in the shooting season. He has taken a lease of a house in London, and spends most of the year there.'

'Ah!' as she showed him the address, 'that is near the old house where I used to stay with my grand-aunt. We thought it altogether in the country then, but it is quite absorbed now, and I have dazzling offers from building companies for the few acres of ground around it. Have you seen her?'

'Oh no; I believe she is quite necessary to her father. I only hear of her through Lady Kirkaldy, who has been very kind to her, but, I am sorry to say, is now gone with her Lord to the East. She says she thinks that responsibility has been very good for Nuttie; she is gentler and less impetuous, and a good deal softened by her affection for the child.'

'She was certain to develop. I only dreaded what society her father might surround her with.'

'Lady Kirkaldy says that all has turned out better than could have been expected. You see, as she says, Mr. Egremont has been used to good women in his own family, and would not like to see her in a slangy fast set. All her own gaieties have been under Lady Kirkaldy's wing, or that of Mrs. William Egremont's relations, and only in a quiet moderate way. Her father gets his own old set about him, and they have not been very choice, but they are mostly elderly men, and gentlemen, and know how to behave themselves to her. Indeed, her cousin Blanche, who was here in the winter, gave us to understand that Ursula knows how to take care of herself, and gets laughed at as rather an old maidish model of propriety, if you can believe it of your little Nuttie.'

'I could quite believe in her on the defensive, unprotected as she is.'

'What did that young lady—Miss Blanche—tell us about that gentleman, Mary?' asked Miss Headworth, hearing and uttering what Miss Nugent hoped had passed unnoticed.

'Oh, I think that was all gossip!' returned Mary, 'and so I am sure did the Mark Egremonts. She said there was one of Mr. Egremont's friends, Mr. Clarence Fane, I think she called him, rather younger than the others, who, she was pleased to say, seemed smitten with Nuttie, but I have heard nothing more about it, and Mrs. Mark scouted the idea,' she added in haste, as she saw his expression vary in spite of himself.

'Do you see much of your neighbours?'

'We are both too busy to see much of one another, but we have our little talks over the wall. What a buoyant creature she is. It seems as if playfulness was really a sustaining power in her, helping her to get diversion out of much that others might stumble at. You know perhaps that when she arrived the work-people had got up a beautiful parasol for her, white, with a deep fringe and spray of rowan. Little Susie Gunner presented her with it, and she was very gracious and nice about it. But then what must Mr. Goodenough do but dub it the Annabella sunshade, and blazon it, considerably vulgarised, in all the railway stations, and magazines.'

'I know! I had the misfortune to see it in the station at Melbourne; and my mind misgave me from that hour.'

'Her husband was prepared to be very angry, but she fairly laughed him out of it, made all sorts of fun out of the affair, declared it her only opening to fame, and turned it into a regular joke; so that indeed the Greenleafs, who were vexed at the matter, and tried to apologise, were quite perplexed in their turn, and not at all sure that the whole concern was not being turned into ridicule.'

'I wonder it did not make him cut the connection,' said Mr. Dutton, muttering 'I only wish it had.'

'Mrs. Greenleaf is very funny about her, 'added Mary, 'proud of the Honourable Mrs. Egremont, as they insist on calling her, yet not quite pleased that she should be the junior partner's wife; and decidedly resenting her hardly going into society at all, though I really don't see how she could; for first there was the Canon's death, and then just after the boy was born came Lady Ronnisglen's accident, and for the next year and a half there was constant attendance on her. They fitted up a room on the ground floor for her, the one opening into your drawing-room, and there they used to sit with her. I used to hear them reading to her and singing to her, and they were always as merry as possible, till last autumn, when something brought on erysipelas, and she was gone almost before they took alarm. The good little daughter was beaten down then, really ill for a week; but if you can understand me, the shock seemed to tell on her chiefly bodily, and though she was half broken- hearted when her husband in a great fright brought me up to see her, and say whether her sister should be sent for, she still made fun of him, and described the impossible advice they would bring on themselves. I had to take care of her while he went away to the funeral in Scotland, and then I learnt indeed to like her and see how much there is in her besides laughter.'

'Did the old lady leave them anything?'

'I believe she had nothing to leave. Her jointure was not much, but I am sure they miss that, for Mrs. Egremont has parted with her nurse, and has only a little girl in her stead, driving out the perambulator often herself, to the great scandal of the Greenleafs, though she would have one believe it is all for want of occupation.'

'Do you think they have taken any alarm?'

'There's no judging from her joyous surface, but I have thought him looking more careworn and anxious than I liked. Mr. Dutton, don't answer if I ought not to ask, but is it true that things are going wrong? I know you have been seeing Mr. Greenleaf, so perhaps you are in his confidence and cannot speak.'

'Tell me, what is known or suspected?'

'Just this, that Mr. Goodenough has been the ruin of the concern. He has been quite different ever since his voyage to America. You were gone, old Mr. Greenleaf has been past attending to business ever since he had that attack, and George Greenleaf has been playing the country squire at Horton Bishop, and not looking after the office work, and Mr. Egremont was inexperienced. One could see, of course, that the whole character of the business was changed— much more advertising, much more cheap and flashy work—to be even with the times, it was said, but the old superior hands were in despair at the materials supplied to them, and the scamped work expected. You should have heard old Thorpe mourning for you, and moralising over the wickedness of this world. His wife told me she really thought he would go melancholy mad if he did not leave the factory, and he has done so. They have saved enough to set up a nice little shop at Monks Horton.'

'I must go and see them! Good old Thorpe! I ought never to have put those poor young things into the firm when I ceased to have any control over it. I shall never forgive myself—'

'Nothing could seem safer then! No one could have guessed that young Mr. Greenleaf would be so careless without his father to keep him up to the mark, nor that Mr. Goodenough should alter so much. Is it very bad? Is there worse behind? Speculation, I suppose—'

'Of course. I do not see to the bottom of it yet; poor George seemed to reckon on me for an advance, but I am afraid this is more than a mere temporary depression, such as may be tided over, and that all that can be looked to is trying to save honourable names by an utter break up, which may rid them of that—that—no, I won't call him a scoundrel. I thought highly of him once, and no doubt he never realised what he was doing.'

Before the evening was far advanced Mark Egremont knocked at the door, and courteously asked whether Mr. Dutton could be spared to him for a little while. Mary Nugent replied that she was just going to help Miss Headworth to bed, and that the parlour was at their service for a private interview, but Mark answered, 'My wife is anxious to hear. She knows all that I do, and is quite prepared to hear whatever Mr. Dutton may not object to saying before her.'

So they bade good-night to Mary, and went on together to the next house, Mr. Dutton saying 'You have much to forgive me, Mr. Egremont; I feel as if I had deserted the ship just as I had induced you to embark in it.'

'You did not guess how ill it would be steered without you,' returned Mark, with a sigh. 'Do not fear to speak out before my wife, even if we are sinking. She will hear it bravely, and smile to the last.'

The room which Mr. Dutton entered was not like the cabin of a sinking ship, nor, as in his own time, like the well-ordered apartment of a bachelor of taste. Indeed, the house was a great puzzle to Monsieur, who entered by invitation, knowing his way perfectly, thinking himself at home after all his travels, and then missing his own particular mat, and sniffing round at the furniture. It was of the modified aesthetic date, but arranged more with a view to comfort than anything else, and by the light of the shaded lamp and bright fire was pre-eminently home-like, with the three chairs placed round the hearth, and bright-haired Annaple rising up from the lowest with her knitting to greet Mr. Dutton, and find a comfortable lair for Monsieur.

'Miss Nugent says that you set everything right that you do but look at, Mr. Dutton,' she said; 'so we are prepared to receive you as a good genius to help us out of our tangle.'

Mr. Dutton was afraid that the tangle was far past unwinding, and of course the details, so far as yet known, were discussed. There was, in truth, nothing for which Mark could be blamed. He had diligently attended to his office-work, which was mere routine, and, conscious of his own inexperience, and trusting to the senior partners, he had only become anxious at the end of the year, when he perceived Goodenough's avoidance of a settlement of accounts, and detected shuffling. He had not understood enough of the previous business to be aware of the deterioration of the manner of dealing with it, though he did think it scarcely what he expected. If he had erred, it was in acting too much as a wheel in the machinery, keeping his thoughts and heart in his own happy little home, and not throwing himself into the spirit of the business, or the ways of those concerned in it, so that he had been in no degree a controlling power. He had allowed his quality of gentleman to keep him an outsider, instead of using it to raise the general level of the transactions, so that the whole had gone down in the hands of the unscrupulous Goodenough.

Annaple listened and knitted quietly while the affairs were explained on either hand. Mark had had one serious talk with George Greenleaf, and both had had a stormy scene with Goodenough. Then Mr. Dutton had telegraphed his arrival, and Greenleaf had met him in London, with hopes, bred of long and implicit trust, that his sagacity and perhaps his wealth would carry the old house through the crisis.

But Mr. Dutton, though reserving his judgment till the books should have been thoroughly examined and the liabilities completely understood, was evidently inclined to believe that things had gone too far, and that the names of Greenleaf and Egremont could only be preserved from actual dishonour by going into liquidation, dissolving partnership, and thus getting quit of Goodenough.

Mark listened resignedly, Annaple with an intelligence that made Mr. Dutton think her the more clearheaded of the two, though still she could not refrain from her little jokes. 'I'm sure I should not mind how liquid we became if we could only run off clear of Goodenough,' she said.

'You know what it means?' said her husband.

'Oh yes, I know what it means. It is the fine word for being sold up. Well, Mark, never mind, we are young and strong, and it will not be a bit the worse for the Billy-boy in the end to begin at the bottom of everything.'

'I hope—may I ask—is everything embarked in the poor old firm?' said Mr. Dutton with some hesitation.

'All that is mine,' said Mark, with his elbow on the table and his chin on his hand.

'But I've got a hundred a year, charged on poor old Ronnisglen's estate,' said Annaple. 'All the others gave theirs up when they married, and I wanted to do so, but my dear mother would not let me; she said I had better try how I got on first. Think of that, Mark, a hundred a year! Why, old Gunner or Thorpe would think themselves rolling in riches if they only heard that they had a hundred a year!'

'You won't find it go far!'

'Yes, I shall, for I shall make you live on porridge, with now and then a sheep's head for a treat! Besides, there will be something to do. It will be working up again, you know. But seriously, Mr. Dutton, I have some things here of my dear mother's that really belong to Ronnisglen, and I was only keeping till he comes home. Should not they be got out of the way?'

'My dear, we are not come to that yet! I hope it may be averted!' cried Mark.

But Mr. Dutton agreed with the young wife that it would be much better to send these things away before their going could excite suspicion. There was only a tiny silver saucepan, valued as a gift of 'Queen' Clementina to an ancestress, also a silver teapot and some old point, and some not very valuable jewellery, all well able to go into a small box, which Mr. Dutton undertook to deposit with Lord Ronnisglen's bankers. He was struck with the scrupulous veracity with which Annaple decided between what had become her own property and the heirlooms, though what she claimed might probably be sacrificed to the creditors.

Mark could hardly endure to see what made the crisis so terribly real. 'That I should have brought you to this!' he said to his wife, when their visitor had at length bidden them good-night.

'If we begin at that work,' said Annaple, 'it was I who brought you! I have often thought since it was rather selfish not to have consented to your helping poor Ursula with her heavy handful of a father! It was all money grubbing and grabbing, you see, and if we had thought more of our neighbour than ourselves we might have been luxuriating at the Home Farm, or even if your uncle had quarrelled with you, he would not have devoured your substance. I have thought so often, ever since I began to see this coming.'

'My dear child, you don't mean that you have seen this coming!'

'My prophetic soul! Why, Mark, you have as good as inferred it over and over again. I've felt like scratching that Badenough whenever I met him in the street. I must indulge myself by calling him so for once in strict privacy.'

'You have guessed it all the time, while I only thought how unconscious you were.'

'Not to say stupid, considering all you told me. Besides, what would have been the use of howling and moaning and being dismal before the time? For my part, I could clap my hands even now at getting rid of Goodenough, and his jaunty, gracious air! Come, Mark, it won't be so bad after all, you'll see.'

'Nothing can be "so bad," while you are what you are, my Nan.'

'That's right. While we have each other and the Billy-boy, nothing matters much. There's plenty of work in us both, and that good man will find it for us; or if he doesn't, we'll get a yellow van, and knit stockings, and sell them round the country. How jolly that would be! Imagine Janet's face. There, that's right,' as her mimicry evoked a smile, 'I should be ashamed to be unhappy about this, when our good name is saved, and when there is a blessing on the poor,' she added in a lower voice, tenderly kissing her husband's weary brow.

CHAPTER XXVII.

THE BOY OF EGREMONT.

The agony of a firm like Greenleaf, Goodenough, and Co. could not be a rapid thing, and Mr. Dutton lived between London and Micklethwayte for several weeks, having much to endure on all sides. The senior partners thought it an almost malicious and decidedly ungrateful thing in him not to throw in his means, or at any rate, offer his guarantee to tide them over their difficulties. Goodenough's tergiversations and concealments needed a practised hand and acute head to unravel them, and often deceived Mr. Greenleaf himself; and when, for a time, he was convinced that the whole state was so rotten that a crash was inevitable, his wife's lamentations and complaints of Mr. Dutton would undo the whole, and it was as if he were doing them an injury that the pair accepted the comfortable prospect he was able to offer them in Australia.

He would have made the like proposal to the Egremonts, but found that Mark held himself bound by his promise to his father not to emigrate, and thought of some kind of office-work. Before trying to procure this for him, however, Mr. Dutton intended to see his uncle, and try whether the agency, once rejected, could still be obtained for him. Learning from Miss Nugent that the Egremonts were in town, he went up thither with the purpose of asking for an interview.

There was a new church in the immediate neighbourhood of his house in a state of growth and development congenial to the St. Ambrose trained mind, and here Mr. Dutton, after old Micklethwayte custom, was attending the early matins, when, in the alternate verses of the psalm, he heard a fresh young voice that seemed to renew those days gone by, and looking across the central aisle his eyes met a pair of dark ones which gave a sudden glitter of gladness at the encounter. That was all he saw or cared to see. He did not take in the finished completeness of the very plain dark dress and hat, nor the womanly air of the little figure, until they clasped hands in the porch, and in the old tones Nuttie exclaimed: 'I've been hoping you would come to London. How is Monsieur?'

'In high health, thank you, the darling of the steamer both going and coming. I hope your charges are well?'

'My father is tolerable, just as usual, and my little Alwyn is getting more delicious every day. He will be so delighted to see Monsieur. I have told him so many stories about him!'

'Do you think I may call on Mr. Egremont?'

'Oh do! He is ready to be called on between two and three, and we always have Wynnie downstairs then, so that you will see him too. And you have been at Micklethwayte. I am afraid you found a great change in Aunt Ursel.'

'Yes; but she is very peaceful and happy.'

'And I have to leave her altogether to dear excellent Miss Nugent. It seems very, very wrong, but I cannot help it! And how about Mark and Annaple?'

'I think she is the bravest woman I ever met.'

'Then things are really going badly with the dear old firm?'

'I am hoping to talk to Mr. Egremont about it.'

'Ah!'

Nuttie paused. Towards Mr. Dutton she always had a stronger impulse of confidence than towards any one else she had ever met; but she felt that he might think it unbecoming to say that she had perceived a certain dislike on her father's part towards Mark ever since the rejection of the agency and the marriage, which perhaps was regarded as a rejection of herself. He had a habit of dependence on Mark, which resulted in personal liking, when in actual contact, but in absence the distaste and offence always revived, fostered, no doubt, by Gregorio; and Canon Egremont's death had broken the link which had brought them together. However, for his brother's sake, and for the sake of the name, the head of the family might be willing to do something. It was one of Nuttie's difficulties that she never could calculate on the way her father would take any matter. Whether for better or for worse, he always seemed to decide in diametrical opposition to her expectation. And, as she was certainly less impetuous and more dutiful, she parted with Mr. Dutton at her own door without any such hint.

These three years had been discipline such as the tenderest, wisest hand could not have given her, though it had been insensible. She had been obliged to attend to her father and watch over her little brother, and though neither task had seemed congenial to her disposition, the honest endeavour to do them rightly had produced the affection born of solicitude towards her father, and the strong warm tenderness of the true mother-sister towards little Alwyn.

Ursula Egremont was one of those natures to which responsibility is the best training. If she had had any one to guard or restrain her, she might have gone to the utmost limits before she yielded to the curb. As it was, she had to take care of herself, to bear and forbear with her father, to walk warily with her household, and to be very guarded with the society into which she was thrown from time to time. It was no sudden change, but one brought about by experience. An outbreak of impatience or temper towards her father was sure to be followed by his galling sneer, or by some mortification to her desires; any act of mismanagement towards the servants brought its own punishment; and if she was tempted by girlish spirits to relax the quiet, stiff courtesy which she observed towards her father's guests, there followed jests, or semi- patronage, or a tone of conversation that offended her, and made her repent it. Happily, Mr. Egremont did not wish her to be otherwise. One day, when she had been betrayed into rattling and giggling, he spoke to her afterwards with a cutting irony which bitterly angered her at the moment, and which she never forgot. Each irksome duty, each privation, each disappointment, each recurrence of the sweeping sense of desolation and loneliness had had one effect—it had sent her to her knees. She had no one else to go to. She turned to her Father in heaven. Sometimes, indeed, it was in murmuring and complaint at her lot, but still it was to Him and Him alone, and repentance sooner or later came to aid her, while refreshments sprang up around her— little successes, small achievements, pleasant hours, tokens that her father was pleased or satisfied, and above all, the growing charms of little Alwyn.

The special grievance, Gregorio's influence, had scarcely dwelt on her at first as it had done on her mother. The man had been very cautious for some time, knowing that his continuance in his situation was in the utmost jeopardy, and Mr. Egremont had, in the freshness of his grief for his wife, abstained from relapsing into the habits from which she had weaned him. When, however, the Canon was dead, and his son at a distance, Gregorio began to feel more secure, and in the restless sorrow of his master over the blow that had taken away an only brother, he administered soothing drugs under another name, so that Ursula, in her inexperience, did not detect what was going on, and still fancied that the habit had been renounced. All she did know was that it was entirely useless for her to attempt to exert any authority over the valet, and that the only way to escape insolently polite disobedience was to let him alone. Moreover, plans to which her father had agreed, when broached by her, had often been overthrown after his valet had been with him. It was a life full of care and disappointment, yet there was a certain spring of trust that kept Ursula's youth from being dimmed, and enabled her to get a fair share of happiness out of it, though she was very sorry not to be more at Bridgefield, where she could have worked with all her heart with May Condamine. Moreover, Lady Kirkaldy's absence from London was a great loss to her, for there was no one who was so kind or so available in taking her into society; and Nuttie, though mistress of her father's house, was not yet twenty-two, and strongly felt that she must keep within careful bounds, and not attempt to be her own chaperon.

But the very sight of her old friend, and the knowledge that he was in the neighbourhood, filled her heart with gladness, and seemed like a compensation for everything. Mr. Egremont was in a gracious mood, and readily consented to see Mr. Dutton—the friend who had been so pleasant and helpful at Paris— and Nuttie gave her private instructions to the footman to insure his admittance.

His card was brought in just as the father and daughter were finishing luncheon, and he was received in Mr. Egremont's sitting-room, where the first civilities had hardly passed before the door was opened, and in trotted the golden-haired boy, so beautiful a child that it would have been impossible not to look at him with delight, even for those to whom his dark eyes and sweet smile did not recall those that had once been so dear.

Mr. Egremont's voice took a fresh tone: 'Ah! here he comes, the old fellow'—and he held out his hands; but the boy was intent on his own purpose.

'Where's black doggie?' he asked in a silver-bell of a little voice, but lisping a good deal; 'Wyn got penny for him.'

'Wynnie must be a good boy. Kiss papa first, and Mr. Dutton,' remonstrated the sister; and Alwyn obeyed so far as to submit to his father's embrace, and then raising those velvety eyes to the visitor's face, he repeated: 'Where black doggie? Wyn want to see him buy bun.'

'There! your fame has preceded you,' said Mr. Egremont, 'or rather your dog's.'

'You shall see him,' said Mr. Dutton, taking the pretty boy almost reverently on his knee, 'but he is at home now. I could not leave him out on the street, and I did not know if I might bring him in.'

'Oh, Mr. Dutton! as if Monsieur would not be welcome,' cried the Nuttie of old times. 'I only wish I had stipulated for him, dear old fellow.'

'Wyn want to see him,' reiterated the child.

'May I take him to see the performance?' said Mr. Dutton. 'I live only at the corner of Berkshire Road, and there's a dairy just opposite where Monsieur has been allowed to keep up his accomplishment.'

Alwyn's legs, arms, and voice, were all excitement and entreaty; and Mr. Egremont himself proposed that they should all come and witness the feat; so Nuttie, in great glee, climbed the stairs with her little brother to get ready; and when she came down again, found the gentlemen deep, not in Mark

Egremont's umbrellas, but in the gas and smoke grievances which had arisen since the lease of the house had been taken, and in which sympathy might be expected from a fellow-inhabitant of the district. Little Alwyn was, however, plainly the lord of the ascendant, and unused to see anything else attended to in his presence. He took possession of Mr. Dutton's hand, and his tongue went fast, nor did his father or sister seem to desire any better music. They reached an old-walled garden, with lilac and laburnum and horse-chestnut blossoming above, and showing a mass of greenery through the iron railing that surmounted, the low wall on the street side, where Mr. Dutton halted and took out his key.

'Is this yours?' exclaimed Nuttie, 'I have so often wondered whose it could be.'

'Yes, it was a country-house when I was of the age of this little man, though you might not think it.'

'The increase of London had not been on that side,' said Mr. Egremont. 'This must be a very valuable property!'

And Nuttie perceived that such an inheritance made Mr. Dutton much more in his eyes than an ex-umbrella-monger; but no sooner was the tall iron gate opened than Monsieur, beautifully shaved, with all his curly tufts in perfection, came bounding to meet his master, and Alwyn had his arms round the neck in a moment. Monsieur had in his time been introduced to too many children not to understand the situation, and respond politely; and he also recognised Ursula, and gave unmistakable proofs of being glad to see her.

Then the halfpenny was presented to him. He wagged his queer tail, smiled with his intelligent brown eyes, took it between his teeth, and trotted across the street in the most business-like way, the others following, but detaining the boy from keeping too close. They found the creature sitting upright, tapping the floor with his tail, the centre of rapturous admiration to all the customers already in the dairy shop. He received his bun, and demurely dropping on his front legs, walked back with it to his master, and crossed the road with it uneaten, rather to Alwyn's disappointment, but Mr. Dutton said he would probably dispose of it in some hiding-place in the garden until his evening appetite came on. It was well he was a dog of moderation, for there was great temptation to repeat the entertainment more than was wholesome for him.

'There, Wynnie,' said Nuttie in a voice of monition, 'Monsieur doesn't eat all his goodies at once, he keeps them for bedtime.'

It might be perceived that the over-supply of sweets was a matter of anxiety to the elder sister. To the nurse, who waited in readiness, Alwyn was consigned for his walk, while his father and sister accepted Mr. Dutton's invitation to look round his domain. It would have been small in the country, but it was extensive for the locality, and there was a perfect order and trimness about the shaven lawn, the little fountain in the midst, the flower- beds gay with pansies, forget-me-nots, and other early beauties, and the freshly-rolled gravel paths, that made Nuttie exclaim: 'Ah! I should have known this for yours anywhere.'

'I have not had much to do to it,' he said. 'My old aunts had it well kept up, even when they could only see it from their windows. Their old gardener still lives in the cottage behind the tool-house, though he is too infirm for anything but being wheeled about in the sun in their Bath-chair.'

'You keep a large amount lying idle by retaining it as it is,' said Mr. Egremont.

'True, but it is well to preserve an oasis here and there.'

Nuttie knew well that it was not for himself alone, and as they entered the little conservatory, and her eye fell on the row of white hyacinths, the very scent carried her back to the old times, and her eyes grew moist while Mr. Dutton was cutting a bouquet for her in accordance with well-known tastes.

'I shall put them in my room. It will feel like home,' she said, and then she saw that she had said what her father did not like; for he was always sensitive as to any reference to her early life.

Mr. Dutton, however, took this opportunity of saying that he had been backwards and forwards to Micklethwayte several times this spring.

'I hope you are well out of the concern there,' said Mr. Egremont.

'Thank you, sir; I have no share in it at present.'

'So much the better!'

'But I am very anxious about my friends.'

'Ah!' But Mr. Egremont's attention was drawn off at the entrance of the house by a new-fashioned stove of which Mr. Dutton did the honours, conducting father and daughter into the drawing-room, where obvious traces of the old ladies remained, and thence into his own sitting-room, smelling pleasantly of Russia leather, and recalling that into which Nuttie had been wont, before her schooldays, to climb by the window, and become entranced by the illustrations of a wonderful old edition of Telemaque, picked up at Paris.

Mr. Dutton made them sit and rest, for this had been a good deal of exercise for Mr. Egremont; coffee was brought in, having been ordered on their arrival, and therewith Mr. Dutton entered on an exposition of the affairs of Greenleaf and Goodenough, which was listened to with a good deal of interest, though Nuttie could not quite detect whether it were altogether friendly interests in Mark's misfortunes, or if there were not a certain triumph in the young man having run into trouble by rejecting his offer.

Mr. Dutton explained that his present object was to induce the friends of the family to prevent annoyance by preserving the furniture and personals at a valuation; and Mr. Egremont readily agreed to contribute to doing this, though he said the sisters and stepmother were well able also to do their share.

'And then to give the young people a fresh start,' added Mr. Dutton.

'There are some men who are always wanting fresh starts,' said Mr. Egremont, 'just as there are some vessels that are always unlucky. And if you observe, it is just those men who are in the greatest haste to hang an expensive wife and family round their necks.'

'I don't think poor Annaple can be accused of being expensive, papa,' said Nuttie. 'Only think, when Wynnie has two nurses always after him, her Willie has only the fraction of a little maid, who does all sorts of work besides.'

'Yes, I never saw more resolute and cheerful exertion than Mrs. Mark Egremont's,' said Mr. Dutton.

'She owes him something,' said Mr. Egremont, 'for she has been the ruin of him.'

'Of his worldly prospects in one sense,' said Mr. Dutton quietly; while Nuttie felt how much better and wiser an answer it was than the indignant denial that trembled on her tongue. 'There can be no doubt that they made a grievous mistake in their choice, and I unfortunately was concerned in leading them into it; but no one can see how they meet their troubles without great respect and admiration, and I am especially bound to seek for some new opening for them. I have little doubt that some office work might be found for him in London, but they are essentially country people, and it would be much better for them if he could have some agency. I suppose the situation you offered him before, sir, is filled up?'

'Not really,' cried Nuttie. 'We have only a very common sort of uneducated bailiff, who would be much better with some one over him. You said so, papa.'

'Did he request you to apply to me?' said Mr. Egremont sharply, looking at Mr. Dutton.

'Neither he nor she has the least idea of my intention; I only thought, sir, you might be willing to consider how best to assist a nephew, who has certainly not been wanting either in industry or economy, and who bears your name.'

'Well, I will think it over,' said Mr. Egremont, rising to take leave.

The carriage had been bidden to await them at the door for their daily drive, and as Mr. Egremont leant back with the furs disposed over him he observed: 'That's a man who knows how to take care of himself. I wonder where he gets his coffee, I've not drunk any like it since I was at Nice.' And Nuttie, though well knowing that Mr. Dutton's love of perfection was not self- indulgence, was content to accept this as high approbation, and a good augury for Mark and Annaple. Indeed, with Mr. Dutton settled near, and with the prospect of a daily walk from church with him, she felt such a complete content and trust as she had not known since she had been uprooted from Micklethwayte.

CHAPTER XXVIII.

A BRAVE HEART.

'One furnace many times the good and bad may hold,
Yet what consumes the chaff will only cleanse the gold.'
Archbishop TRENCH.

Never was there a truer verse than that which tells us that in seeking duty we find pleasure by the way, and in seeking pleasure we meet pain. It might be varied to apply to our anticipations of enjoyment or the reverse. Ursula had embraced her lot as a necessity, and found it enlivened by a good many sunshiny hours; and when she looked upon Mr. Dutton's neighbourhood as a continual source of delight and satisfaction, she found that it gave rise to a continual course of small disappointments.

In the first place, he did not walk home from church with her every morning. She looked for him in vain, even when she knew he was in town. He only appeared there on Sundays, and at intervals when he had some especial reason for speaking to her. At first she thought he must have grown lazy or out of health to have thus dropped his old Micklethwayte habits, but after a time she discovered by accident that he frequented another church, open at a still earlier hour and a little farther off, and she was forced to come to the conclusion that he acted out of his characteristic precise scrupulosity, which would not consider it as correct for her to walk home every day with him. She chafed, and derided 'the dear old man' a little in her own mind, then ended with a sigh. Was there any one who cared so much about what was proper for her? And, after all, was he really older than Mr. Clarence Fane, whom everybody in her father's set called Clarence, or even Clare, and treated as the boy of the party, so that she had taken it as quite natural that he should be paired off with her. It was quite a discovery!

There was another and more serious disappointment. Mr. Egremont had not seemed disinclined to consider the giving the agency to Mark, and Nuttie had begun to think with great satisfaction of May Condamine's delight in welcoming him, and of the good influence that would be brought to bear on the dependents, when suddenly there came a coolness. She could trace the moment, and was sure that it was, when Gregorio became aware of what was intended. He had reason to dread Mark as an enemy, and was likely to wish to keep him at a distance; and it had been Ursula's great hope that an absolute promise might have been given before he heard of the plan; but Mr. Egremont was always slow to make up his mind, except when driven by a sudden impulse, and had never actually said that the post should be offered to his nephew. Nuttie only detected the turn of the tide by the want of cordiality, the hums and haws, and by and by the resumption of the unkind ironical tone when Mark and Annaple were mentioned; and at last, when she had been reading to him a letter from Mrs. William Egremont full of anxiety for the young people, and yet of trust in his kindness to them, he exclaimed, 'You've not been writing to her about this absurd proposal?'

'I have not mentioned any proposal at all. What do you mean?'

'Why, this ridiculous idea about the agency. As if I was going to put my affairs into the hands of a man who has made such a mull of his own.'

'But that was not Mark's fault, papa. He was junior, you know, and had no power over that Goodenough.'

'He ought, then! Never sail with an unlucky captain. No, no, Mark's honourable lady would not let him take the agency when he might have had it, and I am not going to let them live upon me now that they have nothing of their own.'

'Oh, papa, but you almost promised!'

'Almost!' he repeated with his ironical tone; 'that's a word capable of a good deal of stretching. This is what you and that umbrella fellow have made out of my not giving him a direct refusal on the spot. He may meddle with Mark's affairs if he chooses, but not with mine.'

Nuttie had learnt a certain amount of wisdom, and knew that to argue a point only made her father more determined, so she merely answered, 'Very well;' adding in a meek voice, 'Their furniture, poor things!'

'Oh ay. Their umbrella friend is making a collection for them. Yes, I believe I said I would contribute.'

Hot blood surged up within Nuttie at the contemptuous tone, and she bit her lip to keep down the answer, for she knew Mr. Dutton intended to call the next afternoon for her father's ultimatum before going down to Micklethwayte, where the crisis was fast approaching, and she had so much faith in his powers that she dreaded to forestall him by an imprudent word. Alas, Gregorio must have been on his guard, for, though Nuttie was sure she heard her friend's ring at the usual time, no entrance followed. She went up to put on her habit to ride with her father, and when she came down Mr. Egremont held out a card with the name 'Philip Dutton,' and the pencilled request below to be allowed to see Mr. Egremont later in the day.

'He has been denied!' exclaimed she in consternation.

'Hein! Before we go out, sit down and write a note for me.' And he dictated—

> 'Dear Sir—I will not trouble you to call again this afternoon, as I have decided on reflection that there is no employment on my estate suited to my nephew, Mark Egremont.
>
> 'As I understand that you are raising a family subscription for rescuing his furniture from the creditors, I enclose a cheque for £50 for the purpose.
>
> —I remain—'

'Yours—what—papa?—' asked Ursula, with a trembling voice, full of tears.

'Yours, etc., of course. Quite intimate enough for an ex-umbrella-monger. Here, give it to me, and I'll sign it while you fill up the cheque for me.'

That such should be the first letter that Nuttie ever addressed to Mr.

Dutton, since the round-hand one in 'which Miss Ursula wished Mr. Duton to have the onner of a tee with me on my birthday, and I am your affected little Nuttie'!

She hoped to explain and lament the next morning, after church. He would surely come to talk it over with her; but he only returned a civil note with his receipt, and she did not see him again before his departure. She was greatly vexed; she had wanted so much to tell him how it was, and then came an inward consciousness that she would probably have told him a great deal too much.

Was it that tiresome prudence of his again that would think for her and prevent impulsive and indignant disclosures? It made her bring down her foot sharply on the pavement with vexation as she suspected that he thought her so foolish, and then again her heart warmed with the perception of self-denying care for her. She trusted to that same prudence for no delusive hopes having been given to Mark and his wife.

She did so justly. Mr. Dutton had thought the matter far too uncertain to be set before them. The Canoness's vague hopes had been the fruit of a hint imprudently dropped by Nuttie herself in a letter to Blanche. She had said more to Miss Nugent, but Mary was a nonconductor. Mr. Dutton's heart sank as he looked at the houses, and he had some thoughts of going to her first for intelligence, but Annaple had spied him, and ran out to the gate to welcome him.

'Oh, Mr. Dutton, I'm so glad! Mark will be delighted.'

'Is he at home?'

'Oh no, at the office, wading through seas of papers with Mr. Greenleaf, but he will come home to eat in a quarter of an hour. So come in;' then, as her boy's merry voice and a gruffer one were heard, 'That's the bailiff. He is Willie's devoted slave.'

'I hoped to have been in time to have saved you that.'

'Well, I'm convinced that among the much maligned races are bailiffs. I wonder what I could get by an article on prejudice against classes! I was thinking how much beer I should have to lay in for this one, and behold he is a teetotaller, and besides that amateur nurse-maid, parlour-maid, kitchen-maid, etc. etc.—'

'What bailiff could withstand Mrs. Egremont? Perhaps you have tamed him?'

'Not I. The cook did that. Indeed I believe there's a nice little idyll going on in the kitchen, and besides he wore the blue ribbon, and was already a devoted follower of young Mr. Godfrey!'

'However, if the valuation is ready, I hope you may be relieved from him, if you won't be too much concerned at the parting!'

'Mrs. Egremont told us that our people are very good to us,' said Annaple, 'and don't mean to send us out with nothing but a pack at our backs. It is very kind in them and in you, Mr. Dutton, to take the trouble of it! No, I'll not worry you with thanks. The great point is, hope for something for Mark to do. That will keep up his spirits best! Poor Mr. Greenleaf is so melancholy that it is all I can do to keep him up to the mark.'

'I have been making inquiries, and I have three possible openings, but I hardly like to lay them before you.'

'Oh, we are not particular about gentility! It is work we want, and if it was anything where I could help that would be all the better! I'm sure I only wonder there are so many as three. I think it is somebody's doing. Ah! there's Mark,' and she flew out to meet him. 'Mark!' she said, on the little path, 'here's the good genius, with three chances in his pocket. Keep him to luncheon. I've got plenty. Poor old man, how hot you look! Go and cool in the drawing-room, while I wash my son's face.'

And she disappeared into the back regions, while Mark, the smile she had called up vanishing from his face, came into the drawing-room, and held out a cordial, thankful hand to his friend, whose chief intelligence was soon communicated. 'Yes,' said Mark, when he heard the amount entrusted by the family to Mr. Dutton, 'that will save all my wife's poor little household gods. Not that I should call them so, for I am sure she does not worship them. I don't know what would become of me if she were like poor Mrs. Greenleaf, who went into hysterics when the bailiff arrived, and has kept her room ever since. I sometimes feel as if nothing could hurt us while Annaple remains what she is.'

Mr. Dutton did not wonder that he said so, when she came in leading her little son, with his sunny hair newly brushed and shining, and carrying a little bouquet for the guest of one La Marque rosebud and three lilies of the valley.

'Take it to Mr. Dutton, Billy-boy; I think he knows how the flowers came into the garden. You shall have daddy's button-hole to take to him next. There, Mark, it is a pansy of most smiling countenance, such as should beam on you through your accounts. I declare, there's that paragon of a Mr. Jones helping Bessy to bring in dinner! Isn't it very kind to provide a man-servant for us?'

It might be rattle, and it might be inconsequent, but it was much pleasanter than hysterics. Billy-boy was small enough to require a good deal of attention at dinner, especially as he was more disposed to open big blue eyes at the stranger, than to make use of his spoon, and Annaple seemed chiefly engrossed with him, though a quick keen word at the right moment showed that she was aware of all that was going on, as Mark and Mr. Dutton discussed the present situation and future measures.

It was quite true that a man concerned in a failure was in great danger of being left out of the race for employment, and Mr. Dutton did not think it needful to mention the force of the arguments he was using to back his recommendation of Mark Egremont. The possibilities he had heard of were a clerkship at a shipping agent's, another at a warehouse in their own line, and a desk at an insurance office. This sounded best, but had the smallest salary to begin with, and locality had to be taken into account. Mr. Dutton's plan was, that as soon as Mark was no longer necessary for what Annaple was pleased to call the fall of the sere and withered leaf, the pair should come to stay with him, so that Mark could see his possible employers, and Annaple consider of the situations. They accepted this gratefully, Mark only proposing that she should go either to his stepmother or her own relations to avoid the final crisis.

'As if I would!' she exclaimed. 'What sort of a little recreant goose do you take me for?'

'I take you for a gallant little woman, ready to stand in the breach,' said Mark.

'Ah, don't flatter yourself! There is a thing I have not got courage to face —without necessity, and that's Janet's triumphant pity. Mr. Dutton lives rather too near your uncle, but he is a man, and he can't be so bad.'

This of course did not pass till Mr. Dutton had gone in to greet the ladies next door, to promise to tell them of their child at length when the business hours of the day should be over.

Shall it be told? There was something in his tone—perfectly indefinable, with which he spoke of 'Miss Egremont,' that was like the old wistfully reverential voice in which he used to mention 'Mrs. Egremont.' It smote Mary Nugent's quiet heart with a pang. Was it that the alteration from the old kindly fatherliness of regard to 'little Nuttie' revealed that any dim undefined hope of Mary's own must be extinguished for ever; or was it that she grieved that he should again be wasting his heart upon the impracticable?

A little of both, perhaps, but Mary was as ready as ever to sympathise, and to rejoice in hearing that the impetuous child had grown into the forbearing dutiful woman.

CHAPTER XXIX.

A FRESH START.

'Did you say that Mark and his wife were come to Springfield House?'

'They come the day after to-morrow,' answered Ursula. 'Mark could not finish up the business sooner.'

'Well, I suppose we must have them to dinner for once. He has made a fool of himself, but I won't have the Canoness complaining that I take no notice of him; and it is easier done while he is there than when he has got into some hole in the City—that is if he ever gets anything to do.'

'Mr. Dutton has several situations in view for him.'

'In view. That's a large order. Or does it mean living on Dutton and doing something nominal? I should think Dutton too old and sharp a hand for that, though he is quartering them on himself.'

'I believe there is nothing Mr. Dutton would like better, if he thought it right for them, but I am quite sure Mark and Annaple would not consent.'

'Ha, ha!' and Mr. Egremont laughed. 'Their nose is not brought to the grindstone yet! Say Saturday, then, Ursula.'

'Am I to ask Mr. Dutton?'

'Of course; I'm not going to have a tete-a-tete with Master Mark.'

So Ursula had the satisfaction of writing a more agreeable note to Mr. Dutton than her last, and her invitation was accepted, but to her vexation Mr. Egremont further guarded himself from anything confidential by verbally asking Mr. Clarence Fane on that very day, and as that gentleman was a baronet's son, she knew she should fall to his lot at dinner, and though she was glad when this was the case at their ordinary parties, it was a misfortune on the present occasion. She had not seen Annaple since her marriage, except at the family gathering on the Canon's death, when she was very much absorbed by the requirements of the stricken household; and Nuttie expected to see her in the same subdued condition. All Mr. Dutton had said or Mary Nugent had written about her courage and cheerfulness had given the impression of 'patience smiling at grief,' and in a very compassionate mood she started for a forenoon call at Springfield House; but, early as it was, nobody was at home, unless it might be the little boy, whose voice she thought she heard while waiting at the gate.

She was out driving with her father afterwards in the long summer evening, and only found Mark's card on returning just in time to dress. It was a bright glaring day, and she was sitting by the window, rather inattentively listening to Mr. Fane's criticism of a new performance at one of the theatres, when she heard the bell, and there entered the slight, bright creature who might still have been taken for a mere girl. The refined though pronounced features, the transparent complexion, crispy yellow hair and merry eyes, were as sunbeam-like as at the Rectory garden-party almost five years ago, and the black dress only marked the contrast, and made the slenderness of the figure more evident.

Mark looked older, and wrung his cousin's hand with a pressure of gratitude and feeling, but Annaple's was a light little gay kiss, and there was an entire unconsciousness about her of the role of poor relation. She made an easy little acknowledgment of the introduction of Mr. Fane, and, as Mr. Egremont appeared the next moment, exchanged greetings with him in a lively ordinary fashion.

This was just what he liked. He only wanted to forget what was unpleasant, and, giggling Scotch girl as she was, he was relieved to find that she could not only show well-bred interest in the surface matters of the time, but put in bright flashes of eagerness and originality, well seconded by Mr. Dutton. Mr. Fane was always a professor of small talk, and Nuttie had learnt to use the current change of society, so that though Mark was somewhat silent, the dinner was exceedingly pleasant and lively; and, as Mr. Fane remarked afterwards, he had been asked to enliven a doleful feast to ruined kindred, he could only say he wished prosperity always made people so agreeable.

'This is all high spirit and self-respect,' thought Nuttie. 'Annaple is talking as I am, from the teeth outwards. I shall have it out with her when we go upstairs! At any rate my father is pleased with her!'

Nuttie made the signal to move as soon as she could, and as they went upstairs, put her arm round the slim waist and gave a sympathetic pressure, but the voice that addressed her had still the cheery ring that she fancied had been only assumed.

'I'm sorry I missed you, but we set out early and made a day of it; and oh! we've been into such funny places as I never dreamt of! You didn't see my boy?'

'No. I thought I heard him. I must see him to-morrow.'

'And I must see yours. May it not be a pleasure to-night? I've no doubt you go and gloat over him at night.'

'Well, I do generally run up after dinner; but after your day, I can't think of dragging you up all these stairs.'

'Oh, that's nothing! Only you see it is jollier to have my Billy-boy in the next room.'

They were mounting all the time, and were received in the day nursery by the old Rectory nurse, much increased in dignity, but inclined to be pathetic as she inquired after 'Mr. Mark,' while Annaple, like a little insensible being, answered with provoking complacency as to his perfect health, and begged Mrs. Poole to bring Master Alwyn to play in the garden at Springfield with her Willie. In fact there was a general invitation already to Alwyn to play there, but his attendants so much preferred the society of their congeners in the parks that they did not avail themselves of it nearly as often as Ursula wished.

Little Alwyn asleep was, of course, a beautiful sight, with a precious old headless rabbit pressed tight to his cheek; Annaple's face grew tender as she looked at the motherless creature; and she admired him to any extent except saying that he excelled her own. Being more than a year the elder, there could be no rivalry as to accomplishments; but as soon as they were out of the nursery hush, Annaple laughed her way down again with tales of Billy-boy's wonder at his first experiences of travelling. They sat down among the plants in the balcony, as far from the lamps as possible, and talked themselves into intimacy over Micklethwayte. There are two Eden homes in people's lives, one that of later childhood, the other the first of wedded happiness, and St. Ambrose Road had the same halo to both of these; for both had been uprooted from it against their will; the chief difference being that Ursula could cast longing, lingering looks behind, while Annaple held herself resolutely steeled against sentiment, and would only turn it off by something absurd. Nothing was absolutely settled yet; Mark had been presenting himself at offices, and she had been seeing rooms and lodgings.

'The insurance office sounds the best, and would be the least shock to our belongings,' said Annaple; 'but it seems to lead to nothing. He would not get on unless we had capital to invest, and even if we had any, you wouldn't catch us doing that again!'

'Does Mr. Dutton advise that?'

'No, he only thought we should like it better; but we are quite past caring for people's feelings in the matter. They couldn't pity us worse than they do. I incline to Stubbs and Co. One of them was once in the Greenleaf office, and has a regard for anything from thence; besides Mark would have something to do besides desk work. He would have to judge of samples, and see to the taking in and storing of goods. He does know something about that, and I'm sure it would agree with him better than an unmitigated high stool, with his nose to a desk.'

'I should like it better.'

'That's right! Now I have got some one to say so. Besides, rising is possible, if one gets very useful. I mean to be Mrs. Alderman, if not my Lady Mayoress, before we have done. Then they have a great big almost deserted set of rooms over the warehouse, where we might live and look after the place.'

'Oh! but should you like that?'

'Mr. Dutton wants us to live out in some of the suburban places, where it seems there is a perfect population of clerks' families in semi-detached houses. He says we should save Mark's railway fare, rent, and all in doctors' bills. But people, children and all, do live and thrive in the City; and I think Mark's health will be better looked after if I am there to give him his midday bite and sup, and brush him up, than if he is left to cater for himself; and as to exercise for the Billy-boy, 'tis not so far to the Thames Embankment. The only things that stagger me are the blacks! I don't know whether life is long enough to be after the blacks all day long, but perhaps I shall get used to them!'

'Well, I think that would be worse.'

'Perhaps it would; and at any rate, if the blacks do beat me, we could move. Think, no rent, nor rates, nor taxes—that is an inducement to swallow —no—to contend with, any number of blackamoors, isn't it? even if they settle on the tip of Billy-boy's nose.'

'I could come to see you better there than out in a suburb,' said Nuttie. 'But what do these rooms look out upon?'

'On one side into their own court, on the other into Wulstan Street—a quiet place on the whole—all walls and warehouses; and there's an excellent parish church, Mr. Underwood's; so I think we might do worse.'

Nuttie was very sorry that the gentlemen came up, and Mr. Fane wandered out and began asking whether they were going to the rose show. Somehow on that evening she became conscious that Annaple looked at her and Mr. Fane rather curiously; and when they met again the next day, and having grown intimate over the introduction of the two little boys, were driving out together, there were questions about whether she saw much of him.

'Oh, I don't know! He is the nicest, on the whole, of papa's friends; he can talk of something besides'—Nuttie paused over her 'besides,'—'horseyness, and all that sort of thing—he is not so like an old satyr as some of them are; and so he is a resource.'

'I see. And you meet him elsewhere, don't you, in general society?'

'I don't go out much now that Lady Kirkaldy is not in town; but he always seems to turn up everywhere that one goes.'

'Ursula, I'm very glad of that tone of yours. I was afraid—'

'Afraid of what?' cried Nuttie in a defiant tone.

'That you liked him, and he is not really nice, Nuttie. Mark knows all about him; and so did I when I lived with the Delmars.'

Nuttie laughed rather bitterly. 'Thank you, Annaple. As if I could care for that man—or he for me, for that matter! I know but too well,' she added gravely, 'that nobody nice is ever intimate at home.'

'I beg your pardon. I would not have worried you about it, only I think you must take care, Nuttie, for Blanche mentioned it to us last winter.'

'Blanche is an arrant gossip! If she saw a grandfather and great grandmother gossiping she would say they were going to be married.'

'Yes, as Mark says, one always swallows Blanche with a qualification.'

'You may be quite sure, Annaple, that nothing like that will ever be true about me! Why, what would ever become of my poor little Wyn if I was so horrid as to want to go and marry?'

She said it with an ineffable tone of contempt, just like the original Nuttie, who seemed to be recalled by association with Annaple.

That sojourn of Mark and his wife at Springfield House was a bright spot in that summer. If it had been only that Annaple's presence gave the free entree to such an island of old Micklethwayte, it would have been a great pleasure to her; but there was besides the happiness of confidence and unrestraint in their society, a restful enjoyment only to be appreciated by living the guarded life of constraint that was hers. She was so seldom thrown among people whom she could admire and look up to. Annaple told her husband of Nuttie's vehement repudiation of any intention of marriage. 'I am sure she meant it,' she observed, 'it was only a little too strong. I wonder if that poor youth who came to her first ball, and helped to pick us out of the hole in Bluepost Bridge, had anything to do with it.'

Annaple had an opportunity of judging. Mr. Dutton would not have brought about a meeting which might be painful and unsettling to both; but one afternoon, when Nuttie was 'off duty' with her father, and had come in to share Annaple's five o'clock tea, Gerard Godfrey, looking the curate from head to foot, made his appearance, having come up from the far east, about some call on Mr. Dutton's purse.

The two shook hands with pleased surprise, and a little heightening of colour, but that was all. Nuttie had been out to luncheon, and was dressed 'like a mere fashionable young lady' in his eyes; and when, after the classes and clubs and schools of his district had been discussed, he asked, 'And I suppose you are taking part in everything here?'

'No, that I can't!'

'Indeed! I know Porlock, the second curate here very well, and he tells me that his vicar has a wonderful faculty of finding appropriate work for every one. Of course you know him?'

'No, I don't;' said Nuttie.

'Miss Egremont has her appropriate work,' said Mr. Dutton, and the deacon felt himself pushed into his old position at Micklethwayte. He knew the clergy of the district very well, and how persistently either Mr. Egremont, or perhaps Gregorio, prevented their gaining admittance at his house; and he guessed, but did not know, that Nuttie could not have got into personal intercourse with them without flat disobedience.

Annaple threw herself into the breach, and talked of St. Wulstan's; and the encounter ended, leaving the sense of having drifted entirely away from one another, and being perfectly heart whole, though on the one hand Ursula's feeling was of respect and honour; and Gerard's had a considerable element of pity and disapprobation.

'No!' said Annaple when they were gone, 'he will not cry like the kloarek in the Breton ballad who wetted three great missals through with his tears at his first mass. He is very good, I am sure, but he is a bit of a prig!'

'It is very hard to youth to be good without priggishness,' said Mr. Dutton. 'Self-assertion is necessary, and it may easily be carried too far.'

'Buttresses are useful, but they are not beauties,' rejoined Annaple.

The warehouse arrangement was finally adopted, and after the three weeks necessary for the cleaning and fitting of their floor, and the bringing in of their furniture, Mark and Annaple began what she termed 'Life among the Blacks.'

Nuttie had great designs of constantly seeing Annaple, sending her supplies from the gardens and preserves at Bridgefield, taking her out for drives, and cultivating a friendship between Alwyn and Willie, who hadtaken to each other very kindly on the whole. They could not exactly understand each other's language, and had great fights from time to time over toys, for though there was a year between them they were nearly equal in strength; but they cared for each other's company more than for anything else, were always asking to go to one another, and roared when the time of parting came; at least Alwyn did so unreservedly, for Nuttie had begun to perceive with compunction that Billy-boy was much the most under control, and could try to be good at his mother's word, without other bribe than her kiss and smile. Ah! but he had a mother!

CHAPTER XXX.

NUTTIE'S PROSPECTS.

'Three hundred pounds and possibilities.'—Merry Wives of Windsor.

Again Nuttie's plans were doomed to be frustrated. It did not prove to be half so easy to befriend Mr. and Mrs. Mark Egremont as she expected, at the distance of half London apart, and with no special turn for being patronised on their side.

Her father took a fancy for almost daily drives with her in the park, because then he could have Alwyn with him; and the little fellow's chatter had become his chief amusement. Or if she had the carriage to herself, there was sure to be something needful to be done which made it impossible to go into the city to take up and set down Mrs. Mark Egremont; and to leave her to make her way home would be no kindness. So Nuttie only accomplished a visit once before going out of town, and that was by her own exertions—by underground railway and cab. Then she found all going prosperously; the blacks not half so obnoxious as had been expected (of course not, thought Nuttie, in the middle of the summer); the look-out over the yard very amusing to Billy-boy; and the large old-fashioned pannelled rooms, so cool and airy that Annaple was quite delighted with them, and contemned the idea of needing a holiday. She had made them very pretty and pleasant with her Micklethwayte furniture, whose only fault was being on too small a scale for these larger spaces, but that had been remedied by piecing, and making what had been used for two serve for one.

The kitchen was on the same floor, close at hand, which was well, for Annaple did a good deal there, having only one young maid for the rougher work. She had taken lessons in the School of Cookery, and practised a good deal even at Micklethwayte, and she was proud of her skill and economy. Mark came in for his mid-day refreshment, and looked greatly brightened, as if the worst had come and was by no means so bad as he expected. All the time he had been at Mr. Dutton's he had been depressed and anxious, but now, with his boy on his knee, he was merrier than Nuttie had ever known him. As to exercise, there were delightful evening walks, sometimes early marketings in the long summer mornings before business began—and altogether it seemed, as Nuttie told her father afterwards, as if she had had a glimpse into a little City Arcadia.

'Hein!' said he, 'how long will it last?'

And Nuttie was carried away to Cowes, where he had been persuaded to recur to his old favourite sport of yachting. She would have rather liked this if Clarence Fane had not been there too, and continually haunting them. She had been distrustful of him ever since Annaple's warning, and it became a continual worry to the motherless girl to decide whether his civil attentions really meant anything, or whether she were only foolish and ridiculous in not accepting them as freely and simply as before.

Of one thing she became sure, namely, that Gregorio was doing whatever in him lay to bring them together.

In this seaside temporary abode, great part of the London establishment was left behind, and Gregorio condescended to act the part of butler, with only a single man-servant under him, and thus he had much more opportunity of regulating the admission of visitors than at home; and he certainly often turned Mr. Fane in upon her, when she had intended that gentleman to be excluded, and contrived to turn a deaf or uncomprehending ear when she desired that there should be no admission of visitors unless her father was absolutely ready for them; and also there were times when he must have suggested an invitation to dinner, or a joining in a sail. No doubt Gregorio would have been delighted to see her married, and to be thus free from any counter influence over his master; but as she said to herself, 'Catch me! Even if I cared a rush for the man, I could not do it. I don't do my poor father much good, but as to leaving poor little Alwyn in his clutches—I must be perfectly demented with love even to think of it.'

There was a desire on the valet's part to coax and court little Alwyn of which she felt somewhat jealous. The boy was naturally the pet of every one in the household, but he was much less out of Gregorio's reach in the present confined quarters, and she could not bear to see him lifted up in the valet's arms, allowed to play with his watch, held to look at distant sails on board the yacht, or even fed with sweet biscuits or chocolate creams.

The Rectory nursery had gone on a strict regimen and nurse was as angry as Nuttie herself; but there was no preventing it, for his father was not above cupboard love, and never resisted the entreaties that were always excited by the sight of dainties, only laughing when Nuttie remonstrated, or even saying, 'Never mind sister, Wynnie, she's got Mrs. Teachem's cap on,' and making the child laugh by pretending to smuggle in papers of sweets by stealth, apart from the severe eyes of sister or nurse.

That cut Nuttie to the heart. To speak of the evils for which self-indulgence was a preparation would only make her father sneer at her for a second Hannah More. It was a language he did not understand; and as to the physical unwholesomeness, he simply did not choose to believe it. She almost wished Alwyn would for once be sick enough to frighten him, but that never happened, nor would he accept nurse's statement of the boy being out of order.

Poor little Alwyn, he was less and less of an unmixed joy to her as he was growing out of the bounds of babyhood, and her notions of discipline were thwarted by her father's unbounded indulgence. To her the child was a living soul, to be trained for a responsible position here and for the eternal world beyond; to her father he was a delightful plaything, never to be vexed, whose very tempers were amusing, especially when they teased the serious elder sister.

'Oh father! do you ever think what it will come to?' Nuttie could not help saying one day when Mr. Egremont had prevented her from carrying him off in disgrace to the nursery for tying the rolls up in dinner napkins to enact Punch and Judy, in spite of his own endeavours to prevent the consequent desolation of the preparations.

Mr. Egremont shrugged his shoulders, and only observed, 'An excuse for a little home tyranny, eh? No, no, Wyn; we don't want tame little muffs here.'

Nuttie was obliged to run out of the room and—it must be confessed—dance and stamp out her agony of indignation and misery that her father should be bent on ruining his child, for she could not understand that all this was simply the instinctive self-indulgence of a drugged brain and dulled conscience.

She did, however, get a little support and help during a brief stay in the shooting season at Bridgefield. The Canoness was visiting the Condamines at the Rectory, and very soon understood all the state of things, more perhaps from her former nurse than from Ursula. She was witness to one of those trying scenes, when Nuttie had been forbidding the misuse of a beautiful elaborate book of nursery rhymes, where Alwyn thought proper to 'kill' with repeated stabs the old woman of the shoe, when preparing to beat her progeny.

Just as she was getting the dagger paper-knife out of his little hand, and was diverting the pout on his swelling lip, his father became aware of the contest, and immediately the half conquered boy appealed to him. 'Sister naughty. Won't let Wynnie kill cross ugly old woman, beating poor little children.'

'A fellow feeling! eh, sister? Kill her away, boy, tear her out! Yes, give her to sister, and tell her that's the way to serve sour females! I declare, Ursula, she has got something of your expression.'

'Oh Wynnie, Wynnie!' said Nuttie, as he trotted up to her, 'is sister cross and ugly?' and she opened her arms to him.

'Sister, Wyn's own sister,' said the child affectionately, letting himself be kissed as he saw her grieved. 'She shan't be ugly old woman—ugly old woman go in fire.'

So perilously near the flame did he run to burn the old woman that Mr. Egremont shouted to her that in spite of all that humbug, she was perfectly careless of the child, although if she had withheld him she would probably have been blamed for thwarting him.

'Are you quite fair towards Ursula?' the aunt ventured to say when the girl had gone to dress for walking down with her to the Rectory. 'It is hard on her, and not good for the boy to upset her authority.'

'Eh? Why, the girl is just a governess manquee, imbued with the spirit of all those old women who bred her up. A nice life the poor child would have of it, but for me.'

'I am sure she is devotedly attached to him.'

'Hein! So she thinks; but trust human nature for loving to wreak discipline on the child who has cut her out.'

'That is scarcely just, Alwyn. She was greatly relieved to be cut out.'

Mr. Egremont laughed at this, and his sister-in-law indignantly added with all the authority of a successful parent, 'Anyway, nothing is so bad for a child as collision between the authorities in a family. Ursula is doing her best to act as a mother to that child, and it will be very injurious to him to interfere with her influences.'

'She's a good girl enough—gives very little trouble,' he allowed, 'but I'm not going to have the boy sat upon.'

As he spoke the words, Nuttie returned, and as soon as she was out of the house and out of hearing she exclaimed, 'Oh, Aunt Jane, you see how it is! How am I to prevent my boy from being utterly ruined?'

'I have been speaking to your father,' said Mrs. Egremont, 'but he does not seem to understand. Men don't. A child's faults and fancies seem such trifles to them that they can't see the harm of indulging them, and, besides, they expect to be amused.'

'And is that poor dear little fellow to grow up spoilt?' said Nuttie, her eyes hot with unshed tears.

'I hope not, Ursula. I have great confidence in your influence, for I see you are a sensible girl.' This was astonishing praise from the Canoness. 'But you will throw away your chances if you keep up a continual opposition to what your father allows. It will be much less hurtful if Alwyn does get too much indulgence, and does a little unnecessary mischief, than for him to learn to think you the enemy of his pleasures, always wanting to check and punish him. Oh yes,' as Nuttie was going to answer, 'I know it is for his real good, but how is that baby to understand that? Indeed, my dear, I know how it is; I have gone through the same sort of thing with Basil.'

'Oh, it could never have been so bad!'

'No, of course not; but I have had to allow what I did not like for the child rather than let him see the shadow of difference of opinion between us, and I don't think it has done him any harm. The great point is that you should keep that poor little fellow's affection and respect, and make him unwilling to vex you.'

'That he is, dear little man. He is sorry when he sees sister grieved. He is always distressed if anything is hurt or pained. He is really tender-hearted.'

'Yes, but boys are boys. That feeling will fail you if you work it too hard, and especially if you show vexation at his pleasures. Keep that for real evils, like falsehood or cruelty.'

'Not for disobedience?'

'The evil of disobedience depends much more upon the authority of an order than on the child itself. If he disobeys you under his father's licence, you cannot make much of it. You have him a good deal to yourself?'

'Yes.'

'Then make use of that time to strengthen his principles and sense of right and wrong, as well as to secure his affections. My dear, I never saw a girl in a more difficult position than yours, but I see you are doing your utmost; only I am afraid the love of sedatives is the same.'

'Oh aunt, I did think he had given it up!'

'You are inexperienced, my dear. I see it in his eyes. Well, I'm afraid there is no stopping that.'

'Mother—' and Nuttie's voice was choked.

'She did her best, but you have not the same opportunities. It can't be helped with a man of that age. Mark might have done something, but he is out of the question now, poor fellow!'

'Indeed, Aunt Jane, I think Mark and Annaple are some of the happiest people I ever saw. I only wish my poor Alwyn were as forward as their Billy, but I'm not even allowed to teach him his letters, because once he cried over them.'

'I wish they had anything to fall back upon,' said Mrs. Egremont anxiously. 'They are so unwilling to let any one know of their difficulties that I feel as if I never knew in what straits they may be. You will be sure to let me know, Ursula, if there is anything that I can do for them.'

That conversation was a great comfort and help to Nuttie, who was pleased to find herself treated as a real friend by her aunt, and perceived the wisdom of her advice. But the watching over the Mark Egremonts was a very difficult matter to accomplish, for when she went back to London she was warned that Billy had the whooping cough, rendering them unapproachable all the winter, so that she could only hear of them through Mr. Dutton, whom she continued to see occasionally whenever there was anything to communicate. Mr. Egremont rather liked him, and on meeting him in the street, would ask him casually in to dinner, or to make up a rubber, or play piquet, for he excelled in these arts, and still more in chess, and an evening with Mr. Dutton was quite a red-letter time with Nuttie. It gave her an indefinable sense of safety and protection; but it was not always to be had, for her friend had many engagements, being one of the active lay church workers, and devoting two regular evenings in each week to Gerard Godfrey's eastern district, where he kept all the accounts, had a model court and evening class, besides hospitably resting tired clergymen and their wives in his pleasant quiet house.

In the spring Mr. Egremont was laid up with the worst rheumatic attack he had yet had, in consequence of yielding to the imperious will of his son, who had insisted on standing in a bleak corner to see the Life Guards pass by. On this occasion Nuttie did not prove herself the heaven-born nurse that the true heroine ought to be, but was extremely frightened, and altogether dependent on Gregorio, who knew all about the symptoms, and when to send for the doctor and a garde-malade. Gregorio always talked French to Nuttie when he felt himself in the ascendant, as he certainly was at present; but he became much less gracious when he heard that Mrs. William Egremont might be expected, declaring that madame would only excite his master, and that her presence was quite unnecessary. Her coming had been volunteered, but it was a great boon to Ursula, who was thus helped out in many perplexities, although Mrs. Egremont was a great deal at her step-son's, and neither lady was of much avail in the sick-room, during the stress of the illness. It was never actually dangerous, but there was great suffering and much excitement, and for four or five days the distress and anxiety were considerable. After this passed off Ursula was surprised to find her company preferred to that of her aunt. She was a better souffre-douleur, was less of a restraint, and was besides his regular reader and amanuensis, so that as the force of the attack abated, he kept her a good deal in his room during the latter part of the day, imparting scraps of intelligence, skimming the papers for him, and reading his letters.

There was a lease to be signed, and, as soon as might be, Mr. Bulfinch, the Redcastle solicitor, brought it up, and had to be entertained at luncheon. While he was waiting in the drawing-room for Mr. Egremont to be made ready for him, he looked with deep interest on the little heir, whom Ursula presently led off to the other end of the room to the hoard of downstair toys; and an elaborate camp was under construction, when by the fireside, the Canoness inquired in a low confidential tone, 'May I ask whether you came about a will?'

'No, Mrs. Egremont. I wish I were. It is only about the lease of Spinneycotes farm.'

'Then there is none?'

'None that I am aware of. None has ever been drawn up by us. Indeed, I was wishing that some influence could be brought to bear which might show the expedience of making some arrangement. Any melancholy event is, I trust, far distant, but contingencies should be provided for.'

'Exactly so. He is recovering now, but these attacks always leave effects on the heart, and at his age, with his habits, no one knows what may happen. Of course it would not make much difference to the boy.'

'No, the Court of Chancery would appoint the most suitable natural guardians.'

'But,' said Mrs. Egremont, 'I am afraid that the personal property when divided would not be much of a provision for her.'

'You are right. The investments are unfortunately and disproportionately small.'

'She ought either to have them all, or there should be a charge on the estate,' said the Canoness decisively. 'If possible, he must be made to move.'

'Oh, don't!' cried Nuttie, jumping up from the floor. 'He mustn't be upset on any account.'

'My dear, I had no notion that you heard us!' exclaimed her aunt. 'I thought Alwyn was making too much noise with his soldiers.'

'I beg your pardon,' said Nuttie, 'perhaps I should have spoken sooner, but indeed he must not be worried and disturbed,' she added, somewhat fiercely.

'Don't be afraid, my dear,' said her aunt. 'Mr. Bulfinch knows that your father is in no condition to have such matters brought before him.'

'Certainly,' said the old lawyer politely;' and we will trust that Miss Egremont's prospects may soon come forward on a more auspicious occasion.'

Nuttie could have beaten him, but she was obliged to content herself with such a sweeping charge of her Zulus among Alwyn's Englishmen, that their general shrieked out in indignation against such a variation of the accustomed programme of all their games.

Nuttie thought she had defended her patient sufficiently, but she found she had been mistaken, for when her aunt had left them, some days later, her father began, 'We are well quit of her. Those troublesome dictatorial women always get worse when they are left widows—taking upon them to say what their dear husbands would have said, forsooth.'

'Aunt Jane was very kind to me,' said Ursula, not in the least knowing what he was thinking of.

'To you. Ay, I should think so, taking upon her to lecture me about securing a provision for you.'

'Oh! I hoped—'

'What?' he broke in. 'You knew of it! You set her on, I suppose.'

'Oh! no, no, father. She and Mr. Bulfinch began about it, not meaning me to hear—about a will, I mean—and I told them I wasn't going to have you worried, and I thought I had stopped it altogether.'

'Stop a woman bent on her duty? Hein! But you are a good girl, and shall come to no loss when we have to make your marriage settlement.'

'You won't have to do that, father!'

'Hein! What do you keep that poor fellow Clarence Fane dangling in attendance on you for?'

'I don't! I'm sure I don't want him. I would do anything to keep him at a distance!'

'How now! I thought your Grace condescended to him more than to any one else.'

'I don't dislike him unless he has *that* in his head; but as to marrying him! Oh—h—h,' such a note of horror that elicited a little laugh.

'So hot against him, are we? Who is it then? Not the umbrella fellow?'

'Father! how can you?' she cried, with a burning flush of indignation. He —why—he! He has always been a sort of uncle, ever since I was a little girl.'

'Oh yes, adopted uncles are very devout when young ladies rush out to morning prayers at unearthly hours—'

'Father!' with her voice trembling, 'I assure you he doesn't—I mean he always goes to St. Michael's, unless he has anything particular to say to me.'

'Oh yes, I understand,' and Mr. Egremont indulged in a hearty laugh, which almost drove poor Nuttie beside herself.

'Indeed—indeed,' she stammered, in her confusion and suppressed wrath; 'it is nothing of that sort. He is a regular old bachelor—he always was.'

'At what age do men become old bachelors? For he seems to me about the age of poor Clarry, whom you seem to view as a bugbear.'

'I wish you would not think of such things, father; I have not the slightest intention of leaving you and dear little Wynnie! Nothing should tempt me!'

'Nothing? Hein! Then you may as well be on your guard, Miss Egremont, or we shall have pleadings that you have encouraged them—church and world —or both, maybe. You pious folk take your little diversions and flirtations just like your poor sisters whom you shake your heads at, never guessing how Gregorio and I have looked out at you and your adopted uncle parading the street.'

'I wish Gregorio would mind his own business, and not put such things in your head!' burst out Nuttie.

At which Mr. Egremont laughed longer and louder than ever.

Poor Nuttie! It was terrible discomfiture, not only for the moment, but a notion had been planted in her mind that seemed cruel, almost profane, and yet which would not be dismissed, and made her heart leap with strange bounds at the wild thought, 'Could it be true?' then sink again with shame at her own presumptuous folly in entertaining such a thought for a moment.

Yet whenever she actually encountered Mr. Dutton her habitual comfort and reliance on him revived, and dispelled all the embarrassment which at other times she expected to feel in his presence.

CHAPTER XXXI.

SPES NON FRACTA.

Summer had quite set in before Mr. Egremont was able to go out for a drive, and then he was ordered to Buxton.

Nuttie only once saw her cousins before leaving town, for their little boy fulfilled the nursery superstition by whooping till May; and all intercourse was prohibited, till he had ceased for a whole week to utter a suspicious sound. Mr. Dutton had insisted on the family spending a fortnight at Springfield House for change of air, and it was there that Nuttie was permitted to see them, though the children were still forbidden to meet.

Annaple looked very thin, but rattled as merrily as ever. 'No one could guess,' she said, 'what a delight it was not to know what one was to have for dinner?'

'To do more than know, I am afraid,' said Ursula.

'Well, next to the delight of knowing nothing at all about it—and even that is only good for a holiday—is the delight of seeing a pudding come out smooth and comfortable and unbroken from its basin. "Something attempted, something done," you know. It is quite as good a work of art as a water-coloured drawing.'

'Only not quite so permanent.'

'No; it is only one's first pudding that one wants to embalm in a glass case for being so good as not to leave its better part behind in the basin, or to collapse as soon as it is in the dish.'

'Which my puddings always did in the happy days of old, but then I was always hunted ignominiously out of the kitchen and told I wasted good food,' said Nuttie.

'Yes, and waste is fearful when Mark and Billy have to eat it all the same, like the poor cows with spoilt hay. I wonder whether your old experiences recall the joy of finding trustworthy eggs within your price.'

'Ah, I was not housekeeper. I only remember being in disgrace for grumbling when there was no pudding, because the hens would not lay.'

'Though I heard a woman declaring the other day that there ought to be a machine for them. Oh, the scenes that I encounter when I am marketing! If I only could describe them for Punch! I walked home once with our porter's wife, carrying two most brilliant sticks of rhubarb, all carmine stalk and gamboge leaf, and expressing a very natural opinion that the rhubarb tree must be very showy to look at, and curious to know in what kind of fruit the medicine grew.'

'Oh, Annaple! do you go yourself in that way?'

'Mark used to go with me, but, poor old fellow, he has ruinous ideas about prices and quantities, and besides, now he is so hard worked-up and down all day—he wants a little more of his bed in the morning.'

'And what do you want?'

'I never was a sleepy creature, and I get back in time to dress the boy. I generally find him at high-jinks on his father's bed. It uses up a little superfluous energy before the dressing.'

'But surely you have a servant now?'

'I've come to the conclusion that a workman's wife charing is a better institution. No. 1, a pet of Miss Nugent's, was a nice creature, but the London air did for her at once. No. 2, also from Micklethwayte, instantly set up a young man, highly respectable, and ready to marry on the spot, as they did, though their united ages don't amount to thirty-nine. No. 3 was a Cockney, and couldn't stay because the look-out was so dull; and No. 4 gossiped with her kind when I thought her safe in the Temple Gardens with Billy, whereby he caught the whooping-cough, and as she also took the liberty of wearing my fur cloak, and was not particular as to accuracy, we parted on short notice; and I got this woman to come in every day to scrub, help make the bed, etc. It is much less trouble, and the only fault I have to find with her is an absolute incapability of discerning blacks. I believe she thinks I have a monomania against them.'

Still Annaple insisted that she did not work half so hard as her nieces, Muriel and Janet, in their London season, and that her economy was not nearly so trying and difficult as that which Lady Delmar had been practising for years in order to afford them a summer there; nor was her anxiety to make both ends meet by any means equal to her sister's in keeping up appearances, and avoiding detrimentals. The two sisters met occasionally, but Lady Delmar was so compassionate and patronising that Annaple's spirit recoiled in off- hand levity and rattle, and neither regretted the occupation that prevented them from seeing much of one another.

A year passed by, chiefly spent by Mr. Egremont in the pursuit of comparative health, at Buxton, Bagneres, and Biarritz, during which his daughter could do little but attend to him and to little Alwyn. The boy had been enough left to her and nurse during his father's acute illness to have become more amenable. He was an affectionate child, inheriting, with his mother's face, her sweetness and docility of nature, and he was old enough to be a good deal impressed with the fact that he had made poor papa so ill by teasing him to stand in the cold. Mr. Egremont was not at rest without a sight of the child every day, if only for a moment, and the helplessness and suffering had awed the little fellow a good deal. It was touching to see him pause when galloping about the house when he went past the sick-room, and hush his merry voice of his own accord.

And in the journeys, when his father's invalided state would have made a fractious or wilful child a serious inconvenience, his good temper and contentment were invaluable. He would sit for hours on his sister's lap, listening to whispered oft-told tales, or playing at impromptu quiet games; he could go to sleep anywhere, and the wonderful discoveries he made at each new place were the amusement of all his auditors. Sister was always his playfellow and companion whenever she could be spared from her father, and she had an ever-increasing influence over him which she did her best to raise into principle.

Perhaps she never had a happier moment than when she heard how he had put his hands behind him and steadily refused when Gregorio had offered to regale him at a stall of bonbons forming only a thin crust to liqueurs, which unfortunately he had already been taught to like.

'But I told him sister said I mustn't have them,' said Alwyn. 'And then he made a face and said something in French about you. I know 'twas you, for he said "soeur." What was it?'

'Never mind, Wynnie dear. We had much better never know. You were sister's own dear steadfast boy, and you shall kiss mother's picture.'

Nuttie had a beautiful coloured photograph of her mother, finished like a miniature, which had been taken at Nice, in the time of Alice Egremont's most complete and matured beauty. She had taught Alwyn to kiss and greet it every evening before his prayers, and such a kiss was his reward when he had shown any special act of goodness, for which, as she told him, 'mother would have been pleased with her little son.'

Such another boon was his one Sunday evening at Biarritz, when she found that while she was shut up at dinner with her father he had voluntarily gone to church with nurse instead of playing on the beach with some other English children. 'It was all very long and tiresome,' he said, when asked if he liked it.

'Then why did you go, old man? There was no need to drag you there,' said his father.

'She didn't drag me,' said the boy; 'I walked.'

'You need not have walked then, Master Dignity.'

'Poor nursie couldn't go without me,' said Alwyn, 'and sister says there's a blessing on those that go.'

'A blessing? eh! and what idea does that little head entertain of a blessing?' said Mr. Egremont.

Alwyn lifted his soft brown eyes reverently and said, 'It is something good,' speaking, as he always did, in a baby lisp inimitable here.

'Well?'

'And it comes from God.'

'Well, what is it? Can you see it?'

'No'—he looked in perplexity towards Nuttie, who was in agony all the time, lest there should be a scoff that might remain in the child's mind.

'Never mind sister. Can you feel it?'

'Yes;' and the little face lighted with such a reality that the incipient mockery turned into wonder on the next question.

'And how does it feel?'

'Oh, so nice! It makes Wynnie glad here,' and he spread his hands over his breast; and gave a little caper like a kid for very gladness.

'There!' said Mr. Egremont, leaning back fairly conquered. 'Any one might envy Wynnie! Goodnight, my boy, blessing and all. I wonder if one felt like that when one was a little shaver,' he pursued, as Alwyn went off to his bed.

'I think I did sometimes,' said Nuttie, 'but I never was half as good as Wynnie!'

'What?' exclaimed her father. 'You! bred up among the saints.'

'Ah! but I hadn't the same nature. I never was like—*her*.'

'Well—'tis very pretty now, and I don't know how we could stand a young Turk, but you mustn't make a girl of him.'

'There's no fear of that,' said Nuttie. 'He is full of spirit. That old bathing woman calls him "un vrai petit diable d'Anglais," he is so venturous.'

Which delighted Mr. Egremont as much as the concession that the boy's faith was 'pretty' delighted Ursula. Indeed, he went a little further, for when she came back from her few minutes at Alwyn's bedside he proceeded to tell her of the absolute neglect in which his mother, a belle of the Almacks days, had left her nursery. It was the first time he had ever hinted at a shadow of perception that anything in his own life had been amiss, and Ursula could not but feel a dreamy, hopeful wonder whether her sweet little Alwyn could be the destined means of doing that in which her mother had failed. It was at least enough to quicken those prayers which had been more dutiful than trustful.

And then her hope sank again when she realised that her father's days were spent between the lull of opiate, followed by a certain serenity, then in a period of irritability, each being more or less prolonged, according to health, weather, or entertainment, and closed again by the sedatives in various forms. It relieved her indeed, but she felt it a wickedness to be glad of the calm, and she was aware that the habit was making inroads on her father's powers. Between that and his defect of eyesight, he was often much confused, especially about money matters, and was more and more dependent.

Would that it had been only upon her, but she was constantly certain that Gregorio was taking advantage of his master's helplessness, and keeping it up by all means in his power. Yet what could be done? For the valet was absolutely necessary to his comfort, and yet she sometimes thought her father half in dread of him, and afraid to expostulate about personal neglects, which became more frequent. Things, that would have enraged him from others, were only grumbled and fretted over, when Gregorio caused him real inconvenience by absence or forgetfulness, and made very insufficient apology. It seemed like a bondage; Nuttie thought of her mother's efforts, and blamed herself in vain.

It was during this journey that she heard of good Miss Headworth's death. The old lady's mind had long failed, and the actual present loss to Nuttie was not great; but it seemed to close a long account of gratitude such as she had not thoroughly felt or understood before; and the link with Micklethwayte was severed.

For Mark and Annaple prevailed on Mrs. Egremont to install Miss Nugent as governess to Rosalind and Adela. In that capacity Nuttie hoped to see a good deal of her; but of course was again disappointed, for her father would not hear of returning to Bridgefield. It was draughty, and dull, and desolate, and nothing suited him but London.

CHAPTER XXXII.

BLACKS IN THE ASCENDANT.

'Man's work ends with set of sun,
Woman's work is never done.'—Proverb.

It was far on in May when Ursula found herself again in the sitting-room over the warehouse. Somehow it had not the dainty well-cared-for air of erst. The pretty table ornaments were out of sight; the glass over the clock was dim, the hands had stopped; some of Annaple's foes, the blacks, had effected a lodgment on the Parian figures; the chintzes showed wear and wash, almost grime; the carpet's pattern was worn; a basket full of socks was on the sofa; and on the table a dress, once belonging to Annaple's trousseau, was laid out, converted into its component parts. The wails of a baby could be heard in the distance, and the first person to appear was Master William, sturdy and happy in spite of wofully darned knees to his stockings.

'Mother's coming, if baby will stop crying,' he said, 'and lie in her cradle.'

'Your little sister! What's her name?'

'Jane Christian,' said the boy, with a much more distinct enunciation than Alwyn, though a year older, had yet acquired. 'She does cry so! She won't let mother make my new knickies out of her blue gown!'

Thoughts of the suits that Alwyn was discarding came across Nuttie. Could they be offered without offence? She asked, however, 'Do you remember Alwyn—my Wynnie?'

'Wynnie gave me my horse,' cried the boy, unstabling a steed which had seen hard service since the presentation. 'Where's Wynnie?'

'He is at home. You must come and see him,' said Nuttie, who had not been allowed to bring him till secure of a clean bill of health. 'But see, just outside the door, there's something for Billy.'

She had made her servant bring up the parcels to the passage outside, and Billy was soon hugging a magnificent box of soldiers, wherewith he pranced off to show them to his mother, leaving the doors open, so that Ursula could more decidedly hear the baby's voice, not a healthy child's lusty cry, but a poor little feeble wail, interspersed with attempts at consolation. 'Come, won't she go to Emily? Oh, Billy-boy, how splendid! I hope you thanked Cousin Ursula. Baby Jenny, now can't you let any one speak but yourself? Oh! shall I never teach you that "Balow, my babe," is not "bellow, my babe." That's better! Now can't you let Emily have you, while I go to Cousin Nuttie?'

'Let me come! Mayn't I?' exclaimed Ursula, invading the room that served as kitchen, where Annaple was trying to hush off the child and make her over to a little twelve years old maid, who stood in waiting, helping Willie meantime to unpack his soldiers, with smothered exclamations of delight.

'Oh, Nuttie, how good of you! Please to excuse the accompaniment. There never was such a young lady for self-assertion to make up for there being so little of her.'

And Annaple, very thin and tired looking, held up the child, fearfully small and pinched for four months old, to be kissed by Nuttie.

'Does she always go on like this?'

''Cept when she is asleep,' said Willie.

'Poor wee lassie,' said Annaple; 'there's great excuse for her, for the food has not yet been invented that suits her ladyship.'

'You must come and consult nurse.'

'And how are you all? I'm glad you are at hand, Nuttie! Is Mr. Egremont better?'

'As well as ever he is—lame and altogether an invalid,—but he has not had such bad attacks of pain lately.'

'And his eyes?'

'About the same. He can write, and tell one card from another, but he can't read—or rather it hurts him to do so, and he can't bear a strong light. But, Annaple, how are you? That child is wearing you to a shadow.'

'Oh! I'm quite well—perfectly. There, I think she is gone off at last. You had better walk her about a little, Emily; she will break out again if we try to put her in the cradle.'

And having handed over the child with only a very low murmur, Annaple left her combined kitchen and nursery. She flew at the flowers Nuttie had brought like a thirsty person, crying, as she buried her face in them, 'Now for beauty! Now Mark will be refreshed! Ah! here's a pretty pickle for a reception room.'

'Oh, don't put it away! I could help you; I do so like that kind of work. It is so like old times.'

'It must be put away, thank you, for Mark will be coming in. And the saying about the public washing of garments is specially true of one's own husband. Ways and means are worrying to the masculine mind.'

'I thought it was too early for Mark?'

'He has an appointment to keep at Charing Cross or thereabouts, so I made him promise to come in in time to "put a bit in his head," as our Irish charwoman says.'

'Then I can take him. I have the carriage, and I must be at home by half-past twelve. I wish you would come too, Annaple. There's plenty of room. You could show the baby to nurse, and the boys could have a good game. I would send you back in the evening. Mark could come on after his business is done.'

'Thank you, Nuttie, I can't to-day—for a whole heap of domestic reasons; but, if you can get Mark to come, do, it would be so good for him.'

'How is Mark?'

'He is well, quite well,' said Annaple; 'and so good and patient. But you see, it does take it out of a man when that doleful little noise won't stop all night! We are both acquiring a form of somnambulism, but when there's real out-of-door business to be done, it is not like proper sleep.'

'Or when there's woman's indoor business, I am afraid,' said Nuttie, much concerned at the extreme thinness of Annaple's face and hands, and the weary look of her large eyes.

'Oh, one makes that up at odd times!' she answered brightly. 'One thing is, this work suits Mark, he feels that he can do it, and he gets on well with the men. They asked him to join in their club, and he was so much pleased. He gets up subjects for them, and I am so glad he has such a pleasure and interest to keep him from missing the society he was used to.'

'It must be very good for them too. Mr. Dutton said he really thought Mark had kept them from going in for a strike.'

'Besides the glory of the thing,' said Annaple drawing herself up, 'Mr. Dobbs thought so too, and raised us ten pounds; which made us able to import that little Bridgefield lassie to hold baby—when—when Miss Jenny will let her. He has some law copying to do besides, but I don't like that; it burns the candle at both ends, and he does get bad headaches sometimes, and goes on all the same.'

'You must both come and see my Wyn.'

'Ah! I had never asked after him. I suppose he is as pretty as ever,' said Annaple, who secretly thought his beauty too girlish compared with her sturdy Billy.

'Prettier, I think, as he gets more expression. We can't persuade ourselves to cut his hair, and it looks so lovely on his sailor suit. And he is so good. I could not have believed a child could be so quiet and considerate on a journey. You should have seen him standing by my father's knee in the railway carriage, and amusing him with all that was to be seen, and stopping at the least hint that he was chattering too much.'

'Billy is wonderfully helpful. Ah—' and Annaple's eyes lighted up as the step that had music in't came up the stair; and as Mark came in, Nuttie thought him grown older, his hair thinner, his shoulders rounded, and his office coat shabby, but she saw something in his countenance there had never been before. Ever since she had known him he had worn a certain air of depression, or perhaps more truly of failure and perplexity, which kept before her conscious mind the Desdichado on Ivanhoe's shield, even when he was a gentleman at ease at the luxurious Rectory; but there was now not only the settled air of a man who had found his vocation, but something of the self-respect and eagerness of one who was doing it well, and feeling himself valued.

'Is baby—' he began. 'Oh, Nuttie! Are you there? Mr. Dutton told me you were coming. How is my uncle?' And the voice was much brisker than in the days of lawn-tennis.

'Father, father, look!' cried the boy.

'Why, Billy-boy, you are set up! Zouaves and chasseurs! I see where they came from.'

During the mixture of greetings and inquiries, admiration of the flowers, and the exhibition of Billy's treasures, Annaple glided away, and presently placed before him a tray, daintily benapkinned and set forth with a little cup of soup.

'Baby is really asleep, and Emily as proud as a Hielandman,' she said. 'Now eat this, without more ado, for that good Nuttie is going to set you down at Charing Cross.'

'This is the way we spoil our husbands, Nuttie,' said Mark. 'Refections served up at every turn.'

'Only bones! The immortal pot au feu,' said Annaple. 'And you are to go on after you have interviewed your man of steel, and have tea with Nuttie, and pay your respects to your uncle, like a dutiful nephew.'

'No, that I can't, Nannie; I promised Dobbs to go and see a man for him, and I must come back as soon as I can after that.'

He looked—as to figure and air—much more like his old self when he had changed his coat. They fed him, almost against his will, with a few of the forced strawberries Nuttie had brought. Billy pressed on him wonders from a Paris bonbon box, and Annaple fastened a rose and a pink in his button-hole, and came down to the street door with her boy to see him off.

'What do you think of her?' was Mark's first inquiry.

'Think! As Mr. Dutton said long ago, never was braver lady!'

'Never was there a truer word! I meant as to her health? As to courage, spirits, and temper, there is no question; I never saw them fail; but are they not almost too much for the frame?' he asked anxiously.

It echoed Nuttie's fear, but she tried to frame a cheerful answer. 'She is very thin, but she seems well.'

'She never complains, but I am sure her strength is not what it was. She cannot walk out as she did at first. Indeed, she gets no real rest day nor night, and there's no relieving her!'

'She says you don't get much rest either.'

'More than my share,' said Mark. 'The poor little thing never sleeps except in someone's arms, and if awake, is not content for a moment except in her mother's.'

'And that has been going on four months?'

'Three. Ever since we brought her back from Redcastle. I have nearly determined to move into some suburb when I get a rise at Michaelmas, unless she improves.'

'Nurse might suggest something.'

'Or at any rate tell us what to think. We showed her to a doctor, and all he could propose was some kind of food, which was no more successful than the rest. Did you look at her, Nuttie? She is a pretty little thing when she is quiet, but she dwindles away—at least so it seems to me, though Annaple will not see it, and—and if we are not permitted to keep the little one, I dread what the effect may be on her.'

Nuttie said something about bravery and goodness, thinking in her heart that, if the blow fell, it would be better for all than the perpetual suffering of the poor little sickly being.

'Ah! you don't know what her affections are,' said Mark. 'You did not see her when she lost her mother, and there had been no strain on her powers then. However, I've no business to croak. Many a child gets over troubles of this kind, and, as Annaple says, little Jenny will be all the more to us for what we go through with her.'

The carriage stopped, and Nuttie asked him if it would delay him too long if she executed a commission about her father's glasses. He had plenty of time, but she was delayed longer than she expected, and on her return was surprised to find that he had dropped asleep.

'Ah! that's what comes of a moment's quiet;' he said, smiling.

'Fine quiet in the roar of Ludgate Hill!'

'To a Cockney 'tis as the mill to the miller! I like the full stir and tide,' he added, looking out upon it. 'I never knew what life was before!'

'I should have thought you never knew what hardness and hard work were.'

'That's just it,' he answered, smiling. 'The swing of it is exhilaration— very different from being a cumberer of the ground.'

'Oh, Mark, all the privations and anxiety!'

'The privation! that's nothing. Indeed I am afraid—yes, I am ashamed to say—it falls more on my dear wife than myself, but if we can only wear through a year or two we shall get a further rise, and my poor Annaple may get out of this drudgery. Please God, she and the little one can stand it for a time, and I think she has a spring within her that will;' then, as he saw tears in his cousin's eyes, he added, 'Don't be unhappy about it, Nuttie; I have had it in my mind ever so long to tell you that the finding you at Micklethwayte was the best thing that ever happened to me!'

Yes, so far as character went, Ursula could believe that it had been so. He was twice the man he would have been without the incentive to work, and the constant exercise of patience and cheerfulness; but her heart was heavy with apprehension that the weight of the trial might be too heavy. To her eyes the baby's life seemed extremely doubtful, and Annaple looked so fragile that the increase of her burthens, any saddening of the heart, might destroy her elasticity, and crush her outright; while even Mark seemed to her to be toiling so close within the limits of his powers that a straw might break the camel's back!

She longed to talk to Mr. Dutton about them, but she found herself doomed to a day that perhaps Annaple would have thought more trying than her harrowed life. She was a little later than she had intended, and her father had been waiting impatiently to have a note read to him, so he growled at her impatience to run after 'that Scotch girl.' And the note happened to be of an irritating nature; moreover, the cutlets at luncheon were said to be akin to indiarubber, and there was the wrong flavour in the sauce. Ursula let that cook do what she pleased without remonstrance.

Even Alwyn did not afford as much satisfaction as usual, for the boy was in high spirits and wanted to blow a little trumpet, which was more than his father could stand. He was very good when this was silenced, but he then began to rush round the room daring his sister to catch the wild colt as he went by. This had likewise to be stopped, with the murmur that Ursula spoilt the child.

She tried to compose matters by turning out the old toys in the ottoman, but Alwyn had outgrown most of them, and did not care for any except a certain wooden donkey, minus one ear and a leg, which went by the name of

Sambo, and had absorbed a good deal of his affection. He had with difficulty been consoled for Sambo being left behind, and now turned over everything with considerable clatter in search of him. Alas! Sambo could nowhere be found in the room, and Alwyn dashed off to inquire of all the household after him. His father meanwhile growled at the child's noise, and went on trying the glasses Nuttie had brought, and pronouncing each pair in turn useless, vowing that it was no use to send her anywhere.

Upon this, back came Alwyn, terribly distressed and indignant, for he had extracted from the housemaid left in charge, who was as cross as she was trustworthy, 'What! that old broken thing, Master Egremont? I threw it on the fire! I'd never have thought a young gentleman of your age would have cared for such rubbish as that.'

'You are a wicked cruel woman,' returned Alwyn, with flashing eyes; 'I shall tell papa and sister of you.'

And in he flew, sobbing with grief and wrath for the dear Sambo, feeling as if it had been a live donkey burnt to death, and hiding his face on his sister's breast for consolation.

'Come, come, Wyn,' said his father, who did not brook interruption; 'here's half a sovereign to go and buy a new donkey.'

'It won't be Sambo,' said Alwyn ruefully.

'But you should thank papa,' said Nuttie.

'Thank you, papa,' he said, with quivering lip, 'but I don't want a new one. Oh Sambo, Sambo! burnt!' and he climbed on Nuttie's lap, hid his face against her and cried, but her comfortings were broken off by, 'How can you encourage the child in being so foolish? Have done, Wyn; don't be such a baby! Go out with nurse and buy what you like, but I can't have crying here.'

He tried to stop in sheer amazement, but the ground swell of sob could not be controlled. Nuttie was going to lead him away, and console him with more imaginative sympathy than could be expected from the maids, but her father sharply called her back. He wanted her himself, and indeed there was no question which was the worse spoilt child. He might idolise Alwyn, but not so as to clash with his own comforts. The glasses being unsuccessful, Nuttie proposed to drive back to Ludgate Hill for him to choose for himself, but he would not hear of going into the heat of the City, and growled at her for thinking of such a thing.

They took an aimless drive instead in the park, and Nuttie was nearly baked while the carriage was stopped for her father to have a long talk over the prospects of the Derby day with one of his most unpleasant associates, who stood leaning over the door on the shady side of the carriage, no one recking how little protection she derived from her small fringed parasol.

She came home tired out, and thankful that her father went to rest in his own room. She climbed to the nursery, thinking to share Alwyn's tea and comfort him, but she found only nurse there. Nurse had a bad foot, and dreaded hot pavement, so she had sent Master Alwyn out with her subordinate, a country girl, to play in Mr. Dutton's garden till it should be cool enough to go and make his purchase, and a message had since arrived that he was going to drink tea there, and Mr. Dutton would take him out.

His sister envied him the green shades, and had just done her best to cool the back drawing-room and rest herself with a book, when Mr. Fane was announced. He talked pleasantly enough, and lingered and lingered, no doubt intending to be asked to dinner, but she was equally determined to do no such thing. She had heard enough of races for one day, she thought, and at last he took his leave, only just before she dressed for dinner.

'I thought Fane was here,' said Mr. Egremont as he came in; no doubt told by Gregorio.

'He has been, but he is gone.'

'You didn't ask him to stay and dine?'

'I did not know you wished it.'

'You might have known that I should have liked to see him. I suppose you think your sweet self society enough for any man?'

'I am sorry—'

'I'm sick of hearing you are sorry! I believe there's nothing you like so well as doing an ungracious thing to a friend of mine.'

Nuttie had learnt to hold her tongue on such occasions.

Dinner was nearly over, and her father had been grumbling again at having no one to take a hand at cards with him, when the door opened a little way, and Alwyn's pretty glowing face looked in. He was come to say good-night rather later than usual, and he ran up to his sister with a little bouquet of yellow banksia and forget-me-nots. 'Mithter Button'—so Alwyn called him —'sent you this. He said you would like it, 'cause it came from one that grew at Mittletwait. And oh, look, look!'

He was hugging a little ship, which he proudly exhibited, while his father's brow had darkened at the message. 'Did you buy that?' asked his sister.

'Yes, Mr. Button went with me, and we sailed it. We sailed it by the fountain in Mr. Button's garden, And we made a storm!'

He danced about with glee, and Mr. Egremont observed, 'A dear purchase for ten shillings. Did it cost all that, Wyn?'

'They gived me a big silver half-crown, and I gived that to a little boy what came to speak to Mr. Button, and had his toes through his boots, and he was so glad.'

'Your money is not for beggars, Wyn.'

'The little boy was not a beggar, papa. He came with a newspaper to Mr. Button, and he is so good to his poor sick mother,' said Alwyn. 'See, see, sister!' turning the prow of his small vessel towards her, and showing a word on it in pencil which he required her to spell out. It was Ursula.

'Oh Wynnie!' she said, duly flattered, 'did Mr. Dutton do that?'

'He held my hand, and I did!' cried Alwyn, triumphantly, 'and he will paint it on Saturday. Then it will dry all Sunday, and not come off, so it will be the Ursula for ever and always.'

Here nurse claimed her charge; and when the goodnights were over, and a murmur recommenced, Nuttie suggested that if Mr. Dutton was at home perhaps he would come in and make up the game, but she encountered the old humour. 'I'll tell you what, Ursula, I'll not have that umbrella fellow encouraged about the house, and if that child is to be made the medium of communication, I'll put a stop to it.'

The words were spoken just as Gregorio had entered the room with a handkerchief of his master's. Nuttie, colouring deeply at the insult, met his triumphant eyes, bit her lips, and deigned no word of reply.

An undefined but very slight odour, that told her of opium smoke, pervaded the stairs that night. It was the only refuge from fretfulness; but her heart ached for her father, herself, and most of all for her little brother. And was she to be cut off from her only counsellor?

CHAPTER XXXIII.

THE LOST HEIR.

'Seemed to the boy some comrade gay
Led him forth to the woods to play.'—SCOTT.

Though it was the Derby day, Mr. Egremont's racing days were over, and he only took his daughter with him in quest of the spectacles he wanted. When they came back, Nuttie mounted to the nursery, but no little brother met her on the stairs, and she found nurse in deep displeasure with her subordinate.

'I sent him out with Ellen to play in the garden at Springfield, and swim his ship, where he couldn't come to no harm,' said nurse; 'being that my foot is that bad I can't walk the length of the street; and what does the girl do but lets that there Gregorio take the dear child and go—goodness knows where—without her.'

'I'm sure, ma'am,' said the girl crying, 'I would never have done it, but Mr. Gregory said as how 'twas his papa's wish.'

'What was?' said Nuttie.

'That he shouldn't never go and play at Mr. Dutton's again,' said Ellen.

'I told her she was to take her orders off me, and no one else,' returned nurse, 'except, of course, you, Miss Egremont, as has the right.'

'Quite so; you should have told Mr. Gregorio so, Ellen.'

'I did, ma'am, but he said those was Mr. Egremont's orders; and he said,' cried the girl, unable to withstand the pleasure of repeating something disagreeable, 'that Mr. Egremont wouldn't have no messengers between you and a low tradesman fellow, as made umbrellas, and wanted to insinuate himself in here.'

'That's quite enough, Ellen; I don't want to hear any impertinences. Perhaps you did not understand his foreign accent. Did he say where he was going?'

'I think he said he'd take him to the Serpentine to sail his ship,' said Ellen, disposed to carry on asseverations of the correctness of her report, but nurse ordered her off the scene, and proceeded, as a confidential servant, 'The girl had no call to repeat it; but there's not a doubt of it he did say something of the sort. There's not one of us but knows he is dead against Mr. Dutton, because he tried to get master to get to sleep without that nasty opium smoke of his.'

There was bitter feud between nurse and valet, and Nuttie could have exchanged with her many a lament, but she contented herself with saying, 'I wish he would let Master Alwyn alone. It is high time they should come in.'

'The child will be tired to death, and all dirt! His nice new sailor suit too!

Going grubbing about at the Serpentine with no one knows who, as isn't fit for a young gentleman,' moaned nurse.

This, however, was the worst fear she entertained, and it was with a certain malicious satisfaction that she heard her master's bell for Gregorio.

Nuttie descended to explain, and whereas the need was not very urgent, and she looked distressed and angered at the valet, her father received her complaint with, 'Well, the boy is getting too big to be tied for ever to a nursery-maid. It will do him good to go about with a man.'

But as dressing-time came on, and still neither Gregorio nor Alwyn appeared, Mr. Egremont became impatient, and declared that the valet had no business to keep the child out so long; indeed, he would sooner have taken alarm but for Nuttie's manifest agony of anxiety, starting and rushing to listen at every ring at the bell or sound of wheels near at hand. At last, at eight o'clock, there was a peal of the servants' bell, and the footman who answered it turned round to the anxious crowd: 'Mr. Gregory! He just asked if the child was come home, and went off like lightning.'

'The villain! He's lost him!' shrieked nurse, with a wild scream. 'Run after him, James! Catch him up!' suggested the butler at the same moment. 'Make him tell where he saw him last!'

James was not a genius, but the hall boy, an alert young fellow, had already dashed down the steps in pursuit, and came up with the valet so as to delay him till the other servants stood round, and Gregorio turned back with them, pale, breathless, evidently terribly dismayed and unwilling to face his master, who stood at the top of the steps, white with alarm and wrath.

'Sir,' cried Gregorio, with a stammering of mixed languages, 'I have been searching everywhere! I was going to give notice to the police. Je ferai tout! Je le trouverai.'

'Where did you lose him?' demanded Mr. Egremont in a hoarse voice, such as Nuttie had never heard.

'In the Park, near the bridge over the Serpentine. I was speaking for a few moments to a friend. Bah! Il etait parti. Mais je le trouverai. Parker, he seeks too. Fear not, sir, I shall find him.'

'Find him, you scoundrel, or never dare to see me again! I've borne with your insolences long, and now you've brought them to a height. Go, I say, find my boy!' exclaimed Mr. Egremont, with a fierce oath and passionate gesture, and Gregorio vanished again.

'Bring the carriage—no, call a cab;' commanded Mr. Egremont, snatching up his hat. 'Who is this Parker?'

The servants hesitated, but the butler said he believed the man to be a friend of Gregorio's employed at one of the clubs. Nuttie meanwhile begging her father not to go without her, flew upstairs to put on her hat, and coming down at full speed found that Mr. Dutton, passing by and seeing the open door and the terrified servants on the steps, had turned in to ask what was the matter, and was hearing in no measured terms from Mr. Egremont how the child had been taken away from his nurse and lost in the Park while that scamp Gregorio was chattering to some good-for-nothing friend.

To Nuttie's great relief, Mr. Dutton offered to go with the father to assist in the search, and the coachman, far too anxious and excited to let his master go without him in a cab, contrived to bring up the carriage. Some of the servants were ordered off to the various police offices. Poor nurse, who was nearly distracted, started in a hansom on her own account, persuaded that she should see and recognise traces of her darling at the scene of his loss, and she almost raced the carriage, which was bound for the same spot.

Sluggish natures like Mr. Egremont's can sometimes be roused to great violence, and then pour forth the long pent-up accumulations kept back by indolence and indifference. His only occupation during the rapid drive was to vituperate his valet, the curse of his life, he said. To hear him talk, it would have seemed as if Gregorio had been the tyrant who had kept him in bondage all these years, fully aware of his falsehood, peculation, and other rascality, but as unable to break the yoke as if he had been in truth the slave of anything but his own evil habit and helpless acquiescence.

Would it last if Gregorio made his appearance at that instant with Alwyn in his hand? Or even, as Mr. Dutton confidently predicted, a policeman might bring the boy home, before many hours were passed. The chief doubt here was that Alwyn's defective pronunciation, which had been rather foolishly encouraged, might make it difficult to understand his mode of saying his own name, or even that of the street, if he knew it perfectly; but the year he had been absent from London had prevented him from acquiring the curious ready local instinct of the true town child, and he had been so much guarded and watched that he was likely to be utterly at a loss when left alone; and Nuttie was wretched at the thought of his terror and loneliness, even while Mr. Dutton told her of speedy recoveries of lost children through kind people or the police.

They found all the officials of the Park already aware and on the alert, and quite certain of the impossibility of nurse's prime dread that the boy had fallen into the water unseen by any one and been drowned. She was even ready to look into every bush, in case he had been frightened and hidden himself; and nothing would satisfy her but to stay making these researches, when her master had decided on endeavouring to find 'Parker' at the club, and to ascertain from him particulars of time and place.

He was found there. The dinner-hour had brought him back, he being a man in authority there, very well dressed and deferential, declaring himself immensely distressed at the occurrence, and at having accosted Gregorio and attracted his attention. It was about four o'clock, he thought, and he described the exact spot where the little boy had been sailing his vessel fastened to a string. They might have been talking twenty minutes or half an hour when Gregorio missed his charge, and since that time both had been doing all in their power to find him, until half-past seven, when he had to return to his club, and Gregorio went to see whether the child had been taken home.

By this time Mr. Egremont looked so utterly exhausted, that Mr. Dutton availed himself of the hope that the boy might be found safe at home to take him back; but alas! nothing had been heard there.

The poor man was in a restless, unmanageable state of excitement, almost as terrifying to his daughter as the distress that occasioned it. He swallowed a tumblerful of claret, but would not eat nor go to bed; and indeed, Gregorio alone having had the personal charge of him, latterly sleeping in his dressing-room, none of the other servants knew what to do for him. Mr. Dutton agreed with her that it would be better to send for his doctor, as probably he ought to have a sedative, and neither would take the responsibility of giving it; while he himself declared he neither would nor could rest till he had his boy again.

The doctor was dining out, and they had two terrible hours; while Mr. Egremont paced to the windows; threw himself on the sofa; denounced Gregorio; or, for a change, all the system of police which had made no discovery; and Ursula for letting the boy be so helpless. Mr. Dutton sometimes diverted his attention for a few minutes, and hoped he would doze, but the least sound brought him to his feet again, and the only congenial occupation was the composition of a description of poor little Alwyn's person and dress, which set Nuttie crying so uncontrollably, that she had to run out of the room.

Dr. Brownlow came at last, and was very kind and helpful, taking the command, and insisting that Mr. Egremont should go to bed, and take the dose which he mixed. Broadbent, the butler, was to take Gregorio's place, but he was a ponderous man, without much tact, and unused to the valet's office. 'I might just as well have a rhinoceros about me,' said Mr. Egremont, in a fit of irritation; and it ended, Nuttie hardly knew how, in Mr. Dutton's going upstairs to smooth matters. He came down after a time and said: 'I am not satisfied to leave him alone or to Broadbent; I have his consent to my sleeping in the dressing-room. I am just going home to fetch my things. Let me find you gone when I come back. You will hear no more to-night. Even if he is found, they will keep him till morning.'

'It is of no use; I can't sleep.'

'Even if you don't, the mere restful position will make you fitter for the morrow. Will you promise me to undress and really go to bed?'

'Oh yes! if you say I must,' said Nuttie drearily; following an instinct of obedience.

'And remember,' he said, 'though I do not say it will be so, this may be deliverance from bondage.'

'But what a terrible deliverance!'

'Bonds are not burst without something terrible. No; don't be frightened. Remember there is safekeeping for that sweet little fellow, wherever he may be.'

'Oh, Mr. Dutton, if I could pray for him; but the turmoil seems to have driven away all such things! My boy, my boy, where is he now? Who has heard him say his little prayers?'

'His Heavenly Father has; of that we may be secure. You will feel it in the quiet of your own room. Good-night.'

'And I shall know you are praying, better than I can,' murmured Nuttie, as she returned his good-night, and crept up to her chamber.

CHAPTER XXXIV.

FETTERS RENT.

'The gods are just, and of our pleasant sins
Make whips to scourge us.'—King Lear.

There was no real sleep for Ursula that short summer night. She saw the early dawn, listened to the distant roll of market-carts, and wondered when it would be reasonable to be afoot, and ready to hear, if aught there was to hear. At any hour after seven, surely the finders would have mercy and bring the welcome news. And just before seven she fell asleep, deeply, soundly, and never woke till past eight, but that was just enough to revive the power of hope, and give the sense of a new day. But there was nothing to hear—no news. She found Mr. Dutton in the dining-room. He had had to administer another draught to her father, and had left him in a sleep which would probably last for some time. If she would go and sit in the outer room, after her breakfast, he would go out to obtain intelligence.

'You must have some breakfast,' she said, ringing the bell, and wistfully looking over the blinds; then exclaiming: 'Oh, there's Mark! Has he heard anything?' and out she darted, opening the door before he rang. 'Mark! have you found him?'

'Yes,' he said gravely, looking utterly amazed as she clasped her hands, and seemed ready to fling herself on his neck with joy. 'I came because it will be a great shock to my uncle.'

'Then it is so! Nurse was right,' said Nuttie, turning deadly pale, and standing as if before a firing platoon. 'Tell me, Mark, where did they find him?'

'At the Faringdon Station. I was sent for to identify him.'

'Stay,' said Mr. Dutton, as there was a wild horrified look in Nuttie's eyes. 'Do you mean little Alwyn?'

'Little Alwyn! No, certainly not. What of him?'

'Gregorio managed to lose him in the park yesterday,' put in Mr. Dutton.

'That accounts for it, then,' said Mark. 'No, it was Gregorio himself, poor man. He was knocked down by the engine, and killed on the spot, just by the station, at eleven o'clock last night. Our name was found on him, and I was sent for early this morning. There was no doubt about it, so I came on here at once to let my uncle know, little thinking—'

'Oh, it is dreadful!' cried Nuttie, sinking into a chair. 'Do you remember, my father told him never to see his face again unless he found Alwyn?'

Broadbent came in at the moment with the coffee-pot, and stood suspended, as he was told what had happened, Mark adding the detail: 'He was crossing the line in front of the engine.'

'Yes, sir,' said the butler. 'It is an awful dispensation. No doubt he knew it was all up with him. You may not be aware, sir, of the subject of his conversation in the park. Mr. Parker had just seen a telegram of the result of the Derby, and he had heavy bets on Lady Edina. I am afraid, sir, there can be no doubt that he found a voluntary grave.'

'We will not talk of that. We cannot judge,' said Mark, shuddering. 'I said I would send some one from here to arrange what was to be done after the inquest.'

Broadbent immediately undertook to go, if his master did not require him, and this was thought advisable, as his services were certainly not acceptable to Mr. Egremont. Mark had thought himself likely to be detained and had provided for his absence, and the awe-stricken trio were consulting together over the breakfast-table, eating mechanically, from the very exhaustion of agitation, when the door opened, and Mr. Egremont in his dressing-gown was among them, exclaiming: 'You are keeping it from me.' He had been wakened by the whispers and rushes of the excited maids, had rung his bell in vain, dressed himself as best he could after so many years of dependence, and stumbled downstairs, where, as with his daughter, it was something like a relief to know that hope was not extinguished in Alwyn's case. But Mr. Egremont was in a very trembling, broken condition, and much overcome by his valet's end after so many years of intimate association. Certainly, if either of the others had so parted with the man, it would have been a horror in the recollection, but he did not seem to dwell on it; and, indeed, attention was distracted by every sound at the door, since each might bring news of the missing child.

One of these tantalising rings proved to be a policeman with poor Gregorio's keys, and a demand for an investigation into any papers he might have left which would show his state of mind. Mr. Egremont was very much annoyed, declaring that he would have no stranger meddle with them, and that he saw no use in such prying. What difference could it make to any living creature? However, when he found there was no help for it, he said he must do it himself. Nuttie offered to help, but was sharply, strongly refused. Mark alone might and should help.

Then Mr. Dutton volunteered to go and explain matters to Mr. Dobbs, so as to get freedom for Mark for at least the remainder of the day. He would call at the police offices and see what was doing in the search, put forward the advertisements, and obtain that the Serpentine should be dragged, for he saw that only that measure would remove one great terror from these anxious hearts.

'And,' he said to Mark, 'with your permission, I will bring back Mrs. Egremont and the children if they will do me the honour to become my guests. She will be a comfort to Miss Egremont, and then you will be at hand in the evening.'

Mark could only be thankful, and presently addressed himself to the investigation, which his uncle insisted should be made in his own presence, though the opiate kept him for the most part dozing in an arm-chair, only rousing up now and then by some noise at the front door, or putting queries, the replies to which startled him more and more, as he grew more wakeful and Mark proceeded.

All, except a few unimportant bills and a betting-book, was locked into a dressing-case that had once belonged to Mr. Egremont, and had tricks of secret drawers that only he could explain. It was full of papers, and they were a strange revelation that Mr. Egremont might well wish to withhold from his daughter. They went very far back, and of course did not come out in order of chronology, nor would Mark have understood them but for exclamations and comments here and there from his uncle.

Everything seemed to be there,—the old passport and certificate to Gregorio Savelli, when he left his Savoyard home to be a waiter at a hotel; a few letters in Italian, probably from his parents, which Mark could not read, but which soon ceased; the counter-signed character with which he had entered General Egremont's service; and then came a note or two signed A. P. E., which Mr. Egremont regarded with great annoyance, though they only consisted of such phrases as 'Back on Wednesday. Find an excuse,' or in French, 'Envoyez moi la petite boite!' 'Que la porte soit ouverte apres minuit.'

'That was the way,' groaned Mr. Egremont. 'The scoundrel! he kept all those to be able to show me up to the General if he chose! I was a young man then, Mark, not the straitlaced lad you've always been. And the General! A bad old dog he was, went far beyond what I ever did, but for all that he had no notion of any one going any way but his own, and wanted to rein me in as tight as if he had been an epitome of all the virtues. And Gregorio seemed a good-natured young fellow then, and made things easy for me, though no doubt he meant to have me in his hands, in case I tried to shake him off.'

Another discovery affected him far more. It was of a letter in Alice's handwriting, addressed to Captain Egremont, in the yacht Ninon—poste restante, Madeira. He had never seen it, never known of its existence; Gregorio had gone to inquire for the letters, and had suppressed it. Mr. Egremont had wondered how he had become aware of the marriage. His knowledge had from that time been used as a means of enforcing the need of a good understanding with the heir. Mr. Egremont was much moved by the sight of the letter, and its date, from Dieppe, about six months after he had left his young wife there. He made Mark give it to him unread, handled it tenderly, struggled to read the delicate pointed writing to himself, but soon deferred the attempt, observing, 'There, there, I can't stand it now! But you see, Mark,' he added after an interval, 'I was not altogether the heartless brute you thought me.'

Mark, as he told his wife afterwards, could not help thinking of the old preamble to indictments, 'By the temptation of the devil.'

And by and by, out of a pocket-book bearing the date of the General's death, came a copy of the certificate of the baptism of Ursula Alice, daughter of Alwyn Piercefield and Alice Egremont, together with that address which Miss Headworth had left at Dieppe to gratify Alice's forlorn idea of a possible rescue, and which Gregorio had asseverated to be non-existent.

Doubtless he infinitely preferred his master's wandering bachelor life to the resumption of marriage ties, and thus he had contrived to keep Mr. Egremont from meeting the Houghtons at Florence. At the same time the uncertainty as to Alice's fate had prevented any other marriage. Gregorio had taken care that, if Mr. Egremont had been villain enough to make such an attempt, he should know that his secret could be brought to light.

Compared with all this wickedness, the proofs of fraud and dishonesty were entirely unimportant. Gambling had evidently been a passion with the valet, and peculation had followed, and Mark could have traced out the full tide before the reinstatement of Mrs. Egremont in her home, the gradual ebb during her reign, the diminished restraint under her daughter. The other servants had formerly been implicated, but, except a young groom and footman, Mark thought the present set quite free from the taint, and was glad to acquit Broadbent. But the last telegrams and the betting-book in the unhappy man's pocket confirmed Parker's evidence that of late he had staked almost madly, and had risked sums far beyond any means he could raise upon the horse which had failed. The bailiff at Bridgefield had, it had long been guessed, played into his hands, but to what an extent Mark only now discovered.

The result was that what he had learnt in the Park had so astounded him that his inattention to the child had not been wonderful. He had—as Parker testified—sought the little fellow vehemently, and had he been successful, he might yet have made some effort, trusting to his master's toleration; but the loss and reproach had made him an absolutely desperate man. Was it blind flight or self-destruction? That he had money about him, having cashed a cheque of his master's, favoured the first idea, and no one would too curiously inquire whether Mr. Egremont was aware of the amount.

It was only too true that, as he had said, Gregorio Savelli had been the curse of his life, having become one of the whips left by pleasant vices, and the breaking of the yoke had been not only at a terrible price, but, to a man in his half-blind and invalid condition, the actual loss of the person on whom he had depended was a privation. Dr. Brownlow, however, knew of a good man-servant just set at liberty by the death of an invalid master, and promised to send him on trial.

It was a day of agitations and disappointments, a sample of many that were to follow. There was not a sound of a bell that did not make anxious hearts throb. And oh! how many were spent on vain reports, on mere calls of sympathy by acquaintance whom the father and sister could not see, and on notes of inquiry or condolence that Nuttie had to answer.

Annaple came and was a great help and support to her. Poor nurse, oblivious of her bad foot, or perhaps, willing to wreak vengeance on it as the cause of all the mischief, had insisted on continuing her search in the morning under all the thorns and rhododendrons where she thought the dear lamb might have hidden and cried himself to sleep, and at last had been brought home in a cab quite worn out and despairing. But the screaming baby proved to be a much better comforter to her than any amount of reasonable argument. To soothe it, to understand what ailed it, to find suitable food for it, was an occupation which made the suspense less intolerable. The very handling of an infant would have been congenial; and a sickly crying one was only too interesting. Willie was too near her darling's age to be a welcome sight, but he was already a prime pet with the servants at Springfield; and Annaple, secure that her children were in safe and experienced hands, and overflowing with motherly sympathy for the grievous loss, was ready to devote herself to Nuttie, whether by talk, by letter writing, or by seeing inquiring friends. She did not expect to be of any use to Mr. Egremont, who had always held aloof from and disliked 'the giggling Scotch girl,' but who came drearily wandering at an unexpected time into the room where she was sitting with his daughter, and presently was involved in their conversation. Whether it was the absence of the poor familiar, or that Annaple was no longer a giggling girl, but a brave, cheerful wife and mother, it was certain that he found the same comfort and support in her presence as did Nuttie. When fits of restless misery and despair pressed hardest upon him, it was soon perceived that Annaple's cheerful tact enabled her to deal with him as no one else could do. There was the restraint of courtesy towards her, such as had worn out towards his daughter, and besides her sanguine optimist spirit never became so depressed as did poor Nuttie's. Mark went by day to his work, but came back to dine at his uncle's, hear the reports, and do what he could for him; and meantime Annaple spent the chief part of the day in aiding Nuttie and Mr. Egremont, while her baby really showed signs of improvement in nurse's keeping. And so the days went on, while every endeavour was made to trace the child, but with no result but bitter disappointment. Twice, strayed children, younger than Alwyn—one even a girl—were brought as the lost boy, and the advertisements bore fruit in more than one harassing and heartless correspondence with wretches who professed to be ready to restore the child, on promises of absolute secrecy, and sums of money sent beforehand, with all sorts of precautions against interference from the police.

The first of these created great excitement, and the pursuit was committed to Mr. Dutton. When it proved abortive, Mr. Egremont's disappointment and anger were great, and he could not be persuaded that all was not the fault of Mr. Dutton's suspicion and precaution in holding back the money, nor could any one persuade him that it was mere imposture. When another ill-written enigmatical letter arrived, he insisted that it was from the same quarter, and made Broadbent conduct the negotiations, with the result that after considerable sums had been paid in circuitous fashions, the butler was directed to a railway arch where the child would be deposited, and where he found a drab-coloured brat of whom he disposed at the nearest police station, after which he came home savagely disgusted.

Nuttie was not much less so at what she felt as a slight to Mr. Dutton as well as at the failure. 'When you are doing so much for us. We deserve that you should do nothing more,' she said with tears shining in her eyes.

'Do not talk in that way,' he answered. 'You know my feeling for the dear little fellow himself, and—'

'Oh yes,' interrupted Nuttie, 'I do trust to that! Nobody—not the most indifferent person, but must long to save him. Yes, I know it was doing you a wicked injustice to fancy that you could take offence in that way at a father in such trouble. Please forgive me, Mr. Dutton.'

'As if I had anything to forgive. As if there were anything on earth that could come before the endeavour to recover him,' said Mr. Dutton, too much moved for his usual precision of speech.

'Yes; he is *her* child,' said Nuttie, with a trembling tearful smile.

'*Her* child! Yes, and even if he were not, he is *your* brother,' said Mr. Dutton; then hastily gathering himself up, as if he had said too much, he rose to take leave, adding as their hands clasped, 'Remember, as long as I live, you may count upon me.'

'Oh, I know, I know! There's nobody like you, but I don't know what I say in this awful suspense. If I had only seen him lying white and cold and peaceful, it would have been far better than to think of him pining and miserable among wicked people, who would try to bring him up like themselves. Mother's own little boy!'

'It will not be allowed, it will not be allowed,' cried Mr. Dutton. 'God's Providence is still over him.'

'And there are prayers, I know—at our church and Mr. Godfrey's-and all ours, but oh! it takes a great deal of faith to lean on them. I wonder if you would, Annaple, if it were Willy?'

'We will not ask Mrs. Egremont,' said Mr. Dutton, as Annaple made a gesture of something like doubt.

'It is almost as bad,' said she, coming up and putting her arm round Nuttie. 'But indeed, Mr. Dutton, she does trust, only it is very, very sore, for her,—as it is for us all.'

'You are her great comfort,' said Mr. Dutton, as he shook hands with her.

'He could hardly help thanking me,' said Annaple to her husband afterwards. 'Mr. Egremont may well call him an adopted uncle. I should say he was a good deal more, poor man.'

CHAPTER XXXV.

THE HULL OF THE URSULA.

Ten days had passed, and Mark and Annaple were thinking that they ought to return to ordinary life, and leave the bereaved ones to endeavour to construct their life afresh under the dreadful wearing uncertainty of their darling's fate. Still they were detained by urgent entreaties from father and daughter, who both dreaded their departure as additional desolation, and as closing the door of hope. And certainly, even this rest was good for Annaple; and her baby, for whom nurse had discovered a better system, had really not cried more for a whole day than 'befitted a rational child,' said the mother, as she walked back to Springfield with her husband in the summer night, after dinner, on the day that Broadbent's negotiations had failed.

'Nurse will break her heart at parting with her,' said Mark. 'I wish we could afford to have her.'

'Afford, indeed! Her wages are about a quarter of your salary, sir! And after all, 'tis not the nurse that guards the child, as we have seen only too plainly.'

'Do you think he is alive, Nan?'

'I begin to think not. He is not so young but that he could make himself known, and those advertisements are so widely spread. I am sure poor Nuttie would be more at rest if she could give up hope.'

'I did not tell you before, Nan, but Dutton was going to-day to look at a poor little unclaimed child's body that had been found in the Thames. He knew him better than I, so he went.'

'He would have come if—' said Annaple.

'Assuredly. He meant to fetch nurse if he had any doubt, but afterwards he was going to his court about his rents. He always does that on Saturday evenings.'

Mr. Dutton himself opened his door to the pair.

'Well,' said Mark.

'Certainly not. The poor child was evidently much younger, and had red hair. But look here,' and he held out a battered something, black with a white stripe. Mark understood nothing, but Annaple exclaimed, 'Is it his ship?'

'Yes, I could swear to it, for see,' and he pointed to some grimed, almost effaced, but still legible capitals, which, however, scarcely any one but himself could have read as "Ursula." 'I guided his hand to make those the evening before he was lost,' said Mr. Dutton.

'Dear little man! And where did you find it?'

'Where I never thought of doing so! On the bed of a little crippled boy in the next court to mine. He is rather a friend of mine, and I turned in to take him some strawberries. I found him hugging this.'

'How did he get it?'

'Our "Liz" brought it to him. Our "Liz" is a very wild specimen, who has spent her life in eluding the school board officer till she is too old for his clutches; but she has a soft spot in her heart for her little brother, and I believe another for Gerard Godfrey. We must be very cautious, and not excite any alarm, or we shall be baffled altogether. I am not sure that I did quite prudently in giving little Alf a fresh boat in exchange for this; but I could not help bringing it home.'

'You did not see the girl?'

'No. Those girls wander long and late on these hot nights, and I do not think I could have got anything out of her. I have been to Gerard Godfrey, and the next step must be left to him.'

'The next question is whether you will tell those poor things at No. 5,' said Mark.

Mr. Dutton hesitated. 'I should have no doubt of giving Miss Egremont the comfort of knowing that there was a possible clue, but if her father insisted on setting on the police, there would be very little more hope of success. I am afraid it will be more prudent to wait till we know what Godfrey says. He hopes to see the girl to-morrow evening at his mission class, but of course she is a very uncertain attendant there. No, I cannot trust myself.'

Annaple was forced to brook withholding the hope from the fainting hearts all the ensuing Sunday, which was a specially trying day, as Nuttie pined for her dear little companion with the pictures, stories, and hymns that he had always enjoyed, and made pretty childish remarks about, such as she began to treasure as memorable.

As soon as he could, early on Monday morning, Mr. Dutton repaired to Gerard Godfrey's lodgings, and found that the young clergyman had succeeded in seeing the girl, and had examined her so as not to put the wild creature on her guard, and make her use the weapons of falsehood towards one who had never been looked on as an ally of the police. It appeared that she had brought home the ship, or rather its hull, from one of the lowest of lodging houses, where she had employment as something between charwoman and errand girl. She had found it on what passed for a bed in its present condition, one morning, when going to make the extremely slight arrangements that the terrible lair, which served as a common bedroom, underwent, and had secreted it as a prize for her little brother.

At first she had been stolid, and affected utter ignorance as to how it got there, but Mr. Godfrey had entreated her as a friend to try to discover; and had with all his heart made a pathetic description of the girl (he durst not say lady) who had always been a mother to her little brother, and now had lost him, and was in terrible uncertainty as to his fate. That came home to Lizzie's feelings, and she let out what she had seen or picked up in the way of gossip,—that the ship had been left behind by its owner, whether boy or girl Liz was uncertain, for it had long fair hair, wore a petticoat, and had been dosed with gin and something else when carried away. They said it had made noise enough when brought there by Funny Frank and Julia. They were performing folk, who had come in after the Derby day to have a spree, and to pick up another kid to do fairies and such like, because the last they had had hurt his back and had to be left in the workhouse. Yes, she had heard tell that they had got the child from Mother Bet, of whom Gerard had a vague idea as one of the horrible hags, who not only beg themselves, but provide outfits for beggars, including infants, to excite compassion. Either she or one of her crew had picked up the child and disposed of his clothes; and then finding him too old and intelligent to be safely used for begging purposes, she had sold or hired him out to these acrobatic performers, who had gone off into that vague and unknown region, the country. Liz had no notion what was their real name, nor where they would go, only that they attended races and fairs; and as soon as the actual pleasure of communicating information was over, she was seized with a panic, implored Mr. Godfrey to make no use of her information, and explained that the people of the house were quite capable of killing her, if they suspected her of betraying any of their transactions. It was impossible to bring any authorities to bear on the quest; and Mr. Dutton held it wisest only to write a note telling Mr. Egremont that he had obtained evidence that the child was living, and that he was going in pursuit, but thought it safer to say no more at present. He gave the note to Mark at his office. 'I cannot trust myself to see your cousin,' he said. 'I might be tempted to say more than was consistent with Godfrey's honour towards his informant.'

'I think you are right,' said Mark. 'You had better leave me with only indefinite knowledge, for I shall be hard pressed. Do you not go home first?'

'Yes, I go to pack up a few things and fetch Monsieur. A run in the country will do him good, and he may be a valuable auxiliary. I shall find no one at Springfield at this hour.'

'What is your plan?'

'I shall venture so far as to apply to the police for the names of the usual attendants at races and fairs, and for some idea of their ordinary rounds. I have no doubt that these are known at the chief offices. For the rest, I must use my eyes. But tell your cousin that, with God's blessing, I hope to bring him back to her.'

'He will,' said Ursula, when Mark gave her the message, and from that moment she was calmer. She did not fret Mark with questions even as much as Annaple did, she tried to prevent her father from raging at the scant information, and she even endeavoured to employ herself with some of her ordinary occupations, though all the time she kept up the ceaseless watch. 'Mr. Dutton would not have said that without good hope,' she averred, 'and I trust to him.'

Yet when four, five, six, eight, days had passed with no tidings, the heart sickness grew almost more than she could bear, though she still answered with spirit when her father again took to abusing the umbrella-fellow for choosing to keep all in his own hands.

Even Annaple could not help saying to her husband that a precise, prim, old bachelor was the very last person for a hunt in slums and the like. The very sight of him would put the people on their guard. 'And think of his fine words,' she added. 'I wish I could go! If I started with a shawl over my head, yoked to a barrel-organ, I should have a far better chance than he will. I declare, Mark, if he does not succeed we'll do it. We'll hire an organ, whereon you shall play. Ah! you shake your head. A musical education is not required, and I know I shall do something desperate soon, if that dear little boy is not found.'

CHAPTER XXXVI.

NUTTIE'S KNIGHT.

'The night came on and the bairnies grat,
Their minnie aneath the mools heard that.'

'LYNDHURST, 4th July.—Philip Dutton to Miss Egremont. Found. Waterloo, 6.15.'

'I knew he would,' said Nuttie, with a strange quietness, but as she tried to read it to her father her voice choked, and she had to hand it to Annaple. But for the first time in her life she went up and voluntarily kissed her father's forehead. And perhaps it was for the first time in his life that the exclamation broke from him, 'Thank God!'

Perhaps it was well that the telegram had not come earlier in the day, for Mr. Egremont was very restless, showing himself much shaken in nerves and spirits before the time for driving to the station, which he greatly antedated. Nuttie could hardly keep him in the carriage, and indeed had to persuade him to return thither, when he had once sprung out on the arrival of a wrong train.

And after all, when the train did come, his blue spectacles were directed to the row of doors at the other end, and Nuttie was anxiously trying to save him from being jostled, when a voice said 'Here!' and close beside them stood Mr. Dutton, with a little boy by his side who looked up in her face and said 'Sister!' It was said in a dreamy, almost puzzled way, not with the ecstatic joy Nuttie had figured to herself; and there was something passive in the mode of his hearing his father's 'My boy, my boy!' Instinctively all turned to the harbour of the carriage; Mr. Dutton lifted Alwyn in, and as Nuttie received him, a pang shot across her, as she felt how light, how bony the little frame had become in these three weeks.

'Come in! Come back with us! Tell us all!' said Mr. Egremont, as Mr. Dutton was about to help him in.

'My dog,' said Mr. Dutton, while Alwyn looked up from nestling in Nuttie's lap to say, 'Mithter Button come! And Mothu!'

'We have room for him,' said Mr. Egremont graciously. 'Here, poor fellow.'

'He has the right,' said Mr. Dutton, 'for he was the real finder.'

And Monsieur, curly and shiny, occupied with great dignity the back seat beside his master, while Alwyn, in a silent but dreamy content, as if he only half understood where he was, rested against his sister's bosom with his hands in his father's.

'Come, old chap,' said his father cheerily, 'tell us all about it.'

But Alwyn only shuddered a little, raised his eyelids slightly, and gave a tiny faint smile.

'I think he is very much tired,' said Mr. Dutton. 'There was a good deal to be done to make him presentable this morning. You must forgive me for sacrificing his curls, there was nothing else to be done with them.'

'Ah!' and Nuttie looked again. The boy was in a new, rather coarse, ready-made, sailor suit that hung loosely upon his little limbs, his hair was short, and he was very pale, the delicate rosy flush quite gone, and with it the round outline of the soft cheek; and there were purple marks under the languid eyes. She bent down and kissed him, saying, 'Was Mr. Button nurse to you, Wynnie?'

He smiled again and murmured, 'Mr. Button made me boy again.'

After a question and answer or two as to main facts of place and time of the discovery, Mr. Dutton told his story. 'I did not effect much with my inquiries after the circuses. All I heard of were of too superior an order for kidnapping practices. However, I thought the only way would be to haunt fairs and races, and look at their camp-followers. At a place in Hertfordshire I saw a performance advertised with several children as fairies, so I went to see it. I was soon satisfied that Alwyn was not there; but it struck me that I had known the face of the prime hero, a fine handsome supple fellow, who was called in the programme Herr Adalbert Steinfuggen, or some such name. Well, it seemed that he knew me, for as I struggled out after a considerable interval, I heard myself accosted, "Mr. Dutton! Sir, surely I have the honour of speaking to Mr. Dutton of Micklethwayte?" I assure you he was the very pink of politeness. Do you remember, Miss Egremont, Abel Stone?'

'Oh, Abel Stone! He was a choir boy at Micklethwayte, I remember! He was very handsome, and had a splendid voice; but he was a real monkey for mischief, and nobody could manage him but mother. She was always pleading that he should not be turned out, and at last he ran away.'

'Yes; he went off with a circus, and there he found his vocation, rose and throve, married the prima-donna, and is part owner. He seems very respectable, and was so friendly and affectionate that I ventured to consult him; when, on hearing whom I was seeking, he became warmly interested, and gave me just the information I wanted. He said he had little doubt that Funny Frank was a clown called Brag, with whom he had had words some years back for misusing the children. He said he did not hold with harshness to the little ones in teaching them to do the feats, which certainly were wonderful. If they were frightened, they were nervous and met with accidents; but make much of them, and they thought it all fun, and took a pride and pleasure in their performances. However this Brag, though a clever fellow, could not be hindered from bullying, and at last he went off with a girl of the troupe and set up on their own account. Stone, or whatever he pleases to call himself, had met them several times, but he spoke of them with great contempt as "low," and they did not frequent the same places as he does. However, he referred to one of his men, and found that they had been at Epsom on the Derby day, and moreover, that there was a report of them having lately narrowly escaped being in a scrape about a child who had been injured. There was no scruple as to advising me where to look for them, or as to the best means of detection. Stone was very indignant, and made me understand that all his young people were either to the manner born, or willingly hired out by their parents. I saw them in private life, and they looked happy and well-fed, but that was no guarantee for Funny Frank. Well, I followed him up without success, trying each place Stone had set down for me, till I came last night to Lyndhurst, a very pretty place in the New Forest, where there is to be a fair to-morrow, beginning this afternoon. Stone advised me to look about before the affair opened, while unpacking and arranging was going on. Well, after all, it was very simple. I strolled out with my dog round the field where the vans and booths were getting into order. There was what I thought a little girl in a faded red petticoat sitting on the steps at the bottom of a yellow van with her head on her hands.'

'That was me,' said Alwyn, lighting up. 'And Mothu came and kissed Fan!'

'Yes,' said Mr. Dutton; 'I verily believe we might have missed one another, but Monsieur ran up to him and, as I was actually whistling him off, I heard a little voice say, "Mothu! Mothu!" and saw they were—well, embracing one another, and then came "Mithter Button, Mithter Button, oh, take me home!"'

Eager caressing hands were held out to Monsieur, who jumped off the seat to receive the pats and laudations lavished on his curly round pate, and had to be reduced to order before Mr. Dutton could answer the question whether he had any further difficulty or danger.

'I took him up in my arms, and a handsome truculent-looking woman burst out on me, demanding what I was about with her child. To which I answered that she knew very well he was no such thing. Her man came swaggering up, declaring impudently that I had better be off—but I believe he saw that the people who came round would not take his part, for he gave in much more easily than I expected. I explained as loud as I could that this was a gentleman's son who had been stolen from his nurse in the Park. The man began to protest that they had found him deserted, and taken him with them out of charity, requesting to be paid for his keep. So I thought it better to give them a sovereign at once, so as to have no further trouble, and get him away as fast as I could. The woman came after me, making further demands, but the sight of a policeman in the distance turned her back. I went up to him and explained. I found he knew all about the loss and the reward, and looked regretfully at my prize. We went back to the hotel, where I set Alwyn to rights as well as I could, sent out for some clothes, such as the place would produce, and which at least, as he says, made a boy of him again. I'm afraid the process was rather trying from such unaccustomed hands, though he was very good, and he has been asleep almost all the way home, and, his senses all as in a dream bound up.'

The heaviness—whether weariness or content, still continued. Alwyn seemed to find it too much trouble to talk, and only gave little smiles, more like his mother than himself. He clung quite desperately to his sister when Mark offered to lift him from the carriage, but nurse was close behind, and it was good to see the little arms stretched out, and the head laid on her shoulder, the hand put up to stroke her cheek, and the lips whispering 'Wyn's own nursie.' The jubilant greeting and triumphant procession with which he was borne upstairs seemed almost to oppress him. He appeared almost as if he was afraid of wakening from a happy dream, and his lively merriment seemed all gone; there were only beams of recognition and gladness at 'Wyn's own nursery, Wyn's own pretty cup,' touching it as if to make sure that it was real, and pleased to see the twisted crusts, his special treat.

But he could not eat much of them, and soon laid his head down, as one weary, with the exhaustion of content; and nurse, who had allowed that Mr. Dutton had, considering all things, done much for the outward restoration of the daintiness of her recovered child, was impatient to give him the hot bath and night's rest that was to bring back the bright joyous Alwyn. So Nuttie only lingered for those evening prayers she had yearned after so sorely. When she held his mother's picture to him to be kissed, he raised his eyes to her and said: 'Will she come to me at night now?'

'Who, my darling?'

'She, mother dear.'

'Here's her picture, dear boy.'

'Not only the picture—she came out of it, when I cried, up on the nasty-smelling bundle in the van all in the dark.'

'She came?'

'Yes, she came, and made it so nice, and hushed me. I wasn't afraid to go to by-by when she came. And she sang. Sister, can't you sing like that?'

'Not here, I'm afraid, dear, dear boy,' she whispered, holding him so tight that he gave a little cry of 'It hurts.' Then came the prayers, not a word forgotten, and the little voice joined in her murmured thanksgiving for bringing him home.

She was much moved and awe-stricken at these words of her little brother; but she had to dress in haste for dinner, listening the while to her maid's rejoinings and vituperations of the wretches who had maltreated the child.

When she came down she found no one in the drawing-room but Mr. Dutton, whom her father had asked to the happiest meal that had perhaps ever been eaten in that house.

She went towards him with winged steps in her white dress: 'Oh! Mr. Dutton, we have not said half enough to you, but we never, never can.'

He gave a curious, trembling half smile, as she held out her hands to him, and said: 'The joy is great in itself,' speaking in a very low voice.

'Oh! I am so glad that you did it,' cried Ursula. 'It would not have been half so sweet to owe it to any one else.'

'Miss Egremont, do you know what you are saying?' he exclaimed.

'Don't call me Miss Egremont! You never used to. Why should you?'

'I have not dared—' he began.

'Dared! Don't you know you always were our own Mr. Dutton—best, wisest friend of all, and now more than ever.'

'Stay,' he said, 'I cannot allow you in your fervour to say such things to me, unaware of the strength of feeling you are stirring within me.'

'You! you! Mr. Dutton!' cried Nuttie, with a moment's recoil. 'You don't mean that you care for *me*.'

'I know it is preposterous—' he began.

'Preposterous! Yes, that you should care one bit for silly, foolish, naughty, self-willed me. Oh, Mr. Dutton, you can't mean it!'

'Indeed, I would have kept silence, and not disturbed you with my presumption, if—'

'Hush!' she cried. 'Why, it makes me so glad and so proud, I don't know what to do. I didn't think anybody was good enough for you—unless it was dear, dear mother—and that it should be me.'

'It is true,' he said gravely, 'my younger days were spent in a vain dream of that angel, then when all that was ended, I thought such things were not for me; but the old feeling has wakened, it seems to me in greater force than ever, though I meant to have kept it in control—'

'Oh, I am glad you didn't! It seems as if the world swam round with wonder and happiness,' and she held his hand as if to steady herself, starting however as Annaple opened the door saying, 'We've been sending telegrams with the good news.'

Then an arch light came into her bright eyes, but the others were behind her, and she said no more.

CHAPTER XXXVII.

FOUND AND TAKEN.

'Come up and see him,' said Nuttie, as the dining-room door was shut. 'I must feast my eyes on him.'

Annaple replied by throwing an arm round her and looking into her eyes, kissing her on each cheek, and then, as they reached the landing in the summer twilight, waltzing round and round that narrow space with her.

'You ridiculous person!' said Nuttie. 'Do you mean that you saw!'

'Of course I did; I've seen ever so long—'

'Nonsense! That's impossible—'

'Impossible to owls and bats perhaps, but to nothing else not to see that there was one sole and single hero in the world to you, and that to him there was one single being in the world; and that being the case—'

'But, Annaple, you can't guess what he has always been to me.'

'Oh! don't I know?—a sort of Archbishop of Canterbury and George Heriot rolled into one. So much the more reason, my dear, I don't know when I've been so glad in my life than that your good times should be coming.'

'They are come in knowing this! It is only too wonderful,' said Nuttie, as they stood together among the plants in the little conservatory on the way upstairs. 'I always thought it insulting to him when they teased me about him.'

'They did, did they?'

'My father, incited by poor Gregorio. Oh, Annaple! don't let any one guess till we know how my father will take it. What is it, Ellen?' as the nursery- maid appeared on the stairs.

'If you please, ma'am, Mrs. Poole would be glad if you are coming up to the nursery.'

They both hastened up and nurse came out to meet them in the day nursery, making a sign to Ellen to take her place by the cot, and withholding the two ladies. She made them come as far off as possible, and then said that she was not at all satisfied about Master Alwyn. There had been the same drowsiness and disinclination to speak, and when she had undressed and washed him, he had seemed tender all over, and cried out and moaned as if her touch hurt him, especially on one side where, she felt convinced, there was some injury; but when she asked about it his eyes grew frightened and bewildered, and he only cried in a feeble sort of way, as if sobs gave him pain.

She had soothed him, and he had gone into his own bed with the same gentle languid gladness, but had presently begun moaning, and imploring in his sleep, wakening with screams and entreaties, 'Oh, I'll do it! I'll try!' and she thought him very feverish. Would it not be better that a doctor should see him?

Nurse was always an alarmist, and Nuttie could not help thinking that to wake the child to see a stranger to-night would only add to his terror and distress, while Annaple declared her entire belief that though no doubt the poor little fellow had been cruelly knocked about and bruised, a night's rest would probably restore his bright self, and make all that was past only like a bad dream. There was no judging to-night, and sleep was wonderful reparation to those little beings.

Then however the moans and murmurs began again, and now the awakening cry. They started forward, and as Nuttie came to the cot-side the child threw himself into her bosom with, 'Sister! Sister! It is sister!' but his eyes grew round with terror at sight of Annaple, and clinging tightly to Nuttie he gasped, 'Send her away! don't let her touch me! Fan's not here!'

To tell him she was Cousin Annaple, Billy's mamma, had no effect; he did not seem able to understand, and she could only retire—nurse being thus convinced that to let him see another stranger to-night would only do further harm. Nuttie and nurse succeeded in reassuring him that he was safe at home and with them, and in hushing him off into what they hoped would be a quiet wholesome sleep in spite of the hot sultry night, on which Annaple laid a good deal of the blame of his restlessness and feverishness.

Nuttie only came down for a short time before the visitors went away; and then she wrote a note to Dr. Brownlow, which Mark promised to leave as he went to the city in the morning, Mr. Egremont, in his present relief, pooh-poohing all fears, and backing up Annaple's belief in the powers of 'tired nature's soft restorer'; but Mr. Dutton looked grave and said that he had remarked the extreme tenderness, but had hoped that much was due to his own inexperience in handling little children. The parting clasp of the hand had a world of meaning in it, and Nuttie openly said that she hoped to tell him after matins at St. Michael's how the boy was. But she could not be there.

When she went upstairs at night the half-delirious terrors had returned, and there was another difficult soothing and comforting before the child slept again. Nurse fancied the unwonted presence might disturb him, and insisted on her going to her own room.

When she returned in the morning it was to find that since daylight he had been more quietly asleep; but there was a worn sunken look about his face, and she could not be satisfied to leave him alone while the nurses stirred about and breakfasted.

He awoke smiling and happy; he looked about and said gladly, 'Wyn at home! Wyn's own nursery,' but he did not want to get up; 'Wyn so tired,' he said, speaking of himself in the baby form that he had for several months discarded, but he said his pretty 'thank you,' and took delight in breakfasting in his cot, though still in a subdued way, and showing great reluctance to move or be touched.

Nuttie was sent for to report of him to his father, who would not hear for a moment of anxiety, declaring that the boy would be quite well if they let him alone, he only wanted rest, and insisting on following out his intention of seeing a police superintendent to demand whether the kidnapping rascals could not be prosecuted.

Neither by Nuttie nor nurse could much be extracted from the poor little fellow himself about his adventures. He could not bear to think of them, and there was a mist of confusion over his mind, partly from weakness, partly, they also thought, from the drugged spirits with which he had been more than once dosed. He dimly remembered missing Gregorio in the park, and that he had tried to find his way home alone, but some one, a big boy, he thought, had said he would show him the way, took hold of his hand, dragged him, he knew not where, into dreadful dirt and stench, and apparently had silenced him with a blow before stripping him. But it was all very indistinct, he could not tell how Mother Bet got hold of him, and the being dressed in the rags of a girl had somehow loosed his hold of his own identity. He did not seem at all certain that the poor little dirty petticoated thing who had wakened in a horrible cellar, or in a dark jolting van who had been dubbed Fan, who had been forced by the stick to dance and twist and compelled to drink burning, choking stuff, was the same with Alwyn in his sailor suit or in his white cot.

It was Dr. Brownlow who at once detected that there had been much of this dosing, and drew forth the fact. It had probably been done whenever it was expedient that he should be hidden, or unable to make any appeal to outsiders. Alwyn was quite himself by day, and showed no unreasonable fear or shyness, but he begged not to be touched, and though he tried to be good and manly, could not keep from cries and screams when the doctor examined him.

'Then it came out. 'It's where he kicked me.'

'Who?'

'That man—master, she said I must call him. He kicked poor little Fan with his great heavy big boots—'cause Fan would say Wyn's prayers.'

'Who was Fan?' asked the puzzled doctor.

'Himself,' whispered Nuttie. 'Alas! himself!'

'Wyn was Fan,' said Alwyn. 'Fan's gone now!'

'And did the man kick poor little Fan,' repeated the doctor—'here?'

'Oh don't—don't! It hurts so. Master said he would have none of that, and he kicked with his big boot. Oh! Fan couldn't dance one bit after that.'

He could not tell how long ago this had been. He seemed to have lost all reckoning of days, and probably felt as if ages had past in Funny Frank's van, but Dr. Brownlow thought the injury could not be above two or three days old, and probably it accounted for there having been no more obstructions put in the way of removing the child, since he had ceased to be of use, and the discovery of the injury might have brought the perpetrator into trouble. Indeed, as it was, Mr. Egremont caused the police to be written to, demanding the arrest of the man and woman Brag, but they had already decamped, and were never traced, which was decidedly a relief to those who dreaded all that a prosecution would have involved.

And Dr. Brownlow became very grave over the injury. He said it was a surgical case, and he should like to have another opinion, enjoining that the child should be kept in bed, and as quiet as possible, till he could bring his friend in the afternoon, which was no difficult matter, for Alwyn seemed to have no desire for anything but rest and the sight of his friends and his treasures, which were laid beside him to be gently handled and stroked but not played with. Mothu and Mithter Button were among the friends he craved for, but he showed no desire to see Billy-boy, and it was thought best to keep that young gentleman's rampant strength at a distance.

The chief difficulty was with his father, who declared they were all croaking, and that the boy would be as well as ever to-morrow. He went and sat by the cot, and talked merrily of the pony that Alwyn was to ride, and the yachting they would have in the summer; and the little fellow smiled and was pleased, but went to sleep in the midst. Then Mr. Egremont went out, taking Annaple with him, because Nuttie would not go till the doctors' visit was over, though he declared that they were certain not to come till long after her return from the drive. He actually went to the dealer's, and had pony after pony paraded before the carriage, choosing a charming toy Shetland at last, subject to its behaviour with the coachman's little boy, while Annaple hopefully agreed with him that Alwyn would be on its back in another week.

He still maintained his opinion, outwardly at least, when he was met on his return by Nuttie with a pale, almost thunderstruck face. Dr. Brownlow had called her from trying to soothe away the fright and suffering of the examination, to break to her that both he and his colleague thought very seriously of the injury and its consequences, and deemed it very doubtful whether the poor little fellow could be pulled through.

Mr. Egremont was again angry, declared that she had misunderstood, and made the worst of it; that Dr. Brownlow was a conceited young ass; that his friend played into his hands; with other amenities of the same kind, to which she listened with mingled irritation and pity for his unreasonableness, and even at the sympathy which he found in Annaple's hopeful nature.

The young mother never dreaded nor expected what she could not bear to think possible, such as the death-warrant of that beautiful child, while Nuttie's nature always expected the worst, and indeed had read the doom in the doctor's eyes and voice rather than in his words. So Annaple backed Mr. Egremont up when he made his daughter write to desire Dr. Brownlow to call in the first advice in London; and among them they made so sure that this would be effective that they actually raised Nuttie's hopes so as to buoy her through the feverish early hours of the night when the pain was aggravated, the terrors returned, the boy was tormented by his duality with Fan, and the past miseries were acted over again. Even nurse and sister did not suffice, and Mithter Button had to be fetched by Mark before he could feel quite secure that he was Alwyn and not Fan. Indeed, in these light-headed moments, a better notion was gained of what he must have endured than in the day-time, when all seemed put aside or forgotten. After a time he became capable of being soothed by hymns, though still asking why his sister could not sing like that vision of his mother which had comforted him in his previous miseries, and craving for her return. Then at last he fell quietly asleep, and Nuttie was left with a few sustaining words and a pressure from Mr. Dutton's hand.

Alas! the new consultation could only ratify the first opinion. The injury need not have been necessarily fatal, though dangerous to any young child, and here it had been aggravated by previous ill-treatment, and by the doses of spirits that had been forced down, besides which, Alwyn was naturally delicate, and—though the doctors would not say so to father or sister—there were hereditary predispositions that gave him the less chance of battling through.

Yet Mr. Egremont concluded his purchase of the pony, and insisted that Alwyn should be carried to the window to see it; and Alwyn's smile was almost enough to break Nuttie's heart, but his head drooped on nurse's shoulder, he hardly lifted his heavy eyelids, and begged for 'by-by' again. Even Annaple burst into tears at the sight, ran out of the room with her sobs, and never augured recovery again, though still she strove to cheer and while away the poor father's piteous hours by making the most of every sign that the child was happy and not suffering much.

That he would be viewed as a 'pale placid martyr' was his sister's chief comfort. His replies as to the manner of the hurt, as well as his light-headed wanderings, had made it more and more evident that the man Brag's brutality had been excited by his persisting in kneeling down to say his prayers aloud —the only way he knew how to say them. Indeed there was a recurring anxiety night and morning to kneel, which had to be reasoned away, even when he was too weak to make the attempt, and was only appeased by 'Sister' kneeling by his side, holding his hands, and repeating the little prayers with him. It was of his own accord that he added: 'And forgive those people, and make them good.' Annaple burst into tears again and almost scolded when she heard of it. 'Oh dear! oh dear! now I know he won't get well! I'm glad Billy isn't so horribly good! Nuttie, Nuttie, don't! You know I don't mean it. Only I just can't bear it. He is the sweetest little fellow in the world! And oh! the cruelty of it.'

'Yes,' said Nuttie in her dreary calmness; 'he is too sweet and lovely and beautiful and good to be anywhere but safe with mother.'

For it was more apparent that they could not keep him. It did not last long; there were a couple of piteous days of restless pain and distress, and then came the more fatal lull and absence of suffering, a drowsiness in which the little fellow sank gradually away, lying with a strange calm beauty on his face, and smiling feebly when he now and then lifted his eyes to rest them on sister or nurse. His father could not bear the sight. It filled him more with angry compassion than with the tender reverence and hushed awe with which Ursula watched her darling slipping as it were from her hold. So Mr. Egremont wandered wretchedly about the lower rooms, while Mark and Annaple tried their best for him through the long summer evening, darkening into night. By and by Alwyn lifted his hand, turned his head, opened his lips, and whispered, 'Hark, sister, she is singing.' The look of exceeding joy beamed more and more over the pinched little face. 'She's come again,' he said; and once more, 'Come to take Wyn to the dear Lord.' After that there were very few more long breaths before little Alwyn Egremont's spirit was gone to that unseen world, and only the fair little frame left with that wondrous look of delighted recognition on the face.

CHAPTER XXXVIII.

THE UMBRELLA MAN.

Little Alwyn was laid to rest beside his mother in a beautiful summer noontide. His father was not in a state to attend the funeral, and was left under the care of Annaple, his own choice among those who offered to stay and minister to him. It was his own wish that his daughter should be to the last with her little brother. He had even said to her that she had been a good sister, and his boy had been very fond of her, and he would not keep her away on any account.

And, with a man's preference for a young and kindly woman, he chose Annaple to be with him rather than Mr. Dutton, remembering likewise that but for him the boy would have died in some workhouse, unknown and unclaimed, or among the wretches who had caused his death. So Nuttie had the comfort of Mr. Dutton's going down with her, as well as Mark, and poor broken-down nurse, but not a word referring to the confession of that happy evening had passed between them during the mournful fortnight which had since elapsed.

May Condamine and her husband had made all as fair and consoling as they could. There were white-robed children to bear the boy from the churchyard gate, choristers sang hymns, the grave was lined with moss and daisies, and white roses decked the little coffin and the mound. There was as much of welcome and even of triumph as befitted the innocent child, whose death had in it the element of testimony to the truth. And Nuttie felt it, or would feel it by and by, when her spirit felt less as if some precious thing had been torn up by the roots—to be safe and waiting for her elsewhere, indeed, but that did not solace the yearning longing for the merry loving child; nor the aching pity for the crushed blighted creature whom she had watched suffering and dying. It was far beyond her power as yet to acquiesce in her aunt's consolation that it was happier for the child himself, than if he was to grow up to temptation from without, and with an unsound constitution, with dangerous hereditary proclivities. She could believe it in faith, nay, she had already experienced the difficulties her father had thrown in her way of dealing with him, she tried to be resigned, but the good sense of the Canoness was too much for her.

It was a day of more haste than suited the ideal of such a time, for Mr. Egremont could not be left for a night; so there was only time for a luncheon, with little jerks of talk, and then for an hour spent in short private interviews. Mrs. Egremont obtained from poor Nurse Poole all the details, and, moreover, her opinion of Mr. Mark's baby, in whom, it having been born under her auspices, she took a special interest.

Nuttie meantime was pacing the shady walk with her dear old friend Miss Nugent, feeling it strange that her heart did not leap up at the bare presence of one she loved so much, yet conscious of the soothing of her sympathy. And Mary, watching her all through, had been struck with the increased sweetness and nobleness her countenance had acquired during these years of discipline. More of her mother's expression had come than could have been thought possible in features of such a different mould, formed for so much more strength and energy. They had not met since Nuttie had been summoned home to her mother's deathbed, and their time was chiefly spent on reminiscences alike of the old sorrow and the new; but, when the time for parting was nearly come, Mary said affectionately, 'And you, my dear?'

'Oh, I am all right,' said Nuttie, and her eyes shone with a light Mary did not at the moment understand; 'you need not be anxious for me *now*.'

'I suppose that unhappy valet's death makes your task easier,' said Mary.

'I think it will,' said Nuttie. 'Poor man! He was—I can't help saying it— the evil genius of the house. Dear mother knew it, struggled against him, and broke down in the struggle. It seems so strange that what she could not do has been done in such a manner, and at such a price! I wonder whether she knew it when she welcomed her boy!'

'Her influence will aid you still,' said Mary, 'and you have Mr. Dutton to help you too. I was so glad to find he was so near you.'

'Oh, Mr. Dutton!' exclaimed Ursula, in a strange tone that sent a thrill through Mary, though she knew not why; but at that moment they were interrupted, very inopportunely, by Mr. Bulfinch, who could not go away without asking Miss Egremont whether she thought her father could see him on business if he came up to town the next day. She thought that such an interview would rouse her father and do him good, advising him to call on the chance.

Mark's tete-a-tete had been with his sister May, to whom he had much to tell of his wife and her gallant patience and energy, and how curious it was that now the incubus that had weighed on his uncle's household was removed,

the prejudice had melted away, and he had grown so fond of her that, next to
Ursula, she was his best comforter.

'I hope that will lead to more,' said May.

'I don't see how,' said Mark. The more we rely only on a blessing on our
own exertions the better.'

'Even when Annaple works within an inch of her life?'

'Now that she is on a right tack about the baby, that will be easier. Yes, May,
I do feel sometimes that I have brought her down to drudgery and narrowness
and want of variety such as was never meant for her, but she will never let me
think so. She says that it is living in realities, and that it makes her happier than
toiling after society, or rather after the world, and I do believe it is true! I'm
sure it is with me.'

'But such work as yours, Mark.'

'Nonsense, May; I enjoy it. I did not when I was in the Greenleaf firm, with
an undeveloped sense that Goodenough was not to be trusted, and we were
drifting to the bad, yet too green to understand or hinder it; but this I thoroughly
like. What does one want but honest effective work, with some power of
dealing with and helping those good fellows, the hands, to see the right and
help themselves?'

May sighed. 'And yet, now that poor child is gone, I feel all the more how
hard it is that you should be put out of the rights of your name.'

'I never had any rights. It was the bane of my life to be supposed to have
them. Nothing but this could have made a man of me.'

'And don't you have regrets for your boy?'

'I don't think I have—provided we can give him an education—such as I
failed to make proper use of, or Annaple might be luxuriating at Pera at this
moment.'

'Well!' said May, pausing as she looked up the vista of trees at the great
house; 'I can't bear it to go out of the old name.'

'Names may be taken!'

'You don't mean that there's any chance of—Oh! not that horrid Mr.
Fane?'

'Certainly not.'

'Oh!' as a trim black figure appeared walking down the open space. 'That
man!'

'I am not authorised to tell any one so, May.'

'Yes, I understand. The wretch, he is taking stock of the place already!'

'For shame. May, no one has deserved so well of them.'

'I don't care, he got you into that horrid concern.'

'And got me out of it, and found my work for me. I tell you, May, it is the best thing that could possibly happen to your parish, or the estate, or my poor uncle either! And you will soon come to a better mind.'

'Never, while he is to get into your place! Turn back before he comes within hailing distance.'

Before Mark could do anything towards bringing his sister to a better mind he was seized on by his stepmother to propound a scheme she had hatched, namely that, as a mutual benefit, Nurse Poole should be allowed the consolation of bringing her chief comforter, his little daughter, down with her on the visit Mrs. Egremont had invited her to pay at Redcastle. He was very grateful, though doubtful whether Annaple would accept the offer, for she was missing her children's company, though they were only at Springfield House, and she had been with them part of every day. And, sad as this month had been, it had been such a rest from sheer physical toil that she had gained almost as much by it as the little one.

There was a general assembly and coffee-drinking in the verandah,—Mr. Condamine, Blanche, and her two young sisters were all there,—and May had to be duly civil to Mr. Dutton, though he came back with some water-lilies that he had fished out of the lake for Nuttie, and she thought it taking possession. Then the Londoners set forth for the station, and there Mark, having perhaps had a hint from his wife, saw Nuttie and Mr. Dutton safely bestowed by Broadbent in an empty carriage, and then discovered a desire to smoke, and left them to themselves.

They had not been alone together for more than a second since the evening of Alwyn's return, and there was a great shyness between them, which lasted till the first station was past without any irruption of newcomers. Nothing had been said but a few comments on the arrangements and the attendants, but probably both were trying to begin to speak, and at last it was Ursula who crossed over so that her face could not be seen, and said in an odd tone—

'Mr. Dutton—'

'Yes,' and he turned, instantly on the alert.

'Did you mean it—what I thought you meant that evening?'

'Can you doubt it?' he said earnestly. 'But even then I was surprised into the avowal, and I would have held it back if possible, if I had guessed what was going to happen.'

'Ah! but then I should not have had that drop of comfort through it all,' and she laid hold of his hand, which returned the pressure strongly, but he sedulously guarded both words and tone as he said:

'Listen, Ursula, before you speak again. How dear you must always be to me, I cannot tell you, but when I then spoke, it was with the sense that on every account, I should meet with strong opposition from your father and family. And now your position is altered, so that the unsuitability is doubled. I am not a young man, remember, and my thoughts must be for you above all, I want you to consider whether, in the present state of affairs, you would not do better to look on what then passed as unsaid, or only as the ebullition of gratitude towards your old friend. Let me go abroad, and give you full opportunity for— for some fresh beginning likely to be fitter for you—'

'Mr. Dutton, how can you say such horrid things? As if a dukedom would make any difference.'

'Yes,' he said, turning towards her. 'If it is only the old-friend feeling, then it is better dropped, but if your heart is in it, child, then we go on, come what may. It is due to you.'

She raised her face towards him now, and he gave a grave kiss to her forehead. She drew a long breath, and said after a little pause, 'And now I have something to say. One does think of such things even in these sad times, and you can help me. I am so glad it is you, because I know you will, and be rejoiced to do so. You know when Mark found us out first, dear mother and I always felt that it was a great pity he should not have the estate he had been brought up to expect. I believe dear mother thought it would have been the right thing for me to marry him, but I always did mean to give it back to him, even when I didn't like him. Well, then, you know it all seemed settled otherwise, but now, it is so lucky you spoke to me while that dear little fellow was with us, because now you will help me to persuade my father that it is the only satisfactory thing to do to let it go in the male line to Mark and his Willy.'

'I see! I see!' said Mr. Dutton eagerly. 'It would be an infinite relief if it could be carried out.'

'I believe my father would like it,' said Nuttie. 'He cares for the name; and now no one prevents it; he is fond of Mark, and still more of Annaple! And you! Oh, Mr. Dutton, if he will only take it in the right way, I think you will make me able to do what it grieved dear mother never to have brought about for my poor father.'

'My whole self is yours to aid you,' he said. 'You know of course that I could not ask you to detach yourself from one to whom you are so necessary. If he will permit us, we will watch over him together as doing her work.'

'Thank you,' was all Nuttie's lips could utter, though her hand said much more.

And before they reached London they had arranged something of a plan of action for propitiating Mr. Egremont, and bringing the future prospects to be available so as to save Annaple from being worked to death in the meantime.

CHAPTER XXXIX.

ANNAPLE'S AMBITION FALLEN.

'Well, how did you get on, Annaple?'

'Oh! very well, poor old man, on the whole, though it made one pity him doubly that he chose to make as if he forgot everything, and you were all gone on a picnic, taking me out for a long drive in the afternoon—where we were least likely to meet any one—that I will say for him.'

'Forgetting is not the best for him.'

'As if he could forget! But he was very nice and friendly, and put on his best, most courteous self. I think he looks on me rather as a protector from the solemn Mr. Edsall.'

'Surely Edsall treats him well. He was excellently recommended. You know I saw his master's daughter.'

'Oh! only *too* well. He takes the management of him as if he were three years old, or a lunatic. He simply *will* not be offended any more than if he had to do with a baby.'

'What should offend him?'

'That Mr. Egremont greatly resents being allowed nothing but by what Edsall calls medical sanction. He is too blind, you know, to venture to pour out anything for himself, and besides, Edsall has all the drugs under lock and key, and is coolness itself about any amount of objurgations, such as I fancy go on sometimes.'

'Do you think he will stand it?'

'Who? Your uncle? Yes, I think he will. This man really makes him more comfortable than poor Gregorio did.'

'Yes; Nuttie said she was sure that there was neglect, if not bullying latterly. But he must miss Gregorio terribly. They had been together for at least five-and-twenty or thirty years, and had plenty of gossip together.'

'Whereas the present paternal despotism and appalling dignity and gravity will keep him more dependent on his right congeners.'

'If they are of the right sort, that's all.'

'He has been making me read him a whole heap of letters; indeed, as you know, I have been doing that all along, when he could not get Nuttie. There were some from Mr. Bulfinch. Do you know that bailiff of his must be next door to a swindler?'

'Bulfinch is coming up to see him to-morrow.'

'And, Mark, do you know, he has been putting out feelers as if to discover whether we would do—what he asked us to do five years ago.'

'Would you?'

'If it were not for the children, and—and sometimes the extreme pinch, I should say it was more like *life* to work yourself up as a City man,' said Annaple. 'If you were the Squire, with all his opportunities, it would be a different thing, but there's no outlet there, and I have often admired the wisdom of the Apocryphal saying, "Make not thyself an underling to a foolish man."'

'Well, it is lucky you think so, Nannie, for though Dutton is certainly not a foolish man, he will not want an underling. And what do you say to my mother's proposal of having poor Poole to stay at Redcastle, and borrowing baby to comfort her till she goes out again.

'I hate it,' said Annaple energetically. 'It is very horrid, but it is awfully good of the Canoness; and I suppose we shall have to let it come to pass, and miss all that most charming time of babyhood which is coming. But most likely it will quite set the little woman up, and be a real kindness to poor Poole.'

'If we could only keep her for good.'

'Yes, and then our children would not be half so much our own. I do want to be away with them in our own quarters. I wonder when Nuttie can spare us, but I should like to see her through the great crisis with her father.'

That crisis was to involve more than Annaple in the least expected. Nuttie found that the momentous confession could not possibly take place before the interview with Mr. Bulfinch, at which her presence was needed to help her father with his papers. The principal concern was to show the full enormity of the bailiff, and decide upon the steps to be taken, the solicitor being anxious for a prosecution, while a certain tenderness for poor Gregorio's memory, or perhaps for the exposure of his own carelessness, made Mr. Egremont reluctant. There was also a proposal, brought forward with much diffidence from Mr. Condamine's mother, to rent Bridgefield House, but on this, as well as respecting a successor to the bailiff, Mr. Egremont was to give his answer the next day, when Mr. Bulfinch would call again.

Nuttie was thankful for the business that had filled up the hour after luncheon, when Alwyn used to play in the drawing-room and delight his father; but she was feeling desperate to have the crisis over, and resolved to speak when she went out driving with him. It was he, however, who began. 'I sounded Mark's wife yesterday, Ursula. She is a nice little thing enough, and a good wife in her way.'

'A very good wife.'

'Except when she persuaded him to turn up his nose at the agency. D'ye think he would take it now, since he has tasted the sweets of his umbrella business?' then, as Nuttie paused, taken by surprise; 'Five hundred a year and the Home Farm would be better than, what is it, a hundred and fifty and a floor over a warehouse! I don't like to see old Will's son wearing himself out there, and the lad is a good honest lad, with business habits, who would do justice to you after I am gone.'

'Father,' said Nuttie, trembling with the effort, 'I want you to do something better than that. I want you to let Mark take the agency with a view to himself— not me. Let him be as he would have been if he had never hunted us up at Micklethwayte, and put me in his place.'

'Eh!' said Mr. Egremont. 'It is not entailed—worse luck; if it had been, I should not have been bound to dance attendance at the heels of such an old sinner as the General.'

'No, but it ought to go to the heir male, and keep in the old name. Think— there have been Egremonts at Bridgefield for four hundred years!'

'Very pretty talk, but how will it be with you, Miss. We shall have Fane, and I don't know how many more, coming after the scent of Bridgefield now,' he said with a heavy sigh, ending with a bitter 'Hang them all!'

'And welcome,' said Nuttie, answering the thought rather than the words. 'Father, I wanted to tell you—'

'You don't mean that any one has been after you at such a time as this!' he cried.

'It was before—I mean it was the evening when we were all so glad, before we began to be afraid.'

'The umbrella man! By Jove!'

'And now,' went on Nuttie, in spite of the explosion, 'he would hardly have ventured to go on with it but for this—I mean,' as her father gave a little laugh of his unpleasant sort, 'he said it would be the greatest possible relief, and make it all right for the property to go to the heir male.'

'Hein! You think so, do you? See how it will be when I come to talk to him! A shrewd fellow like that who got out of the Micklethwayte concern just in time. Catch him giving up a place like that, though he may humbug you.'

'Then you will see him, father?'

'If you turn him in on me, I can't help it. Bless me! umbrellas everywhere! And here you mean to turn me over to the mercies of that solemn idiot, Edsall. I should have been better off with poor Gregorio.'

'No, father; Mr. Dutton would not take me from you. We would both try all we could to make you comfortable.'

'Convert the old reprobate? Is that his dodge?'

'Don't, father,' for the sneering tone returned.

'Come now,' he added in a much more fatherly manner, for her voice had struck him. 'You don't mean that a well-looking girl like you, who could have her pick of all the swells in town, can really be smitten with a priggish old retired umbrella-monger like that. Why, he might be your father.'

'He has been getting younger ever since I knew him,' said Nuttie.

'Well. He plays as good a game of whist as any man in England,' muttered Mr. Egremont, leaving his daughter in actual doubt whether he meant this as a recommendation, or as expressing a distrust of him, as one likely to play his cards to the best advantage. She had to remain in doubt, for they overtook Clarence Fane, who came and spoke to them in a very friendly and solicitous manner, and showed himself willing to accept a lift in the carriage. Mr. Egremont, willing to escape from perplexities as well as to endeavour to drive away if possible the oppression of his grief, invited him in, and he had some gossip to impart, which at first seemed to amuse the hearer after this time of seclusion, but the sick and sore heart soon wearied of it, and long before the drive was over, Mr. Egremont was as much bored as his daughter had been from the first.

When Mr. Fane got out, he paused a moment to hold Ursula's hand in a tender manner, while he told her that he had not ventured to intrude (he had left a card of inquiry every day), but that if ever he could be of the least use in amusing Mr. Egremont, he was at her service, and would give up any engagement.

'Hein! my fine fellow! No doubt you would!' said Mr. Egremont, when his daughter had uttered her cold thanks, and they had driven on. 'I see your little game, but it is soon to begin it. We may as well let them know that she is booked before the running begins.'

It was a remarkable intimation of his acceptance of her engagement, but Ursula was contented to take it as such, and be thankful.

Mr. Dutton had his interview as soon as Mr. Egremont had rested after his drive, and the result was satisfactory.

No doubt much was due to the Egremont indolence and want of energy, which always preferred to let things take their course. And now that Gregorio was no longer present to amuse, and take all trouble off his hands, Mr. Egremont could hardly have borne to part with his daughter; and, despite of umbrellas and religion, was not sorry to have a perfectly trustworthy son-in-law in the house, able to play at cards with him, manage his household, and obviate all trouble about suitors for the heiress. Moreover, his better feelings were stirred by gratitude on his poor little son's account, and he knew very well that a more brilliant match for his daughter would not have secured for his old age the care and attention he could rely upon here. He was obliged likewise to believe in the disinterestedness, which disclaimed all desire for the estate, as involving cares and duties for which there had been no training; and he was actually glad to keep the property in the direct line. The old liking for Mark, and sense of the hardship of his exclusion, revived, strengthened now by regard for Annaple; together with the present relief from care obtained by making him manager of the estate.

When once brought to a point, Mr. Egremont was always sudden and impetuous, chiefly for the sake of having it over and being unmolested and at rest again. So that very evening, while Nuttie only ventured on sharing with Annaple the glad tidings that Mr. Dutton was accepted, and in his marvellous goodness, undertook to make his home with her father. Mark was almost stunned by the news, confirmed to him by Mr. Dutton as well as his uncle, that he was to be acknowledged as heir of Bridgefield Egremont, and in the meantime manage the estate with an income suitable to an oldest son.

Presently he came upstairs by himself, and beckoned to Nuttie, rather to the alarm of his wife.

'Ursula,' he said, and took both her hands, 'I cannot have you do this for me.'

'Can't you, Mark? You can't prevent it, you see. And don't you know it is the beginning of all my happiness?'

'But indeed, I cannot feel it right. It is a strained sense of justice. Come and tell her so, Nannie.'

'What?' said Annaple coming forward.

They both paused a moment, then Nuttie said, 'Only that the estate ought to go in the male line.'

'Oh, is that all?' said Annaple, 'I was afraid Mr. Egremont had a fit!'

'Ah! Don't you see what it means,' said Mark. 'They want it to be as if there were an entail—to begin treating me as an eldest son at once. It is Ursula's doing, putting herself out of the succession.'

'I always hated being an heiress,' said Nuttie.

'It would be more dreadful than ever now. Annaple, do be sensible! Don't you see it is the only right thing to do?'

'Billy!' was the one word Annaple said.

'Yes, Billy and Jenny and all,' said Nuttie, 'before you've all died of your horrid place—Oh! you haven't heard that part of it. Of course Mark will have to go down to Bridgefield and look after the place, and live like a gentleman.'

'Eight hundred a year,' murmured Mark, 'and the house at the Home Farm.'

'Oh! dear,' gasped Annaple, 'I wanted you to be Lord Mayor, and now you'll only be a stupid old country squire. No, no, Nuttie, it's—it's—it's the sort of thing that one only laughs at because otherwise one would have to do the other thing!'

And she gripped Nuttie tight round the waist, and laid her head on her shoulder, shaking with a few little sobs, which might be one thing or the other.

'It will save her youth, perhaps her life,' whispered Mark, lifting Nuttie's hand to his lips for a moment, and then vanishing, while Annaple recovered enough to say, 'I'm tougher than that, sir. But little Jenny! Oh, Nuttie, I believe it has come in time. I've known all along that one straw more might break the camel's back. We've been very happy, but I am glad it is over before Mark got worn down before his time. Grinding is very wholesome, but one may have too much; and I haven't Mark's scruples, Nuttie dear, for I do think the place is more in his line than yours or Mr. Dutton's.'

'Yes,' said Ursula, 'you see he was always happy there, and I never was.'

The next thing was for Mr. Dutton and Ursula to keep Mr. Egremont up to the point of making his long deferred will; nor did they find this so difficult as they expected, for having once made up his mind, he wished to have the matter concluded, and he gave his instructions to Bulfinch the next day. Of course Mark had to give full notice to his employers; but the allowance was to begin at once, so that Annaple only went back to the warehouse to pack up, since she was to occupy No. 5, while Mr. Egremont and his daughter were going under Mr. Dutton's escort to the baths in Dauphine, an entirely new resort, free from the associations he dreaded, for he could not yet bear the sight of little Willy— the rival 'boy of Egremont.' But the will was safely signed before he went, to the great relief of Nuttie, who, according to the experience of fiction, could hardly believe his life safe till what she called justice had been done.

After all Mr. Egremont became so dependent on Mr. Dutton, during this journey, that he did not like the separation at its close, and pressed on the marriage even sooner than either of the lovers felt quite reverent towards the recent sorrow. He insisted on Bulfinch having the settlements ready for them on their return, and only let them wait long enough to keep their residence, before there was a very quiet wedding in their parish church, with the cousins for bridesmaids. Then Mark and Annaple took care of Mr. Egremont for the fortnight while Mr. Dutton showed his wife his old haunts in France, returning to Springfield House, where there was plenty of room for Mr. Egremont to make his home with them.

Said Annaple to Miss Nugent, 'I never saw Nuttie so youthful and bright. She is more like a girl than I ever saw her since the first.'

'Yes,' said Mary, 'she has some one to rest on now.'

Mr. Egremont lived between three and four years, more contented and peaceful than he had ever been, though frequently suffering, and sometimes giving way to temper and impatience. But Mr. Dutton understood how to manage on these occasions, and without giving up his own extensive usefulness, could give him such care, attention, and amusement as beguiled his discomforts, and made his daughter's task an easier one.

How far the sluggish enfeebled nature was capable of a touch of better things, or whether his low spirits were repentance, no one could judge. At any rate sneers had ended, and when he was laid beside his wife and boy at Bridgefield, Ursula stood by the grave with a far more tender and hopeful feeling than she could have thought possible when he had rent her away from her old home. She looked up at her husband and said, 'Is not her work done?'

THE END.

www.ingramcontent.com/pod-product-compliance
Lightning Source LLC
Chambersburg PA
CBHW021646110726
47902CB00007B/1849